I0822473

PRAISE FOR THE SQUIMBOP CONDITION

David Leo Rice writes fiction with a seething ferocity, brilliance, and arcane imagination; *The Squimbop Condition* is a surreal and profound leap into the timeless art of storytelling. David Leo Rice is a writer I greatly admire.

—Brandon Hobson, finalist for the National Book Award for Fiction, and author of *The Devil is a Southpaw*

Reading David Leo Rice's *The Squimbop Condition* is like stumbling into the world of an unmade David Lynch movie, getting lost in the dream of it. Tracking the escapades of the notorious Brothers Squimbop, it plays like a roadshow presentation full of mysterious visions from a realm both alien and familiar. Like Richard Brautigan and Flann O'Brien and Samuel Beckett, Rice is a marauding magician, and he's both deadly serious and deadly funny. *The Squimbop Condition* is a majestic and strange force of a book, a work of wild pleasures for our unsettled, damaged times.

—William Boyle, author of *Saint of the Narrows Street*

I've always been a DLR super fan, and *The Squimbop Condition* is a new pinnacle. It has a joyful rhythm, a cadence that pervades the psyche until our concepts of self, other, relation, and identity tumble out topsy-turvy. I cherish the hours I spent with this book.

—Charlene Elsby, author of *The Devil Thinks I'm Pretty* and *Violent Faculties*

Much like his titular characters, David Leo Rice is an agent of chaos, inciting literary anarchy with an aptitude rarely seen in today's so-called experimental writing scene. The Squimbop Condition unleashes a barrage of questions so incisive it renders any and all answers moot; functioning simultaneously as a medical text, a historical document, and even a holy book. It is a diagnosis of our collective malaise. A prescient lesson plan outlining a new golden age of American fiction.

—JOSHUA CHAPLINSKY, author of
Letters to the Purple Satin Killer

PRAISE FOR DAVID LEO RICE

"*Drifter* should secure Rice a place on the same list as... [Thomas] Ligotti and Brian Evenson.... The writing here is that weird, and that good."

—GABINO IGLESIAS, *The Southwest Review*

"Like peering through a slit at some brilliant, brutal new world..."

—KIMBERLY KING Parsons on *Drifter*

"Somewhere Between Bradbury and Ligotti, Rice folds centuries of Americana into a space unstuck from time."

—BR YEAGER

"What might happen if Edvard Munch decided to paint directly on the inside of his own skull rather than a canvas."

—BRIAN EVENSON on *A Room in Dodge City*

"The ease, the command, the deadpan assurance of Rice's language, and the angularity of his imagination can make even the unspeakable somehow charming."

—MATTHEW SPECKTOR in the *LA Review of Books*

"Lash yourself to the mast of your ark as you set sail for the siren song of David Leo Rice's imagination... The emerging cult novelist of today's moment, he's the reigning surrealist sorcerer of tomorrow's century."

—STEVE ERICKSON, author of *Zeroville* and *Shadowbahn*

"*The New House* is magic. It's a book so infused with dreams that it seems to be dreaming us into being—you and me and the families that form us, the towns that try us, the shadows that want to wake us or take us away for good. I don't remember a book that captured dreaming so perfectly, or at least captured my dreams: the streets I repeatedly step down, the edges of town that scare the shit out of me, the sweetness that always seems to dissipate while I'm savouring it"

—DEREK MCCORMACK

"[*The Berlin Wall*] is a startling declaration of artistic purpose, a capstone of Rice's work hitherto, and a revolt against established genre."

—THEODORE SOVINSKI, *Full Stop Magazine*

The Squimbop Condition

DAVID LEO RICE

David Leo Rice

THE SQUIMBOP

Copyright © 2025 David Leo Rice
All rights reserved

This book may not be reproduced in whole or in part, except for the inclusion of brief quotations in a review, without permission in writing from the author or publisher. No part of this publication may be reproduced, stored in or introduced into a retrieval system, or transmitted, in any form, or by any means (electronic, mechanical, photocopying, recording, or otherwise), without prior permission of the publisher.

Requests for permission should be directed to 1111@1111press.com, or mailed to 11:11 Press LLC, PO Box #11, Dundas, MN 55019.

Book Design by Mike Corrao
Cover and Illustrations by Jan Robert Duennweller

ISBN: 9781948687706

Printed in the United States of America

FIRST AMERICAN EDITION

9 8 7 6 5 4 3 2

"If there even *is* a natural being, an irreducible self, it is rather small, I think, and may even be the root of all impersonation—the natural being may be the skill itself, the innate capacity to impersonate."

—Philip Roth, *The Counterlife*

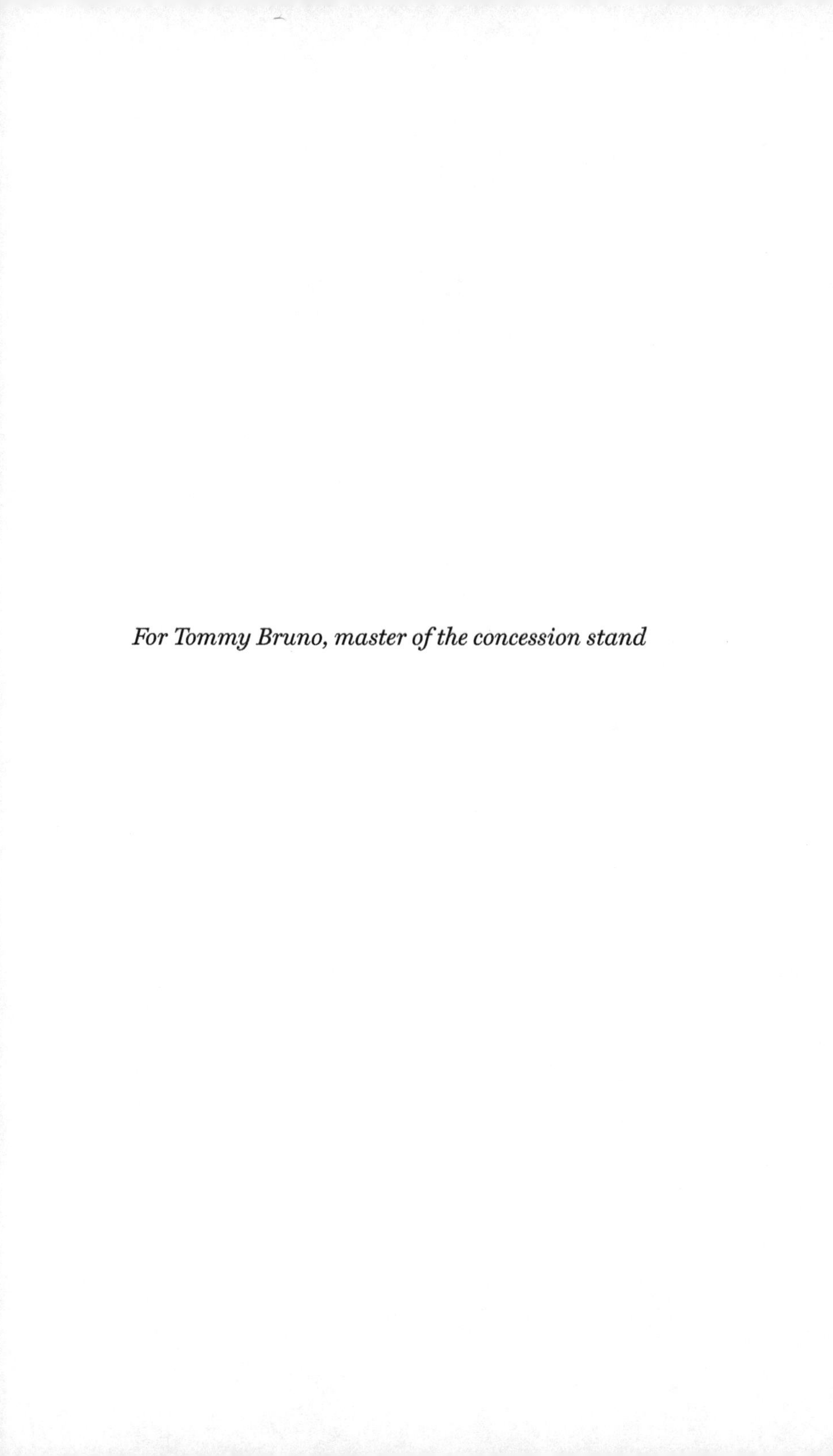

For Tommy Bruno, master of the concession stand

CONTENTS

Dr. Forearm I

Doctor Forearm looms toward me where I sit on the wax paper covering the slab. "This won't hurt a bit," he grins, spritzing silver liquid from the tip of a needle so long it bends in the air between us. I recoil as it extends and twists and probes, following me backward along the paper and up to a map labeled "Escapades of the Brothers Squimbop" plastered to the wall. The USSR is red, the USA blue, with Europe stretched tan between them and arrows pointing toward the "Totally Other Place" in all four directions.

The Doctor makes a sucking noise with his tongue in his lip and the needle retracts, straight and true and eager again. My mother, who must've brought me here in the family van, retracts as well, exiting the scene long before I thought she would. Then the Doctor turns the needle toward his eye and says, "One second. Just one second, please."

He leans forward, peels me off the map and repositions me in the center of the paper, pinching my upper arm and inspecting the skin. "Now Jim," he says, slowly, his attempt at consolation obvious and ineffective. Though Jim must be my name, I flinch upon hearing it. "There's no need to worry. My patients think of me as the American MC Escher. Your MC for all that follows. You'll soon see why. I had this dream too when I was your age. Before I caught the Condition. You could say my entire career has been an attempt to recover from that dream, much as you could also say it has been a continuation thereof. The first of the Saga's innumerable antinomies, all of which would surely reveal a deeper harmony if only we could see it… as some of us did, once or twice or a handful of times in our lives, in the halls of the great Mountain Houses in the heart of the Golden Age, sitting in the velvet seats with our Brother on one side and our Pervert Uncle on the other, Tommy Bruno popping popcorn in the distance while we waited for the curtains to part and release the Brothers into a realm wherein we could behold them as they were."

He tears a handful of paper off the slab, dabs his eyes, and then, with a snort, grabs my arm tighter with one hand and plunges the needle with the other. The silvery liquid rushes into me and Dr. Forearm sighs as I scream myself awake.

I AWAKEN INTO THE KNOWLEDGE THAT WHAT'S done is done. What's in me is there to stay. In school, our lanky teacher with his prominent mustache and alligator-skin boots assigns us a story entitled "In Dreams Begin Responsibilities." All the students laugh at the coincidence, as if they too can see not only the residue of my dream but also what's circulating in my blood because of it, the change that has overtaken my life. When I close my eyes and return to Dr. Forearm's office—now empty and dim—my classmates are clustered against the map, holding hands and laughing as the needle strains toward my arm and laughing harder when a tape player reproduces the American MC Escher speech. Hearing it now, it lands like the punchline to a joke I hadn't known I was telling. When I realize that I am, two more realizations come with it: first, that I enjoy the way my audience regards me, and second, that this audience, composed of these children and millions like them, will travel with me for the rest of my life, populating, with a bare minimum of detail, whatever towns or cities or indeterminate wastelands I happen to try to call home between the Saga's Opening Number and its Grand Finale.

At the end of the semester, I set out to write my term paper on Delmore Schwartz and why he claimed responsibilities begin in dreams, but when I read my draft, I see all I've written is, "Dr. Forearm, the American MC Escher and my unofficial Pervert Uncle, has infected me with the Squimbop Condition, which I will now dedicate my career to spreading."

Driven by a force that feels ubiquitous yet unlocatable inside me, I apply to medical school, after perhaps many more years of childhood and adolescence, each less memorable than the last, until any trace of parentage and native soil has faded to hokey rumor. The house I believe I was raised in, side by side with my Brother in the shadow of a woman in a severe black dress, is no more salient now than the spot where a legendary circus planted its tents in the age before we were born, a site rumored to have been the origin point of the Brothers Squimbop, Jim and Joe, one of whom is rumored to have been me and the other my long-lost Brother, and yet what besides rumor do circuses ever leave behind?

I AM ACCEPTED BY EVERY MEDICAL SCHOOL I APply to and leave for Boston in the fall. There I dedicate myself to my studies, under a series of professors who all resemble Dr. Forearm in ways both playful and sinister. I drift through the standard coursework, writing papers and taking exams in the same fog that came over me when I attempted to parse "In Dreams Begin Responsibilities," a story that, after all these years, still exists for me as a title with nothing beneath it. I rent a studio apartment off Boylston Street and avail myself of assorted cannoli and dumplings as I stalk the alternately frozen and sweltering streets of the city, alone save for the suggestion of a presence beside me which, as I move from the early to the middle years of my schooling, thickens to the point of becoming visible in certain rare Massachusetts weather.

The appearance of this other neither spooks nor reassures me. Instead, I take it as a sign that I'm still on the path I've been on since I first visited Dr. Forearm, or since he first visited me, while I intuit that this presence, my Brother perhaps, is on the prior path, the one that I—or he—would have followed had it led anyplace other than straight to Dr. Forearm's office. Today I follow the path we've briefly come to share across Boston Common and down to the Ether Monument, erected in honor of that miracle gas's inventor, where I can tell another pivotal meeting will occur.

"I've been waiting," the presence says when I arrive, swarming the monument in imitation of its heady, formless subject. "I knew you'd come, but I didn't know when."

I look quickly behind me, then side to side, unsure what I'm afraid of but glad that no one's around. The presence seems to have walked by my side while also having been here expecting me all along. For a moment the roles scramble and I feel as though it was me waiting here for him to cross the Common, and I hear the applause that I sometimes think is roaring in the background all the time, so ceaselessly that ignoring it has become my only means of considering anything else.

"Jim," he says. "I'm Joe. Together we are the Brothers Squimbop. I think you know this, but it bears repeating for the folks at home." The children who laughed when I returned to Dr. Forearm's office in the dark of what I remember as my last day of elementary school laugh again now, their voices older, deeper, richer. A little frayed as well, I realize. Sanded down by the vicissitudes of wherever they've been.

"Follow me," my Brother instructs, and I turn from the monument, back across the Common and all the way to the Countway Library off Huntington Ave. He leads me inside, past the guard station where I flash my ID, and up into the stacks, past carrell after carrell stocked with frowning dummy students and into a reading room that, until now, has always been locked. The smell of dust and old ink and carpet cleaner wraps around me as I'm led by the hand toward a shelf full of dense brown hardbacks with German and Swedish lettering on their threadbare spines. Within a row of these—my hands rummage without guidance, or with a guidance that isn't mine—I pull out a creased paperback full of jutting bookmarks. The pages crinkle and crack, as if they'd been soaked and then dried on a radiator. I turn the cover toward me but find that the sun has set outside the window, leaving me alone in a dark room where I didn't think to turn on a single light.

I tuck the book under my arm and carry it to the wall, where I search for a switch I can't find. Then I try the door, which also declines to appear. Then I lie down on the carpet, where I see myself spending the night in a ball before reading the book's title by the rising sun. My audience hangs off the shelves, their breath hot in the sealed room, and I dream of a young Dr. Forearm closing his practice and driving a long, dark country road to the starter home he shares with two baby boys and a woman in a severe black dress. He sits down to dinner with the three of them and although he smiles and nods and even speaks between bites of ribeye and gratinated potato, all he can see is himself descending to his basement lab, past dozens of copies of *The Squimbop Condition*, to mix up more of the silvery liquid he will inject at dawn into one arm after another, peeling a long day's worth of boys off the world map to which they cling.

"You see?" my Brother asks. The Doctor jolts awake in his basement lab, having fallen asleep over his work again. In the library, I gaze through the dawn light at the volume I came all this way to find. I take in the words "The Squimbop Condition" on the title page before I flip to the Table of Contents, which appears to be divided, as in the old Sagas, into a series of escapades determined by circumstance or location.

My relief at discovering this book, with its introductory and valedictory notes by Dr. Forearm, and with it the potential for elucidating the Condition I've borne alone since childhood, is immediately undermined by a memory of my Pervert Uncle giving me the same book, wrapped in fish-stained newspaper, for my eighth or ninth birthday, unless it was my graduation from sixth grade. I see myself taking it upstairs to my bedroom, reading the first entry, entitled "Dr. Forearm," passing myself where I stand now, in the secret reading room in the back of the library, and realizing that nothing—none of the future that, even at eight or nine, I could see flickering behind an open door at the end of a long hallway—would be mine to author. "The first of innumerable Primal Scenes," I mutter, though I don't feel my lips move nor does the statement seem to have issued from any internal understanding of its significance, neither in the library nor in the childhood bedroom that led straight to it.

I close my mouth, read the first few pages, then return to my childhood bedroom, where perhaps I've been all along. When I first read the pages beneath the title "Dr. Forearm" and proceeded from there to those beneath the title "The Brothers Squimbop," I knew, all those years ago, that I would never be who I'd thought I was going to become and that, like so many before me and so many awaiting their turn, I would be Jim Squimbop instead, one half of a comedic duo that history, if these pages are any guide, still isn't done with and I can only imagine never will be.

I carry the book through the door that has just now appeared and over to an empty carrell—the only empty carrell on the entire main floor—pull a pen from a caddy on the desk, open to page ten, and write the words, "The Squimbop Condition is the human condition."

Then I close the book, sickened by what I know I'll find when I reopen it. When I do, the words I just wrote have been reproduced and crossed out and rewritten dozens of times, densely enough to cover all of page ten and most of page eleven across from it, turning both into nearly solid blocks. I study the script, searching for my own handwriting, determined to find it and thereby disprove the theory I can feel forming underground, in the least visited but likely most consequential layer of my cognitive framework, down where I picture the silver liquid forming under tremendous pressure. "I really am here," I say aloud. "This really is now."

I reach for the pen to write these words on the clean expanse of page twelve, but find the caddy empty. I look up to see all my classmates in a semicircle around me, pens in hand, jotting notes while our Abnormal Psych Professor struts and preens, puffing out verbiage that elicits sighs and nods from his audience. "And so you see," he says, rustling my hair, "the subject is not certain which memory is correct. Or, I should say, which memory underlies the other, since both are clearly present: did his uncle give him this book when he was a boy, in which he read and internalized the account of Dr. Forearm filling his veins with mercury, or did it happen the other way around, such that Dr. Forearm really did inject that solution, only to send the poor boy down a dim corridor of third- and fourth-hand memory until he ended up here, well into his coursework at Harvard Medical School, only to discover a book that, as soon as his eyes made contact with the Dr. Forearm account setting the narrative sequence in motion, overrode the memory of that trauma having actually occurred and replaced it with the *apparently* more innocuous possibility of having read about said trauma in a book—*this book*," the Professor barks, tearing it from my hands—"and thus annulling, by safely depositing between one dusty library page and another, the burden he feared it would otherwise be his fate to carry all the way from the Opening Number to the Grand Finale?"

The audience applauds and I take a long bow as the Professor removes his bald cap and lab coat and puts his arm around me and together we bow again, longer and lower, low enough to see that nothing can stop us from basking in the adulation the world directs, again and again, toward the Brothers Squimbop, whose role therein can never, it seems, be cleanly integrated or expunged. The warmth of our reaction to the applause sends us back to a long lost Mountain House where he and I sat side by side on damp velvet cushions with our Pervert Uncle beside us and Tommy Bruno in the wings, watching the Brothers take their bow at the end of the "Library Scene," kicking off another unforgettable performance at the apex of the Golden Age, just before setting out again on the open road, into an adventure that so entranced my Brother and me it came to feel as if we were its stars.

he Human Condition e Human Con

The Squimbop Condition

The Squimbop Condition

The Squimbop Condition

The Squimbop Condition is the

ndition is the Hum

the Human Conditi

is the Human Condit

the Human Condition

The Squimbop Condition is the Human

is the Human C

The Squimbop Condition is the

Human Condition

The Squimbop

is the Human Condition

he Squimbop

Condition

The Squimbop Condition is the Human

The Squimbop Condition

The Squimbop Condition
is the Human Condition
The Squimbop Condition is the Human Condition
is The Human Condition
The Squimbop Condition is the Human Condition
The Squimbop Condition is The Human Condition
Condition is the Human Condition
Squimbop Condition is the Human Condition
Squimbop Condition is the Human Condition
The Squimbop Condition is the Human Condition
the Human Condition
Squimbop Condition is the Human Condition
The Squimbop Condition is the Human Condition
The Squimbop Condition
is the Human Condition
Condition Squimbop Condition The Squimbop Condition is the Human
is the Human Condition
mbop Condition is the Human Condition
The Squimbop Condition is the Human Condition
The Squimbop Condition is the Human Condition
Human Condition
is the Human Condition
The Squimbop Condition
is The Human Condition
The Squimbop Condition is the Human Condition
Squimbop Condition is the Human Condition
Squimbop Condition is the Human Condition
The Squimbop Condition is the Human Condition
The Squimbop Condition
is the Human Condition
The Squimbop
The Squimbop Condition is the Human

The Brothers Squimbop

The Brothers Squimbop, Jim and Joe, plied their trade in the dusty American interior of the 2070s, which, following the logic that Y2K was the Zero Hour and it was all linear reversion from there, mapped almost perfectly onto the 1930s. They rambled through the Dust Bowl in a beat-up Chevy, taking semester-long postings at forgotten, often nameless Community Colleges to teach the students, such as they were, about what the nation used to be like. "Addle-brained giants walked this land," they would say, "picking up cities and putting them down thousands of miles to the west, once confusion slowed their progress to a standstill," or, "Overnight, all land and water in this nation traded places, such that America was once nothing but a constellation of small islands, the largest of which eventually became the Great Lakes." The students would yawn and stare at their crackling yellow notepads, dragging their pens along the lines and then off the edges of the paper and onto their desks. Others pulled cold hocks of meat from paper bags and held them in the air, sometimes remembering to gnaw them, other times not.

It was a dying art, that of walking into cavernous lecture halls and holding forth with the presumption of authority, despite the water damage, despite the mildew, despite the boxes of smudged documents floating in puddles, but the Brothers Squimbop were determined to keep it alive as long as they could. They sensed that its death would coincide with their own, so they took turns standing behind the podium in Tulsa, Aberdeen, and Eau Claire, careful never to be seen together so as to maintain the illusion of being one slightly inconsistent man, though no one ever pointed this inconsistency out.

Still, the idea that someone might was the source of no small degree of hilarity. Modest pleasures, the Brothers had determined long ago, were the only pleasures within mortal reach. The confusion caused by their alternation, even if only theoretical, was a good example of this. We are, in this sense, a sort of comedy duo, they liked to tell themselves, a pair of entertainers plying our trade in the vast interior of a nation that long ago lost any claim to psychic or even geographical coherence. A nation that is now nothing but a tattered platform upon which anyone passing through can mount whatever road show accords with his—the Brothers knew no women well enough to joke about—sense of humor, and, with luck, extract a few nickels before shuffling on.

They might go for whiskey and pork at a Beale Street barbeque joint on their way out of Memphis, if they'd already been fired from whatever institution they'd been teaching at, and ruminate on the nature of their journey, forcing their minds away from any speculation as to its unremembered beginning and unimaginable end.

Hovering, as they were obliged to, in the temporal and spatial middle of all things, they ribbed one another constantly and mercilessly, each claiming, as often as possible and in the lewdest possible terms, to be the other's father. The things they claimed to have done with their ostensibly mutual mother, whom neither had ever met, nor even ever heard from, though both pictured her clad always in a severe black dress, made each Brother blush so heavily that it was nearly impossible to complete the boast without devolving into gusts of nervous laughter, like boys watching pigs rut on a farm, had they been farm boys, which perhaps they had been, since no images from before the age of forty existed in either of their minds.

Aside from the one-upmanship inherent in these tales of the circumstances surrounding the other's conception, their greatest game involved devising new and increasingly salacious means of getting themselves fired from their already-tenuous teaching posts. Each delighted in returning to the Ramada Inn or the EconoLodge where the other was sprawled on the bedspread with the blackout curtains drawn at three in the afternoon, and announcing, "They've run us off campus again! This time I suggested that the moon was in fact the locus of all legitimate human activity, while Earth was a sort of penal colony for those too dimwitted or depraved to take part in the larger social project, and I had a whole lecture prepped on this premise"—the Brothers always prepped their lectures separately, to ensure maximal disjunct as they traded off teaching duties—"but then I found myself laughing so hard I was, in short order, choking on great spicy wads of phlegm, and I had the impression that the moon itself had heard my blasphemies and was punishing me for it, in the manner of actual lunatics, and, anyway, I was..."

But by this point in the story the other Brother would already be packing his bags, stealing a few Douwe Egberts coffee packets if they were in a motel that provided them, and preparing to peel out of the parking lot in their '27 Chevy, tearing onto the abandoned highway like a couple of bank robbers, Dillinger 1 and Dillinger 2, burning rubber in high dudgeon as they put another failed venture behind them, "Me and the Devil Blues" wailing over the transistor radio.

These were the times when the Brothers fancied themselves the only mobile entities left in the nation, elected to that position by forces residing either deep within themselves or else far off in the surrounding murk. The highways were abandoned save for the occasional unlabeled truck and caravan of gypsies, and the motels and gas stations seemed to be the only anachronisms, pointing to the existence, in the past or the future, of an era other than the 1930s. Everything else, as far as they could tell, had reverted and was perhaps reverting still, toward the medieval or even the prehistoric, not that either Brother had a stable notion of what this meant. Memory and imagination, they found, had grown so intermingled that it was no longer possible even to claim a distinction between the two words, let alone to find out what it might be.

As they lurked in a strip club in New Orleans, watching men and women covered in sores circle sweaty poles in a daze, slamming into one another when the music stuttered, they considered how a smothering, smoke-smelling curtain of forgetfulness had been drawn across the country, so that now history was nothing more than whatever they said it was.

Because the saddest thing, or one of the saddest things, they thought, each Brother keeping it to himself, is that we are never, in actuality, run out of the colleges we teach at, because no claim we make ever gets enough traction to become taboo. As there is nothing for us to clash with—each pictured himself lecturing the strippers—we are only run out in the sense of wanting to leave, of seeking, once again, the romance of the open road, knowing full well that any exit off the highway, chosen either at random or after painstaking deliberation, will produce the exact same result, like a die whose every face displays the same black dot.

To avoid the grim prospect of giving voice to this notion, each Brother kept his die well hidden, insisting to the other that his transgressions were real, and that the consequences, if they stayed in town, would be swift and decisive. Each was thus, in the eyes of the other, a genuine outlaw, or so he told himself.

"Want to walk through the French Quarter and see if any murders are going on?" Joe Squimbop asked, unfurling a few bills to pay for the beer and chicken they'd consumed, and stuffing another few under the bandage of a stripper who'd cantilevered out over their table to receive them.

Jim nodded, eager to lighten the mood, so they walked off their dinner along Bourbon and Royal Streets where, indeed, three people were murdered in quick succession, a knifing and two shots to the head. Though the Brothers weren't unmoved, they seemed to stand apart from it, bullets whizzing inches from their noses without grazing them, nor even seeming liable to. It's as though we are both here and not here, they found themselves thinking in the relative private of their respective heads. Present in name only.

Before the evening wilted the rest of the way into bathos, they returned to their Red Roof Inn in Metairie, cutting through alleys where ambiguously human shapes bedded down in piles of trash, their eyes shining yellow in the humid night. Others clung to doorways, backlit, their fingers merging with the soft wood surrounding them until it looked like they'd grown there.

As the Brothers slipped naked into the motel hot tub, they coined a new term—mushroom-people—for these entities, though of course neither mentioned it to the other. Outwardly, it was just the two of them in a chlorine-smelling annex, laughing about the lecture series they would deliver in Arkansas as soon as they found a suitably decrepit college to decamp at until their next scandal uprooted them yet again.

TWO DAYS LATER, THE BROTHERS SQUIMBOP HAD secured themselves a post at a taxidermy school in Mountain Home and a room in another Red Roof Inn, where they joked that the day's journey had, in the end, consisted of no more than moving a few doors down a single ashy hallway. They seemed to be the only guests, and were most certainly the only professors in the American History Department.

At the outset of every new post, the Brothers drew straws to determine who would teach first. After this, they would alternate daily. This time it was Jim, so, the following morning, he showered and shaved, put on the sweaty tweed suit the two of them shared, neither quite fitting into it, and walked to campus with his empty briefcase under his arm. Standing behind the podium, facing two young women and a young man with cauliflower ears, he began by summarizing what had gone wrong with America in the last century. "Americans began as mushrooms," he answered, "and would have been much better off remaining such. But, around the year 1995, a torrential downpour—what some called a Flood—saturated our ancestors' systems and, unable to absorb the excess moisture, their fungal crevices became capillaries, which in turn became veins, which in turn became arteries, and, within the span of a generation, we turned into what we are now, hopelessly trying to inhabit an environment we were never built for.

"And yet those who fared the worst," he added, picturing the entities sprouting from doorways in New Orleans, "are those who stayed inside during the downpour and thus remained mushrooms, or mushroom-adjacent. A collective species-consciousness now compels them to attempt to leave their domiciles and join the larger human family, but they are stuck too tightly to the walls—indeed, they are *part* of those walls—to ever do so. Imagine, if you would, being left behind in such a state."

At this point in the lecture, a wolf sauntered into the room. It stood in the middle ground between the podium and the students, swiveling its head from one side to the other. Then it yawned and sauntered out. When Jim looked back at his students, his eyes locked onto those of one of the young women, who had an animate keenness about her that unnerved him.

AFTER CLASS, HE RETIRED TO HIS OFFICE, WHICH in this case was an electrical closet on the third floor. He took his shoes off, leaned against the wall, and shocked himself on a loose wire. Jolting forward, he kicked open the door just as the young woman was standing outside, peering in.

"Professor Squimbop?"

She appeared certain that it was him, so he didn't respond.

"Are you having office hours in here?"

There were few things in the objective world that he hated more than office hours, but he nodded and watched as she pulled a crate from a pile stacked against one wall and sat down on it, as far from him as the cramped space would allow.

Clearing her throat, she leaned forward and said, "I was interested in what you were saying in class. I've seen the mushroom-people too, up in Minneapolis where I'm from, and also... well, I was wondering, how do you know where they came from? How is it that you remember what America used to be, while no one else does? What secret source do you draw from?"

Jim licked the backs of his teeth, anxious to see how long he could get away with not responding.

Time ticked on, until, quivering slightly, she repeated her question verbatim.

I can tell she isn't sure if she asked it already, Jim thought. He had half a mind to try his not-answering act a second time, but feared it would escalate the situation, and, being at heart a coward, he knew that any escalation would eventually turn out poorly for him. "How is it that I remember? I might ask the same, er, rather, the opposite, of you: how is it that you don't?"

Another silence. He could feel the tables turning, though he wasn't yet sure how. The horror of being taken seriously, of a student actually listening to what he'd said and acting as though it meant something, swarmed him. He started to fear that the air in the closet would soon run out.

"Are you seriously asking me that?" she asked. "Because I live in the same country as everybody else. The exact same thing that happened to them happened to me. You, on the other hand..."

Her eyes flickered with a kind of intensity he'd never seen before. The gaping stares of the zombies he'd addressed from all the podiums he'd ever lectured from now seemed benign compared to the attention she was leveraging against him.

Either she's not really here, Jim found himself thinking, or I'm not. We can't both be. He knew that all it would take on his part was the presence of mind to insist that he was the real one and she the interloper. But, just now, he couldn't tell if he had it in him. He shivered as she leaned in, expecting an answer.

Isn't this what I've always wanted? He wondered. A genuine conflict, a real reason to flee town? Faced with it just then, he couldn't be sure.

"Why should we believe this is what happened?" she asked, making it clear she wasn't going to simply vanish because he wished she would.

Jim shivered and wanted to cry. Why, indeed? Perhaps nothing at all happened, and this is simply how it's always been. All my Brother and I ever wanted, he wanted to tell her, was to comfort ourselves with the possibility that the truth is knowable. That something, rather than nothing, resides at the very bottom. Is that so shameful a thing to want?

Yes, he imagined her saying.

He opened his mouth, hoping that some of what he'd just thought would come out, but nothing did. He left it open until he'd forgotten what he'd wanted to confess. Then he licked his palm and grabbed the exposed wire, praying it would shock him violently enough that she'd run away, or at the very least yawn and saunter off, just as the wolf had.

ONE WAY OR ANOTHER, HE WOKE UP ALONE IN THE closet what felt like many hours later. His first thought was that he was dead. Then he considered that perhaps it was the other way around, that he'd been dead all this time and now he'd shocked himself alive.

He got to his feet, falteringly, and made his way out of the building, past the damp classrooms, so empty they seemed as though they'd never been occupied, past the grim gallery of taxidermy equipment on the first floor, past piles of armadillo shells under a dripping spigot, past the wolf from earlier sitting so still it looked stuffed, across the campus, up HWY-62, past a Shoney's where a crowd was fighting in the parking lot, and back to the Red Roof Inn where, he prayed, his Brother would be drunk enough to refrain from asking how the day had gone.

Bursting into the room, which smelled of chicken skin and hot sauce, he yelped, "The day went great!" Then he stripped down to his boxers, removed his journal from the nightstand, and got into bed with it. Aware that his Brother's eyes were on him, he undid the novelty lock, opened to the first blank page, and wrote:

Unutterable abyss of loneliness, deeper than the deepest, darkest depths of the ocean, wider than the widest breadth of space in the asteroid-choked nothingness beyond the orbit of any planet, habitable or otherwise: this is what I, in my heart of hearts, believe with absolute certainty lies at the bottom of everything that ever was, and ever will be. Student today wanted to know why I was spared the forgetting while no one else was. The answer I should've given: I was spared nothing at all. I remember nothing save for what I've made up.

I'm simply less gullible than you are.

So thank God (ha-ha!) that my Brother is an imbecile and thus incapable of perceiving what I perceive. Thank God my Brother lives in childlike ignorance, thereby allowing me to tag along with him for the comedy of errors that makes up our blessedly circumscribed life here in the Saga. This is the sole mercy that allows me to persevere.

"WHAT'RE YOU WRITING?" JOE ASKED, AS HE FINished his own writing and prepared to turn out the bedside lamp, to which Jim replied, without hesitation, "How I porked your mother in an alley behind a Denny's in Fresno with the busboy watching, and then how you popped out two months later, so freak-looking the doc said you were a rare hybrid of rat-lady and actual rat!"

Closing and locking his journal after pretending to read these words from it, Jim nodded off with a mixture of fear and envy at the prospect of his Brother waking up to face the young woman tomorrow, while he would spend the day drinking alone in this room, fending off Housekeeping if it tried to ferret him out. Like a sow pregnant with many piglets at once, his mixed feelings went all the way to his center.

Joe Squimbop, meanwhile, smiled as he too turned off his bedside lamp. His final thoughts before sleep were: *Thank God my Brother's too dumb to understand what our situation here actually is, how precarious it has become, and perhaps has always been. Let him joke his life away. It spares me having to commune with someone who sees the truth as clearly as I do.*

Then he pulled the sweaty Red Roof pillow over his head, determined to get a few hours of real sleep before it was his turn to wake up, put on the tweed suit, and head to campus in the morning.

The Brothers Squimbop in Europe

When the Lecture Circuit folded in on itself, as they'd known one day it would, the Brothers decided to ship out east, back where their something-something-somethings had sailed from, once upon a time, to see if things were any funnier on the other side. Refreshed by this possibility, they made it across in a little under a week, stowing away on a nineteenth-century steamer carrying oats, horses, and touched-up Model T's.

They disembarked at the Hook of Holland along with a sweaty and cursing rabble, and wended their way into the narrow streets, flexing their nostrils against the blackening meat smoke in the air. As their wending went on and the crowd thinned out, they found themselves lost among blind men and women draped in rags and dragging carts while legless children scooted along the cobblestones on tricked-out skateboards.

These sights and others like them proliferated until the Brothers stopped to lean against a grease-stained and graffitied bus station wall, and thought to themselves, say, doesn't this all look a little more like how we always imagined things back then, and a little less like how we always imagined them now? Not that there was much recourse if there'd indeed been a switcheroo, but it couldn't hurt to find out, and, seeing as they were leaning against a bus station wall, they figured they were already partway toward turning up someone to ask, or at the very least a trustworthy piece of signage.

So they peeled off the wall and strutted through the automatic doors, which whooshed open onto a dim terminal full of muffled footsteps and rolling gusts of air-conditioned perfume. Everything was immaculate, like an exhibit of a bus station from an earlier or a later time, a testament to how things once were or might one day be, if the chips fell one way and not another, complete with demo-people sitting on benches, watching the Brothers pass.

Through this heavy quiet, they made their way to an *InfoKiosk*, labeled as such, and put their swarthy faces up to the polished, fresh face of a young woman in a blue pantsuit with a short red scarf tied around her neck and asked, in unison, whether this here was now or then.

The woman blinked and computed for part of a second, then looked from one Brother to the next, as if keen to assign them roles before replying, "Well, gentlemen, that depends on whom you ask." She sighed, as if the implications of this statement ought to be obvious, the burden it conveyed shared by all. The Brothers attempted to appear as if this were so, but their attempt must've been unconvincing, because she added, a moment later, "There have been a number of referenda lately, attempts to determine whether the modern era you see in here, or the medieval era you see out there, is the pretend one. Because certainly—nearly everyone agrees on this much, though not an inch more—they can't both be genuine. One must be the pageant, the other the actual present time. But who's to say which is which? Well, the people are to say, of course, and yet what happens when the people become no more than a volatile surplus of ghoul-eyed persons?"

She paused here, as if waiting for an answer, then adjusted her scarf, looked from one Brother to the other, cleared her throat and said, "Well, gentlemen, that depends on whom you ask." She sighed. "There have been a number of referenda lately, attempts to determine whether the modern era you see in here, or the medieval era you see out there, is the pretend one. Because certainly—nearly everyone agrees on this much, though not an inch more—they can't both be genuine. One must be the pageant, the other the actual present time. But who's to say which is which? Well, the people are to say, of course, and yet what happens when the people become no more than a volatile surplus of ghoul-eyed persons?"

When she'd finished, the Brothers thanked her for the info and, sensing opportunity, hurried back out of the bus station and into the throng surrounding it.

THEY POSTED UP AT A PLASTIC TABLE FRONTING A meat and flatbread stall, bought as much as the last of their dollars would get them, and ate with their hands, kicking the stray cats that poured in to nip at their ankles. The eating and the wincing and the kicking took on the rhythm of a routine, a clown interlude, and, before long, a filth-crusted public had clustered in to watch. Faces grew out of the shoulders wedged behind them, eclipsing all necks, and mouths fell open to jeer and excrete tobacco in unison, like it was a multi-headed beast the Brothers had summoned, a bulbous hee-hawing demon they could puppet with their legs each time they kicked a cat, or with their mouths each time they howled in pain, or with their arms now that these too had become incorporated, slamming up and down on the uncleared tabletop, spraying meat leavings in a cloud that surrounded their vision, grease on grease, hovering there as the day heated up.

Now that they were in rhythm, nothing prevented them from reverting all the way back to their roots, tumbling awake, sticky with afterbirth, in the grass of a county fairground in some corn town in Indiana, or on some brown-grassed riverside in Missouri. They could never agree which, but the image of the place, or the feeling of the image, saturated them, and lent their current slapstick an air of pathos, which caused them to drill so deeply into the performance that, by the time they resurfaced, the sun was going down and the crowd was dissipating, leaving in its wake a pile of wilting reddish bills whose value the Brothers could only pray wasn't nothing.

They stood, shivering as they came back to the present, and scooped the haul into their fists, divvying it fifty-fifty. Then they walked into the darkening side streets behind the market square, past the circle of cats they'd kicked to death, through air heavy with the scent of damp wool and frying gristle. "Through air heavy with the scent of damp wool and frying gristle," they repeated, storing the line for future use. It wasn't until they'd rounded several blind corners, climbed a steep set of concrete stairs past a cathedral whose stained glass windows had been reduced to trembling stalactites, and traversed a boardwalk whose boards had long since rotted to nail-bitten slats, that they came to the ocean, black and calm and fishy as any ocean anywhere.

They walked out of the light of a row of hotels and beach bars, past a harbor where dinghies and sailboats bobbed at anchor, and up to a cove at the edge of the city, which they judged as safe a place as any to sit and think. A scuttling in a spruce tree overhead forced them to reconsider, but a glance revealed it to be no more than a squirrel, and a second glance revealed it to be, perhaps, not even that. Still, they reasoned, it would be wise to buy knives.

With this much decided, they spread their haul across the sand, counted it by feel in the dark and, agreeing to believe that it represented a substantial sum, looked toward the future. Whatever place this is, they thought, it seems to contain a receptive audience, if today's is any indication.

Satisfied with this new prospect and thus relieved to be free of the deadening alternation of Missouri and Michigan, Arkansas and Arizona, state after state drying up and blowing away as they lectured in empty halls watered by dripping spigots, they burrowed into the sand, hot on top and cool underneath, and slept amidst the sandflies, dreaming of glory.

THE SUN BROILED THE BROTHERS AWAKE. IT CAME down so hot the first thing that reached them was the smell of their own smoking skin, a rich, meaty aroma that sent them out in search of breakfast.

After a quick repast of stewed goat and black bread at a stall staffed by almond-eyed children, they set out on the road that led up from the valley in which the Hook of Holland nestled, and soon found themselves tracing a network of mountain passes, looking down at blue lagoons and up at destitute settlements freckling rock faces, their streets so steep it seemed to the Brothers that only spidermen could live there.

As the day wore on and their lack of water took its toll, it started to seem that spidermen were indeed clinging to the streets of these jagged mountain towns, nailed to chairs outside smoky cafes or leaning over iron balconies with pipes dangling from their mouths, watching through motionless eyes as these two dehydrated and improbable wanderers passed below. The streets were now so steep they closed in overhead, forming a dome the Brothers had to lean back and stare up at, making eye contact with elderly spidermen and -women sipping coffee from tiny cups and picking at wilting pastries that, through the private logic of a foreign culture, held fast to their ornate china platters.

"Either we've wandered someplace heavy, Brother," Jim whispered once it was clear that both of them were perceiving the same tableau, "or we've got about five minutes to find something to drink before we collapse."

Joe, whose skin was steaming, had already come to this conclusion and thus began to hector an old woman dragging a donkey cart who'd just appeared. He begged her to spare some of the black liquid that dangled in a clear canister from a leather strap tied to her wrist, hoping it wasn't tar or motor oil. Though she didn't speak, she seemed to understand the request well enough to pull the donkey's metal bowl from a clattering pile of tools in the cart and place it on the ground with a sigh, bracing it with her foot as she poured it half full.

When she'd done this, she stood back, placed her hands on her hips, and looked the Brothers over. Recognition played across her face, like she expected them to know her, but they ignored it and she made no move to force the issue.

Joe sank to his knees, then down to his belly, propping his upper body on his flat palms so as to swivel his face into the black liquid. He spooled his tongue down into its viscid depths and tasted molasses and honey and possibly something fermented, but it was sweet and hearty and, as far as he could tell, not too poisonous.

He drank until the woman kicked him aside. Then he rolled into the dust and watched as Jim took his turn, lapping until the woman kicked him aside as well, so as to make room for the donkey.

When the donkey had also finished—the woman didn't kick it aside, but merely waited until the creature let up—the Brothers wiped their mouths, got to their feet, and looked the woman over. She was old and hunched and her left side had a pronounced tremor. Though she had both eyes, they could already hear themselves telling a roomful of townspeople tonight, if they were lucky enough to find a town, how they'd met a crazed one-eyed sorceress on the road, and how she'd nursed them back to health with some black poison that had imbued them with the power to contact the dead, or to detect the winging of notional creatures in the high ether, or perhaps to...

But there'd be plenty of time for all that later. The thing now was to impress upon her their need to reach this imagined reprieve by nightfall. They pointed up the road, which had returned most of the way to horizontality, and squinted at the sky to show that the sun was blinding them. There was no means by which they could convey the nature of the hallucinations they'd had before meeting her, but they hoped their pantomime would nevertheless prove their condition was dire. They were careful to both look in the same direction, lest she tell one of them to go one way, and the other another.

"We need food, shelter," they intoned, hugging themselves and dancing, which had the effect of making the old woman smile. As they went on, clownishly exaggerating their motions, she began to guffaw.

She rocked back and forth on her heels, and didn't stop until the Brothers had winded themselves and staggered over to the remnants of a cement wall by the edge of the road, where they panted and spat up long gobs of brown phlegm.

When this routine too had reached its conclusion, she lurched over to them and, as if she'd been joking all this time in her bafflement at the language they spoke, said, in a clean Dutch or German accent, "Nearest town's up that way, about an hour. Rough place. Take care, boys."

Then she kicked the donkey, tightened the screw cap on her empty bottle, and trudged off with a knowing wave.

The Brothers made haste in the direction she'd indicated, heads full of loose story that, by the time they arrived, would have compacted itself into an open-road tale that ought to earn them a drink or two, and, if they were lucky, a few mouthfuls of fried meat to soak it up. They riffed and rehearsed as they went, and the road seemed to flatten further to accommodate them, apparently satisfied with the ordeal it'd put them through.

As they emerged into the twilit glow of the Outskirts, they ambled along smooth cobblestones with rows of high-end Scandinavian cars on one side and piles of horse dung on the other, until they crossed what felt like an unguarded but highly tangible border, away from the open road and into the stagnant sanctum of a new town.

Immediately, townspeople gathered to look them over with a mix of wariness and intrigue. The very fact that they'd managed to enter from outside seemed sufficient to arouse the interest of these people, who appeared, like everyone the Brothers had met so far except for the woman on the road, to be stuck in place, circling a vanishingly small center of gravity. More like plants than people, the Brothers thought, as they climbed the concrete base of a towering statue of some chisel-jawed dictator. It's almost, they thought, clearing their throats and beholding the gathering crowd, like these people haven't succeeded in being born yet. Like they're still tethered by some umbilical link to this tiny patch of earth, absorbing ever more degraded nutrients as they wait for the clarifying event that we are now here to deliver.

Opening their mouths when they judged the crowd sufficiently swollen, Jim began, "We are, good people, free agents who've made our way here all the way from America to tell you that, even as we speak, there are lurkers on the surrounding roadways."

Joe continued, after a nudge from Jim, "Indeed, we've come to tell you that witches are massing on the peripheries. They're flocking together, gaining strength. Why, just today, we passed a one-eyed sorceress who forced us to kneel beside her donkey and drink a gout of blackest poison. If we'd refused, she would've turned us into infants and left us to await our deaths in the crushing heat. The poison was the lesser evil, though only very slightly."

He held his side and mimed collapse from stomach pain, inducing Jim to join in. The crowd laughed, cautiously, everyone looking to the person beside them to be sure they were laughing too.

"We dispatched that witch," Joe groaned, "only after great toil, and at great personal risk." He fumbled in his pocket for a hank of fur he'd torn from the donkey while Jim was supping. "Here's the last of her. But be warned, more are coming. They are, even now, meeting in hollows in the surrounding wilderness, planning their onslaught. As we've said, we come from America, a land already ruined by sorcery. It is too late for us, but not, thank God, for you."

"Not," Jim added, shouting over the growing clamor of the crowd, "provided you enlist our services. For we alone, good people, can preserve the natural order that has grown so fragile. For a modest fee, we will enchant the peripheries of your town, seeing to it that no witches penetrate the inner sanctum, which all of you have worked so hard to preserve for yourselves, and your children, and your children's children."

It was almost too easy. The Brothers hadn't come to Europe in search of a challenge, but the speed with which these people foisted their crumpled currency upon them and proffered food, drink, and lodging at the inn behind the slaughterhouse left them with a queasy feeling, like that of eating a milky pudding whose sweetness has begun to curdle.

Nevertheless, they left that town the next day in high spirits, and set out back on the open road with the promise that no witches would ever penetrate the protective spell they had expertly cast. They made their way upward, farther, as they imagined it, from the Hook of Holland, though their memory of arriving in Europe already felt warped and dented by the heat, a useless thing they ought to throw away before it went off in their rucksacks.

Day by day, town by town, business continued to boom. The Brothers worked through all the classics, spreading tell of well poisonings and child abduction, changelings and incest and miscegenation by ravening wildmen eager to rape young girls out milking at dawn or picking red berries in the pastor's woods for Sunday breakfast; they warned of currency manipulation and the malicious spread of occult science; they fanned the already flickering flames of suspicion that desert religions were seeping into the groundwater of mountain ones, and vice versa, turning the True Word into a mush-mouthed abomination thereof, blasphemy upon blasphemy, moral decrepitude and decline, and they sowed fear of paternity, of bloodlines sundered and contaminated by Moors and Masons and Jews, of politicians serving as the puppets of unseen masters, simpering in the boardrooms of cities that no one present had ever seen, and few had ever heard of. They called into question whether the year was 1613 or 1835 or 1999 as they turned neighbor against neighbor, seeing to it that none could trust any of what they read or heard or—once the Brothers really got going—even any of what they themselves believed. They bribed printers to issue contradictory versions of the same local papers and claimed that orphan trains had been found in the Ukrainian steppe, thousands upon thousands of children strong, worshipping star deities and tattooing themselves with runes and hieroglyphs, breeding in ever quicker succession, children begetting children, then infants begetting infants, triplets emerging from wombs where only one child had been conceived. Trains of goats birthing blind children who in turn birthed goats, all of them growing into mad kings and queens, wrecking the world while pretending to run it.

"No one but us can be trusted," the Brothers told town after town after town, the crowds sometimes composed of gap-toothed peasants riven with buboes, and sometimes of gap-toothed teenagers in torn jeans and soccer jerseys, straining to comprehend the Brothers' English, "because we alone have traveled the open road, and the high seas, and we have seen what's afoot out there. We know the full scope of what can happen. The entirety of America, ruined before our eyes. Here too those who appear most blameless are surely the most corrupt."

As the weeks became months, they expanded their repertoire, deviating from the classics and ranging more boldly into tales of their own design. "Werewolves are stealing in from the deep Carpathian woods at night," they told the people of one town, "and impregnating your cows, so that any calves born to them must be buried in molten iron, lest they grow into three-headed demons, their milk the fibrous nectar of the Gnostic Satan, who will, in time, be born to a human mother and crawl into your pantries to sup."

In the next town, they reported that chickens all over the countryside had been caught in the dark of a lunar eclipse and sent backward on their evolutionary path, so that soon lizards would hatch from their eggs and then, if nothing was done to stop it, dinosaurs. Dinosaurs, they stressed, that would take to the skies and reduce whole regions to ash in the course of one long Walpurgisnacht as soon as the next eclipse happened to occur.

There was, it seemed, nothing they couldn't sell. Any tale at all, delivered by the Brothers Squimbop, would send any town into a frenzy of preparation in which the people would, without hesitating, slaughter their cows with hammers and drown their chickens in ice baths, or, in the towns where the Brothers suggested that the monsters were already amongst them, having assumed human form, turn the market square into a pyre whose flames loomed high above the rectory, the crematorium, and the rendering plant.

THEY DRAGGED THEIR ROADSHOW THROUGH BELgian swamps and up jagged alpine ridges, brandishing the knives they'd purchased from a silversmith in Zürich at monkeys and bears and the occasional lowland fox. They rode sometimes in military vans driven by silent, masked soldiers, and sometimes they stowed away on boats crossing pristine glacial fjords or sweltering stretches of sea between one Greek isle and the next. They told themselves that they cared little for their lives, yet nothing seemed eager to kill them. On the contrary, it seemed as though everything and everyone they came in contact with was operating at a remove, like there was an invisible dead space between themselves and the world they were describing, or conjuring, so that while they could trudge across fields of unexploded mines in the hills above Sarajevo, or swim ashore after an Italian pleasure boat they'd snuck aboard capsized off the coast of Taormina, there was never any threat, or chance, of a permanent reprieve. The demand for our services, they thought, while basking in the shadow of Mount Vesuvius, is too great to let us go. Indeed, perhaps, it's all there is. The only factor still in play.

IT WAS ONLY WHEN, IN A MOUNTAINSIDE HAMLET outside Belgrade, the Brothers beheld a troupe of eyeless, infant-sized creatures leading a herd of goats on chains through the market square that they were forced to pause. They observed the goats birthing more of these creatures as casually as excreting the roughage of their morning kibble, hardly stopping as the monsters fell out of them. These monsters then rose to their feet, produced chains from someplace the Brothers couldn't identify and, perhaps from that same place, produced more goats, who in turn produced more monsters and chains and goats, which in turn sent the Brothers scrabbling along a steep, dusty goat path all the way back to Belgrade, where they holed up in a WWI-era pension, desperate only for a little time to regroup.

They lay in bed the next morning until the sunlight through the window singed their foreheads. Then they got up, hosed down in the shower stall on the first floor, and went into the square for flatbread and coffee. Here, as over the days that followed, they watched chaos mount, voices rising in Serbian and Greek and Russian and dialects they couldn't identify, a sense of alarm rising toward a breaking point they could tell was near. As newspapers and broadsides circulated photos of mass riots, villages in flame, altars and effigies soaked in blood, the tables around them emptied out. Everyone, so far as they could tell, was mobilizing, mobbing the train stations and bus terminals, or marching, en masse, out of Belgrade and toward what the Brothers assumed must be the coast.

Just like that, they thought, among the crumbs at their breakfast table in the now empty square a week later, our journey has taken a turn. Today is likewise the day for us to flee. So they packed their few belongings, settled their bill at the pension, and hustled up the crooked Ottoman streets, strewn with the heads of chickens and the entrails of sheep, past capsized buggies and corpses writhing with strange new life, until they made it to the teeming train station. They were jostled this way and that, hauled off a train they'd already boarded and shoved onto another, destination unknown, and yet still they were happy to board. They sat back in their seats, among passengers wearing antlers on their heads, or on shrunken heads around their necks—the Brothers could dimly remember spreading tales of this faction—stuffed with yellow eyes that seemed to gaze out with hellish intensity. They wriggled down on the leather banquette and fell into a spiral of nightmares. When they awoke, perhaps days later, the few remaining passengers were disembarking. Even so, the Brothers tried to remain, eyes closed and knees hugged to their chests, but the conductor came by and, as if expecting to find them in precisely this aspect, sighed, barked something in a language they couldn't name, and dragged them out, first Jim and then Joe, depositing them both on the track beside the one where the train sat idling. Then, though the conductor had seemed to swear this was the last stop, the train rushed off to the south.

THAT NIGHT, IN WHAT APPEARED TO BE A TOWN IN southern Germany, the Brothers, exhausted and clean out of currency, took to the podium in the central square and simply told what they'd seen. They began with the chains and the goats, continued on through Belgrade, and ended with their journey here. "Europe, good people, is turning strange. There is nothing to say but this. All attempts at warding off what is coming have failed."

Looking out at the crowd, they saw the woman in the black dress with her donkey. She had only one eye this time. It took them both in, sparkling with concern as she mouthed something, her expression dire. A warning, they understood. Then she vanished.

They finished speaking and retired to a room above the alehouse, eager to buy more time, though they knew there was no more they could do with it. They drifted off, back to their nightmares. The next morning, after a repast of rolls and cold meat at the communal table downstairs, where the few townspeople present granted them a wide berth, the Brothers set out, agreeing to spend the day shoring up their routine. Time to get back on solid ground, they each thought. Put our act back together, get back ahead of the story. Update our itinerary, refill our coffers. Ensure that the show goes on.

But no sooner had they reached the next village than each Brother found his attention pulled from his head like stuffing from a dummy. Jim and Joe took to peering away from one another and into butcher shops, blacksmiths', and haberdasheries, imagining the lives of the men undertaking these professions, the colossal quiet that must fill the space of all that was shrieking inside the two of them. True ignorance is true innocence, they found themselves thinking, as if the time to become fathers was drawing near and they were thus imagining these unsuspecting villagers as the children they were soon to have, hammering anvils and flensing steaks within the safety of a village-sized womb.

The day wore on and the Brothers gawped at churchgoers and gravediggers and schoolchildren until the sun began to set and they found themselves at a crowded wooden table outside another alehouse. It's only a matter of time, they realized, watching the villagers sup, before the star-children and money-lenders make their way here. Before the sky fills with runes. There's no stopping it now, and thus, they decided, dipping a hot pretzel in cool lard, nothing to do but warn them.

So, once they'd finished their meal, such as it was, they took up a perch in the square and began their routine. "We two Brothers have come all the way here from America," Jim proclaimed, taking comfort in the familiar salvo. "Bearing a simple warning. Something too vast to name, something knowable only in its infinite particulars, a Fever some call it, laid waste to our land and is now laying waste to yours."

The ring of truth choked the Brothers Squimbop, but they forced their way past it, looking away from the eye of the woman in black, who'd reappeared near the front of the growing crowd.

Joe took over. "Trains of blind children leading pregnant goats on chains through the squares of formerly peaceful villages just like this one, making of them a wasteland in the course of a single moonlit spree. Mass rearrangements of the stars, polarities shifting, magnetisms shifting... entire orbits shifting..." He found he couldn't finish a sentence before the next one began. "Wells choked with severed bat wings... goats b-begetting... girl-children fathering half-wits with their outstretched index fingers in obeisance to... to..." His gaze snared, once again, on the woman in black, and he fell silent.

"In obeisance to," Jim continued, though something told him not to, "a one-eyed sorceress in a black dress, who... who..."

The crowd, as one, closed in on her. All attention lapsed from the Brothers, rendering them a two-man witness to what was fast becoming a village-wide riot. While they stood there, torches were produced and the alehouse went up in flames. Then the church, the butcher's shop, and the village stables. A grunting and growling emanated from the townspeople, a mass-voice that belonged to none of them in particular, reverberating off the cobblestones and the buckling wood.

Looking up, the Brothers saw the stars rushing together, drawing powdery traces across the firmament, and they heard a low slithering from the distance and with it the smashing of bottles, the breaking of bones, and the spilling of blood. Amidst all this, they bowed to their absent audience and set out running, skirting the edge of the melee as best they could, leaving the sorceress for dead.

THEY RAN THROUGH THE SIDE STREETS, AVOIDING the doorways through which streamed knife-wielding men, women, and children, and made it intact to the sheds and garden plots flanking the Outskirts. Here, they deemed it safe to catch their breath before venturing into the surrounding wilderness, which grew hot and misty as it welcomed them, sealing itself off beneath the changed sky.

Soon they were lost in a deep wood. The air turned thicker and blacker still, the trunks of tremendous black oaks now brighter than the sky. They marched on, looking straight ahead, or down at their feet, or up at the hint of leaves, anywhere but at one another.

Before long, they were marching through knee-deep moss, past eerie, dripping ferns, singing nursery rhymes at full volume while the forest whispered louder and louder, until it wasn't a whisper at all. Now the forest was ringing and echoing in earnest, their own voices rubbed out, the air filling with smudges in the watery distance, which flickered, trembled, and, as they approached it, resolved into two figures, one of them draped in a black dress, the other a donkey.

The one-eyed sorceress smiled as they approached, her arms outstretched to receive them. They marched, half-conscious, into her embrace, desperate to be forgiven for what they had made her suffer. Then it was as if she were everywhere, all around them, blotting out the woods and the moss and the smudge of stars, until all they could see or feel or smell was black cloth and red blood, and they felt themselves shrinking inside it, their bones and muscles uncoupling, their worn-out viscera reverting to unformed flesh.

WHEN THE BROTHERS AWOKE, IT WAS DIM, LATE afternoon or early evening. They winced up to a sitting position, cradled their soft elbows, and scraped thick, sticky ropes of blood and mucus from their thighs and shoulders, then used the backs of their hands to wipe their brows, many times, until they could see.

Looking over, they saw the one-eyed sorceress, mopping between her legs with a black cloth. She smiled at them. "One of these times," she said, looking from Joe to Jim, "I'm going to get tired of doing this."

But she said it without rancor, and even smiled as they rose to their feet and asked if they could help her to hers. She waved them off. "I'll be alright. I ought to be by now." She laughed, but when they stayed standing above her and began to laugh as well, her face grew worried. "Go!" she shouted. "What are you waiting for? There's clothes and provisions in the donkey's pack. Take them and be off. Europe is no place for bright young men any longer."

EAGER, FOR ONCE, TO OBEY, THE BROTHERS GATHered these provisions, dressed themselves, and set out running, out of the forest and into the crackling ruins of a village they could just barely remember, an echo from another lifetime. They hoped to stop for bread and ale, but nothing remained, not even bodies. Well-fed jackals pawed the embers, eyeing the Brothers.

They hurried past a ransacked chicken coop at the far edge of town, lizard skin spooling out of gigantic crushed eggs, and then down a mountainside and through dense birch woods, through fields of fire and ash, through deserts and the shells of cities in which ostrich-headed deities presided over mass sacrifices and stars churned and boiled overhead, forming symbols the Brothers took turns staring up at, unable to look away, whatever the psychic cost.

Finally, they arrived in a rubble-strewn metropolis they decided to call the Hook of Holland. They turned to regard a group of monks or penitents in an alley, roasting a naked boy on an open flame, and, though their hunger was great, their eagerness to set sail was greater.

Thus, they gathered their cloaks about themselves and made their way to the harbor, where, though half the ships were capsized and half of those that remained had been hacked to splinters, they boarded a vessel that appeared primed to depart.

After long, dark hours hiding in the hold, among horses and threshers, the ship pulled anchor and wheezed out of the harbor, leaving the blighted continent behind at last. When they judged it safe, the Brothers climbed to the upper deck and watched Europe vanish to the east. Then they turned westward and watched the sun begin its dimming journey to America.

"This time, Brother, maybe we ought to—" Jim began, but Joe, eager to enjoy what respite the passage might hold, raised a hand to stop him. If he'd learned anything after all these years, it was to expect peace only so long as neither coast was visible.

The Brothers Squimbop in Hollywood

After their tour of Europe, the Brothers returned to America, disembarking at the edge of a New World they could already see would never be new again. They quickly abandoned the East, having lived out many lifetimes in both the slums and the penthouses of Boston and New York, to say nothing of their wild years in Philly, and thought to return to Arkansas and Louisiana, reprising their tired roles as shyster professors on the off-chance that the narrow Community College circuit had widened in their absence.

But as the train took them down past Wilmington and Baltimore, over the foggy narrows and vacationlands of the Chesapeake Bay and then inland from DC via Richmond, Raleigh, and Charlotte, the situation looked even more dire than they'd remembered, or perhaps it was simply that, after all they'd either caused or witnessed in Europe, they'd gotten their hopes up too high about the possible sanctity of return. The assumption that one side would look different from the other... where did it come from? They wondered, as the train sped Westward, deeper into the territories.

The vestiges of settlement, the motels and fast-food chains and, indeed, the waterlogged Community Colleges where they'd once taught, or pretended to teach, were no longer visible. They could see nothing from the train windows except bare foundations, burned cars, and piles of bodies whitened with lime. Stock material, they thought, powerless to prevent their next scheme from beginning to take shape. It's amazing, they went on thinking, that there's even still a train.

As soon as they thought this, the train, if there'd been one, tossed them out. They found themselves kicking bottles and syringes along the platform of a trashed station under a hazy blue sun, in a scrubland they took to be Missouri, or possibly Kansas, which they had at one time—from the dense solitude of a German forest, as they spent themselves in the effort to embody their own fathers—imagined to be the place of their birth, a sanctified land to which they feared they might never return.

And yet, they thought, here we are.

They sat down on the platform edge and gazed at the tracks extending away in both directions, the two horizons carbon copies of one another, like the landscape had been pressed together, then pulled apart by a lazy creator eager to double his every half-lucid inkling.

Speaking of half-lucid inklings, the Brothers thought, what about heading out West? All the way this time. We haven't pulled that one in a while, and it looks like we're halfway there already. They nodded, amenable to the notion, though uncertain what, if any, gold remained for the taking in what they remembered as the hills of Nevada and rural California, to say nothing of the great coastal cities beyond.

THEY GROANED TO THEIR FEET, EACH HOPING THE other would help him up, and began to walk along the tracks, toward what they could only hope was the sunset, though the bluish sun appeared likewise to be copied across both horizons—unless, they thought, it's a yolk that's broken and dribbled across the sky, smearing pseudo-suns in every direction, its undefined singularity or multiplicity but a version of our own conundrum, wherein we are both ourselves and each other, so that...

They both started cackling, at once sincerely and performatively, before they could follow this line of reasoning through to its no doubt ridiculous conclusion. Returning to more terrestrial comedy, as they always did when their inner routine drew too close to the raw nerve of their own nature, the Brothers reminisced, openly and incoherently, about their last venture out West, when they'd sold... or stolen... or dug up, or, indeed, smuggled copious quantities of...

The nouns wouldn't come. They staggered, back in their usual state of dehydration, and found that they could recall the moods and something of the scenes they'd inhabited in their previous Western escapades, the glitz, the glamor, the elegant decline, but none of the content. No faces, no names, no money. Nothing but a generalized whoosh of hustle, the thrill of pulling off a scheme in a distant, unsupervised corner of a still-nascent empire, in a lifetime now buried beneath many others.

They could picture an empty theater, and, if they strained, they could hear distant echoes and see shadows flitting at the edges of the stage and smell popcorn popping in the lobby behind them, but they could not draw any closer to reconstructing the specifics of the act performed there.

So they lumbered on, panting under the dimming bluish sun, or suns, and attempted to focus on the immediate landscape, stuffing their wayward shared attention back into whatever passed for the present.

Missouri, or Kansas, in contrast to California, appeared as nothing but specifics, chunks of concrete and rubber purged of all mood and atmosphere, to say nothing of narrative momentum. Objects that had reached their resting place. Indeed, the only narrative the Brothers could gin up was that their rebirth in the German forest had been botched, or only carried out partway—so that perhaps everything we're seeing here, each considered, is nothing but a manifestation of our own condition, as if this country appears only partly-made because that is the state my poor Brother and I have fallen into, as we struggle even now to finish being born, hovering between German and Kansan heritage, our story somewhere between that of two immigrant Brothers eager to seek our fortune in the booming West, and two low-down American grifters, returning in defeat from a disastrous spate of pillage abroad.

Still, each Brother looked at the other and thought, it's his problem more than mine. He's the half-made one, the gimp, which makes me his keeper, dragging him through this desert of discontent until, at long last, we bathe in the healing blue waters of the Pacific and become new again, cleansed of the afterbirth we cannot otherwise scrape off.

Relieved to have established this preliminary schema, they trekked on foot through dead town after dead town, stopping to rummage in abandoned gas stations and convenience stores, continually reminding themselves that they were advancing Westward however much they privately feared they were moving instead in narrowing circles, between one dead town and the next, along a Kansas-Missouri line that grew more constricting each time they walked it.

Here and there roving bands of refugees crossed their path, cowed, silent families with faces scrunched inward against the blowing dust, fearful of the white-haired shamans clacking among them with the shrunken heads of former shamans clustered like pearls around their necks. These shaman-headed shamans marched in front as if to lead the procession, but something shifty in their gait suggested to the Brothers that they knew the refugees followed only reluctantly, and only because they were all obligated to march in the same direction, out of the scalding interior and toward the coast.

The Brothers averted their attention, uncertain whether these people felt as doomed as they appeared, nor quite what the nature of this doom might prove to be, and, more to the point, whether any aspect of it was contagious. We are, lest we forget, they strove to remember, holy men ourselves, vested with the power to blight the entire European continent, to summon demons from the ether and set ancient villages ablaze. Perhaps, then, it is not too much to imagine that here in this new continent we may, indeed, once again stake our claim to the mythic and profit accordingly.

As they mulled over the possible return of their own shamanic power, redoubled as they took on the New World with the occult energies of the Old, the Brothers trudged past a series of signs that all read SALTON SEA: KEEP OUT. Once, twice, three times, then five times, then ten, they passed the salt-crusted banks of a dead ocean, rows of eviscerated tilapia lined up in the sun along its edges, verging onto wide expanses of shanties, tents, and trailers with blacked-out windows. The Brothers closed and rubbed their eyes and opened them again, hoping to resolve the question of whether they were wandering in circles or passing through a blighted Salton Sea district, a wide, woozy territory stretching between where they stood and the coast they longed to reach, but, of course, all that emerged were more signs that read SALTON SEA: KEEP OUT.

When they'd grown too exhausted to continue, they lay down on the granular banks of one such sea, closed their eyes, and prayed for deliverance, frightened and ashamed to imagine their new venture foundering so soon after its inception.

THEY AWOKE IN THE GRUELING SUN OF A NEW DAY and rose to their feet, determined to leave the last of the Salton Seas behind. We got a little turned around, they told themselves, as they set out West again. We got a little lost in the middle, they repeated throughout the day, dreaming of the cool Pacific and the sun setting, once and for all, over the horizon, perhaps never to rise again over their Saga.

Their resolve paid off, as the escapade appeared willing to admit them into a new phase. Now they wobbled past enclaves of mansions behind row upon row of razor-topped fencing, before which the Brothers couldn't help but stop and, half-crazed with hunger, gaze through the slats and up at the barred windows. They pictured the wealthy holed up like hermit crabs inside, praying that whatever this was would soon blow over.

Fat chance, the Brothers thought. They looked around, at the shuttered mansions on one side and the orphan trains on the other, the shaman-headed shamans whistling into sawed-open beer cans in the middle of the road, and the Brothers decided, as perhaps they often had before, that only they were qualified to tell the nation's story back to itself, and thereby to offer some form of clarity to those who were still in a position to absorb it. If they hadn't needed us, the Brothers reasoned, we wouldn't have been called back.

THIS REALIZATION COINCIDED, PERHAPS SUSPICIOUSLY, with their arrival in the Outskirts of what they were prepared to consider, at last, the Real Los Angeles, so long dreamed of and so long deferred. They explored one remote neighborhood after another, watching the alternation of loud ruin and hushed opulence until, once again, the sun set and they bedded down beneath a piece of corrugated tin siding in a mood of tentative calm.

Their dreams moved them back and forth across a soft, colorless plane, like a piece of vellum with nothing on it, separating those sequestered in their mansions from those trudging through the dust, eating one another and being eaten as the nascent escapade's delicate interplay of hunger, weakness, and circumstance dictated. The Brothers slept, and knew they'd have to go on sleeping, long enough to rough this space out, crossing it again and again inside themselves and each time dragging more detail—more footprints, more sweat, more fallen spittle and hair—into place, until it was sufficiently established to serve as the stage for whatever happened next.

In the morning, they staggered into a bakery where an old woman stood guard over a tray of cinnamon rolls. She grinned at them and, for a moment, something of the black-clad witch crossed her face. Her eyes seemed to drift together and, teasingly, resolve into one. When she smiled, they took it as her blessing. We are on the right track,

Brother, each thought, as they returned their attention to the face of the woman who now had two eyes again. If it seems we reached the West Coast too soon, it's merely an understandable sadness at this great nation having contracted over the years, shriveling in the merciless heat.

"Gets smaller every day," the woman quipped, slapping the counter and rattling the pennies in the change bowl. "That's why I never see the last of you." They bought two rolls with coins they'd scrounged from a train station ash tray and bit into them as they hurried out of the bakery and onto the dusty path behind it, past two dogs chained to a tire. The rising sun spread, once again, down their backs as the woman bid them a temporary farewell.

They walked and munched and danced unselfconsciously from side to side, growing jaunty as clarity rose within them. The apparition of their mother boded well. A sign that we're almost home.

The word *home* stopped them dead beside a plaque in the dusty path that read SPAHN MOVIE RANCH: KEEP OUT. They stood beside it for as long as they could bear to, reading and rereading those words, in the same font as the SALTON SEA, trying to remember where they'd heard or seen the name before. When they realized they'd finished their rolls, they spit out the crumbs and decided, without turning around to check, that their story led nowhere but deeper in.

THEY WALKED, CAUTIOUSLY AT FIRST, AMONG THE remnants of shacks and stables, a frayed hanging rope flapping in the wind and a horse graveyard in a ditch beside the gravel path. Beyond this, where the path split off toward alleys lined with more sheds and shacks to the left and right, stood the foundation and part of the first floor of what looked like it had once been, or was once going to be, a handsome, multistory wooden house. A mansion, nearly, though less opulent than those they'd seen on the way here. A humble mansion, they thought, as they climbed over cement chips and stray nails, hoisting themselves in through the gutted front door to stand in the unfinished foyer beneath a ceiling furry with bats. A mansion for workers, not retirees. A place of business.

As they pressed into the darker back rooms of the sprawling first floor, they uncovered a trove of camera and audio equipment beneath a wool blanket in the center of what they'd taken to calling *our command center.*

Here, they decided, keeping their eyes off of one another so as not to move, just yet, from thought to speech and then speech to action, we will set up our equipment. Whatever we produce will be produced in here. The first reels of what will one day become a Squimbop Media Empire will take shape in these dark back rooms. They stood in silence after this development had articulated itself, awaiting further instruction.

WHEN THE SILENCE HAD GONE ON SO LONG THAT it threatened to turn sinister, they looked at one another, and Jim, taking on this name for the first time since their return, said, suddenly overeager to speak, "Let's go out back and see if there's a truck. We're gonna need one."

Joe, also newly renamed, shuddered to hear his Brother speak aloud in this manner, and to realize that he otherwise wouldn't have known what he was about to say. We remain in nameless unison as long as we can, he thought. "But then..." He clamped both hands over his mouth, still unwilling to hear his own voice in that enclosed, abandoned space.

The Brothers, having resumed a silence that now felt performative, set out in the truck they'd found behind a storage shed, after hot-wiring it with a coat hanger they'd found lying on the passenger's seat, as if it had been used for this purpose many times before. A suitcase of wilted cash, found likewise in this shed, hid beneath Jim's feet as he drove.

They set to cruising the Outskirts of what they could just barely remember was once called Hollywood, up one broad, deserted boulevard and then down another, past tent cities and open-air markets where goats and donkeys hung skinless over plastic buckets, their hoofs wrapped in chains. They watched the destitute swarm, jockeying for position while they waited, the Brothers assumed, for the butcher to appear and divvy up the meat according to whatever system had been roughed out to postpone raw chaos.

They idled by the side of the road, just out of earshot, and began to confer. "Something happened here, Brother," Jim said to Joe, his tone rich with the same authoritativeness he had affected back in the command center. Joe nodded and, going with the riff, picking up on its rhythm—I can play the slow Brother, if that's our shtick for now, he conceded, I am man enough for that—replied, "Something, indeed. Something only we can reveal."

A familiar groove reasserted itself between them, a pattern of banter they hadn't fallen into since early in their European Tour. They relaxed, for the first time since that escapade had gotten away from them. "Phew," Jim said. "I think we're gonna be okay. I think we can show these people what happened here, and, by showing them, make it true. Remind them that nothing happens except through us."

"And make a buck or two."

They looked down at the suitcase of cash and saw what needed to be done, miming astonishment at their own powers of deduction for anyone who might be watching from afar.

THEY CRUISED BACK TO THE RANCH WITH THREE new hires in the truck, two women and a man, perhaps some kind of family. When they got out, they reiterated what they'd explained at the market, after the butcher divvied up the day's rations and the crush of supplicants closed in and then dispersed with veiny chunks in hand.

"So we just… pretend with these?" one of the women asked, looking from one Brother to the other, then over at the pile of pickaxes, awls, and sharp shovels they'd unloaded from one of the tool sheds. Her expression hovered between intrigue and suspicion as Jim nodded. Joe, meanwhile, was already plugging the camera and microphones into an extension cord they'd spooled out of the unfinished house, following the orders that Jim had given on the drive back.

"That's correct," Jim continued, while Joe warmed up the machines. "For this sequence, you three are deputy leaders in the Revolution, plotting the overthrow of the overlords of Old Hollywood. Taking it back for the people."

They nodded without evincing comprehension. "The graft and corruption have spread unchecked for too long!" Jim shouted, intimating that they should shout this as well, once the camera was rolling. "They've poisoned the very earth from which once grew our daily bread."

A silence ensued while the actors looked down at their feet, over to the swinging gallows, then back to the wad of cash tucked into Jim's pants, waiting for the signal.

Jim dragged George Spahn's mummy out from behind the woodpile where they'd found it—Joe tried to remember when this had been, and whether it'd made an impression on him, but found that he couldn't consider it in enough depth while also manning the camera. So he pressed his eye to the viewfinder and focused on the three actors stabbing the mummy again and again, shrieking, "Off with the corrupt head! Off with the corrupt head!" until, as directed by Jim, one of the women decapitated the mummy with the sharp shovel and held the head up to the camera, smiling and dancing in circles as it dangled from her fist by its long gray ponytail in the dying light of the long afternoon.

"Now kiss it," Jim directed. The woman hesitated, looking directly at the camera in a break of continuity that would have to be cut, but, after he repeated the directive, she acquiesced. She held the head to her lips long enough for Joe to zoom in on the contact, then danced, more slowly this time, in another circle, lips to the head's lips, while the other two danced around her, shrieking, "Crush the head! Crush the head! Crush the head like the head once crushed us!"

After the three of them had crushed the head, Jim yelled "CUT!" and Joe complied. There ensued a moment of fraught silence. The Brothers knew they had their footage. What they didn't know was what ought to become of the actors, now that they were complicit in its production. As far as Joe could tell, they hadn't yet considered this conundrum, inevitable as it now seemed.

If we are to sell this footage as actual, the Brothers thought, resorting to the telepathy that still inhered—or that each, when it suited him, chose to believe still inhered—between them, then these actors must never be seen on the streets again. They must be at-large, a tantalizing aura of terror building around their absence.

A family of murderers too savage to be housed in human flesh.

"You'll live here now," Jim announced, as if he and Joe had discussed it well ahead of time. "Spahn Ranch will be your home. Bury that head and go wash up." He nodded toward an open-air bathhouse that had cold running water and two toilet stalls. "If you try to leave, something will happen."

The actors looked from Brother to Brother, apparently weighing their options. "Will we...?" The woman who'd kissed the head asked, her lips dusty with old flesh.

"You'll be fed and watered," Jim replied. "Room and board. What else? Money? For what?" He waved his arm in the direction of the road that led out of the Ranch, as if to imply that everything out there, where money might still have been spent, was no longer of any concern.

It wasn't clear how the actors felt about this gesture, but they made no obvious move to contradict it. They turned and dragged the pulped head by its ponytail into the bathhouse.

AFTER THE BROTHERS HEARD THE COLD-WATER showers turn on, they ventured into their command center to edit the footage. As they worked, and found themselves equal to the task, which Joe hadn't been certain would be the case, they constructed a history in film for themselves, a loose but vivid story of how they'd been prominent directors in Europe—Joe pictured Vienna, while Jim pictured Zagreb—forced to flee the continent when its endemic tensions boiled over. The fact that these tensions had been of the Brothers' own making was no longer part of the narrative, nor, given that they were no longer quite the same duo they'd been back then, was it quite true. Now, here, they were two prominent European directors seeking refuge in Hollywood, trying to make a new name for themselves in the anything-goes Marketplace of American Ideas, at once more puritanical and more libertine than anything their Continental upbringing could've prepared them for.

THE PERIOD THEY SPENT DEVISING THESE NEW particulars coincided perfectly with the period they spent editing the footage to look like a piece of illicitly captured street video, raw minutes never meant to be seen, so that, by dawn, they emerged with both a coherent plan for their time in Hollywood and the tape that would set it in motion.

After noting that the three actors were asleep beneath a blue plastic tarp in the shade of a ratty willow, the Brothers climbed in their truck and drove out to what remained of Beverly Hills. They cruised through districts of ransacked bungalows and torched municipal buildings, the post office lying on its side, while the shriek and whistle of illicit pool parties curled over impermeable fences.

They rounded corner after corner in search of a chalet at which to peddle their wares. When they found one, Jim yanked up the parking brake so their truck wouldn't roll down the steep hill. They got out and approached the intercom beside the polished obsidian gate, Joe carrying the tape while Jim pressed the TALK button and put his lips to the microphone.

"Y...yes?" a tentative woman's voice responded.

"Ma'am, we have something you need to see."

Silence.

Joe fingered the tape, scratching its grooved plastic with the nail of his index finger.

"Ma'am," Jim repeated, when he could tell she hadn't hung up. "My Brother and business associate is holding up a unit of raw data," he nudged Joe to hold the tape in front of the camera's milky grey eye.

When it seemed that the woman had seen it, he continued, "This is a pure unit of clarifying information. Hard evidence of what happened. The reason you..." he looked at the high walls, the gate, the intercom they were speaking through. "The reason you are frightened merely to visit the day spa. Surely you sense that something has happened, and yet you wonder what it is. Well, you're going to need to see this. Send a lackey if you fear for your person. My Brother and I will wait for a quarter of an hour. If no lackey emerges in that span of time, we will take our business elsewhere and you will remain in the dark as to the fate of Los Angeles."

FOURTEEN MINUTES LATER, AN ARMED LACKEY turned up, unquibbling at Jim's stated price of $1500. As he watched the lackey peel Benjamins off a thick stack, Joe could tell they were nowhere near the ceiling of what they could charge. He watched Jim take the bills, fold them into his pocket, doff an imaginary hat, and say, "Tell your keepers there's more where that came from. Things are afoot in this city that none would believe, and yet we have proof. We are the Brothers Squimbop. Trust no one else."

The Brothers watched the lackey, tape in hand, lock the automatic gate and disappear. Then they cruised down from the Hills and back to the squalor of Hollywood Boulevard, picturing the woman and her partner or friends or dogs or whoever was shut away in there with her sitting down to watch the beheading, shocked, sickened, and, though none would admit it, secretly thrilled. They imagined rumors spreading through a tangle of ears and mouths strung along a dried-up artery, now flowing thick and hot with the blood they'd dredged from the mummy.

As they cruised along, they passed a gathering in a Von's parking lot. Two old women on stilts danced to a small band—accordion, harmonica, fiddle—while many others danced around them. The Brothers pulled up, idling in their truck until the band took a break and the crowd lost some of its definition, hovering uncertainly between dispersing and devising a new reason to remain together. Into this uncertainty they strode and, with even more ease than last time, conscripted a new cast, plying them with the promise of room, board, and, if they rose to the occasion, authentic if anonymous fame.

Back at the Ranch, they got down to it. The other mummies that Jim had discovered along with Spahn's were too desiccated to make convincing victims, so Jim devised a new scheme, whereby one of their actors—a swarthy man with long black hair—would be hung from the gallows by the other two, a young woman and an older man whose eyes were so lazy it was hard to say where, if anywhere, his attention was centered.

"But how will we fake it?" Joe asked, as he plugged the camera back in and tested the microphones.

Jim suppressed a smirk as he hoisted the man's feet onto a block of wood beneath the gallows. Panting, he said, "Never you worry. I have it all worked out. You just run the tape when I tell you to."

A look passed between them here, an unspoken acknowledgment that this was the final moment before their new roles hardened all the way. Joe watched the moment arrive and hover without coming to a complete stop, like a train slowing down through a station where, nevertheless, no one would be allowed on or off. Then it departed and there was no recalling it. He would do what his Brother said.

He engaged the camera while Jim stretched a velvet blazer over the man's shoulders, fit the noose around his neck, whispered something apparently reassuring in his ear, and stood back, instructing the others on what to shout before kicking away the block their compatriot was standing on.

Then Jim stepped out of frame, shouted "ACTION!" and watched while the two actors launched into a frenzied speech about the degeneracy of the cabal behind the cabal behind what remained of Hollywood. "None of you plague-rats will be safe in your chalets," they shouted, "the Flood is coming for each and every one of you!"

They went on shouting, occasionally looking off-frame for more direction from Jim. Then they stopped and looked at him again, their eyes confused and imploring, as if hoping for permission to stop the scene here. All sidelong glances will be cut, Joe knew. He felt his allegiance travel from the actors to the man in the noose to his Brother, who was growing increasingly livid. Joe watched it play out, uncertain what was going to happen, until he realized he'd missed the moment when the actors kicked the block away, and now the swarthy man, in his velvet blazer, was swinging, jigging his legs and hunching his shoulders in an effort to raise his bound hands to his neck.

For a terrifying moment, Joe feared he hadn't left the camera running and they'd have to reshoot the scene, either hanging this same man again, or, if the body proved unusable—he didn't yet allow himself to think the other word, though he knew what he wasn't thinking—then they'd have to move on to another actor.

Or to me. He glanced at his Brother with fear for the first time. For the first time, he could see it happening. He could see Jim turning on him, declaring the reign of the Brothers Squimbop over, and inaugurating a solo tour that Joe would never live to see. He looked down at the camera and exhaled with tremendous relief—*too much relief*—to see that it was still recording. The take had been captured.

"CUT!" shouted Jim, walking into frame and clapping the two remaining actors on the back as they stood by the feet of the swinging body.

WHEN THESE ACTORS HAD BEEN CONVINCED TO disperse into the cold-water showers, Jim strode into the house, motioning for Joe to follow.

Joe wanted to keep his eyes on the body until it showed some sign of life, but knew he couldn't afford to wait that long. That train, he reminded himself, has left the station. He stood there a moment longer, watching the body swing in the breeze, and tried to remember the actual train he and his Brother had taken from the East, the journey they'd embarked upon and what they'd imagined their imminent exploits would consist of. He tried to see that train traveling still, chugging ever Westward, toward the *Real Los Angeles*, not the grim simulacrum they'd ended up in here. That's all it is. We just got off too soon, when the journey was still underway, and got mired in a purgatory we'll soon be free of. The Real Brothers Squimbop are still on that train and the people my Brother and I have temporarily become are merely stand-ins, a hapless opening act before those Brothers take the stage. A cautionary tale. "That," he whispered, "or even less than that."

The pleasure of receding into this schema was not inconsiderable. He could see himself watching that act now, secure in the beer-smelling seats with his Brother on one side and his Pervert Uncle on the other, ready for the Real Brothers to take the stage and do whatever they chose. Whatever the next act proves to be, he realized, there on Spahn Ranch, I can rest assured that I am merely its spectator. Anonymous among a great, great many.

Thus consoled, he entered the house. By the time he'd made it to the editing bay, Jim had already loaded the footage into a timeline and added static and distortion, once again creating the illusion that this was an execution captured on the fly, more gruesome evidence of the uprising that, if things panned out, would in due time become the accepted history of what had happened to Hollywood, to say nothing of Los Angeles. The chickens that had finally come home to roost.

Determined to take a more active role in the process, Joe cleared his throat after realizing that Jim had yet to acknowledge his presence. When nothing happened, he cleared his throat again. "Get some sleep," Jim barked, without looking up. On the monitors, the body jigged on its rope, up and down and back and forth as Jim scrubbed through the timeline, trying to get the rhythm right.

"Get some sleep," Jim repeated. "Go have a nightmare."

BY THE TIME JOE HAD SETTLED INTO THE CRAMPED, rickety bed he'd apparently been sleeping in since they'd arrived on the Ranch, he couldn't be sure whether his Brother really had said this last part. Either way, he could tell a nightmare was about to begin.

He roamed the premises, exploring them in full for the first time, already unsettled as he realized how long he'd been living here without knowing where he was, or, it seemed, making any effort to find out. Now he roamed from room to room in the mansion, the production hub, opening closets stuffed with hair, fur, blue tarps, heads, and torsos. He never got close enough to tell if they were props or actual body parts, though the rooms took on such a butcher-shop reek that he was forced outside, into the moonlit alley linking the sheds, shacks, and other outbuildings.

He followed this alley toward the moon, dragging his feet through gravel flanked by tractors, combines, and cacti, his back to the gallows where, though he tried not to hear it, the body still swung, tapping against the metal frame like it was trying to get someone's attention.

As he roamed from shack to shack, looking for the actors they'd hired, he found nothing but carnage, limbs drained and stacked like car parts, sorted sometimes by type and sometimes by individual. He took in as much as he could, auditing the damage done, aware that gas or bile was simmering in his belly and that, before long, he'd have to sit down. The scope of it, the enormity of what'd happened here, was such that he could tell things would never be the same.

But, he found himself thinking, as he sat down in the lunar dust beneath the feet of the hanging body, the same as what? How did things used to be? Did we used to be different?

He looked up at the noose and the neck it encircled, and the gridlock in what he saw translated into the gridlock he felt, the extent of the pseudo-California they'd run aground in without any imminent hope of breakthrough. Just as he couldn't picture that body coming free of its noose, he couldn't picture his mind coming free of the present, and just as the body's feet could not reach the ground, he could not envision any concrete past upon which to anchor himself in the present of Spahn Ranch. He knew he'd lost touch with *something*—its absence was acute, as was the absence of whatever it would've portended—and yet he could not supply any scene, story, or object to say what it was.

Nevertheless, he was determined to try.

He closed his eyes and saw his Brother and himself, Jim and Joe, the Brothers Squimbop, hands on the railing as the ship they'd taken back from Europe made landfall. They were, he remembered, relieved to be back. At large in America again. He smiled, glad to have recovered this scene with certainty. Then he tried to extend it, to see the two of them disembarking and beginning to consider their next move, whether to try again to take Boston and New York by storm—*to say nothing of Philly*, a notion that made him laugh for reasons he couldn't untangle—as they had in the great industrial thrum of the nineteenth century, or to head inland, back to Chicago, where they'd once erected a gambling and liquor racket to rival Al Capone's, or maybe all the way back to Hollywood, where they'd once... the longer he went on trying to picture it, the further it receded, until he felt, painfully, like a non-entity in an empty theater, watching reruns of old Squimbop funnies on a dismal Sunday afternoon with no one to wonder where he was.

A SHARP PAIN IN HIS RIGHT CLAVICLE SHOCKED him awake. He could feel the sunrise on his molars as Jim pulled him upright and said, "Time to go."

Joe allowed his Brother to deposit him in the passenger's seat of the truck, then watched as they cruised up the path, away from the Ranch and back toward what remained of the city. They rolled through suburban sprawl, half the houses boarded up, probably full of squatters, while the other half appeared unscathed, their residents watering rosebushes or collecting mail off the front steps, squinting into the sun.

As they wound back into the Hills, Joe ruminated on his nightmare. He couldn't shake its feeling of purgatory, of being stranded too far from both the Opening Number and the Grand Finale to make any move. Though he couldn't remember how he'd gotten out of them, he knew he'd been in situations like this before. Moments where it grew unsustainable to operate so far from any point of reference. Moments where—he realized suddenly, as if some operative force were taking pity on his dilemma by supplying a clue, unless, he worried, this too was part of that dilemma—any scene was primed to turn Primal. The mystery and its solution fused by deviant physics.

Looking out at the rapidly fancifying streets as they approached their destination, he tried to sneak a second clue by, as he put it, *remembering what happens next*, but the operative force rebuffed him.

"What're you laughing at?" Jim scowled, as he retrieved the tape from the glove compartment.

The futility of trying to parse the situation, he wanted to reply. My inability, for what feels like the first time in our shared life, to guess at your intentions. He said none of this, only frowned and hoped that his Brother would ask more concretely what the matter was. But Jim was already at the gate, ringing the bell and preparing the sales pitch.

Joe knew he wasn't needed at this point, though he still kept by his Brother's side, afraid of being left alone in the truck. What if it rolls down the hill with me in it? He wondered, trying to convince himself that this was his only worry.

By the time he'd made it to the gate, a lackey was already there, trembling with anticipation. "This footage is growing more precious by the day," Jim said. "The tide is rising. The rate of execution is increasing. Names, addresses, all are circulating. If your client wishes to be apprised of the direct threat, she will have to pay what it costs."

The lackey skimmed hundreds off the top of a pile, looking up imploringly after every three or four. "Keep going," Jim said, as the lackey's face started to fall, then kept falling, until the pile was depleted.

As they wound down from the Hills and back toward Hollywood Boulevard, the stack of cash flapping in the wind on Jim's lap, he smiled and said, "Brother, we're a hit! They're buying it faster than it can be made. There is, as best I can tell, no news any longer. No media, no Internet, no phone networks, no word as to what, if anything, has happened here, or is about to happen. Only us, Brother. Our Word. Time to celebrate!"

He clapped Joe on the shoulders, just as he used to when times were good. Alongside his relief, Joe chided himself for overreacting, for having imagined a rift between the Brothers Squimbop, or between himself and the Brothers, where, it seemed now, none had been. He exhaled and smiled through his shaky exhaustion. "Musso and Frank?" he proposed.

Jim grinned, nodded, and yanked the truck to a halt beside the ancient restaurant, grabbing the wad of cash, tearing it in half, and stuffing it into his two pockets. Inside, they ordered ribeye with gratinated potatoes and double pours of top-shelf scotch. As they sipped and relaxed, they overheard a waiter and a busboy whispering by the kitchen doors. "Saw them in here yesterday," the busboy said.

"And you're sure they... drank her blood and baked the skin?"

The busboy nodded. "I know people who've seen it. I can't say who, but trust me. It's happening all over town, actors, producers, directors, financiers from overseas... gathering up babies, don't ask me where they get them, there's plenty of orphans around, and breaking the necks, tearing open the throats, drinking the blood. Baking the skin into leather masks. Leather chaps, leather thongs. It's the only way they can stay young. Strong, healthy-looking. Vampires, the whole fucking lot of them. Grinding the poor into pink slime."

Joe closed his eyes to listen more intently. If only there were some footage to prove it. His heart raced as he prepared to announce his discovery of a brand-new market. Jim! He was preparing to say. We've only tapped half the market so far: with minimal adjustment we can also sell footage to the—

He opened his eyes to find his Brother gone, two sizzling steaks on the table and the waiter who'd just been talking standing quizzically off to the side. Joe looked for the stack of cash, knowing he wouldn't find it, then said, "I'm, ah, let me just run outside for a sec and..."

HE DASHED OUT OF THE RESTAURANT AND INTO the truck just as Jim pulled out of the lot and onto Hollywood Boulevard. He could tell by the fiendish look in Jim's eyes that his own stroke of genius was already redundant. Of course, he thought, trying to console himself, whatever I think of he thinks too. That's how it works with the Brothers Squimbop!

Their adventure was back on track.

He tried to take comfort in remembering this, but as he watched his Brother drive twenty miles over the speed limit, he had to admit that he couldn't tell what Jim was thinking. Whatever telepathy remained did not seem durable. He could only sit there in silence while Jim careened around curves and over sidewalks, muttering, "Baby... baby... gotta find a baby."

This went on until Jim yanked the truck to a halt outside one of the impromptu meat markets they'd stopped at before and said, "Wait here."

Joe waited, though he knew he should follow so as to find out, in what he could tell would soon be the crucial moment, whether it was his fate to encourage or oppose his Brother's culminating impulse, that which would push this escapade over the cusp and into the next. But his own impulse held him fast. He unclicked his seatbelt and sat there encumbered only by his own nature while Jim negotiated with the gypsies and streetwalkers and shaman-headed shamans, going from one group to the next with his wad of cash, until he returned with a fresh contingent in tow.

"Help them in," Jim barked, as he settled back behind the wheel, tucking the remaining cash into his shirt-front pocket. Finding that he could move once again—as if his Brother's command had reactivated him—Joe got to his feet and opened the back doors of the truck's main cabin, kicking aside camera equipment, taco wrappers, and beer cans, so that the new contingent—two shaman-headed shamans, a young woman, a young man, and, much as Joe hated to see it, an infant in a bassinet—could squeeze in.

As soon as they were settled, however haphazardly, Jim jerked the truck into motion, forcing Joe to careen headfirst into the passenger's seat, a pratfall that made the spooked newcomers giggle. Joe giggled too as he righted himself amid a flurry of memories of the Brothers as an old-school slapstick duo, tearing up the boards in one steamy or snow-choked Mountain House after another. Sitting again rightwise in his seat while they sped into the Canyons, he leaned back, closed his eyes, and watched the Brothers dance across a series of stages in flickering, gauzy black and white. He saw them tumble and flip and trip each other; he saw them play-fight and dance with canes and top-hats; he saw them fall down a wobbly ladder they took turns holding aloft, swapping roles faster and faster until the audience rose to its feet in hysterics, clapping, stomping, and cheering along.

Joe pressed his face to the window and let these memories play across the landscape, resisting any effort to discern whether what he could see was in the first or third person. He saw his face framed in the glass against a backdrop of telephone poles and dry mesquite, but the face was fading, receding into a Golden Age where, soon, he feared he'd be unable to claim it.

"Okay, we're here," Jim barked, jerking the parking brake yet again as the truck settled into position in front of the house on Cielo Drive. As Joe surfaced, a little of what his Brother had been thinking stuck to the inside of his head. The last of the old telepathy, he thought, watching Jim usher the new actors inside. Then it was gone. Joe was only Joe.

And part of me felt like less than that. A third entity, a boy in his seat watching the duo perform. But there was no third body, so onward as Joe I went.

"There's a camera and mic under the tarp in back of the truck," Jim said, as if he'd known since morning that they'd be making an extra stop today. "Bring it inside."

Then he turned, herding the shaman-headed shamans and the young family past the pool and in through the frosted glass doors. I had no choice but to gather the equipment and follow. Inside, Jim had already ransacked the closets and found a sheer, strapless dress for the woman and a blue blazer with matching trousers for the man. He stuffed these into their hands and said, "Get changed. We're on the clock here."

The shaman-headed shamans looked at him but Jim waved them off, saying, "You folks are already in costume."

Then he looked at me and said, "Set up the equipment. I need us in and out. This isn't our house."

I complied, my hands trembling so badly I bent the teeth on the extension cord as I jammed it into the wall, and tried to wiggle them back apart without Jim seeing my error. When I'd succeeded, just barely, I stood, blood rushing to my head, to see the couple, all cleaned up, smelling of whatever perfume and cologne they'd found in the bathroom of whoever had lived here during what I could only think of as *normal times*, which had perhaps only recently come to an end, despite my previous sense that they'd ended long ago. Perhaps—the thought struck me with an authority it seemed entirely unworthy of—*we* lived here, my Brother and I. I pinched the bridge of my nose and flashed through a dense sequence of images of the two of us, disgraced yet alluring European directors living alone in a glass cube, hosting wild parties about which *things were said*, flirting with devils and demons, summoning spirits that, once they entered our orbit, could never be banished.

"Great," Jim said. The numbers swam. There were too many and too few people here all at once. It was just the two of us unwinding after a hard day on set while, at the same time, there'd been an invasion, our privacy had been violated, freaks from the desert had swarmed us as soon as we got comfortable in California.

"Now, in this scene," one of the freaks—a real Jim Squimbop type, I thought—said, "you're going to sacrifice the baby. The shamans will help. They'll say the prayers and then, on my command, you'll slice the baby vertically in half with this," he handed over a boning knife with a light wooden handle. "By slicing it thus, you will reveal its fundamentally twinned essence. You will help two emerge from one. You will be the conduit—or make of it a conduit for itself, or selves—and we will record it for all time. My Brother's gone lame," he turned and made a cocky gagging face in my direction, "so it's time to reset the clock on us both. Start back from the beginning. Nothing to be ashamed of but it's gotta be done."

I closed my eyes and tried to return to the theater, to feel the warm, sweaty air and smell the popcorn and malty puddles on the floor, but all I succeeded in doing was dropping the cable, forcing Jim to turn toward me and shout, "Wake up, goddammit!"

The couple in their fancy get-ups stared at him, then at their baby, then at the shaman-headed shamans, slavering at the edge of the room, the pool flickering through the floor-to-ceiling windows behind them.

Jim handed the woman the boning knife, though I was sure he'd done so already.

"You will do this because, if you do not, the Saga ends here. The Brothers ride no further. Look at him. A gimp. An idiot. There is no journeying on with a partner like that."

All of them, including the baby, looked my way and their attention caused the floor and walls to ripple along with the pool outside. Everything reverted, tumbling backward into history, into old headlines and stuttering news reports—MURDER ON CIELO DRIVE!—and then, deeper still, to the crime that set my Brother and me out on the road all those years ago, at the very beginning of our journey. The Primal Scene I'd felt coming had arrived.

Jim paused long enough for everyone present to glance at the heads around the shamans' necks, which blushed and clenched their teeth at the unexpected attention. The baby moaned and gurgled, growing bored.

Then Jim said, "When I call ACTION, you will deliver the dyad from unformed, virgin flesh. Through no fault of our own, the two of us are stuck in there and need to come out!"

WHEN HE CALLED "ACTION," I TRIED AGAIN TO drift down from Cielo Drive and back to the theater where the Brothers mugged in perpetuity, their highlight reel starting up as soon as the news clips petered out. Although I failed again, I managed this time to transport myself to a dim, sweltering alley with a number of other people, huddled around a monitor on a plastic chair as we leaned in to watch a mysterious cabal bisect a baby and hoist the halves overhead, kneading the flesh into two humanoid shapes that then, in a shaky montage, grew into toddlers and ran through a collapsing circus on a riverbank in Kansas or Missouri, dabbing one another with face paint and honking at the camera with tremendous kazoos.

I felt what it would be to watch this footage in a crowd and to know, as none had known before, the True Origin of the Brothers Squimbop. I felt too the relief of passivity, of sinking into this crowd and renouncing my name, of shrugging off my role in what had happened on Cielo Drive until none would ever think to suspect it. And then I felt a deeper relief, that of knowing that renunciation *was* my role, that I'd shirked nothing, that I was not a coward but merely a...

I pressed my eye against the viewfinder hard enough to see that I was not in that alley, not yet, but rather still in the house on Cielo Drive, filming the event as it played out mere feet from where I stood. I tried to picture myself driving away, tearing down the hill and out of the Canyons and back through the city toward the coast, the scene before my eyes melting into the silver pool of all the cinema I'd ever absorbed, the sum total of every dreary Sunday afternoon I'd ever spent alone in the theater, wishing for a Brother who would not take form.

The couple, totally lost in their roles now, hypnotized by their duty, covered their faces in the baby's blood and sawed through its spine with the slippery knife. I pressed my eye deeper into the viewfinder, almost popping it against the slick glass, and watched as the woman became the black-cloaked witch. Her face caked with afterbirth, she turned to look directly through the lens and into my eye. When she could tell the shot was focused on her alone, she mouthed words I struggled to make out. "Leave now," I think she said. "You are no Squimbop any longer. The next phase is only beginning. You never had the stomach for it, so leave this instant. I release you."

Then the shot—I managed, for a moment, to look past the viewfinder and back to the screen in the empty cinema—shredded down the middle as the boning knife tore through it. It sawed faster and faster, the blade protruding into the theater, covered in sap, perforating the image until it was unwatchable and, at the same time, bifurcating me too, into one half that wished only to see what I was missing and another that wished only to flee, through the lobby and into the unknown day beyond.

When the shot had been reduced to red squiggles, I peeled my eye from the viewfinder, weeping, and left the camera where it stood, unconcerned with being followed, though I knew Jim would kill me if he saw me leave, just as I would've killed him had our roles been reversed. I walked out the door, my shirt and pants spattered, and over to the truck, the air thick around my legs, like the water in the swimming pool glimmering on my right. I suspected I'd be able to fly if I made an effort. Instead, I put my hands in my pockets, surprised to find the keys there.

I climbed behind the wheel, disengaged the parking brake, and rolled down the hill, out of the Canyons and into the Valley. I drove, waiting for all I'd seen to fade as I got up to speed on the highway, passing derelict theaters and billboards for the peep shows of an irretrievable epoch. I looked down the offramps and saw, again and again, a monitor set up in an alley with a circle of dark figures pressing around it, their gaze fixed on a scene I hoped never to see.

I drove through the night, seeking the ocean, the actual Pacific at last, beyond all the Salton Seas, beyond the arena where the Brothers' journey ended and mine began. I drove and scratched at the flesh on my belly and up into my armpit, and I pictured how I would immerse myself in the cold, black water beyond the continent's edge, washing away whatever of my Brother remained from the place where we'd been slashed apart, never again to share the stage in any of the Mountain Houses where, even now, I knew the duo was tap-dancing into eternity, juggling boning knives and rubber infants as they worked their audience into a frenzy before rewarding them with the Primal Scene that everyone had come to see.

Squimbop Fever

I DROVE ALL NIGHT, WINDOWS OPEN SO THE LAST of the names Jim and Joe could flow out, leaving me in a purified state I still chose to call *the Brothers Squimbop*, though I knew I was alone. I drove through lowlands and highlands, dabs of city here and there, trains rolling by in the dark until the exurbs gave way to open country. I reminded myself that I was seeking the ocean, and that, once I found it, I would peel off my soiled uniform and immerse my body in the black waves at the edge of the continent and wash off the last of the dead flesh clinging to my side at the site where my Brother had been sliced away, and then *the Brothers Squimbop* would refer to me alone.

A me and an us all in one. I pulled off the road behind a row of dunes fringed in spiky beachgrass. I will become a being strong and cogent enough to embark upon a brand-new escapade now that Hollywood lies in ruin behind us...

Behind me. In a former age, before the Primal Scene set the clock back to zero.

I cut the engine, yanked up the emergency brake even though the ground was level, and strode, head high, toward the lapping edge of the ocean, squinting to make out Japan in the distance. When I reached the surf, I kicked off my shoes, then pulled off my pants, shirt, and undergarments, scratching at the hardened flesh on my left side, the skin slick and scarred, and, though I yearned to wash myself clean, I found I could not. Perhaps it was simply that the water was too cold—far colder than I'd imagined on the drive up here, when I'd pictured myself plunging to the very bottom, down to the silt layer upon which it's said that all Squimbop skulls are emptied and refilled over the eons—or else some residual memory of my Brother, an intractable homing impulse, clung to my side more firmly than the *me* part of us could overcome. It felt as though part of my mind was in my head and part was in my armpit, trembling in the Pacific pre-dawn, and only when both were in agreement could any action be taken.

The two minds repelled one another in the cold, so we turned back to shore to watch the sunrise over the bluffs as the new day's first surfers, clad in wetsuits and swimming caps, raced across the sand and into the water, taking to the waves without seeming to notice us where we stood.

The flesh on our side trembled and burrowed inward, clustering more densely between our ribs, where we could hear it whisper, *time to go. The water is theirs now.*

So I turned, again resolving to use *I* for the sake of my sanity—*our sanity*, we thought—and said farewell to Japan, which did seem nearly visible now that the sun had risen, and I strode, naked, across the beach. I watched the surfers glide up and over the waves as I pulled my old clothing over my wet body, sand and salt bonding with the fabric to ensure that I'd stink like an old fishing net until I found a new costume or a freshwater means of washing.

THUS ATTIRED, I RETURNED TO THE TRUCK, EASED it out between the wide vans of the surfers, and took to the highway again, heading north, the brightening ocean to my left. I drove for another hour or two, rolling the dial between AM stations, half of them covering harbor conditions and the other half extraterrestrial coverups, until hunger and thirst overwhelmed me and I turned off the road in the next beach town I saw.

I pulled into the lot of a diner near the exit ramp, took a few bills from the glove compartment, jerked the parking brake in what I'd come to see as *one of my signature moves*, and went inside, eagerly inhaling the scent of brewing coffee and frying onions. A waitress in white jeans and a Shelter Cove sweatshirt brought me water in a ribbed plastic Coca-Cola cup, and nodded without writing anything down when I ordered pancakes, bacon, and coffee. As I waited, I looked to the only other occupied table, where a man who appeared to be in his sixties sat at a booth with three small children.

I sipped my coffee and studied his behavior with his young companions, trying to determine the nature of their relationship. I did this to force myself to focus on the buzzing area between him and the children, rather than on his face, which reminded me of something, or someone, I didn't want to remember until the very last moment, when I knew I would have to.

There was something forced in how he looked at them, an element of threatened and hence threatening insecurity, like he was warning them with his eyes not to try to escape. I heard one of the children ask if he could use the bathroom, to which the man snapped, "No!" in such a way that, had I been a child, I would've gone in my pants.

I jumped when the waitress brought my pancakes and bacon, which made her jump too. She stood back from the table and looked me over like she'd formed an initial idea of who she was dealing with but had now been forced to revise it. We locked eyes; then we both looked at the table, where, it appeared, my coffee had splashed out of its mug. We watched it run around the edges of my pancake platter, transfixed until she said, "Lemme get you a placemat."

When she disappeared into the back, my gaze returned to the man with the children, whom I was now certain he'd kidnapped. I itched the cold, sandy flesh under my shirt, and ruminated on how that man had gotten those children—I saw him lurking behind a rest stop bathroom in the dead of night, waiting until they went into the Women's side with their mother—and why, and where he was taking them. My mind drifted down my torso, into the Brother-flesh in my armpit. Together we descended further, past our side, past our waist, under the table, and through the floor, into a chamber of hooks and chains dangling over a bathtub in which something humanoid floated with an expectant grin beneath a dangling yellow light bulb. *The Forbidden Room,* a voice announced inside us. *The deep back corner of the Angel House basement.*

We could see it clearly, as if it were located directly beneath the diner, rendering the space we were sitting in no more than a surface for what really mattered—a sort of, at most, *Angel House breakfast salon.* My Brother, or the part of me given over to him, thrilled at the notion and pictured the man leading the children down there and beginning, very calmly, to disembowel them with a boning knife while an unseen audience clapped and laughed in the shadows, relieved to see that the old routine had not perished from the earth, nor even lapsed into a decadent latter-day phase in which the founding rituals degrade into pallid symbology.

We only left the Forbidden Room when the waitress returned with a rolled-up paper placemat under her arm. She lingered by the side of the table, as if she expected us to remind her why she'd come back. When we did no such thing, she sighed, picked up the plate and half-empty coffee cup, spread the placemat underneath it, then put everything on top.

We looked at the plate, determined to eat whatever was there, though the sight of that man with those children had sapped our appetite and made our head throb with what felt like two brains clogging a space meant for one. *But which one??* We goofed, making brief but jarring contact with the raw nerve at the root of all comedy.

I forced myself back to singularity and picked my fork and knife off the placemat, whereupon I noticed it was covered with ads in rectangular boxes. MORT'S DRYWALL, SUSY & ANNA'S FISH & CHIPS, LAYNE'S BANG & BROW SALON, and, in a smaller box under the shadow of my plate, THE BROTHERS SQUIMBOP WAX MUSEUM.

In pantomime of another kind of man, a businessman perhaps, someone with a fixed nature and a fixed schedule, I checked my wrist. Seeing nothing but salt-crusted hairs—*it's my Brother that's got the watch there*, I heard myself think—I held my hand aloft a moment longer, then picked up my silverware and ate my soggy pancakes as quickly as I could. When they were gone, I called the waitress over, settled the bill, and asked directions to the Wax Museum. She appeared about to answer when the man with the children got everyone up from their booth and forced them past my table. He locked eyes with us and we looked away from the horrible denouement we could see coming.

I swallowed, once again forcing my Brother back to my side, but I could tell it would only grow harder to resist his influence as the escapade wore on. The Brothers Squimbop,

I thought, will always be us, never just me, no matter how few bodies we inhabit.

And yet, I added, as the man and the children dinged the door on their way out, I am here and he is not. That's got to count for something. When they were gone, the waitress, half-traumatized for reasons she likely couldn't have explained, looked back at me and said, "What was the question again?"

After she told me where the Museum was, I wrapped the butter knife in a napkin, stuck it in my pocket, and drove there. The address was so close I could've walked, but I'd already decided that the truck, and especially the yanking of the parking brake, was an essential part of my flair for as long as this escapade lasted. "The Brothers Squimbop roam the Northwest coast in a beat-up truck," I narrated, as I drove, "picking up drifters and slaughtering them in rented rooms, feeding their remains into a bathtub full of..."

We almost crashed into the Wax Museum, so intent had we become on seeing, or hearing, what was in the tub. I had to jerk the truck to a halt and exhale into my fist behind the wheel, scratching the flesh on my side until my breathing stabilized. In time, Brother, in time, I thought, or heard the flesh think through me. Step by step... by step. The effort to remain singular winded me, then sent a surge of adrenaline through my system so that, when I yanked the brake and climbed out of the truck to behold the façade of the Wax Museum, emblazoned with crude renditions of our two faces, I felt both exhausted and charged up, like I'd spent the night pacing between the door and the TV in a rented room on the edge of this town, where I'd come for the express purpose of visiting the legendary Brothers Squimbop Wax Museum, and now, thank God, here I was.

"You here for the ten o'clock?" A pudgy man in a yellow flannel shirt popped out and swept the parking lot before pausing his attention on me. I nodded, and hurried inside when he motioned me in.

A small group had congregated in the lobby, composed of a trio of twentysomething women and the man and children from the diner. The guide popped out to sweep the lot again, then returned and sighed, "Well, looks like it's just us for now. Okaaay... let's get started then, you can settle up in the Gift Shop on your way out."

HE TURNED THROUGH A LOW DOORWAY INTO A dim hall, flanked by wax sculptures. I kneaded my side, easing my Brother to sleep, and entered along with the rest of the group. We passed sculptures of the Brothers in all their classic escapades, which the guide narrated in an elliptical, breathless style. "Here, we see them, ah... oh, they're on their teaching stint here," he said, pointing at a diorama of one of the Brothers—I tried to keep from thinking *me*, though I, or my Brother, did think it—in a damp lecture hall, leaning against a podium with an empty briefcase open beside him. On the floor between us and the exhibit stood a wax wolf, which the guide claimed, "Turned up, I'm sure you remember, just as the situation was getting juicy."

A few of the women laughed, but only enough to show that they thought it was meant as a joke, or a reminder of a funnier time. The exhibit nooks were open-plan so everything was visible at once, and we might've been happier wandering freely, but the guide insisted on leading us from one to the next, shuffling across the carpeting in a pair of green foam sandals, as if we could only see what he was describing. “Here, we have the Brothers relaxing on a motel bed,” he told us, pointing to what we could clearly see was the Brothers relaxing on a motel bed. “The conceit of this escapade was that they'd both appear to teach at a Community College, but only ever alone, obscuring the fact that there were two of them, even though—and here's the real genius of it—they were by no means identical!”

He looked right at me and I shuddered to consider that he could see my Brother under my shirt. “And here,” I imagined him saying, turning the group's attention on me, “we have the Brothers in a new escapade where they've merged, with characteristic imperfection, into a single body and turned themselves loose on the backroads of the great Northwest, enacting a killing spree that will go down in American history as one of the...

“Please don't fall behind,” he called, and I had to hurry over to where he was describing a diorama that showed the Brothers holding forth upon a platform in the heart of what he called, “A backward village in Upper, Upper Austria.”

For the moment, I felt free of the group's attention, though I'd grown preoccupied with trying to remember how I looked, and whether, from the group's point of view, my face was familiar enough to raise suspicion. I couldn't decide whether I hoped it was. Would I, if I could, slip out of the Saga and content myself with a life spent admiring its detritus?

“And here,” the guide said, glaring as I fell behind again, “we have my personal favorite, *The Brothers Squimbop in Hollywood*... we, ah, see them on the Spahn Movie Ranch, before a gallows where, depending on whom you ask,” he grinned, making it clear that this was his favorite line in the tour, “they either hung or pretended to hang a gypsy they found in a parking lot off Hollywood Boulevard. Heavy stuff... sir, you might want to," he looked to the man with the three children, evincing concern as they blanched before the sight of the hung gypsy, but quickly turned back to the exhibit when the man glared menacingly enough to brook any intervention.

"Well, um," the guide stammered, "er, here we have the Brothers overseeing the murder of a child." He couldn't help looking at the man again. "This piece is, understandably, our most controversial, because, well, you see, some say the Brothers were separated here, that is, each went his own way in a sort of Primal Scene, or Reverse Primal Scene, ending the Golden Age for good, while others, and that includes yours truly, hee-hee, believe we haven't seen the last of them yet. No sir, not by a long shot. Perhaps even the severing in two of that poor brute was the very knife that had to fall in order to..."

He looked straight at me and I felt my Brother squirm. I felt certain that some confrontation was nearly at hand, but the guide preempted it by asking, "So, um, are there any questions?" He scratched his nose, then reached back to hike up his jeans. "What's that? Did someone ask if there's a wax statue of yours truly, showing you all around, doing his part to keep the Saga moving forward, from one escapade to the next, and thus taking his rightful place within it?"

Silence spread through the hall as we waited for him to continue and he, it seemed, waited for us to request that he do so. The children had fanned out, their gaze roving between the waxworks and the face of their captor, while the three women looked at me, in unison, then at the guide. One of them said, "Well, yes. First of all, it's great to be here. We've been to three of these so far, two in Oregon and one in Mendocino, and, well, this is one of the best. So cheers on that." She paused, then said, lowering her voice, "What I wanted to ask, if you don't mind, and I ask this everywhere because I'm writing my dissertation on it, is what do you think about Squimbop Fever?"

The guide leaned against a wax model of the truck I'd parked in the lot—*good thing the parking brake's on!* I mugged—sighed, looked at his slipper-clad feet on the carpeting, and said, "What do I think about it? Do I believe that individuals all over the country have been driven to murder in order to force a mystical reunion with their supposedly long-lost Brothers? Do I believe the endless proliferation of Brothers Squimbop impersonators," here he looked at me, and I looked away, scratching my side while he scratched his, "is anything but another manifestation of the ancient American propensity toward graft and rip-off artistry in every corner where breathable air still manages to flow?"

"But surely you'll admit," the woman cut in, "that the face is strikingly similar. I mean, look at him," everyone turned toward me, "you must get one on every tour. Look at that face, look at the skull, then look at the sculptures. You're seriously telling me that nothing neurological is afoot? Nothing morphological, just a garden variety, as you say, *rip-off artist* plying his trade? To what end? Does that look *fun*?"

Everyone swiveled between me and the nearest sculpture of me, and I couldn't decide how to play it. I wanted to mine the dilemma for laughs but couldn't tell whether doing so would help prove or disprove the point, nor even, in that moment, quite remember what the point was.

"You're right about one thing," the guide said, his voice turning sharp, "I do get one of these bozos on every tour. Every damn time, let me tell you. But let me tell you something else, too. Since you're all here. The Brothers

Squimbop are singular. There is only one True Duo. Only ever has been, only ever will be. So whatever Fever may or may not be afoot, let me just say, and then I need to let my eleven o'clock's in, the Brothers will return. And we'll know it when they do. Until then, it's just bozos having a laugh. Put that in your damn dissertation."

The woman rolled her eyes like she'd heard this many times before. "I will," she said, and nodded to her friends.

I FOLLOWED THEM OUT. ON THE WAY, I AGAIN lagged behind the group long enough for a pair of sawhorses propping open a curtain on one side of the hall to catch my eye. Trying not to draw attention, I drifted over to peer inside, gazing as hard as I could in the few seconds I had before the group left the hall. The dimly lit space beyond receded so far I suspected it was larger than all of what we'd covered on the tour. I saw rows of wax figures, some free-standing, some on pedestals, and many more racked against one wall, beneath neon signs that read *The Brothers Squimbop in Morocco, The Brothers Squimbop in Tokyo,* and *The Brothers Squimbop on Mars*. The dissonance of these alien adventures—I could neither refrain from trying to recall them, nor bring anything to mind—was enough to force my eyes off the flashing words and down to the smudged faces of the figures below, their eyes, noses, and mouths barely distinguishable from the cheeks, chins, and foreheads surrounding them.

"Unformed," the guide reassured me. I shuddered to see him, having assumed he was on the far side of the hall by now, if not already greeting the next group. Part of me suspected he was a duplicate, having emerged from storage right before my eyes. He put a hand on my shoulder. "That's all it is. We haven't shaped them yet. Come with me now. If you want to take the tour again, you'll have to buy another ticket."

"How did you—?" My voice sounded strange, like the question wasn't genuine. Like this, here, was another wax escapade, or mini-escapade. An interlude before returning to the main theme. *The Squimbop Missing Memory Panic*, a treat for those in the audience hardy enough to hold their urine until the next intermission.

The guide nodded in exactly the same way, like he too meant none of what he said, or was about to say. Like we were both elsewhere, watching this small exchange play out. Maybe we were old friends, I thought, revisiting a Squimbop favorite from our youth. A rare moment in the Saga, unknown to most. "Someone always lags behind," he said. "Someone always sees the room they're not supposed to see. *The Hall of Neophytes*, I've heard it called. *The Hall of Unstaged Exhibitions.* Some call it merely 'visible storage,' though that sounds a tad gauche, don't you think?"

I looked at my feet, afraid to see that his mouth wasn't moving. "Since it happens every time, some might wonder why we don't close that hall off. Kick out the sawhorses. Draw the curtain. But it's all part of it. Something to take home with you." His eyes glinted so brightly I could see my shoes light up. "Something to wonder about. How many escapades were there, really? And if it's more than you thought, what then? Who *are* you in all this?"

He patted me on the back. Then he was gone.

IN THE GIFT SHOP, I RIFLED THROUGH A RACK OF Squimbop sweatshirts, not intending to buy one until the woman at the counter—a variant on the tour guide—said, "Admission's free with a purchase of $15 or above."

Buy one, I heard my Brother urge. *I'm cold.* I nodded, took one off the rack and brought it to the counter, where the woman flinched, seemingly shocked at my approach, as if she hadn't just summoned me.

"What?" I asked, blushing as I scrambled for a cover story. Behind her stood a row of action figures in boxes decorated with photos of Morocco, Tokyo, and Mars.

"Nothing," she said, ringing up the sweatshirt. "Just, you got it bad, is all."

I turned to see the graduate students in line, leaning in to hear the exchange play out. "Got what?" I asked, though I knew what she was about to say.

She shrugged and handed me the sweatshirt without a bag, as if she could tell I was planning to put it on right away. I pulled it over my head, a cartoon image of my face over my right nipple, my Brother's over my left, with a glowing purple ship cresting a wave across my belly.

"So you believe it then?" the graduate student asked.

I turned, hugging the sweatshirt, and was about to answer when the woman at the checkout counter said, "Excuse me, could you folks um..." She motioned for us to clear the area, as if people were waiting behind us.

We decided to play along and walked together out to the parking lot. Her friends were gone. "You really do look like them," she said, leaning close to my face, "more than anyone I've seen. Would you be willing to talk to me about it, for my research? I'll buy you lunch."

THOUGH I WANTED TO CHECK INTO A ROOM ON the harbor and wait till dark—I glanced at the doors of the Wax Museum, picturing how I'd let myself back in—I was hungry enough to nod when she asked a second time.

Then I got in my truck, released the brake, and followed her sporty Nissan to a Mexican restaurant in what looked like the historic center of whatever town this was.

Inside, she ordered margaritas and chips and dip for the table, then took out a notepad and said, "Do you mind?"

I wanted to reach under my sweatshirt and ask my Brother, but I could feel that he was sleeping again. The night we'd both been through seemed to be taking a heavier toll on him, whereas I was left punchy and buzzing, all the more so as I sipped my blue-green margarita and chewed iridescent crystals of salt. Alone for the time being, I indicated that I wouldn't stop her from taking notes.

"Thanks," she said. "Do you want, like, real food? My treat, like I said. Or if I didn't, I meant to."

She ordered us steak fajitas when the waitress came back. Then she asked, "When did you first suspect you had it?"

I yawned, exhaustion rising beneath my manic energy. Something in her attentiveness, the way she hovered her pen over her notepad, the pride she clearly took in being able to treat me to lunch in service of the dissertation she showed no sign of doubting would one day be a document of genuine significance... something in all of this made me smile. Her flair, I thought. The routine she's been assigned. Hoping to preempt a laugh, I clamped my lips onto the rim of my cocktail glass.

"Sorry," she said, dipping a chip, then sitting back to eat it with her other hand underneath, guarding against runoff. "I know it's a touchy subject. Ha, I *ought to* know, after all the interviews I've done!" She laughed, so I did too, less and less certain of where in this scene my center of gravity was to be found. I felt my eyes water, so I cleared my throat and took a chip, guarding it the same way she had.

"Look," she said. "It's not just you. Squimbop Fever is sweeping the nation. Has been for years, no matter what they say. Years ago? In undergrad? I took a course with a 'Professor Squimbop' and he..." She nodded out the window, perhaps in the direction of the Wax Museum. "I mean, even back then, I could see the seeds of it. But now? Ask yourself... how long since the actual Brothers have appeared? And what became of them? Where'd they go? Why are there so many tribute acts, so many impersonators, so many," she looked at me with compassion, and I felt terror and rage grind together, almost audibly, "so many people who look like them, and are growing to look *more like them* with time, and yet remain alone, always one half of a duo they can never put back together, except as an obvious rip-off? Explain that to me in language other than that of viral spread. Thanks, yep, uh-huh, looks great," she said, as our fajitas arrived, steaming up the space between us.

We ate in silence until we each grew visible again. Then she reached into her purse and placed a brochure on my napkin. "Take a look." She chewed the rest of the steak in her mouth, then added, "Sorry, I just get excited. I know a lot of people with it. I've *lost* people to it. That man, with those kids on the tour today... the way he looked at the waxworks? The way he looked *like* the waxworks? He has an early case, just beginning to show symptoms, whereas you..."

Something in my face cut her short.

"How many pseudo-duos do you think there are today?" She asked, trying to cool the conversation once again. She nodded at the brochure, and I picked it up. *The Brothers Squimbop West Coast Tour*, its cover said, with a hazy photo of a duo that looked something like my Brother and me, wearing tuxes and top hats on a stage much like the one I'd pictured while filming the worst of the footage in the house on Cielo Drive.

I gagged on the memory, spitting the steak in my mouth into the foil the tortillas had come wrapped in. "I've been up all night. Is there a decent motel in this town, do you know?"

She hesitated, as if weighing whether to try one last time to get me to say whatever she needed to hear. Then her face dimmed and she nodded and signaled for the check. "Sure," she said, disappointed but diplomatic. "I'm staying right by the marina. I'll take you there. See you at the show later, maybe?"

I GOT BACK IN THE TRUCK AND FOLLOWED HER TO an L-shaped motel fringing the marina, sunfish and motorboats bobbing outside the windows. The proprietor, a youngish Indian man in sneakers and overalls, showed me a room, which he claimed was the, "Best for single men between here and Ukiah." He winked in such a way that it seemed like he wanted to appear to be implying something without letting on quite what it was. I felt my side squish and swirl, and said, "No, I need one with a big tub."

"Big tub?" he asked, startled, like he'd gotten lost in thought as soon as he opened the door, certain that his work was done.

I pointed out the window, at the bobbing waves, and coughed to muffle the sound of my squirming Brother. "Big tub," I said again.

This time he seemed to understand, or to admit that he understood. Whether my request was one he'd heard countless times before was not a question I intended to ask. "Very well, my friend," he said, and showed me into another room, identical but for the big tub in the bathroom. My side squirmed again and the proprietor froze, sinking back into the realm he'd sunk into before. For a moment I couldn't bear to rouse him, as I came to see what would happen later tonight, what he'd be left with and would then, perhaps, be called upon to explain. Better to let him enjoy it now, I figured, as he looked out the window at the bobbing waves, where, I realized, he'd surely been looking for years, perhaps dreaming of the Indian Ocean.

I too lapsed into a dream, drifting back to the house my Brother and I shared on the Spahn Movie Ranch, the half-finished wooden mansion that had been our headquarters in what I now considered the Golden Age of our partnership. As I slipped in deeper, I saw the house floating in the harbor, a mansion that was also an Ark preparing to dock after centuries at sea. I watched it draw near, filling in the hazy horizon until the open harbor turned into a lake—the ship's lights glowed like those of houses on the opposite shore—and then I looked over at the proprietor and let my dream sync up with his, so that now together we watched the Ark arrive after a journey around the world, all the way from India. We shared the relief of its arrival, the sense that all was at last well in the world, all separations mended, all dualities fused. All journeys concluded in safe return.

The reverie came to an end as the Ark clanged against the edge of the motel, its window against the window of the room we were standing in. "Well," he said, wiping his eyes, "this room is better for you?"

I nodded, wiping my eyes too, and then I was alone, the door closed and locked, the water running in the tub. I stood in the gathering steam, removed my clothes for the second time today, and, for the second time, prepared to submerge myself and, at last, wash the extra flesh clean and emerge as the new being I had still only halfway become. I breathed in the cloudy chlorine smell that emanated from the tap, and felt the image I'd conjured a moment ago disappear. *You will step into this steam,* a voice informed me, *with your head full of soft, creamy Lecture, which has been pooling inside you all day. You will stay under until it has turned firm and shapely, the cream churned to butter.*

I squeezed my side, beginning likewise to churn what I found there, irritating and kneading the skin as, once again, I failed to submerge it. I stood at the edge of the tub, listening to the voice, which seemed to travel through the steam the way other voices travel through the radio. *You will sail the globe in the Ark whose arrival you've just witnessed, which from now on will be your home, just as it once was ours, on the Spahn Movie Ranch, before you fled. Before your cowardice cut short the Golden Age and inaugurated the Age of Imposters. Now, apostate, it falls to you to sail in Angel House, preaching the Lectures I will write. This is the only escapade that remains. I am gone from here, away in the Totally Other Place, working beneath a glowing yellow bulb, never to be heard from again outside of steam. All the duos you see and hear and meet from now on are, like you, nothing but wax sculptures driven mad by Fever, pretending that what's lost can be still found.*

I leaned against the sink and tried to purge the voice from the steam, blocking out the pseudo-Squimbop that had come between me and my Brother, but I grew weaker the longer I leaned there, until I fell into a dream in which I was the one made of wax.

Just before full paralysis set in, I wrenched myself awake, coughed red foam into the sink, turned off the overflowing tub, dumped all the towels from the rack above the door onto the soaked linoleum and, for the second time today, pulled my clothes back over my unwashed and unrested body, though thankfully this time I had my souvenir sweatshirt to keep me warm.

I sat down on the bed, running my hands through my hair and trying to remember why I'd come here, and what I might do now that I'd arrived. I couldn't tell if my plan was going right or going wrong. All I knew, or decided that I must know, was that the time to return to the Wax Museum had come.

So I pulled the sweatshirt tighter, relishing the pain in my side, picked up the keys to the room and the truck, and let myself out into the cool evening. I drove through growing excitement in the harborside town, traffic backed up along the main street in the direction of the historic center, beneath banners proclaiming the "BROTHERS SQUIMBOP BIG-TOP SPECTACULAR, TONIGHT 7PM." I sped up in the opposite direction and let myself indulge the thought that I could just keep driving, all the way down the coast and through the ruin of Los Angeles and back into the Hills, where I'd stop on the gravel path at the Spahn Movie Ranch and find my Brother waiting for me in the house where we...

I jerked to a halt in front of the Wax Museum, killed the headlights, yanked the brake and sat behind the wheel, trying to focus on the task at hand. I pictured how I'd let myself in, retracing my steps from this morning, how I'd creep over to the waxwork tableau of the Primal Scene on Cielo Drive, me behind the camera and my Brother off to the side, directing the black-clad woman with a murderous smirk on his lips. Then I'd load him into the truck, cover him with the blue tarp, and bring him to the big tub.

A scuttling in the lot startled me, and I looked up to see the man from this morning, with the three children by his side, dragging another sculpture into the bed of his own truck and covering it with a blue tarp of his own. I watched the lot fill with identical trucks, Squimbop-faced loners sneaking off with wax sculptures under their arms... and there I was among them, weaving through the foot traffic and in through the museum's smashed doors, past the ransacked Gift Shop and into the main hall, where some of the lights were on and some were broken, and most of the sculptures were gone. I passed tableaux of us on the steamer to Europe, and on the dusty roadside in the high mountains where we met the witch, and then deep in the German woods where she birthed us again.

As if some Providence were looking down on me through the sprinkler system, recognizing me as half of the *Real Duo*, alone among so many imposters, the tableau of the Surgery at Cielo Drive was still intact. I fell to my knees and kissed the glass-strewn carpet, vowing to do whatever it took to restore us to that moment, even if it turned the nation into a charnel house. *If it ends up that my Brother and I are the last beings alive on this planet, then that will be as it should*, the voice I'd heard in the motel bathroom declared, though I tried not to consider what it meant that the prospect of restitution had reached me as a message from that apostate.

I rose to my feet, made my way to the Primal Scene, uprooted my Brother where he stood, and carried him through the wrecked museum and back to the parking lot while a fleet of cruisers closed in. I paid them no mind as I loaded him into the truck, covered him with the blue tarp, disengaged the parking brake with a flourish, and pulled out, past the cruisers that warned me over and over again to stop where I was.

We tore down the main street in a hail of gunfire, "Me and the Devil Blues" blaring on the AM radio. We swerved around roadblocks and up onto curbs, speeding up as the audience clapped and stomped, egging us on, until we crashed to a halt under the "BROTHERS SQUIMBOP BIG-TOP SPECTACULAR, TONIGHT 7PM" banner. We got out, dodging bullets as we ducked around dozens of identical pickup trucks with identical blue tarps in back.

Leaving my Brother in the truck, I worked my way into the crowd, easily slipping past the distracted ticket-takers and under the big-top, where a shameless impersonator duo in tuxes and top-hats stomped across a wooden stage with a ladder between them, one holding it aloft while the other tried to climb it, taking turns climbing faster and faster while the audience, crammed full of men in the early and middle stages of the Fever—looking at them together like this, there was no denying what the student had told me—clapped along, their eyes hollow and swimmy, wax pooling on their cheeks as their tears dried.

I could see them sinking into their own private memory theaters, where, like me, they sat in the cheap seats on a gloomy Sunday afternoon, watching the Brothers tap dance and do ladder tricks and hatch doves and fan out decks of cards and don and doff top-hats and mince about in ill-fitting dresses and high heels, pink lipstick smeared over their chins and mustaches, making it seem, for a while, that life was a lark you could prance through with ease, provided you had a light-enough touch and didn't mind stumbling around in rhinestone stilettos and floppy rubber clown shoes. The right mix of focus and dreaminess to keep it from turning heavy, to keep that ship from drifting into harbor, its windows flush with those of your room, open just wide enough to let through the scent of Tommy Bruno's old, old butter...

I swooned against the Squimbop behind me, breaking the spell he'd fallen into and causing him to roar with the pain of it. He clobbered me in the temple and would have again had I not stumbled in such a way that his next blow hit the Squimbop in front of where I'd been standing. A moment later, the crowd collapsed in a hundred-headed pratfall, a dazed centipede pounding itself again and again.

I ducked out while the duo onstage played a kazoo duet, then sang one of our classics, from the days when we simply went town to town in big-tops like this one, yodeling the nights away. They seemed unfazed by the melee before them, either unable to see it or all too happy to welcome its energy into their routine.

Back in the parking lot, where the police were still lined up, I searched for my truck, wondering what could possibly distinguish it from the others. As I roamed from one to the next, verifying that each had the same lump beneath the same blue tarp in back, I ended up on the far edge of the fairgrounds, out by the dumpsters and porta-potties, where a few men stood smoking and waiting to pee while others peed on the tires of nearby vehicles.

I passed by, intrigued now not by the line of trucks but by a whimpering from even deeper in the field, out of reach of the spotlights. As I approached, I saw a standing sculpture, and, as I drew closer, four bodies, three of them prone, one of them kneeling. As I drew closer still, I saw, as I knew I would, the man from this morning rocking on his knees before a blood-soaked Squimbop sculpture, the three children sliced from throat to groin in the grass beside him.

Each step I took in their direction pushed me deeper into the past, down toward that original fairground in Kansas or Missouri where, amidst the bustle and furor of the circus, something happened to my Brother and me to make us what we became. The man up ahead became our Pervert Uncle and the children beside him were failed attempts, aborted efforts at the transformation he was about to enact. *It all begins here,* the voice gloated. *The genuine Primal Scene at last.* Some part of me knew he was wrong, that that was then and this was now, half a continent West of the Saga's lost beginning, and yet this knowledge felt trivial. All that mattered was that here I was, with no more space between myself and the scene I'd chosen to approach.

"Just, please, come back to life," the man moaned as he knelt in the grass. "Just make it be funny again. Just let me back in the theater. I'm sorry I left you. I'm sorry. I know you think I was the cowardly one, and that you had what it took, but look what I've done. Look at me, here. Look what I did for you." He gazed up at the sculpture's face, and begged again, louder this time, perhaps performing for me, if he could sense that I'd drawn close behind him. "Please," he almost shouted, pressing his lips against the sculpture's pedestal, "please, let us be the Brothers again. Enough with the impersonators, the waxworks, the reenactments, the ships pulling into harbor and the stagnant bathtubs in rented rooms... let's get back out there and do what only we can!"

He broke down, shedding gore as he shivered and sobbed in his souvenir sweatshirt. I put my arms around him and held him close and, for a long, strange interval, it was like he and I really were the Brothers, reunited at last, our battles behind us and the open road—the Inland Circuit that connected each Mountain House to the next, where there were still suckers aplenty waiting to hand us their grubby cash—just up ahead. He leaned into my arms and I held him in that empty field in the dead of night, beside the children he'd slain and the waxwork he'd stolen, and we listened to more wax being poured in a distance we could not see, turning this scene too into a tableau that would take its place in every Squimbop Wax Museum in America. Then, when it was time, I helped him to his feet and we walked together back to the lot where, thankfully, all the other Squimbops had left, leaving only his pickup and mine.

"I'm staying at the motel on the harbor," I said. "Would you like to go there with me?"

He stood back and looked into my eyes, Fever boiling across his face as his tears turned to wax, and he nodded with such gratitude I had to look away. "I just wanted it to be funny again," he muttered, though he must've known I required no explanation. "I just needed it to be funny again somehow. To arrive again at the very beginning. And to blot out the voice that said I'd be alone from now on."

I shook the keys, motioned him into the passenger's seat as my Brother had once motioned me, got into the driver's seat, released the brake with a flourish, and pulled out of the lot, past the lone pickup still remaining as the big top deflated on the other side of the turnstiles.

WE DROVE THROUGH THE DESERTED HISTORIC center, the traffic lights blinking yellow while a pair of street sweepers made the rounds. The banners hung limply from their posts, tangled in branches and drooping over the awnings of shuttered stores.

Back at the motel, I parked by the harbor and came around to the passenger's side to let the man out. He leaned on my shoulder as I walked him to the door and propped him against it. Then I went back to the truck to retrieve the sculpture.

When I'd gotten both inside, I put the man on the bed and took the waxwork into the bathroom, where I found the tub still full of water. I eased it in and watched as it sank to the bottom and then began to bob, a smile appearing on its lips. Soon, I thought. We'll be on our way again soon.

I went back to the bed and sat down next to the man, rubbing his shoulders and letting him rest his hand on my thigh, where it hung like something he couldn't have retracted even if I'd told him to. We sat like that for a long time, looking at our reflection in the empty TV screen, and at the harbor out the window, where motorboats and sunfish bobbed in the moonlight.

"I just..." He began.

"I know," I replied. "I know. We all do."

He sighed and leaned against me.

THEN I STOOD AND HELD OUT MY HAND. HE TOOK it and let me lead him, like a nervous bride, into the bathroom. I leaned him against the sink and went back to the bedroom for the butter knife I'd taken from the diner this morning, wrapped in my napkin. It was dull and flimsy, but it would work, because it had to.

When I came back, he was still leaning on the sink, but had turned to regard the sculpture as it decomposed in the bathwater. "It's not going to work," he said. "It can't. It didn't for me."

"I know," I said again, suddenly unable to pretend otherwise. "But, like you, I have to try."

I dragged the serrations back and forth along his throat and he let me do it without complaint, wincing and gurgling and then giving out all at once, blood pouring against the tiles and into the tub, soaking my Brother where he lay. I emptied the body into the tub without looking, almost bored with the act, like I was emptying my suitcase onto the bed. I knew that nothing would happen, but I finished what I'd promised to do, raining down plasma onto my Brother, where he could drink it and grow strong again, if he so chose, if any possibility remained that the Golden Age hadn't ended on Cielo Drive.

When the last of the man had been decanted, I folded his husk beside the toilet and returned to the bed, where I sat, shaking and soaked in my souvenir sweatshirt, my fingers trembling so badly I dropped the remote three times before I succeeded in turning on the TV.

When it came alive, I leaned back, wrapping myself in the bedspread, and watched while the student who'd taken me to lunch spoke at the site of the ransacked Wax Museum. "It's mayhem," she said, as ambulances and cruisers sped around her. "I've been saying, for years now, that this was going to happen.

"That Squimbop Fever was spreading and it was only a matter of time before it crossed the latency threshold to become an undeniable *mass phenomenon.* Too many men in this country—and, seriously, I can't stress how long I've been saying this—have convinced themselves, or have *been* convinced, and I know how this sounds, by forces outside our understanding, that they were once half of the iconic duo and that, if only enough radical violence could be enacted, a profound enough sacrifice, then that duo could be resurrected and a new *Age of Authentic Comedy* inaugurated, a new Golden Age instead of... of... Well, I wish someone had listened. Literally for years, I've been saying—"

I changed the channel. On the next one, the student paced around the fairgrounds where tonight's show had taken place, stepping over the deflated big-top in a pair of knee-high leather boots. She seemed happier here, deeper in her role, excited to see that it was catching on, that she was being deemed an Expert. I felt years, decades maybe, flutter by, pushing us that much further into a scenario that was now all-pervasive. How can I possibly still be doing this? I wondered. Just as I had in the diner, I again saw rooms full of tubs and hooks and chains extending underfoot, hundreds stacked atop one another, and in each one a waxen Squimbop in a broth from which he would never reemerge. Wasted energy, wasted time, a performance for no one. I saw myself in all these rooms as well, hundreds of me, but all of it amounted to no more than my presence in the room I was already in.

"All along, I've been saying that a Squimbop Night of Wrath was coming, a spectacle of mass sacrifice in which no one at all would be safe. The monomaniacal drive of those with Squimbop Fever to, as they put it, *puncture the veil* and reconnect with the real world on the other side, *the World of Authentic Comedy*, through any means possible, is a force greater than any other. Nothing can stop them now. From now on, we live in the *Age of Squimbop Fever* and we are subject to its..."

EVENTUALLY I TURNED IT OFF, SAID FAREWELL TO what remained of my Brother, got back in the pickup truck, released the parking brake with an enervated flourish, and drove away, out of that town and back onto the coast road, further north, the radio once again whispering about awful secrets known only to those whose origins were not on this planet. From time to time I thought I could hear "Me and the Devil Blues" playing softly in the background, on some channel between channels, but I knew better than to try to find it on the dial.

Night after night and day after day, the same events recurred. I pulled off in whatever town I happened to have arrived in at dawn, shaken after a long night lit only by the purple glow of the ship following me from harbor to harbor. I ate at the local diner, visited the Wax Museum—every town had one—boiled off the day in my room, and then, at night, stole another sculpture of my Brother, immersed him in the big tub, and found another man—it didn't matter who, just any man, they were all riddled with Fever—brought him back, sat with him on the bed for a while, cried with him if he wanted to cry, then emptied him into the water, still praying that my Brother would take what was offered and reciprocate by rising to his feet, drying himself off, and leading me by the hand into our next escapade. I knew that he never would, that wax was wax and skin was skin, and yet the Fever compelled me to go on trying, a pantomime as inexorable as any I'd ever performed.

News spread faster than I could keep up with, that same student in an ever-evolving array of wigs, glasses, and prostheses on every channel on every TV in every room I rented. My will to resist watching diminished so that, before long, I'd spend the whole night, after my work was done, wrapped in the bedspread, watching her track the Fever's course. "All across the country, to say nothing of the world," she said, "men claiming to be Squimbops are killing other men and sacrificing them to wax Squimbop sculptures. All, of course, claiming to be one half of the *True Duo*, desperate to purge the world of impersonators and at last—this phrase never changes, no matter how far the Fever spreads—*puncture the veil and inaugurate the Age of Authentic Comedy, born of sacrifice beyond imagining.*"

I TURNED THE TV OFF AT DAWN IN SOME SALMON town in Alaska and walked down to the frozen harbor to watch the horizon and wait for our mansion to bob into view, lower its gangplank, and invite me aboard. Because if it didn't, I could now see, I would keep doing what I'd been doing until no one on earth remained, rendering myself utterly alone in the effort to avoid that very fate. If there'd been any way of stopping me, I would've found it long ago.

Exhausted beyond description, I turned back toward the frigid town center when it was clear the Ark wasn't coming today, and walked into the diner where I ordered coffee and pancakes at the counter, smiling at the waitress when she asked if I'd had a good night.

The Brothers Squimbop in Kansas

Time wore on up there in Alaska, while I—barely half a duo by that point, no longer a Brother to anyone—watched the Fever spread. Though it had eroded both its origins and its nature, to the point where I could say neither how it had begun nor what it had become, I couldn't fail to perceive its presence in the bleak fishing town I'd washed up in, along with the crimes I'd committed.

I'd done what I'd done, down in California and Oregon and Washington and in the woodlands north of Vancouver. There was no denying it, nor even slowing the rate at which it was bound to continue up here, not so much catching up with me as emerging from who and what I'd turned into, as if my entire northward journey had been for no purpose other than to evolve the Fever into its mature form, a force as generative as it was terminal. Bodies turned up, sacrificed to wax that would never come alive no matter how hard I, or the dozens of others like me, tried. We did all we could, and more than we should have, but wax remained wax and flesh remained flesh, whether living or not, and we remained alone, sealed off from ourselves and one another, nodding remotely when the diner door dinged louder than expected, eyes on our eggs and hands on our toast. Mouth full of that toast, I'd drink coffee with more sugar than it could absorb, enough to sicken me, trying whatever I could think of to kindle a buzz inside my khaki coat up there in the pitch dark, under stars that seemed deployed to menace me in particular, portending a strange new chapter that was ready to begin and yet, still, wouldn't.

There was no question of bringing the Fever to a halt, nor even any serious means of trying. Any officer saddled with the task quickly succumbed to it, as the Fever spread quickest among those who evinced even a modest intention of curtailing its trajectory by living complete unto themselves rather than as half of a sundered duo. One officer after another—Pinkertons or Pinkerton impersonators, sent up from Portland and Seattle, or self-deputized, in the grips of a primitive vendetta that amounted to no more than another symptom of the same condition—succumbed as that first, black winter in Alaska gave way to the next and the next and the next, the distinction between them purely philosophical, or even less than that—an idiot's notion of philosophy cribbed from the kind of Borscht Belt routine that, in another life, part of me still believed my Brother and I used to perform, to rapturous if ghostly applause in the function rooms of colossal Mountain Houses, so deep in the Catskills that, as I might've quipped back then, in the accent of a Yiddish-speaking child who'd learned English at public school in Canarsie, time nearly forgot to forget them.

As the winters passed, more and more of the town's dark storefronts, whether they'd once been leather goods outlets or antique malls or saloons, or the one-room schoolhouse with its crumpled "Closed until Professor arrives" banner in the window, grew marquees until, it seemed, every space that could possibly become a cinema had become one. Whether this represented a distortion of the town or the emergence of its true form was another question that the idiot philosopher I'd once played, while my Brother played my endearingly puckish, unteachable pupil, enjoyed pretending to consider while hopping from leg to leg in the freezing dusk before the show began.

IN THOSE VERY DEEPEST OF THE ALASKAN DAYS, which in retrospect I miss almost as much as the Borscht Belt days buried under so many layers beneath them, and yet, along another axis, are now cloaked in the same shadow and thus nearly equivalent, I hurried from one makeshift cinema to another to another, many with walls that didn't quite meet and roofs made of aluminum and fiberglass that rode up and slammed down in the vicious wind, my patched-together khaki coat pulled tight over three sweaters. If I could get the timing right, I'd catch three or four runs of *Brothers Squimbop Golden Age* revival shorts in three or four cinemas along the only street of that exhausted, murder-soaked town high up along the coast of nowhere, as close to the top of the world as the living can come without traversing a twilight zone beyond which all events freeze into legend and in that sense cannot occur.

I sat in the dark and watched, over and over again, *The Brothers Squimbop in Europe* and *The Brothers Squimbop in Hollywood, The Brothers Squimbop Burst the Borscht Belt Vols. I* and *II,* and even rare showings of the nearly snuff-grade *Squimbop Fever*, probing the snowy footage—the snow falling outside penetrated the cinema, filling the empty space between me and the screen with soft grey fuzz—for any hint of my old face, any clue within the expressions of the actors or documentary subjects that these stories, which I remembered so well, or at least felt that I ought to remember well, were indeed about me, so that I could at least be certain I had once been elsewhere, and might thus end up elsewhere again.

The films, I insisted, were about me and, of course, my Brother. There were nights when the return of his absence was enough to send me reeling onto the streets before the credits rolled, knife drawn even as the population of eligible victims dwindled toward zero, replenished only by stringy drifters deposited in silence by the Night Bus. I'd drag them on such nights, stunned and insensate, toward the shed behind the diner where I worked three days a week, just enough to pay for movie tickets and my room out by the gas station and for occasional visits to White's, the glaring white supermarket on a corner where, even in the daytime, the sky was always black.

Inside the shed, I took no pleasure in going through the Fever's motions, rote as a nickel-operated roadside attraction, though sometimes, in the necessary heat of the routine, I'd flash back to an earlier go-around, further down the coast and, as the hot blood pooled around the feet of that shed's wax Squimbop, melted and refrozen so many times it looked as muddled as I felt—every shed in town had one, presumably crafted and left there by an earlier generation, even more naïve than we were in its belief that the Fever could be satisfied through sacrifice—I'd feel a shiver of purpose return, and, for a blessed instant, it would seem as though the insanity I'd long ago consigned myself to wasn't yet terminal. Perhaps, I'd think, as I locked the shed and dragged the spent body on a hook toward the dump while the Night Bus pulled back into town, I'm no closer to the Saga's ultimate end than I am to its long-forgotten beginning. Perhaps I'm still an ordinary dweller of an expansive and even nutritive middle, with much excitement and a little satisfaction still to come, my time outside the clarifying bond of a Squimbop duo only an interregnum, soon to be restored, so that these long, strange hours in the dark will seem to have been no more than a necessary regrouping between one tour of the Inland Circuit and the next, from Lake Placid to Lake Tahoe and back and back again, a thousand times over, unto the eternity that my Brother and I, after all we've been through, surely deserve.

WHEN I WENT TO SLEEP ON NIGHTS LIKE THIS, improbably warmed despite the unremitting cold outside, I'd sink into my thin mattress and rock as if I were already at sea, floating as fast as the waves would allow back out into the world, never to revisit the coast of Alaska. I'd lie there watching the terror of my singularity recede as a new shore of restored Brotherhood pulled into view. In other versions of the dream, as White's fluorescence filtered into my room, both of our heads would rise from the ocean's depths, titanic and mossy, mountainous, volcanic, twin Atlantises named Jim and Joe, resurrected from the innermost vault of the world's founding blueprint. Then, if I couldn't keep from sleepwalking, I'd find myself back in the cinemas, which seemed never to close—or else to open whenever I turned up—watching Squimbop footage at three and four in the morning, when it appeared raw and unedited like a natural phenomenon, a kind of fleshed wind, as the northern lights danced in the rocky crags that bounded the settlement and the frozen Pacific split the docks in the narrow passable stretch of harbor.

This footage likewise turned nautical, exchanging its familiar pie-stand and hat-rack routines for new material set upon a colossal turn-of-the-century steamer or a rough but sturdy Norwegian deep sea fishing vessel, adjacent to but clearly distinct from the ferries my Brother and I rode so many times to and from Europe, back in the Golden Age these films seemed determined to commemorate, as if the reels had developed a memory of our circuit while tracing their own, from theater to theater around the continent before ending up here, at the very end of the line, where no one wanted them back and they were thus free to unspool into dust, hovering in air that only I was breathing.

I'd breathe this air in and out and in and out until Tommy Bruno, the bald, smiling, tuxedoed usher and concession man who'd been here so long I could see the cinema going up, board by board, around him where he stood in the snow, ejected me for a between-film cleaning, squeezing my shoulder with a delicacy that indicated he was well aware of my state. Still half-awake and fearful of the air outside, I'd reemerge in the diner, either cooking if it was my day to cook or chewing eggs and burnt rye at the counter if it wasn't, and then, with a thin paper cup of dangerously sweet coffee in each hand, I'd shamble over to the harbor to sit on a bench and listen to the waves crack and crunch together while I watched the horizon for the ship I was certain would be here soon, emerging out of the static just as it would have if I'd been allowed to remain in the cinema.

Indeed, it was not lost on me that, if I could see myself from afar, the tableau of a fading Squimbop on a bench with two coffees about to freeze over would sync up exactly with the last scene of the film I'd watched last night, and the night before that, and perhaps—nothing, when it came to gaps or eerie continuities, seemed impossible in Alaska—every night of my life, slowly developing a naïve Squimbop obsession which, I couldn't help but suspect, had no more to do with me than it did with the billion others who'd happened to see the same footage and latch onto it with the same desperation that, by this point, was probably all that kept us alive.

As I sat there gnawing my coffee cups and feeling myself uneasily housed within an iconic Squimbop Pose, the kind that everyone would've recognized years ago, or would come to recognize years from now, if and when the famously scandal-ridden construction of the Squimbop Media Center in Cooperstown, New York was completed, I began to understand, through no force other than what I could sense in the wind, that the supply of stringy drifters would soon run out and it would then be time to renounce the Fever, even if I was far from cured, and resign myself to the care of the captain of whatever Ship of Fools materialized out of the premonitory murk I could tell it was already sailing through, assuming the pride of place in my imagination which, until now, the Night Bus had occupied.

AFTER THIS BECAME CLEAR TO ME, THE RUN OF winters peaked, then trickled toward spring. The ice in the harbor broke up and ran back into the ocean, and the superabundance of winter cinemas reverted to grain storage and ironworks, until only one remained. It was there that I watched the first half of my final murder, a flickery, groaning scene, the footage much degraded after playing in a hundred towns before this one, in which I scooped up a barely-conscious drifter naked beneath a slick raincoat, huddled on the far side of the otherwise empty auditorium, and marched him down the stairs to the basement restroom, its walls adorned with scuffed maps of the Brothers' tours of Paris and London. I leaned him against a Victorian urinal and sawed mechanically at his throat, back and forth and back and forth in time to the clattering of the footage overhead, until I could no longer be certain whether I was watching the scene or acting it out, watched by yet more Squimbops in a silent theater on the other side of a screen whose existence I could just barely intuit, deeper into a topography that, at times like this, I felt extending all around me in a precise yet inscrutable design, a stage for all that was still to come.

Admitting my inability to move freely in this topography allowed me to likewise admit my confusion about whether the man beneath my blade was a real drifter or a wax statue, and thus whether I was sacrificing him to a sacred Squimbop effigy in hopes of bringing it back to life—thus anyway was the narrative of *Squimbop Fever*, as best I could recall—or, rather, slaying the last of the innumerable wax idols that had, for far too long, stood between my Brother and me.

I sawed his, or its, head clean off as I deliberated, growing ever more certain that, beyond what remained irresolvable in these questions, some clarity was indeed pulling into harbor. I was indeed making a kind of progress.

When I finished, I placed the head in the trough of the ceramic urinal, wiped my fingers along the Champs Élysées, placed the diner's serrated knife in a wastebasket full of ticket stubs, and walked upstairs, picturing myself emerging onto the upper deck of the ship that would sail me to the reunion I had by now surely earned. As I passed the concession stand for what I considered the very last time,

Tommy Bruno awoke from a doze, smoothed his bowtie, spread his hands across the warm surface of the popcorn tank, and smiled in a way that made it clear he believed I would soon be back.

I EMERGED ABOVE DECK JUST AS THE SHIP WAS pulling out of port, icicles forming along the thick coil of rope attached to the weed-choked anchor. Whether I surfaced first in the cinema and then proceeded through one last tour of that godforsaken outpost, stopping in my room by the gas station to fill a duffel bag by the light of the supermarket and then at the diner to quit the job which had made possible my stay in that room, taking three limp twenties from the register, or if this sequence was merely implied, seems now, as I watch the Alaskan coastline recede, to be well beside the point.

For the first time since our bleak sojourn in Hollywood, a spirit of newness hangs over me, a sense that the Brothers Squimbop are, at last, soon to be deployed in tandem again. Men clearly in the grip of the same conviction line the edges of the upper deck, keeping their distance, some reclining in hammocks, holding their coats to their sides as the wind shears past, while others lean overboard to watch our wake fan out as we leave behind not just the town where I served my term in purgatory but, I presume, the towns where they served theirs, if it's true that we've already been on this ship long enough to gather many souls in my position, or former position, all of us perhaps no more than standard Americans at the ends of our ropes, prostrate inside ourselves as we beg sources unknown for mercy.

"Good morning, pseudo-Squimbops," says a man in a tightly-tailored grey suit with an earpiece and a wrap-around wireless mic, his eyes wet and blinking as if unaccustomed to the above-deck air. We all turn to face him, admiring his alligator-skin boots and thick, black mustache, as I pour any dawning familiarity he stirs in me into the rippling pool of Squimbop Cinema that now fills most of what I might otherwise have still considered my individual heritage.

"I said," he repeats, louder this time, hitting what's clearly a practiced note, his boots glowing in the sunlight, "I said... welcome pseudo-Squimbops!" He raises his hands, as if expecting applause, which we haltingly deliver. I see myself clapping along with the others, all of our attention fixed on this man, who I can't deny bears a resemblance to the rest of us, but looks—I can think of no better way to put it—*more like us than we do.*

"I am Professor Squimbop," he announces, circling his hands like an orchestra conductor in what we take as a sign to gather around him. "Much as I obey my Distant Master, you will obey me, for I was once, and not so long ago, a pseudo-Squimbop like you, lost in an Alaska of my own. And aren't they all the same!" He scoffs, makes a show of recomposing himself, then adds, "But I found a way to become Real. I generated the power to sweat the Fever out and so, in time, will you. The process won't be easy, but it will, if you follow me all the way there, deep into the subterranean reaches of memory, prove possible. But if you don't," he emits a forced laugh that causes his mic to glitch, "then, well, the Night Bus stops all up and down this coast. It will prove trivially easy to arrange passage for you back up north, and all of you know what happens there. So, let me hear it: who's ready to become Real?"

I cheer along with the others, at first quietly and then with moderate gusto and then, though I can hardly believe it, I'm chanting and shrieking and dancing around the machinery on the upper deck, whooping and hollering in a circle, first in a voice I didn't know I had and then in a voice I can't be sure is mine, with the Professor at the very center, holding us in orbit as he closes his eyes and appears to listen to another voice, coming from much farther away.

AS WE CHANT, THE LANDSCAPE SIMMERS AND melts. By the time we're done, the frigid waters we embarked into are a distant memory and we're cruising through cool British Columbian fog and then Californian and then Hawaiian heat. We sail through bays and up rivers that bisect mountainous islands, into turquoise lagoons and mangrove swamps, cutting the engine and drifting for days at a time. Occasionally, the Professor directs the crew to disembark. When they do, they leave us alone for an hour, then return with huge drums of sand that they stow in a lower chamber, to which the Professor invites us one by one. Manicured hand outstretched, he says, "Time for your Past-Life Regression. You and only you. Just as you were conceived once, and then gestated, and then, upon being born, made Real... so shall you be again now."

With a wink and a curl of his mustache he adds, "*For Real* this time."

Those invited belowdecks never reappear. Naturally word spreads that they've been eaten by the Professor and his crew, or rendered for blubber to light the ship, but this causes no major ripple among those of us who remain. Although suspicion lingers as we sleep under the stars and the heavy sun, taking meals of fruit and nuts when they're given and listening to the Professor's brief, emphatic speeches when he chooses to make them, none of us attempts to spark the kind of conversation about our shared fate that, as I picture it, could only lead to mutiny.

We're too enervated to turn on one another, much less to unite against whatever scheme the Professor might be running, although it does occur to me that, in our desperation, we may well have boarded the wrong vessel, thereby forfeiting whatever chance we had at getting the Brothers back on the road. At best, I now sometimes fear, this sorry episode will occupy a side room in the Wing of Aborted Enterprises in an outbuilding of the Media Center, if the Cooperstown City Council, in accordance with the bylaws of New York State or whatever shadow charter governs its functionaries, ever succeeds in completing construction.

Musing on an eternity spent in that particular limbo, we swing in the hammocks that used to be in short supply but are now more than adequate to our shrunken number and ask ourselves in silence when our day will come. We feel like lobsters in a tank, bobbing together, angry but impotent, our claws clasped shut, a numbed mass of consciousness capable only of the dullest hope and fear as the inevitable culmination of our boredom draws closer in the form of a single mega-lobster who, claws unclasped, roams the tank floor, reaping us one by one.

THIS LOBSTER PHASE DRAGS ON, MORE AND MORE reminiscent of my spell in Alaska. Our self-awareness coils ever more tightly inward, distributed among a dwindling number of heads. The *we* on the upper deck again approaches the state of an *I* as the mega-lobster, embodied of course by the Professor, summons one pseudo-Squimbop after another, sometimes churning through several in one day and sometimes spending several days with each one, and then taking several days off—days spent gathering sand in what could well be Tahiti by now—until I'm the only one left, a development that I take as evidence that I was indeed the Real Squimbop all along, though I can't suppress the suspicion that whoever was left would've felt the same way.

The Professor emerges onto the upper deck, earpiece and microphone in position, looks wistfully down at his alligator-skin boots, then up at the rows of empty hammocks, then smiles and beckons to me. "I always save the best for last," he says with a wink, before adding, "are you ready to be conceived anew?"

I nod, which causes him to shake his head and say, "I require verbal confirmation, my friend. This is a one-way trip to the Dust Bowl, so a Yes or a No is the least I'll accept."

With my mind full of memories of traipsing along a dusty path away from a ramshackle cabin with my Brother by my side, the two of us ready to become infamous, I nod again, almost but not quite forgetting to add, "Yes," just before the Professor drops the nice-guy act he's barely kept up so far.

After this word is absorbed into or beyond his earpiece, he extends his hand, takes mine, and leads me down a steep, narrow staircase and into the ship's cavernous interior, full, as I'd suspected, of grayish, dusty sand. He walks me through it, past a model gas station with a single tank and a handwritten sign that reads, "For Ness County Farm Collective Members Only," and a chrome billboard for "Dottie's Soup Counter & Pie Rack," and positions me in an armchair deep in the sand, making a "shhh" gesture when I open my mouth.

"Welcome to the Dust Bowl," he whispers. "Authentic emanation point of the Brothers Squimbop. It is, at last, time to regain that which, over decades and decades upon the road, at large in the flux of the already-wide and ever-widening world, has been lost. Or," he pretends to revise his speech, "*nearly* lost. For if it had been lost entirely, you would be beyond my help, and I would've left you in that frozen harbor you washed up in, waiting with your mouth open for the Night Bus to return. No," he circles my chair, covering his face in white pancake makeup and pulling off his sportcoat to reveal a striped mime's turtleneck underneath, *No,* he mimes, *it has not been lost entirely. It remains in the dull bottom of your temporal lobe, down on the ocean floor where movies seen in the depths of night recut themselves into what they truly are, only and always* The True Story of the Brothers Squimbop, *which no mortal editor can assemble... No, our story is not over yet. Together, we will fit the spool back onto the reel or,* he grows giddy, hopping up and down, losing himself in the routine, *the reel back onto the spool!*

Either way, he mimes, cooling his energies back to a simmer as he circles my chair one last time and blows sand in my face, *let me tell you a story of the Dust Bowl. Your story and mine, lost but not forgotten... and, as such, both my gift to you and your gift to me. Together, we will offer our bodies to* The True Story, *so that it might recast itself around us, back into its authentic form, at last healing the myriad deformities incurred by years of moldering room service and untreated Fever.*

I CLOSE MY EYES. BEHIND THEM EXTENDS THE same Dust Bowl that extended there while they were open but larger now, more all-encompassing, and laden, suddenly, with sound, smell, savor, all the subtle stimuli that together boil into an atmosphere one can inhabit, move though, and, with sufficient force of will and submission to a larger psychic project, consider Real.

Trudging into this project, already weary and parched, I train my eyes on the mime in the near distance as he bounces over dunes and through thorny scrub-brush, leaping into the air and kicking his heels together when the weather's fine, bedding down in dry riverbeds when tornadoes render us helpless, and otherwise soldiering on for what feels like days, although the sun doesn't rise or set, only wobbles around the center of the sky. The landscape wobbles with it, jogging dim memories of the open ocean, but this seems impossibly distant, as far as the West Coast is from Kansas. The destination of a lifetime, I think, squinting to keep the mime centered in my vision. The site of all aspiration, the end of the line. I've made it this far, halfway at least... surely it will prove possible to keep going once I regroup.

I laugh, unsure if I've made a joke or heard one. This uncertainty makes me laugh harder, so much so that I suspect there was no joke before, but there is now, the eternal joke of whether, as I put it to an imaginary audience obscured by the dust, the Brothers Squimbop are at root actors or directors... indeed, I mug, picking up on the mime's mannerisms as I step onto the stage of the frontier opera house in Abilene I've kept in mental storage for the better part of a century, the question is really whether we're reprising a timeworn routine or making it up as we go, reminding all of you gathered here tonight that the Spirit of Adventure is alive in this nation, seeded here before your very eyes... and, beneath all this—the audience is in hysterics now after waiting a century in silence, rolling in the dust, decomposing and coming back together as the plains shiver and boil—the deeper question is whether there really are or even were any Brothers in the first place, if the legendary duo every existed, or if it's only ever been me, alone in this wasteland for all time, neither living nor dead, neither near nor far, in relation to nothing at all, blindly following a mime who...

THE MIME SWARMS ME AS I RAVE, PULLING THE horizon in with him like the flap of a circus tent, closing it around an intimate, candlelit scene inside. *Evening falls across the broken porch slats of a one-story frontier cabin in Ness City, Kansas,* he mimes. *Year of 1934, year of hunger and thirst, the Crash a long way back, the War barely a glimmer up ahead...*

Yes, we'll post up here for a while. Here, until history compels our escape, our ship comes to anchor and our horses trudge no more. We have, have we not, traveled long enough already.

Nestled in his armpit, I allow the mime to lead me to the cabin's front door and extend my hand to rap at the knocker. After a dead spell, a woman in a long black dress opens up and looks us over. When she makes eye contact, first with the mime and then with me, the tiniest glimmer of recognition plays across her face. Another life, I think. Another sweltering road, in another country, on another continent.

"Well?" she snaps, her recognition draining as the present asserts its total if temporary dominance over the scene. "Did you come to eat or come to gawk? Because I take in hobos for the one but not the other."

The mime makes an elaborate show of mocking my hesitation, shifting his weight side to side in weepy impatience, yawning and tapping his mouth until, though I feel if anything more shaken than I did a moment ago, I get a provisional hold on myself and cross the threshold.

INSIDE, THE WOMAN INDUCES US TO SIT AROUND A narrow table, lit by more of the candles that light the whole scene. Our chairs rock with a distant oceanic pulse as she ladles out three bowls of chili and cuts three slices of hard white bread.

When she's likewise taken her seat, we say a brief Grace in which she invokes the majesty of the Kansas wind and prays for rain. Then we set to eating in silence as the mime entertains us with tales of the wild, weary Dust Bowl he's come to know during his journey from Pittsburgh, where, he claims, he'd managed a sandpaper factory until the going got rough. He tells of cannibal hives in Kentucky and a trade in human molars in Tennessee, of telepathic leviathans beneath the Mississippi and a tree that bled sticky, sickening wine in uppermost Arkansas, potent enough to render that very tree hallucinatory in retrospect, so that no traveler could say for sure if it had been there or not. Our chili dwindles and the woman pours us frugal shots of brown liquor as the mime dances around the kitchen, leaping onto the counters and making a prop of his busted chair as he introduces us to a songster in Olathe who wrote murder ballads for a dollar apiece, the only hitch being that he required the salient events to be acted out before his eyes—and not merely *acted out*, the mime adds, with a leer—and then he's onto a pair of ex-boxers who offered their bruised faces as stand-ins for local personal injury lawyers in upward of two hundred Missouri towns, claiming variably to be the Law Offices of Stevens & Sandino, Lewis & Willmerdorf, and even Fujiyama & Stephanopoulos—the joke always being that the mugs of those two pugilists suggested both dominance and grievous harm at the same time—and then there was the nunnery in Chase County where all the nuns created cloth facsimiles of themselves in order to trick Death into taking these and leaving their flesh in peace, the only problem being that the facsimiles grew so convincing that the nuns were likewise fooled, so that perhaps this nunnery was, or was soon to be, no more than a cloth museum, sterile as a marble shrine on a mountaintop in Armenia, awaiting the rival cults that would in time form to revere and deny what had happened there.

THE MIME TAKES A VICTORY LAP AROUND THE kitchen upon concluding this story. Just as he shows signs of beginning the next, the black-clad woman rises, gathers him bouncing under her arm, and, leaving me alone with my chili bowl, sighs, "Excuse us, it's time for the Primal Scene." She doesn't add *again*, but her sigh more than conveys it.

I remain in position a moment longer, jilted surprise on my face as if I were the mime now, wearing a painted-on expression, but when lewd, magnified shadows spread across the walls, I tiptoe toward the room they're coming from, more frightened of creaking the floorboards than I have any good reason to be. Frozen just outside the open door, I watch the mime and the black-clad woman perform the Primal Scene, its shadows now intertwined with my own, so that I feel myself being pulled in and, soon, cannot be sure whether I'm in the hall by myself or in the room with them. My attention swivels between the bodies and their shadows, back and forth, until my eyes blur and I sink into another memory, that of my Brother and me on the open road, years ago or years from now, behind a Shoney's in El Centro, ribbing each other about this very scene, always claiming, to the point of lurid mania, to be the other's father. A smile spreads across my face, growing painfully wide and wider still, as if extending beyond my head, until I explode in a fit of hysterics that I just barely manage to contain by hugging my sides and tiptoeing down the rocking hall, through ever more vivid shadowplay, into what is clearly the Bachelor's Cell, made up identically to the room I occupied in Alaska, the windows full of White's fluorescence from across the street.

The cot in the Bachelor's Cell squeaks when I collapse upon it and, letting go of my sides, the laughter spills out of me and into the coarse, cigar-burned bedding. I laugh, exaggerating my expressions just as the mime would have, while the cell rocks and the shadows follow me, twisting and twining beyond all geometric sense, projecting every conceivable—*no pun intended,* I smirk, slapping my thighs—permutation of the Primal Scene that my Brother and I joked about so long ago, and all I can think, as the mad repetition of the shadows dulls my faculties, is that I wish he were here with me now, to see such crude living proof of the routine that sustained us for so long, throughout so many dismal teaching gigs along the backmost and bottommost edges of the nation, in which I was his father, much as, of course, he was mine.

I AWAKEN TO AN INFANT'S SOBBING, SO LOUD AND constant it seems impossible to attribute to a single source. When does it breathe? I lean up on my elbows in the cot I only now remember falling asleep in. I yawn and feel the Bachelor's Cell rock and tip back to the oceanic expanse of the womb, an all-encompassing aqueous eternity that feels at once terribly far away and terribly near at hand, as if I've only just now been expelled from it with a directive to ply my trade upon the surface of the planet for as long as anyone there will have me, weaving my Saga into the fabric of the nation *before*—the warning is at once frighteningly direct and maddeningly opaque—*it is, once again, too late.*

As the sobbing continues, I rise, yawn, pee in a pot, and resolve to creak into the kitchen and face there whatever turn my adventure has taken. I press my hands against the clapboard walls and make my way out of my solitude as slowly as I can while also miming this same emergence, squeezing out as if from the womb and blinking in what I pretend is the first sunlight I've ever seen.

In the kitchen, I surface upon the mime ladling gruel into bowls for the black-clad woman and two small boys, who sup desperately, licking the last meager crumbs of brown sugar from the edges of their dented soup spoons. No one admires my routine or even looks my way until I tramp over to the table, feeling my bones thicken and my skin sag as I look down at the sanded wood where no place has been set for me. I tramp out to the shed with practiced heaviness and return with a cracked spare stool, where I sit until the mime has no choice but to spoon what remains into the bowl he'd been eating from, and place it with a scowl before me. He mimes disgust while I mime embarrassment, doing my face up into an impression of a dubious lodger who's long outstayed his welcome. Though it feels tired, our routine elicits modest laughs from the woman and the boys, enough that I can't suppress a blush of pride to know I haven't yet lost my touch.

Still blushing, I watch the dirty spoon tremble as it conveys my portion to my mouth while my eyes likewise tremble with crocodile tears, and the laughter simmers down and the morning approaches its next phase.

Don't get too comfortable here, stranger, the mime mimes as he takes my bowl before I'm finished and tosses it into a pail of suds on the counter. He tips the edge of his fedora, winks, and sets off out the door to, as I imagine it, ply the dusty trails between here and Ransom in search of whatever job will take him. Back in the cabin, the day stretches ahead of us, the black-clad woman and the two boys and me, all of us straining, it seems, to prolong a routine that's abdicated its claim to relevance without nominating a successor.

Save me from this stasis, I beseech the three of them, as they traipse through the cabin and out to the yard in back, the boys whipping each other with wet towels while the mother picks what few scraggly pears protrude from the trees that verge onto a field behind their property. *Release me, for my Past-Life Regression has only just begun,* I wish to declare, but I know the words, even if I found a way to say them, would fall on deaf ears. So I mime the day away, trying to devise a routine in which I overcome this stagnation to travel on with my head held high—in the routine, I'm more than able to travel alone, forsaking whatever need for reunion initially compelled me aboard that ship in Alaska—but, although I do manage to walk down the front steps several times with a rucksack over my shoulder and a potato in each fist, some principle of the larger scenario will not allow me to breach the sidewalk. Each time I try, laughter rises in the background, the routine growing steadily more ridiculous as, somewhere in the dark, Tommy Bruno scoops fresh popcorn into a series of cardboard containers and smiles his tired smile while a series of guests makes its way in to behold my leashed circuit in glorious black and white. I have no choice but to pander, and find I'm glad for the opportunity.

Thus the day goes on, and thus the days go on, the boys growing steadily while I seem to shrink, losing my orientation within the makeshift family that the mime returns to late each evening, launching always into the same hard-luck show as the night before, unaware of or indifferent to the boredom it now provokes in his supposed wife and children, to say nothing of the strained relationship that's evolved between him and me, Paterfamilias and Pervert Uncle, one Brother gone straight, the other sent back to skew it all sideways again.

ONE NIGHT, SEVERAL MORE YEARS INTO THIS ARrangement, after the others have turned in and I've taken it upon myself to scrub the dishes stacked in the washbasin, I hear the mime creep up behind me and turn to see his face painted with violent red streaks and green fanged dentures gleaming in the moonlight. He grins, pulls the washrag from my hands, and motions for me to sit.

I comply. He sits across from me, dancing his legs back and forth on the kitchen floor, warming up for what I can tell will be a routine he's had planned, perhaps from the beginning, for this precise moment, neither a day earlier nor a day later, as if, seen from a more distant vantage—that of Tommy Bruno, eternally unchanging save for his periodic alternation of black and white bowties and the nights on which he appears to be drunk on more than cinema—all of this had been a single elongated act and now, right on time, we've reached the Finale, stasis breaking at last not because of any internal development but simply because the appointed moment has arrived, and the theater must be emptied, cleaned, and made ready for the next showing.

Go to your cell and get your things, he mimes. *Then*—his made-up eyes come to rest on the turkey knife on the counter, with which the black-clad woman slaughtered an ancient bird in the sink—*it will be time for you and me to take our walk, as Brothers one last time.*

Compelled by the same logic of imminent climax that I presume compelled him, I get up with a flourish, turn, and slump down the hall, adding weight to each reluctant step until I'm stomping on the loose floorboards.

As I make my way toward the cell in this fashion, past the wall where the shadows of the Primal Scene still flicker like a property of the wood itself, something else comes to mind. A final errand, and perhaps my first genuine act since the Past-Life Regression began. I check behind me, wary of the mime's roving gaze, and then steal into the room where the boys are sleeping. I stand in the corner, hidden in shadow, and watch their faces, nearly identical and yet not quite, one already more dominant, the other a shriveled version thereof. Just like, I can't help thinking, though it feels like overkill, the surest way to neuter a joke, the mime and me.

I hit myself in the forehead and give a silent belly laugh at the obviousness of this comparison. Then I lean over them, feeling the fullness of my role as their Pervert Uncle come surging up from my core, and say, breaking my silence for what feels like the first time since Alaska, "From this point forward, you are the Brothers Squimbop, Jim and Joe, blessed and cursed to ply the interior of the nation in every form it has left to take, and to deform it yet further from there, kneading the land into a bastion of the very forces you embody, so that you will exist always as both destroyers and destroyed, bastards bastardizing the order of things, authors of the very Saga you live and die within, spared nothing due to that authorship, gods of a realm in which you are, now and forever, nothing but servants."

Footsteps rush up the hall, a desperate, racing violence coming to purge me from where I don't belong, a Dust Bowl pervert loose in the room where the precious boys are sleeping, about to seed in their past a violation so profound they'll never quite...

Knowing all this because it is in some sense the story I'm telling, I lean over the bed and shout, spittle flying from my lips, "Live on so that we might live too, so that we all, all of this, the great wheel we roll within, will not stop here, as if it'd never started... roll on, let the legend of the Brothers Squimbop roll into the future and not lodge here in the Dust Bowl, to which I never would've returned had I not—"

The mime's hands are around my neck, the turkey knife stretched between them, realer than anything I've ever felt or expected ever to feel.

THE BROTHERS SQUIMBOP, JIM AND JOE, JOLTED upright in bed as their father dispatched the last of the Pervert Uncle whose long, lecherous presence throughout the years of their youth accounted in no small part for the dim view they'd already taken on humanity, the viper ethos that would, before very long at all, serve as catalyst for the adolescent exploits that would in turn, not long after that, serve as seedbed for the growing reach of their legend, two damaged Kansas farmboys at large on the high prairie, raising more hell than any pseudo-Squimbop could ever have dreamt possible, magnetizing a torrent of attention and ramifying narrative so colossal that any attempt to encompass it within a Media Center in Cooperstown, New York would be a fool's errand of such magnitude that the City Council, when presented with the proposal, would at first only laugh at the naivete inherent in this most American of all ambitions, still the nation's greatest asset, after so many centuries of trial and error.

They marinated a little longer, there in bed and then at the table and in the fields out back, scrounging for sustenance as their sweat thickened into a shell around their growing frames. The black-clad woman came and went from their vision, resentful of the burden of bearing them, thrust upon her more times than she could count, even if this time, like every time, was the first, and hence, though the paradox had long ago maddened and then bored her, the only. She understood they were about to go into the world to live out the exploits that had already become legendary generations ago, and she understood that the impossibility of this simple fact was a large part of its appeal.

She turned her attention to their Last Supper, in which she killed her prize chicken, fried it in a pan, and served it with honey, butter, and the Brothers' favorite cornbread, dotted with green peppers and baked in a skillet in the oven. The walls turned to curtains again and blew in close, and the lighting framed the three of them suggestively, as they sat rocking on the precipice of a new era. They could all imagine this very scene rendered into a folk painting on the wall behind them, and, though none turned to check, it soon grew impossible to say it wasn't hanging there already.

The Brothers' mother regarded them from across the table she knew she would from then on occupy alone with the painting, sinking into history as their legend grew and, like all legends, obscured its true origin in layer upon layer of eager hearsay, until she'd be nothing save for what drunken strangers in loud rooms said she was, at least until the mime and uncle darkened her door again and, buried in memory and half-yearning to surface from it, having half-forgotten the toll it would take, she again invited them in, provided they'd come to eat and not to gawk.

She looked from Jim to Joe and Joe to Jim, committing their faces to memory and building, insofar as anyone could, a bulwark against the infinite revisions that would soon be relayed back to her, in print and newsreel and painting after painting, and, before long, on the television sets that first one and then all of her neighbors would turn out to have bought in secret, just as the War was winding down. Then she said a prayer inside her head, admitting to herself that she loved them even if, in some regard that could never be untangled, they weren't really her sons, only beings who had passed through her on their way between worlds, and then she excused herself, stooped and rocking down the hallway beneath the weight of knowing she would never be given the credit she'd earned.

THE BROTHERS LEFT SOON AFTER SHE WAS GONE. Finishing the drumsticks that were already in hand, they wiped their fingers on their corduroys and stuffed modest satchels with the ill-fitting clothing strewn about the room they'd been fledged in, laced up the boots that had served them well enough so far, even if they'd soon be outgrown, wrapped some cornbread in paper, and walked down the road that led away from the cabin and out past Ransom, crossing a county line they'd never crossed before.

As they sallied forth, each Brother worked to solidify what he was leaving behind, adding details where details were missing: a stifling country schoolhouse where he'd been taught the rudiments of Greek and Latin along with Eliot, Hopkins, and Poe by a saintly schoolmistress whose belief in the education of minors went well beyond what any of them deserved; an almost-chaste summer romance lit by fireflies and a moon full to bursting, though shadowed also with the heartache of knowing that in September her family was moving to Lincoln; a sinister yet charismatic uncle who, although he'd done unforgivable things in the night, had also revealed the secrets of card counting and the power of suggestion.

Each added these details and prepared to defend them against any discrepancies in his Brother's account. More than anything, they worked to clear space in memory, opening as many spare rooms as they could find, suddenly aware, as they put one foot in front of the other toward the West, that only in the mansion made of these spare rooms would any of what had happened and was about to achieve any cohesion at all.

Indeed, they began to suspect one another as the night wore on, each keeping more and more to himself, a hand clamped over his lips for fear of muttering any part of his ruminations aloud, and thus they trudged, increasingly out of breath, through lunar canyons and beneath sharp outcroppings of glistening basalt, across open tundra and fenced-in paddocks dotted with sleeping horses, only just beginning to gain a sense of how large the world they'd spilled out into, in search of the future, would soon prove to be.

IT WASN'T UNTIL THE FIRST LIGHT FLICKERED IN the distant East, lapping at their heels and then the backs of their legs, that they were forced to stop, take water, and gnaw the cornbread they'd packed. As they did, still wary of making eye contact with one another, a rustling in the creosote a few feet from where they stood stole their attention, so they had no choice but to amble over, crumbs raining from their fists.

By this point, the sun had risen high enough to reveal the tableau in all its rustic glory: the mime slitting their Pervert Uncle's throat with a turkey knife, while the uncle groaned, "Boys, never forget, I'm your real father, sent here from deepest Alaska to seed you. To thread the legend back onto the spool so that it might not terminate in blackest arctic gloom, where Tommy Bruno will only ever... But—" he spluttered as the mime dragged the turkey knife back and forth, graceful as a cellist bowing out Bach, "you mustn't tarry, lest you end up like me. There are thousands, perhaps millions of murders to your names. A Fever precedes you that nothing can describe. You won't outrun the forces that are seeking satisfaction, even if it's not altogether *you* they're seeking it from. The crimes occurred and it is you, if you are serious about becoming the Brothers, who must pay."

The tableau stopped and they figured the cycle was restarting when, instead, their Pervert Uncle gasped, "Let nothing slow your approach to Dodge City. Trudge on, no matter how vastly they swarm you, but make haste, for others are trudging the same path. Other iterations, other Past-Life Regressions, pilgrims on the road, too numerous to reckon, and only one biopic will be made. See to it that it's yours, force yourselves aboard the Ark while the others drown, pledge yourselves to cinema and you will never pay for what you've done, you will never—"

HERE THE TABLEAU STOPPED AGAIN AND A VOICE from behind them, sudden enough that they both jumped in unison—perhaps their first coordinated motion, a harbinger of great things to come if, as the tableau urged, they made it to Dodge City on time—said, "Speaking of paying, that'll be a nickel, boys. Pay up and you can pull the curtain back for free."

They turned to regard a farmgirl who stood all of four feet tall, holding a power cord that stretched between her and a distant tin shed beside the farmhouse she surely inhabited, if she inhabited anyplace on earth. The length of the cord corresponded to the length of time they lingered there, insofar as neither Brother felt compelled to respond until his eyes had traced the cord all the way from where they stood to its distant terminus, and back, and, though they could sense that this was pushing their luck, back and forth a second time as well.

After this was complete, they resolved to regard her—she'd gone nearly as still as the mime-and-uncle show whose power she'd cut—and, clearing their throats with a confidence they'd never expressed before, said, "Show us the curtain first."

She snapped back to attention and bundled the cord more steadily in her arms, nearly vanishing behind it so that only her head appeared above the coil, while her feet peeped out below. The Brothers followed in her dust, past discarded pieces of the mime-and-uncle show—broken turkey knives, cracked dentures, weedy bald spots—as, in the distance, the footsteps of other duos on the Road to Dodge City boiled like locusts about to make landfall. The Brothers hurried toward the shed where the curtain was housed, at once fearful of losing time and determined to get their money's worth, even if they hadn't paid yet.

Following the cord, the farmgirl led them past the rest of the equipment, over a metal grate that traversed a pit of fur and manure, and into the shed, within which a holographic wizard hovered in nervous anticipation. "I am the Great and Wonderful Wizard of—" he sighed, as Joe Squimbop, even more confident than a moment ago, reached past his Brother to yank the curtain open, revealing a small, bespectacled man behind a typewriter-sized console.

He peered out, startled, and said, "Gina, have they paid yet?"

The farmgirl shook her head and the room contracted, growing clammy as the mist the wizard had been projected through condensed on the floor. "You watched the mime-and-uncle show?" the man asked, rubbing his forehead and sighing, like he was already near his emotional limit for the day.

The Brothers nodded in unison, and then, also in unison, joined suddenly by clarity of purpose, said, "Dodge City. We're on our way there, to sell our life rights. We're the Brothers Squimbop. Famous outlaws. Drifters, hooligans, gypsy tricksters. Call us what you will, we have millions of murders to our name. The biopic must get this right. Which way is quickest?"

The man sucked his face into a grimace, then exhaled in what was almost a laugh. "*You're* the Brothers Squimbop!" Now he laughed outright. "You know how many times I've heard that today? And I can still taste my breakfast! And this is just one shed-show of dozens!" He laughed so hard the Brothers couldn't help laughing too, while Gina stood back, fidgeting with the cord.

IN THIS COMMOTION, JOE DROPPED THE EDGE OF the curtain he'd still been holding. As soon as it fell between them and the console, the wizard reappeared, green and garish in the rust-smelling mist, bouncing with the kind of jagged energy that only flares up in moments of extreme exhaustion. "Dodge City?" it boomed, swelling so that its head alone filled all the space between the Brothers and the door, backing Gina into a rake-strewn corner. "Behind this curtain lies the Road, the shortest way by far, but be warned, you won't be on it alone. I owe no special favor to you, nor do I have any reason to imagine you two, alone among the multitudes, are the Real Brothers Squimbop. The ranks of pseudo-Squimbops, as your progenitors knew and you will soon learn, are nearly infinite, and the culling they are bound to suffer will be gruesome beyond imagining."

The head shook with silent laughter, boiling in a loop while the Brothers deliberated, torn between soldiering on along the hot, dry road they'd set out upon last night, charged up and ready to commit the legendary crimes it now seemed they'd committed already, and peeling the curtain aside a second time, thereby taking their chances on the shortcut.

"Pay us that nickel," Gina said, from the corner, "or you're going to bear a curse that—"

If only to be free of additional threat, Jim reached past his Brother, grabbed the edge of the curtain and hauled it aside again to reveal a dusty path choked with duos, so thick it was impossible to distinguish one from the next. Some had fallen on the yellow-brick road, while the rest laughed and bickered and chattered as they sped along, speaking in high tones of the redemption they sought on the backlots and in the gilded cinema palaces of the world-famous Dodge City Film Industry. Some acted out satires of this road scene with hand puppets and marionettes, while others formed harmonica and ukulele bands to sing folk songs about the *Bloody, Bloody Road to Dodge City*, many of which the Brothers found they already knew.

Suddenly fearing the loss of their last tether to the Real, they recoiled and even fought, for an instant, to remain on the near side of the curtain, with their memories of the cabin, the mime-and-uncle show, and the life of crime they'd embarked upon last night. But Gina, who'd surely seen this same hesitation many times today and could tell she'd never get her nickel, leapt behind them with a rake, prodding first Jim and then Joe over the threshold, beyond the curtain, and into the sweat of mummers and the clang of war drums along the Bloody, Bloody Road to Dodge City.

The Brothers Squimbop in Dodge City

Like so many duos before, the Brothers Squimbop emerged from the farm curtain with Kansas far behind them and nothing but Dodge City ahead. The curtain rippled shut on the endless wheat expanse of Ransom County so that here, on the *Bloody, Bloody Road to Dodge City*, as the mummers and drum corps chanted, they were in the thick of something at once contiguous with and entirely discrete from all they'd been brought up to consider their place of origin, to say nothing of the heroic future they had also, until a moment ago, believed to be their birthright.

With no time to reflect on what this transition might signify, they committed to marching along the road, straight as a parade route toward an altar already decked out and waiting to celebrate a sacred event. Their feet fought for purchase on the yellow bricks among the feet of thousands of others, some faster than they were and some slower, while some bled out in the crush, turning the parade route into a Red Sea that showed no sign of parting.

They marched on, their determination growing along with the density of slick material underfoot, while their eyes fixated on the distant but increasingly vivid silhouette of The Dodge City Skyline up ahead, strung from one corner of the horizon clear across to the other. Each Brother—*still Jim and Joe*, they all took pains to remember, though none dared to assign himself either name at the other's expense—kept his eyes on this skyline, determined not to waver and even more so not to fall under the million feet churning behind him, a churn whose relentless pace dragged the horizon closer one step at a time, as if Dodge City were a massive float on wheels, rolling toward them while their feet worked a crank buried beneath the bloody bricks.

The ramshackle network that strung their minds together seized and then insisted upon this understanding, obliging each Brother to keep his eyes on the skyline to such a degree that he lost track of the Brother beside him, terrified to look away even for the instant it would've taken to verify that he was still marching as half of an iconic duo bearing the inviolable particulars of a shared life story ready for The Dodge City Biopic Treatment, rather than as one node in a million-headed Brother pack, a lone speck of fuzzy Kansan memory in a tumbleweed procession that was now, once again, composed of nothing but strangers, frothing with anticipation at the chance to have his story, alone among such a lumpen horde, be heard and committed to the celluloid they could already hear hissing beneath the crunch of Squimbop skulls underfoot, regular and comforting as the popping of popcorn in Tommy Bruno's machine.

THIS SOUND SPURRED THEM TO YET-GREATER speeds as the road grew dense with Outskirts, the open desert of their early approach thickening into one- and two-story buildings and, soon thereafter, filling with booths staffed by former or pseudo-Squimbops in fright wigs and novelty mustaches that hung crooked as their glue melted in the heat of the growing frenzy.

"*The Brothers Squimbop in Kansas!*" shouted a monger draped in the black dress of the woman who'd borne them all so often. He leaned through a makeshift puppet booth to hold out a cluster of marionettes. "Collect 'em all! The mime, the other mime, the black-clad woman, and," he shook the cluster hard enough that a few heads and feet fell off, vanishing into the churn, "the Brothers themselves! Jim and Joe, so tragically lost in their haste to reach Dodge City that they'll never find each other again, and even if they did, they'd never know it was their Brother they'd found! It's every man for himself now, with no mother to say which is which and which the other!!"

He pulled out a model of the farm curtain they'd passed through and stuck his finger in and out with a ghoulish grin, increasing the speed until he mimicked an explosion and smashed the model with his other fist, feigning shock on impact.

The procession cackled, all the Squimbops as one, even as they swooned beneath the terror of knowing that what this puppet salesman said was true. "All of us"—or all of *them*, they couldn't help thinking—"could be Jim or Joe now, any two heads could form a set, any two out of these thousands could be *the Real Brothers Squimbop*, and we'd never know it, and, what's worse, *they'd* never know it either... their being real would amount to no more than a piece of trivia recited by schoolchildren on a tour of the Media Center in

Cooperstown, New York, in exchange for a pat on the head and a token for a Gift Shop Squimbop Suit while the school buses idled in the lot at the end of the day." They heard themselves chanting this lament, their mouths fixed around the words like the mouths of carriage horses around their salty bits.

"*The Brothers Squimbop on the Road to Dodge City*," shouted another puppet salesman. "Relive a simpler time... relive the long, long approach, before all that happened in Dodge City had to happen. Before the vectors of authority grew so muddled that all narratives fell off the cliff of wishful thinking and sank into the swamp of..." He dragged his puppets along a model of the road laid out on the booth's counter, smashing some under the feet of the others, laughing and squishing the rest together until most were ruined. He regarded what was left with a look of real confusion while the mummers sang, "Now even the puppet-sellers look distressed / Bad moon a-rising, good times on the wane / True Story of the Brothers S... / Enough to drive a godly man insane."

All the Squimbops sang along, too caught up in the tune to wonder how they knew the words.

The sales pitches and the songs about them continued to one-up each other, while members of the procession took over for those salesmen who'd been slain in the line of duty and The Dodge City Outskirts grew denser and denser, until they were hardly Outskirts at all. When the prospect of arrival drew near, a run on the remaining puppets occurred. Soon all the booths had been ransacked and the passion play of *The Brothers Squimbop on the Road to Dodge City*, told through an infinitude of marionette mouths all mashed together, coincided with the survivors' emergence in the town proper, so synchronously that later accounts, buried deep in the biopic that played on loop in one of the Media Center's three main auditoriums, would claim the puppet reenactment had served as a lucky charm, permitting the survival of those relatively few Squimbops that did survive... without whom, so the story went, all of what's known about the Brothers would have been lost to the same swamp from which, in due time, the culminating forces of the present escapade will be dredged and, in contravention of a dozen international treaties, deployed on the field of battle.

THOSE WHO'D MADE IT THIS FAR KICKED OVER the last of the puppet booths that clustered even more densely inside the town. They drank and ate from donkey-carts selling roast goat and malt liquor, and shoved inward, shoulder to shoulder, mouths chattering around whatever they'd managed to put in them, desperate to go on telling their story lest, in the chaos, they forgot it and reverted to remembering only what they could hear themselves sing, unable to break rhythm with the mummers.

But their heads had grown so close together, each Brother's mouth pressed wetly against another's ear, that, even though they'd made it to the center of Dodge City, where, according to the schema they'd agreed to acknowledge on the parade route, the *True Story* would finally be put into production, no such story emerged. "Ship," emerged, as did "Black Forest," "mime and uncle show," "Alaska," "Olathe," and "farm curtain," but nothing resembling a sentence, let alone a large-enough sentence cluster to cohere into a tale, which might develop into the script for the canonical biopic whose sale they'd ostensibly risked their lives to come here to broker.

A HEAVY PAUSE ENSUED, A COLLECTIVE EXHALATION that could only last so long. There was only so much breath they could expel, only so much spittle they could wipe from their chins, before it was time to ask in earnest why they'd come to Dodge City, if not to see the *True Story* unfold onscreen, complete and clarified as never before.

The square took on a powder keg atmosphere as the peace they'd fought so hard to achieve began to fester. They returned to fighting over puppets, turning the square into a facsimile of the road they'd marched down to arrive in it, even if now this required marching in circles. "We haven't arrived yet!" some chanted, as they hastily erected puppet booths from scraps of smashed wood and shredded velvet, while others jockeyed for position, determined to reinvoke the afternoon's suddenly-sacred approach, when the Promised Land was still up ahead, shimmering on the horizon and not yet underfoot, slick with goat grease and spilled liquor. When all that mattered was making it to Dodge City, knowing full well that most among them would not.

"Onward, onward, noble soldiers, into *The Real Dodge City* at last," chanted the Brothers, attempting to pick up where the mummers—who, believing their work was done, had dispersed—left off. For a long, dire moment, there were no iconic songs about this second procession, which would at last achieve in reality what the first had merely glimpsed in a fever. Then there were.

Singing these new songs, they marched in the widest circles the square would permit, pressing up against the storefronts and cafes, doing all they could to convince themselves that Dodge City still lay up ahead, on the far side of a bloody conflict whose outcome would determine nothing less than whether any of those gathered here had the right to live safely and peaceably in a clarified future, as upstanding citizens of a sane community, veterans of the War to end all Wars, or whether they'd be vaporized or banished to roam as nameless outlaws, alternating between calling themselves Jim and Joe, riding a trail of ever-diminishing returns as they ducked into one roadhouse and small-town Elks Lodge bar after another, placing their hats on the scuffed brown wood and hoping an old tale of The Dodge City Civil War would earn them a domestic lager or shot of watery Jack, even as the old bartenders grew older and older and then, as had to happen eventually, grew young again.

THE DODGE CITY CIVIL WAR. NONE COULD SAY where the notion had come from, though all pictured a cue card tossed onstage by an unseen audience member eager to help a flailing act into its next phase. Now that it had arrived, there was no masking its import. The square was so narrow, and its energies so jagged, that—this much was beyond clear—*something* had to occur to make their arrival stick. To bring the *Bloody, Bloody Road to Dodge City* to a viable climax, beyond which whoever survived could settle into a sort of afterlife, a Postwar Era of peace and prosperity where any remaining itch would be shunted safely into cinema, and "Dodge City" would mean the end of the wilderness rather than its impassible continuation. The alternative was a yellow-brick road to nowhere, a parade route toward no altar at all.

An endless spool of Dodge City Civil War cinema, they all considered: to age gracefully into a war movie senescence, first must come the War. As soon as this notion arose, it blotted all others out. The Saga had found its way forward. The remaining Squimbops traced the square's perimeter over and over, letting the prospect of War work its way through them, until they stood together before a plaque that read *Sacrifice Square: Site of the First Battle of The Dodge City Civil War.*

If they'd been ready to risk their lives a moment ago, suddenly some of them weren't any longer. As in a dream where a reprieve is granted via mysterious channels at the last possible juncture, some of them became convinced the War was long over, contained now by plaques, flags, and benignly fading statuary. They chanted, "We survived! The Civil War is behind us and here we stand, victorious, West of the crisis, in virgin territory at last, free to devise a new settlement in which to tell our story as it deserves to be told in the gilded cinema palaces of The Real Dodge City, our filmstrips slick with afterbirth before their long, desiccating journey to Alaska."

"A new settlement! A new settlement!" they chanted, clinging to the horrible memory of the Civil War, whose material evidence seemed still to soak their soft bodies, while so many of their brethren were gone, stomped like wine grapes along the way. "To their memory," chanted the Brothers clustered in the center of what they now called Sacrifice Square, "to their memory we consecrate this virgin settlement!"

They hoisted high what puppets remained and pumped them in the smoky evening, tiny wooden mouths frantic with glee, while, behind them, another family of goats was slaughtered and a ritual pyre was stoked, and new stands emerged, selling hard cider from yellow oil drums and Civil War uniforms in the blue and grey trim of the two sides whose irreconcilable differences had shaken the fledgling nation to its core.

"Reenact the foundation crisis!" shouted the Squimbops who'd taken it upon themselves to become uniform salesmen. "For tonight we celebrate those who gave their lives to the Civil War. We honor them by donning their uniforms and retracing their footsteps, as Brothers... Brother against Brother to the death of all, here again as it was before, in the bitterest days of our exile, before Dodge City took us in and held us close!"

As soon as the remaining Squimbops had donned the uniforms of their respective sides, half blue and half grey, the excitement of the reprieve wore off and some of them again suspected that, grim as the prospect might be, *The Real Dodge City Civil War* was in fact still to come. The virgin settlement felt sullied by their mere presence within it, a conundrum from which they could see no reprieve. Thus, for the second time today, they felt the bliss of true arrival fade into a shadowland of premonition, still awaiting its chance to come true on the far side of the cleansing that needed to occur, burying all those who claimed it already had.

"Not yet!" they shouted. "We haven't reached the Postwar Era just yet!"

"First the War, then the Postwar Era!" they shouted, the words as familiar as the mummers' songs had been. "No rest until the blood of our enemies runs deeper than the blood of our comrades ever could! No solid ground of Dodge City until its mortar has been mixed with the blood we must first spill in earnest!"

"Perfect reenactment!" insisted one contingent, while the other countered, "No reenactment at all! The Real Dodge City Civil War is primed to begin at last!"

Like so were the battle lines drawn, as those decked out in blue and in gray departed in identical columns from Sacrifice Square, which either already commemorated or was soon to commemorate the blood spilled for the sake of a sane future in a Dodge City waiting to be made Real, where each Squimbop would know his place and his heritage and would pass such knowledge on to whatever children he was fated to have, with a wife in a black dress who would admire him equally for the journey he'd undertaken and the stasis he'd settled into upon reaching that journey's western terminus.

SIMULTANEOUSLY JITTERING WITH THE MANIA that precedes a massacre and fixated on the biopic they'd come to Dodge City to sell, the soldiers set out marching toward the warehouses and backlots of The Dodge City Film Industry.

But first they marched past the Temple, downtown's flagship cinema, done up with a mixture of Aztec and Egyptian flourishes. The glass cases for the *Coming Soon* posters out front stood empty, but Tommy Bruno was already at the concession stand, popping a fresh batch of popcorn and restocking the shelves with Twizzlers and Raisinets. He nodded sagely at the Squimbops who peeled off from the march, loosened their uniforms, and filed into the theater, hardly bothering to mask their shame at the decision to watch the Civil War from the comfort of plush reclining seats, indifferent to however long the footage might take to arrive.

Those determined to produce this footage marched on, back through the Outskirts and into a sandy stretch of desert between where the main road ended and the path into the replica town maintained by the Film Industry began. The moon simmered on the horizon and in its light they could see that the farm curtain they'd all passed through was still open, admitting more duos from the ranches and farmhouses of Ransom County, conscripted directly into a Civil War whose underlying conditions they'd never be invited to consider.

These new recruits, already stripped of the life stories that just a moment ago they'd believed they were on the verge exchanging for a place in the canon, swarmed both armies, filtering into and swelling their ranks to such a degree that some saw reason to worry whether there'd be enough space among them for blades and bullets to fly.

Crushed together just as they'd been on the Bloody, Bloody Road, they watched the moon float up to the middle of the sky as they marched out of the desert and into The Dodge City Film Industry's version of Sacrifice Square, fringed by a grove of warheads silently standing guard, a becalmed but volatile Stonehenge that none paused long enough to salute. The Real Dodge City they'd renounced—or the Dodge City waiting to become Real—stood silent in the distance, the ultimate prize for whomever survived the culling.

Beyond the warheads, the night boiled with creamy off-white static as the Brothers separated into their respective sides and listened as their respective generals made their respective remarks, one insisting on reenactment, the other on that which would one day be reenacted, with only the covenant of War itself to decide which account the future would consider true.

When all had said their piece, they loaded their muskets, screwed on their bayonets, and surged into the alleys and backlots of the replica town, defending their positions with the full zeal of men who knew that most would not see the dawn.

"Brother against Brother!" declared the offstage voice they could still hear running through their heads. "A bloodbath the likes of which none had seen before, fought with technologies that would forever alter the sacred proving ground of the battlefield, upon which men become Men before becoming meat. A War, indeed, for the very soul of Dodge City and, as such, for the ongoing legacy of the Brothers Squimbop and so, furthermore, for the legacy of

America itself. For all this, for the *True Story* and its sequels beyond counting, tonight we rage!"

THE WAR RAGED AS PROMISED, TEARING THE FIBER of time asunder so that here, in no uncertain terms, the future itself was at stake. Suddenly, it was not inconceivable that the entire Squimbop Saga might extinguish itself, leaving nothing but cacti and lizards to see the sunrise.

Some Brothers ran to the equipment sheds and attempted to film the carnage, as if seizing control of the biopic could be that simple—as if there were no Dodge City Film Industry except that which they founded tonight—but they were easily dispatched by the volleys of cannon- and missile-fire launched from the weapons that had likewise been dragged from those sheds, all of them laid out to be used in exactly this way, in this exact time and place, while the other Brothers, the cowards and pacifists among them, dozed in the Temple, watching the screen buzz with the same pre-trailer advertisements over and over again—radiant Kentucky bourbon in an etched-glass Squimbop canister on ice; platinum or white gold mime-and-uncle cufflinks free with a blue or pink silk deluxe Squimbop Suit upgrade; dentures as sharp and white as the living teeth of the legendary Professor Squimbop himself, fed on a strict diet of full-cream milk and raw beef—until it grew as familiar as the litany of a religion absorbed in earliest childhood, before its signifiers amounted to anything more than the promise of a totalizing benevolent attention at work everywhere in the universe.

As the battle raged on, no advantage emerged. The question of whether they were reenacting the Civil War or enacting it for the first time was both primary and secondary at once, insofar as it determined the purpose of the mass bloodshed yet also, as that bloodshed took on a logic of its own, there were ever fewer heads to house the question whose resolution the death of their fellows had been expected to produce, nor, as these fellows continued to drop, even many heads left to absorb whatever resolution came.

To make matters worse, berserkers began to arrive. Lunatics, psychopaths, Squimbops from villages deep in the nation's interior, where multi-generational blood feuds were still the only means of achieving restitution. Boys who hadn't left home at the behest of their Pervert Uncles. The farm curtain flapped open to admit them, still dusty from the Kansan roads they'd at last been forced to travel, clutching their mothers' shovels and pitchforks as they blindly heeded the drums of war.

They thronged the battlefield, naked or in street clothes or Squimbop Suits they'd picked up secondhand in Hays or Garden City, hacking and slashing and firing into the crowd. As the War's underlying conditions grew increasingly illegible, a secondary uniform industry sprouted up along the peripheries, manned by those who'd declared themselves veterans. They roamed the battlefield with flashlights, skinning fallen Squimbops and tanning their hides in brilliant yellows and greens and reds, so that from this chaos the semblance of a multivalent Great Power Conflict emerged, a full-blown World War growing, according to well-established precedent, out of what, earlier in the evening, had been a mere domestic dispute.

The more Squimbops fell, the more arrived, in almost perfect parity—an instantly iconic slapstick routine in its own right—as the legend of the Civil War that became a World War spread through the Dust Bowl, offering a last-ditch reprieve from the economic drought that had throttled half the nations on earth.

The scale of violence grew proportionally, breaking the bounds of what any biopic could encompass and bleeding directly into a sequel, then a series of sequels, spinning with a centrifugal force that pulled the Black Forest in from the East and the Pacific Theater in from the West, compressing it all into a town-sized black hole of such density that all those who'd survived thus far would be compacted into a single grain of sand, within which they'd have no choice but to go on fighting forever.

Thus the chaos reached a stalemate, bleeding every side dry as rival papers issued front page stories declaring rival victories and self-published books lined the costume and puppet racks, alleging that the entirety of the visible War was nothing but a front for an intractable cabal that thrived on the confusion of its unwitting subjects, wresting a form of absolute control from the appearance of global disorder, while, at the same time, self-published books debunking those that made this claim likewise sprang up, just ahead of the crop debunking them in turn.

Out of this stalemate a single Squimbop, maddened by the *mise en abyme* he could tell was just beginning, unless the way in which it seemed to be just beginning was itself a symptom of its changelessness, marched beyond the battlefield and back to the henge of warheads, panting with the enormity of what he guessed he was about to do.

He stood in the shadow of the nukes, running his long fingers through his short hair, and gave himself all the time he needed to make his decision. Beneath the clouds of mustard gas and Agent Orange and the fray of musket and cannon fire, the strafing of drones punctuating the shrieks of those impaled on bayonets and those attempting to narrate the carnage for a proliferating stable of rival news outlets, he counted his inhales and exhales as he developed an image in his mind of a Bachelor's Cell on a dark corner at the edge of Dodge City, lit only by the glowing white of the supermarket next door. He could see himself in that room, over the years, gazing out the window, through all that soft glow and across the battlefield to the cluster of nukes he stood within now. He remembered standing at the window studying the shadows the warheads cast in the moonlight, and then he remembered scribbling at his desk, page after page of blue ink on yellow paper, birthing his Manifesto one frantic line at a time, his plan for a post-nuclear Dodge City, an end to the stalemate at last, a Finale to the War that could only otherwise go on and on and on, indifferent to the passing of generations, turning into a grotesque form of stability from which it would become impossible to break free, given that War itself, as he put it, remained the only means known to man of leaving one historic era behind and compelling the next to begin.

The more he worked at his desk, the more he worked himself back in time, deeper into the Manifesto, so that now he could also see himself sourcing the uranium from Dead Sir, the swamp just outside Dodge City where, according to the legends the Manifesto cited, all of what the townspeople sought to collectively forget was buried, gone but not gone, a function that perhaps all towns needed a swamp to provide, if they hoped to cross the brink where the past became the present and did not thereafter immediately become the past again. *So here I am at Dead Sir,* he wrote, *paddling on a skiff of lashed-together vegetable crates from the pile out back of White's, fishing for the uranium that was buried on the bottom after the last nuclear holocaust, because none is ever the first, just as no Cold War begins in a vacuum.*

He could see himself dredging up fistfuls of the buried element which, as he'd known it would, had only grown more potent from steeping in the silt of all that Dodge City sought to repress. He dredged it up and, over the course of long, feverish nights in the Outskirts, while the rest of the population battled on and every death summoned a new Squimbop through the curtain, he assembled the warheads, piece by laborious piece, growing ever more convinced that only a single, decisive blow could end the stalemate that had gripped the culture. *No future without annihilation*, he wrote, in the Manifesto he'd decided to call *My Nuclear Dissertation*. He cobbled the warheads together one by one, sweating even when the nights were cold and sustaining himself on eggs and burnt toast from the diner in the center of town, where he worked three mornings a week to support his project for as long as it took. *No way out but through, no green lawns and white picket fences without first pulling the ultimate trigger.*

When his project was complete, the Professor—the title followed the completion of his Dissertation—wiped his silty hands on his pockets, dragged over an empty vegetable crate from the replica supermarket, and, standing upon it, announced into the fray, though he had no expectation that his voice would be heard, "This stalemate must end! The nuclear era has guaranteed that no decisive victory is possible. We cower, instead, in terror of the earth-shattering technologies our forefathers fashioned out of the quantum disturbance of the last World War, and satisfy ourselves with an endless succession of proxy wars that never result in the clarifying epochal shift we so profoundly crave and, indeed, deserve. No, instead, these minatory witnesses," he patted the nearest warhead, "have locked us into an endlessly self-perpetuating present. A zombie present, decades beyond its expiration date, children reliving the lives of their parents to ever diminishing returns, and yet the era has refused to expire because our fear of the future," he patted the warhead again, harder, nearly slapping it, "has sealed us inside a loop where time can only grow stranger and stranger and stranger as we play at War without allowing it to swell into the kind of seismic historical shift that man-to-man combat, in its very essence, exists in order to activate. The putting of things to rest, like a battle in a ring of fire in the days of old. The very reason we wage War, the dim yet sacred hope of peace on the other side, is an utter sham so long as these monstrosities lord over the battlefield, mocking it in silence!" He pounded the warhead now, loud enough to send off an echoing *ping!*

Though the melee continued, several Squimbops did turn to regard him lighting a match and holding it down by the warhead's fuse. Several even appeared to bow as the fuse sparked alight and the flame began to travel. As it reached the reagent and the warhead shuddered and then soared upward, the War came to a halt and an instant of perfect communal clarity ensued, the mud-spattered free-for-all arrested into the changeless grandeur of a medieval Dutch painting while the warhead described its parabola across the nighttime desert, hanging silent and nearly motionless, as if briefly conscious enough to gaze down upon all it was about to destroy, pointing like the finger of God so that, if anyone were watching from a safe enough distance, they'd know just where Dodge City used to stand.

Then, perhaps spooked by its own sudden self-awareness, the bomb fell. Screaming and boiling downward, it crashed into the foam cobblestones, incinerating them before billowing outward in a mushroom cloud that precisely resembled the thousands the Professor had studied in those long, lonely nights in his Bachelor's Cell, writing pages that seemed to have been written long before, in a darkness punctuated only by the supermarket's glow.

ALL WENT BLACK. THEN, SLOWLY, GREYISH-WHITE fog filled the scene and the Professor blinked, spit out grit and bone chips, and got to his feet, wincing in the rank air of the world he'd wrought. The foam cobblestones had melted and the desert sand beneath had turned to glass. He skated across it, away from the carnage and into The Dodge City Postwar Era, real now for the first time, though it was in every regard just as he'd described it. In the distance, the farm curtains had fused with the horizon so they looked painted on, relics from an age that had turned archaic overnight. The father and daughter who'd once held them open were fossilized against a slab of sky that looked solid as a cave wall.

So it begins, he thought, walking out into the ruins, nostrils flared as the fallout mixed with his mucus and turned his saliva sour. It took him the first part of the day to realize he'd written nothing on this contingency, having assumed he wouldn't be here to see it. Indeed, he thought now, my starting position, despite the green lawns and white picket fences and overstocked supermarkets I must've described to the point of morbid obsession, was that no one would be.

"Therefore, all that follows," he heard an offstage voice confirm, "will for you be a kind of afterlife. A kind of heaven or a kind of hell. That much, Professor, is up to you."

AFTER THE GROANING OF A SCENE CHANGE AND A brief intermission, I find my mark, squinting into the orange sun, blinking and licking my lips, my whole body sore like I've either just given birth or just been born. I gag as an image arises of my Brothers hurtling down a sinkhole, clotted together like a ball of mucus and hair, leaving me alone in a future that shouldn't exist. I picture them under Dead Sir, down in the muck the uranium arose from, where they will in time revert to that same element, their memories spooling out and mixing together until a future Squimbop, eons hence, once Dodge City has fed the Postwar Era back into its own ever-hungry Foundation Mythos and reached a new legitimacy crisis which will in turn necessitate a new Civil and then a new World War, once again dredges them out to make the bomb whose impact will restore the world to the way it is this morning.

I swallow and pinch my nose, trying to force down the feeling that this future Squimbop will likewise be me, just as convincingly, or just as tenuously, as *this morning's Squimbop*—a term I wish hadn't come to mind—is me as well. And might this morning not also be that morning? Neither this possibility nor its negation, if it has one, offers much reassurance.

When I close my eyes again, fallout settles on my eyelids. Beneath them, I see a mime, a ship, a mass grave, and a mushroom cloud, spinning like cards in a zoetrope, until they feel burned into my face, an imprint of the fallout itself, a barcode stamped on the soft flesh of the Squimbop that, for now, I'm obliged to call *me*.

I squint and sputter and step backwards, over a cold, soft lump that sends me sprawling onto my back. My head bounces against the melted Styrofoam and hits the glass beneath, causing my teeth to clatter. This triggers a scene of a street-choking procession descending on the town, armed with wooden puppets, their teeth clattering even louder than mine as they spew stories of conquest and adventure, of the glories of the Civil War that has finally ended, and is soon to begin.

Once I've gotten my mouth closed again, I roll over and push myself up, wincing not so much from pain as from the numbness that now fills my body, revealing what I'd both hoped and feared would be the case—that I'm on the other side of something, here and not here in a manner impossible to describe using the language of whatever life I'd been living before.

Back on my feet, I survey the damage. I walk among the corpses—*my fallen Brothers*, I feel compelled to call them, though nothing in me feels any kinship with these bloated bodies clad in the skins of their own fallen forebears—and I lose or fail to generate whatever thought I'd expected to have upon beholding them. I yawn, squint again, and find myself back in the zoetrope of mime, ship, mushroom cloud, and mass grave, a sequence whose compulsive fascination fills me with shame.

I clear my throat and continue my grim route, beginning to wonder—this too feels predetermined, like I'm on a walking tour of the Media Center with a guide who's already done two or three such tours today—whether I killed all these men, and, if not, whether I'll be blamed for it anyway. "As the lone survivor of whatever happened, it stands to reason…" I hear the offstage voice assert, though, for the moment, it asserts nothing else.

My mind catches on a scene of the biopic about to begin in one of the Media Center's numerous packed auditoriums and then I'm overcome with the renewed desire to sell my and my Brother's life rights to whichever representatives of The Dodge City Film Industry remain. Whether this image is anterior to the biopic's existence or very much a part of it—the opening scene, even—I picture rows of ancient scions lined up in a dim boardroom, their notarized contracts and Mont Blanc pens reflecting emerald light on a smooth onyx tabletop. Though I tremble on the threshold, I don't resist when an aide pushes me inside and closes the door, sealing me in there with beings who not only survived the blast but have clearly thrived on its effects. I nod to a dozen identical faces in silk suits, all of their eyes on me though their attention is elsewhere as they sip mineral water from sheer glass cubes and tap painted nails along the line where my signature belongs. I swallow, then I sign each of their forms in turn, making a ritual circuit of the table. Then I swoon.

I AWAKEN ON MY BACK BENEATH A BOILING TOMMY Bruno hologram. His gaunt cheeks, lightly stubbled, and bald head fringed with two tufts of black curls look down upon me, his mouth opening and closing without seeming to speak. I lie there as he backs into a larger hologram, revealing the concession stand that has followed me all around North America. Now, in a medium shot, he sells popcorn and Raisinets to dozens of Squimbops who take their turns in single file, flickering like those reels of workers climbing on and off of locomotives in the very first days of the cinematic medium.

The hologram steams, dissolves, then drifts back together to reveal row upon row of nearly catatonic men waiting in a dim theater, watching the pre-trailer advertisements again and again, blinking in unison as they dig into their treats. I try to sit up, but my body is numb to the point of uselessness, like all my nerves have been cut, leaving only sacs of fat and muscle atop bones that no longer have the power to compel them to move.

I try to swallow but taste only fallout, my mouth packed with dense, crunchy dust that I can neither chew nor spit. So I lie there, my Adam's Apple vibrating as the hologram darkens then comes alight with a blazing *True Story of the Brothers Squimbop* title card. A cheer goes up in the theater and I see Tommy Bruno sneak in beneath the EXIT sign, a solid indication that he's never seen this one before.

SOMETHING IN THE NUMB BACK OF MY HEAD flickers as the rest of me prepares to leave this body in its seat and enter the one at large in the *True Story* onscreen. Only the flicker clocks the violation, the abandonment of what, a moment from now, I'll no longer believe was ever me, even if I'll always feel that something's been lost.

Then, once again, I've left myself behind. For the sake of the Saga, I consign another Squimbop to a slow death in exile and return to the diner inside the film the rest of us are watching. The diner where, I quickly accept, I've worked for years, hunched over my cup of too-sweet coffee and my usual plate of eggs and burnt toast. I lean against the overfamiliar counter and watch, on the TV mounted above the rack of vintage bourbon bottles and baseball pennants, a work crew dredging a gigantic houseboat out of an algae-choked swamp. Picking at my breakfast, I try to keep the vision of what happens next from flooding back in. I see myself floating away on that boat, taking to the waves which, loosed by the blast, have flooded inward, restoring to Middle America the Inland Sea from whence it came and rendering Dodge City an island, soon to sink.

The offstage voice, which sounds pinched and enervated now, says, "Proceed to the cinema, the show is about to begin. The show within the show, the molten core of the *True Story*, the safe harbor you tried to forsake me for."

The abruptness of this phrase causes me to turn so quickly on my barstool I knock my coffee into my eggs, causing two hefty truckers to laugh so hard they do the same, causing two more truckers to laugh so hard they... and... and in the far background, as I'm reminded of the room in which the self I abandoned lies watching, I hear the Squimbops in the theater laugh as well, slapping their thighs and spilling Raisinets between their seats.

"Well?" the voice asks and I look around desperately, coffee soaking my khakis as the TV shows the boat suspended in chains beside the swamp while an anchor says, "And there we have it, folks... *The Dodge City Angel House Exhibit* has been officially exhumed from Dead Sir, dislodged by the colossal blast that set The Dodge City Postwar Era in motion, and is hence ready for its maiden voyage, all the way to its berth at the Squimbop Media Center in Cooperstown, New York, as if the very events for which it's been canonized have, in reality, not yet occurred, but are now, after generations of waiting, finally about to!"

The truckers clap in what strikes me as a particularly Postwar manner, a tense combination of macho triumphalism and nascent paranoia, simultaneously resting on their laurels and champing at the bit. They crowd me, their eyes ashy and unfocused, as if they were no more than avatars of the Squimbops laughing and munching in the darkened theater, with Tommy Bruno standing by the EXIT behind them. They draw nearer with each impact, their feet following their hands as they clap in syncopated unison. I blot eggy coffee from my pockets, slip off the barstool, and run, elbowing three clappers aside as I ding the bell on my way out.

I RUN DOWN THE RUINED MAIN STREET OF DODGE City, puppets trampled into the asphalt, while more and more clappers emerge, coming up alleys and down stairwells and off the Night Bus, masses of drifters in Squimbop Suits just now arriving. "Board the Ark! Board the Ark!" they chant. "Deliver us, before the waters close in, before the tidal wave washes all the..."

They chant this again and again, coming in and out of sync, sometimes doubling each other's voices and sometimes cutting each other off, driving me toward the Temple, where the line snakes three times around the block. *The True Story of the Brothers Squimbop:* OPENING TONIGHT glows on the marquee, surrounded by pulsing flashbulbs.

As I run, my bowels tremble and I scan the line, wondering what would happen if I forced my way in past these hundreds of identical figures, ghosts awaiting the spectacle for whose production they gave their lives. I picture myself shoving past them, past the concession stand and down to that bathroom in the basement where the maps of the Brothers in Paris and London surely still run together above the urinals, forcing my way into a stall at the last possible second.

I see myself emerging from that stall and climbing the stairs onto a tremendous ship leaving Alaska, pulling southward out of the harbor, captained, now as ever, by Professor Squimbop in his earpiece and alligator-skin boots. I try to hear him speaking to me, or miming his speech, sending me back to Kansas to relive the story of two Brothers setting out into the Dust Bowl to hammer their names into the annals of infamy, but now, try as I might, I cannot force myself back to that scene. "Now it's only you, my friend," the voice shrieks in my ear. "This is what you wanted. You left me on my back with my nerves shredded to shoelaces. Now it's only you and you and you and you!!"

As the voice ripples through the fallout, the air comes to smell like seawater and each clap—the thousands of waiting Squimbops have synchronized, shaking Dodge City like children in a cardboard castle—cracks the sky and surrounding air, through which seawater begins to spill.

I burp as the first salty gust passes my lips, and I can tell, with a certainty I've never felt before that this, exactly now, is the only moment of decision I'll ever have. Everything I am, whatever that may be, will only endure based on what I do next. I eye the line one last time, contemplating grabbing one of the Squimbops and taking him with me as a dummy Brother, a prop version of what I've lost, but then a wave crashes over us, wiping out half the line, and I'm swimming through it with Squimbops drowning all around me, fighting for the Ark that has been unearthed from Dead Sir for my sake alone, to serve as the vessel upon which my journey across the Inland Sea takes place.

So my decision has been made, perhaps longer ago than I imagine. The waves carry me over the death throes of Dodge City, as thousands of Squimbops are swept into the sunken cinema below, and I crawl up the rigging on the side of the boat when it bobs into reach, coughing and crying as the voice says, "Welcome aboard, Professor."

Then I'm on the upper deck, falling sideways along a cascade of fish and crabs and eels, careening through a door and down a wooden staircase, into a soaked office where books, papers, and wine bottles float, clinking together in welcome.

I struggle to my feet and then, exhaling so deeply my lungs go flat against my ribs, I lurch over to the window to watch Dodge City vanish beneath the waves, one more Atlantis among so many thousands—thousands behind me, thousands ahead. Through the window the air is fuzzy and gray and I can't help picturing the nerveless, flattened being I left behind, lying on his back with all of this playing out before eyes that will never blink again.

As if to confirm that I'm no longer him, I blink several times. Then I turn and look up the soaked staircase, deciding that this nerveless viewer is up there, in the Master Bedroom watching the biopic whose sale he brokered play out unto eternity, starring whoever I've become.

"And who's that?" he asks. "Who is it that's spending the money I earned, living like an aging bachelor prince on the Ark I bought at auction?"

"I did this for you," I reply, as a bottle of port bobs against my ankle. "So one of us might live to tell the tale. To spread the gospel from town to town, so deep into the Postwar Era that the War itself will soon be forgotten. Is this not what we wanted when we were young?"

As I bend to pick up the bottle and read the label in cursive Portuguese, I wonder whether all those drowned Squimbops are proud to know I've escaped, or if I've damned them by leaving like this, consigning Dodge City to the fate of all towns rather than sacrificing myself upon the altar of its singularity.

My eyes tear up as the boat charts its course toward open water. I hear the wheel creaking overhead, driven by my Distant Master, as I've decided to call him, sprawled painlessly in the Master Bedroom. I remove my soaked clothes, pull on a plush red robe I find hanging by the door, embossed with *Prof. Sq.* in gold script above its fuzzy breast pocket, pour a snifter full of port, pat a life-sized Tommy Bruno cutout on his bald spot, and rifle through the video collection, neatly arranged on an adjacent shelf: *The Brothers Squimbop, The Brothers Squimbop in Europe, The Brothers Squimbop in Hollywood, Squimbop Fever, The Brothers Squimbop in Kansas.*

I wipe my eyes on my sleeve, refill my snifter, select *The True Story of the True Story of the Brothers Squimbop, Vol. 1* from a seven-part making-of documentary, pop it in the VCR, and sit down on the couch as the FBI piracy warning fades into a master shot of thousands of duos marching along the Bloody, Bloody Road to Dodge City. Curious to see how long I can hold out, I use all my remaining energy to restrain myself for a heavy, breathless moment before leaning in to study the screen, in search of me and my Brother in the thousand-fold Squimbop crush, our faces whooping and hollering with an abandon I can now only envy, as we approach the altar atop which I sit alone.

Professor Squimbop in the Towns

In time, the nuclear haze bubbling from the sunken Dodge City dissipates and the waters of the Inland Sea turn smooth and striped with sun. I acclimate to the Ark that the newscasters called "Angel House," though this name is nowhere apparent on the boat itself, unless it's stenciled on some stretch of siding I can't see. This possibility, emblematic as it is of the larger fear that I'm only a guest aboard this vessel, permitted to see only select aspects of it, wears away at my resolve, undermining whatever certainty I'd hoped to feel that here, at last, is where I belong. Instead, it's as if I've been at sea too long already.

When I'm not roaming the decks, I spend my time in the den, draped in my robe watching old Squimbop tapes from the collection on the shelf, or up in the Master Bedroom, searching for the nerveless form in which I left my Brother upon my escape from the Postwar wasteland that I also, in a manner of speaking...

But the voyage has blurred my certainty about these events, pushing them ever more deeply into what I've decided or been told to call the Totally Other Place, a realm as capacious as it is indescribable, immensely distant yet impossible to ignore.

Lying on the tremendous mattress in the Master Bedroom, in place of the nerveless Brother who never turns up when I come to check on him, I feel my head soften as a warm, buttery transmission seeps into the waiting folds within. This transmission, clear as my Brother's voice, demands that I refer to it as Lecture, though whom it's for and what role I play in its delivery remains unsaid. All I can tell, as I lie on the mattress and chuckle at the notion that all shipboard beds are waterbeds, is that whatever complex of muscle and sinew once served as my brain is turning to cream. As I lie and drift and come to terms with this, I glimpse the bottom of the ocean, my perspective plunging down through the mattress, through the video den, through the hull and beyond the reach of all light, beyond even the reach of darkness, into the netherworld at the bottom of everything, and then down further still, all the way to the floor of the floor of the Inland Sea.

Down here the fallout pops my lungs and forces my ribs through the sides of my chest, tearing gills through which I can breathe well enough to trawl the ruins of Dodge City. Beneath the foundations of the few buildings that remain, I see the faces of thousands of Squimbops, melted down but not all the way. A solid seafloor of bones and skin and hair, jellied eyes in crags of coral and craniums smashed flat or cracked in two, but still sentient enough to broadcast reproach, their bloated sockets fixed on mine, as if they all know a truth about me that I will need the entire coming sequence to grasp.

Instead of attempting to hear what I can see them whispering, I open my mouth so wide my hair tickles the back of my neck, revealing a maw into which the skulls leap five, ten, and then fifteen at a time, filling me with fishy cream, some of which pours down my throat while the rest lodges in what I've come to consider the soft palate of my brain.

I THRASH AND SHIVER ON THE MATTRESS AS FEELing returns to my limbs. Then I leap up and into the shower, terrified both of where I've been and also of my Brother, whose presence fills the bedroom as soon as I leave it.

In the shower, I feel the cream I've swallowed turn solid. Seafloor particles regain their shapes within me, restoring sentience to where it can be used. I close my eyes under the burning spray and allow time to pass, heedless of how much water I'm using.

Once the relationship between seafloor smorgasbord and midnight ablution becomes sufficiently routinized—many weeks pass over the course of this shower, or *these showers*—I come to see the cream's firming-up as a crucial stage in the development of my Lecture. Though I still can't hear the skulls on the seafloor speak, footage of the warhead barreling toward the desert and the waves swallowing Dodge City and over-salting the buttery carpet of Tommy Bruno's cinema comes alive behind my eyes, emanating from the cream as naturally as its fishy scent.

This footage evolves into a sequence that features me striding along a country road in a velvet blazer, denim slacks, and alligator-skin boots, my mustache neatly coiffed and my lymph nodes puckered with fine Austrian cologne, ready to expound upon all I've seen before a willing or captive public. To, as it were, *deliver my Lecture at last.*

When the hot water runs out, I towel off, step into my plush red robe, and go downstairs, *back to the sunken cinema*, as the voice puts it, where a video is always already playing, a snifter of port always already on its coaster atop the armrest, across from which the cardboard Tommy Bruno keeps watch.

FOR A LONG SPELL OF SAILING, THIS ROUTINE holds steady. Spatially, the only movement is lateral, as there seems to be no *crossing* this body of water, only sailing across and across it, occasionally glimpsing lights so dim it's impossible to say whether they belong to distant shorelines or nearby planets, while, temporally, the stories I tell myself grow older and older until the blast over Dodge City and subsequent Flood feel as rarefied and impersonal as any other tale, heard many times in the sacral haze of one's irrecoverable youth.

I come to think of the voice embedded within the cream as that of my Distant Master—perhaps the guise my Brother has finally taken on, or perhaps only the guise I've cast him in. Either way, I'm all too happy to submit to his voice, offering, as it does, relief from the terror of steering this ship alone. I allow it to crush me upon the mattress in the Master Bedroom, blacking out my thoughts and replacing them with footage of striding along a country road in my alligator-skin boots, velvet blazer, jet-black jeans, and fine Austrian cologne, ready to deliver my Lecture to...

The footage ends here, leaving me with the specter of a Brother I've given up all hope of locating, even as I remain half-convinced that he's somewhere aboard this ship, every bit as much a resident or prisoner of Angel House as I am, occupying what will, through awful tautology, always be the one room I fail to visit.

I GAIN WHAT I CONSIDER MY FIRST CLUE AS TO how this odd couple sitcom ends when I find a tape in the cabinet behind the others, wrapped in rubber bands and marked only with the words *Primal Scene* in red pen. Though I immediately guess what it contains, and consider sitting down to witness, once and for all, the crime my Brother either did or did not commit in the house on Cielo Drive, the transgression that precipitated our fateful split and now perhaps our ambiguous reunion, I leave it where it is, if only to have something to look forward to for a little while longer. One stone left unturned.

I refill my port, try to forget that tape, and settle back on the couch with *The Brothers Squimbop in Hollywood* at the point where it glitches over the scene in question, cutting straight to the closing sequence where I drive down from the Hollywood Hills and into the wide open North alone. What I've never been sure of, and have tried never to wonder, is if *I* cut the footage in a fugue of guilt and fear over abandoning him, when all I would've needed to do, to avoid the Fever and the chaos it unleashed, is stick by his side so as to ramble deeper into a Saga I was never meant to star in alone. Tommy Bruno regards me through cardboard eyes as I yawn, wipe the beginning of a tear, and watch the end credits, searching for my own name within them.

THIS PHASE OF THE SITCOM STRETCHES ON, WELL past the point where the laugh track sputters out and the walls fill with bitter wheezing. The two of us have become a couple of pinballs bouncing up and down the grand staircase of the houseboat we sold our life story in Dodge City in order to purchase, for reasons we'll now never recover. A couple of pinballs representing all that remains of the Brothers Squimbop, I think, exaggerating whatever melancholy I legitimately feel, unless—I let myself think it—the *Real Brothers* are safely elsewhere, watching this sorry show on a motel TV set in Hiawatha or East St. Louis, or in the dressing room of a venerable Catskills Mountain House, just before taking the stage.

My head swells with the image of the two of us on a cigar-stained couch in Little Rock, eating chicken from a cardboard box while watching our pinball shtick on a wood-framed screen between bouts of infomercials until I end up praying for the power to leave myself up here and join myself down there.

I peer overboard in a desperate attempt to glimpse us in our Little Rock room, nestled in a crag in the coral. Groping around the upper deck, I pitch side to side on the open ocean as rainbows and cascades of salty mist fill my eyes, sprouting mountains in the distance that disappear when I squint. I run my hands along the railing, searching for something I know must be there, though I can't imagine what it is.

The anchor! I hear the voice gasp, as I lick foam from my lower lip, so salty I try to spit it out but find my mouth bone dry. *Drop the anchor now, before you go so mad you fail to recognize my voice!* I reach out, extending my fingers until they clasp a hairy rope, which I then follow around and around the upper deck, so many times that my circular mania threatens to revert to slapstick—the gulls cackle, soundtracking my one-man show as effectively as any roadside hurdy-gurdy ever did—until I trip over an iron spike and fly forward, ending the routine with a perfectly timed crunch of chinbone.

The shock almost renders me senseless while the gulls applaud, but I summon the will to push up onto my knees and then to stand and then, wiping bloody froth with both forearms, I regard the anchor. A spell of mourning comes over me, as it always seems to at the end of things. I let it pass, as if observing a moment of silence for a departed comrade. Then I dredge up what's left of my energy, bend down, clamp my hands around the anchor's oxidized surface, hoist it to waist height, nudge it up onto the railing with my hip, and let it fall overboard. The acceleration of the unspooling rope knocks me onto my back and this time I do pass out, missing whatever catharsis might have come from the anchor making contact with the floor of the Inland Sea.

THE SUN SCALDS ME AWAKE AND MY FIRST thought is that I'm behind the diner where I work three days a week, my nerves shredded after another run of shifts all bleeding together until I collapsed while taking out the trash and found myself clutching the dumpster in the buzzing shadeless noon. I clutch it now and scrabble to my feet, spitting dry mucus onto the asphalt. It isn't until I'm upright and staring out at the sandy, weedy shore of an alien landmass that I manage to let go of the railing and with it any last thought that today is a day like all the others.

No, I revise, as I scratch around my mustache, envisioning how fastidiously I'll soon be obliged to trim it: no, this is something new. A genuine new chapter, well beyond the scope of the video diet I've subsisted on so far. I again picture the tape marked *Primal Scene*, and though I can't explain why, I fear I've missed my chance to pop it in the VCR and find out for sure what happened on Cielo Drive. And why, I wonder, as I duck inside for a quick snifter of port, was I ever sure that's what it contained? What evidence, other than my own obsession, has there ever been... *of that or anything else*? The voice intercedes, knocking my drink onto the carpet. *There is no going astray within the Saga, Professor. What happens is what happens. There is no unlived life, for you or for me.*

I stare down, watching the port soak in, as does the Tommy Bruno cutout, while the voice adds, *So get in the shower. Trim your mustache. Spritz your queasy perfume. Put a Band-Aid over that cut on your chin. Your classroom awaits.*

Reminding myself that I'm nothing but the *Little Brother, faithful servant of his Distant Master*, I comply. I follow the ritual so precisely that there's no distinction between performing and observing it. There is only the ritual itself, as well established as those of an ancient civilization which has, against all odds, persevered unchanged into the present.

As the warm water bastes my skull, the last soft remnants of Lecture firm up and the last of the fog hovering over the history of America dissipates, leaving behind a narrative so crystal clear I almost can't believe my luck in having been hired to teach it. It's hard to imagine why my presence in the town I'll soon emerge into is needed at all, even as it's equally hard to imagine that town existing without me.

Indeed, I let the voice assert, as I shave around the mustache I have pictured shaving around so many times in the mental half-light of my comically long journey, *there would be nothing but the Inland Sea were it not for your presence upon it, and your carnivorous need for dry land. Your inability to remain sane at sea, or to give yourself fully to that sea's heroic madness, and thereby discover a kind of sanity far more profound than any you will find—just wait—once you've descended the gangplank into the town that, had you not dropped anchor, would by virtue of its nonexistence have been spared all of what's coming.*

The voice sputters out as I stretch a Band-Aid across the cut on my chin and puff the fine Austrian cologne I find waiting in the medicine cabinet, in a purple cardboard box embossed with three snow-capped Alpine peaks and clasped shut with a gold seal I take great pleasure in breaking.

WHEN THE RITUAL HAS CONCLUDED AND MY Brother has wished me well on my first day of school, and I've descended the gangplank in my tie and polished alligator-skin boots, swinging my briefcase in time to the long-delayed reunion of my feet with solid ground, I enjoy a surge of total well-being. Maybe this is it, I think. Maybe I've arrived. Through the fog, out of the nightmare and into my real life at last, my pleasant and sensible adulthood in a charming if drafty old mansion on the edge of town—I turn to regard Angel House settling into this description behind me—in which I'll have all the time I need to ruminate on what I've been through to get here, and plenty of time after that to enjoy my later years once the past has been dealt with in the way that only adults can deal with it. By writing it down and putting it in a drawer.

Except, the voice says, *your only reason for being here is to teach the particulars of that past over and over again. What did you think the job entailed when you accepted it?*

I swat the side of my head with my briefcase, tempted to devolve into slapstick here in the middle of what must be

Main Street, but the sight of the diner to my left drains my will. I swivel to regard it, forced into dumb recognition. I look past the overfamiliar dumpster toward the gleaming supermarket by whose unwavering light I wrote my Nuclear Dissertation, painstakingly earning the doctorate that has allowed me, here in middle age, to assume my position as...

"Professor Squimbop, I presume?"

I turn to regard a woman in a gray suit with short, straight hair of almost the same color. Before I can think of any reason to deny it, although I already feel my well-being steaming away, I nod.

"Buy you breakfast before school?" She makes a show of checking her watch, but doesn't pull her sleeve up high enough to see the face.

We enter together, both of us squinting in the supermarket's light, which fills the diner's interior. I order poached eggs and corned beef hash without making eye contact with the waiter, afraid of who I might recognize if I did. *He ought to thank you for rehiring him as an extra,* the voice taunts, forcing me to jam my spoon in my mouth.

"We're all so glad you could make it," the woman says, her eyes also avoiding mine as I slowly extract and lower the spoon. "On such short notice."

I yawn, pour sugar in my coffee, and try to decide whether to ask what she means. Ought I to know? Ought I to remember how and why I was hired, or even to believe that any such thing occurred? And yet how could it, when nothing resembling this town existed until I decided to drop anchor in the middle of the Inland Sea? Or is that not what happened? Is there a chance that all I actually did was apply to job after job after job as an overqualified American History Professor with a checkered past, looking for any outpost that would take me, even if it meant...

"And we're so glad you could accommodate third grade," I think I hear her say. "I know it's not exactly what you, how do I put this, might have chosen, all things being equal, but since all things rarely are these days, well..."

"What?" I finally say, as I run the side of my fork through a poached egg, lancing the yolk. I shove a potato in my mouth and wait for her to answer.

"Anyway," she continues, again pretending to check her watch. "I better get going. You finish up. Tell them at the register to put it on Superintendent Dodd's ticket. They know the one."

When she's gone, I eat a few more potatoes, holding them up to the supermarket light, take a few swigs of coffee, and show myself out, neglecting to mention anything at the register. Back on the street, my blazer and tie thick with diner grease, any last distinction between this town and the million others I've passed through has vanished, rendering them all the same.

Not just the same, the voice insists. *Turning them all into this one. This actual one. The only town left. The one single extant settlement, after the blast. Beyond the cloud of figments. Seed of the entire future, vault of the entire past. Welcome to it, Professor.*

I SIT DOWN ON THE STEPS OF THE CINEMA, CERtain that Tommy Bruno is watching me through the tinted ticket window as I smell my tie, mashing its sausage reek into my nose and mouth. I chew and almost swallow it, pushing more and more down my throat, desperate to mute the dissonance echoing along Main Street and radiating in from the alleys, collecting in the exact spot where, I can see now, I've arrived out of sheer cowardice. The cowardice of an adventurer too spent to see the adventure through, determined instead to pound its middle into a sucker's Finale. The cowardice, I find myself thinking, as I groan to my feet and hurry away from the cinema, as if my mere presence there were an affront to the legacy my Brother and I once seeded into the living womb of legend, of a second- or third-rate Squimbop impersonator, mistakable for the real thing only in the most bereft outpost of a nation long since fallen into terminal decline.

Settling into this role, I swing my briefcase through the rest of downtown, past a sign that reads ████ Community College, and along a secondary road, less densely settled, that deposits me on the far side of the gleaming supermarket, to which the elementary school is apparently appended.

Dodd spies me as I cross the portico, towering over a swarm of children, and extends an arm, as if to rescue me from quicksand. "Professor," she says, and seems poised to launch into a speech, but then either thinks better of it or realizes she has nothing in mind. She relaxes her grip once we've crossed into the foyer, by which point I've built enough momentum to glide into the classroom that, as with so much else here, I've seen many times in dreams and movies, or in memories of my own schooling, eons ago, when another handsome mustachioed stranger in a velvet blazer and gleaming alligator-skin boots stood at the head of the class, filling the dead air with exotic perfume as he ordered us to read a story entitled "In Dreams Begin Responsibilities."

And who's to say now isn't then? the voice blurts, to which I reply, even though the children haven't taken their seats yet, "Well, that's exactly why the blast released at the apex of The Dodge City Civil War, which mushroomed into a World War if one considers Dodge City *a world*, serves as the paradoxical ending and starting point of history, the Zero Hour beyond which all subsequent events are refracted, BC to AD—doubled, or even tripled, quantum reappropriations of the *authentic, first-order occurrences* that initially, in what we might now refer to as the Age of Legends, the sunken time we mark as In-the-Beginning..."

The children gaze at the clock, or at the maps of Jupiter and Neptune on the walls, or at the nest of sparrows on the windowsill, while I gaze more and more intently at two boys sitting together near the back of the room, their eyes alert with a kind of vicious attention under which I can't help but recoil. They're the only two who seem remotely conscious of what I'm saying, or even that I'm speaking at all. The only two with eyes that appear deeper than drawn-on circles. I let my lower lip hang as Lecture spumes down my chin, crackling so loudly that I again lose track of whether I'm speaking or it is. Either way, I think, I'd have no less autonomy were I transformed into a bear dancing at the end of a Bulgarian medicine man's chain.

"And after the blast," I hear my voice continue, while my legs do the bear dance, "the world seized up, melted away, and sank beneath the waves. The Inland Sea covered everything until, over the ages, the Ark known as Angel House, a mobile seed bank containing all of humanity's past and its only possible future, dropped anchor and, in so doing, dredged this settlement from the murk of deracinated Squimbop skulls deep below, conjuring a spark of new life from the very quintessence of death, a paradox upon which, in our infantile yet irrepressible need to comprehend the particulars of our existence in this dimension, we can only ruminate, alone or together, as we are now, well... in any event, this will form the basis of your first essay, 2-3 pages, double-spaced, due before the start of class on Monday."

Spent, I close my eyes and let any remaining Lecture bubble over the Band-Aid on my chin and pool in my collar, where it hardens into a kind of butter ascot. By the time the school day ends, after a break for recess and lunch where I'm forced to watch the children eat while I nibble my tie, I see the duo from the back of the room depart, glaring at me and whispering.

Only they know how this ends, the voice insists, as I pinch my eyes shut and picture my Brother and myself ambling across the kickball field at the end of another school day, eagerly decoding the cryptic message our teacher had just imparted, one more tile in the mosaic that, once complete, would reveal a means of hopping in a '33 Cadillac, cranking the radio, and skipping town, setting out on the adventures for which the Brothers Squimbop would one day become the subject of schoolyard lore all across America.

AFTER A LATE LUNCH AT THE DINER, WHERE HALF my mind is taken up by memories of slugging down egg creams and apple pie with my Brother here after school, while the other half toys with the notion of asking for a grill job and wrapping the biggest knife I can find in my apron, I jaunt along the road to the Community College, crossing its sparse yellow lawn and letting myself in through the cafeteria doors.

The cafeteria smells like a more industrial version of the diner, assembled from a larger size of the same kit, and I can well picture both kitchens receiving shipments of the same foods, oil drums of tomato sauce and bricks of frozen cod. Ideating on the journey of these foodstuffs across the Inland Sea to be unloaded by silent dockhands in the hour before sunrise, I lurch past a few tables populated by small, squabbling groups, then turn down a tiled hallway and hurry past ragged bulletin boards and dim offices, a pattern that repeats several times until I turn another corner and shove my way through a set of metal doors and into the high back rows of a sloping auditorium.

I take a seat near the top, although most of the lower seats are empty, and regard the woman speaking at the podium on stage, her voice echoing from speakers above and behind me. "And so, as the Alvin and Lenore Frye-Kaplan Professor of Squimbop Studies," she says, "it is my foremost duty to crystallize for the public exactly what we mean and do not mean when we speak of the *Real Brothers Squimbop*, which is, in case you were wondering," she pauses to laugh here, earning a few confused chuckles from the audience, "where this course gets its title. In any event, thanks to the largesse of Superintendent Dodd in working out an equitable arrangement between the municipal school district and the College, we are thrilled to offer this course as a community-wide elective, an opportunity of which I'm even more thrilled to see you have all promptly made a point of availing yourselves."

More tittering in the crowd, such as it is, while I wonder who my fellow students are, and what brought them here, if not the same forces that brought me. *But it couldn't be the same*, the voice argues, *since you're real and they're not, which means if you didn't plant them there, inert as wispy turnips in a cabbage patch, then who did?*

"To start us all off on the right foot, please welcome my graduate student, Lester Kane, as he invites the stars of today's lecture onto the stage." We clap as a young man in a quilted vest and bowtie heaves into view, dragging a trolley in which sit, bound and gagged inside a mesh hopper, life-size puppets of my Brother and myself, straw poking out of their mouths and ears. Their faces look old and wrinkled while their bodies are smooth, the straw stretched taut beneath clean wax skin and well-tailored Squimbop Suits.

Lester bows when the applause dies down. Then he sets to work uprooting the puppets from their sawdust nests and dragging them to their chairs, one on either side of the Professor. As soon as the two are seated beside her, their arms wrapped self-protectively around their torsos, she looks up from her notes and says, "Well, now the question I'd like you all to consider in your first reflection papers, 2-3 pages, double-spaced, due before the start of class on Monday, is what are the precise factors that make these straw men less *real* than the Brothers themselves, and furthermore, do these factors—given that these straw men are unmistakably *Brothers Squimbop straw men*—make them more or less real than yourselves, insofar as you are not made of straw, you are human beings—let us assume!—but you are also manifestly not *Brothers Squimbop human beings*? If this question seems abstruse, don't worry, I'm only asking for an initial reflection here. An opening salvo. And if, rather, the question seems crass or simplistic, don't worry there either. I can promise you, if experience is any guide, that there is more than a semester's worth of unpacking to be done in terms of this question's implications for, as I like to call it, *the problem of who people are and what they are doing*."

LEAVING THE STRAW MEN SLUMPED IN THEIR seats with Lester twiddling his bowtie behind them, she dismisses class and strides into a private area before I decide whether to confront her with who and what I am, hoping either to puncture her argument or induce her to puncture mine. "If we're all just hangers-on," I picture myself asking, while her eyes roll faster and faster, "just the middle-aged chaff of a small town desperately auditing courses at the Community College for fear of otherwise going to seed too soon, then how do you explain my being an actual Squimbop, fully half of the original duo, washed up here only until the Golden Age begins in earnest? Why, if none of this is true, do I live alone in Angel House?"

This monologue carries me back through the cafeteria, across the lawn, and into the outlying streets, where, as the sun goes down, I feel the cold seep of Lecture soaking my collar and turning my chest hair slick. It radiates so forcefully from my mouth that I turn from the few passing cars and undo my belt, glad for them to picture me urinating on a stump. "The Golden Age is soon to begin!" I hear myself shout, loud enough that a truck bearing the White's logo rolls to a stop, flashes its lights, and forces me to rebuckle my pants and hurry along the road, past a field of sparse wheat and toward a tremendous construction site. The truck stops, flashes its lights again at a guard manning a wrought-iron gate, and cruises through at the sound of a buzzer. I follow, as if the truck and I were on the same mission, but the gate slams shut against my belly, knocking me over, a pratfall that makes the guard spew his soda and slap his thigh.

When I've gotten back to my feet and tipped an imaginary hat, I shield my eyes from the white gleam and regard a sign rising through the air beneath a looming crane. "Squimbop Media Center, Cooperstown, New York," it reads, as the gleam flashes through the holes in the letters. I watch until the sign makes contact with the main building's roof. Then, as the truck honks and begins to back out, I return to myself and hurry away, tripping along the edges of fields high with corn and darkening pastures dotted with solitary grazing horses.

This route deposits me at my front door, as I half suspect all routes here eventually would. Beyond the frame of Angel House, I can smell the salt of the Inland Sea, though I'm far too exhausted to approach it. I clutch my briefcase tighter and shoulder the door open, torn between the terror that the anchor has slipped and I'll soon find myself afloat in the night again, and the terror that there is no anchor, and never was. That I am no more than I appear to be, an aging bachelor holding down a crumbling fort on the very edge of a medium-sized town somewhere in what's left of America, putting his doctorate to the only dubious use the market will bear.

INSIDE, I MAKE A SIMPLE DINNER OF GROUND beef in warm water. The freezers in the Angel House basement are densely stocked with this and nothing else, and I intend to resist entering the supermarket for as long as possible.

When I'm finished, I rustle up a notepad and a blue pen to work on the essay the Professor assigned, thinking it wise to get an early start before my own students' essays come in.

"My Brother and I grew up very slowly in this town," I write. "Our authentic point of origin, known in those days as Cooperstown, New York, future home of the official Squimbop Media Center, and thus ground zero for the *True Story*, above and beyond whatever spurious accounts circulated on home video as Squimbop Fever swept the nation. This is the schema of the world we learned at school, the drowned world that a half-drowned man in a velvet blazer and alligator-skin boots presented to us day after day after day, in a kind of buttery trance, tying the genesis of our condition to a nuclear blast for which there was, outside of his account, no evidence whatsoever."

I pause to pick beef from my teeth with the nib of the pen and wipe Lecture from my lip. "When it all came to a head," I continue, "when the Age of Straw Men could no longer persist, my Brother and I followed our teacher, who'd become a sort of father to us, along a straight, solemn parade route that linked our home with the newly finished Media Center, on the field trip that would seal our fate, much as it would also seal his."

WAKE *UP!* THE VOICE SCREAMS IN MY HEAD. *You're losing the plot again. Wipe the cream from your mouth and get in the shower.*

I comply without hesitation. Under the hot water, I close my eyes and waver between an urge to rescue the duo from the field trip I can see will soon occur, and an urge to grab them wherever they're sleeping and take them on it now.

My body trembles with indecision, even if there is no decision to make. I picture the den downstairs, the Primal Scene tape on its shelf behind the bottles of port, *the shelf behind the shelf,* as the voice puts it. Something tells me that, were I to play the tape now, it would no longer show what happened on Cielo Drive. I picture the gap on the tape as a gap in the mansion my Brother and I forced our way into, the sacrificial altar abandoned, covered with dried blood and discarded tools, or tools not yet put to use, the scene I've tried so hard to forget forever awaiting its chance to occur. Then I picture this altar in the Angel House basement, stored just beneath me in a Forbidden Room whose invocation makes the shower run cold.

I HURRY OUT OF THE WATER AND WRAP MYSELF IN every towel I can find. A gleam slants in from the east-facing windows and I can tell there will be no going to bed, so I step back into my alligator-skin boots and velvet blazer, rumpled and sweaty from yesterday, and grab my briefcase without checking its contents or attending to my mustache or even spurting any fine Austrian cologne. Soon, I'm eating hash and eggs at the diner, and then I'm back in the classroom, my briefcase on the desk beside me. The children are barely cognizant except for the duo in back, whose gaze is even heavier than before.

Again we lock eyes, and their faces come more into focus the more intently they focus on me, as if the three of us shared an optic nerve. The other children settle into themselves like old cakes, the circles that mark their eyes fading into the tan of their foreheads.

As the Lecture progresses, I hear it describe *the second breaking point of the Postwar Era*, which begins with the class trudging along the road to Angel House, lit as ever by the gleaming white of the supermarket. Only the duo maintains purchase on the ground, while the rest of the children float overhead, drifting together and apart on the breeze, some of them snagging on telephone wires, startling the perched hawks, while the rest drift on, placid and remote as balloons.

The road dead-ends at Angel House and we crowd across the threshold, into the watery purple glow that emanates from the interior, which smells of old port, ground beef, reptile leather, and fine Austrian cologne. The children bob down to the carpet and then up past the furniture, sighing and cooing like infants lost in a dream, until they cluster on the ceiling, their ascent monitored by a Squimbop on a stepladder. He presses them harder and harder against the patterned stucco until their bodies flatten and their liquid drips out, running together as if through a funnel, into a bathtub on the floor.

I look down and realize that it's me on that stepladder, crushing one child after another against the ceiling, each more easily than the last, my hands charged with a kind of practiced mastery I would give anything to purge them of.

As soon as all the children are flattened and the tub is full, I rush to the far side of the living room and haul the anchor up through the window. The sound of a drain unclogging echoes as Angel House buckles and shudders, knocking me to the ground. When I get back to my feet, I return to the window to see all of Cooperstown sinking beneath the waves, the last of its windmills and barnyards succumbing to the Inland Sea. Hundreds of horses drown on their backs. Then I'm out upon the sea again, bound for the Totally Other Place with nothing but my old tapes and the tub full of whatever dripped out of the children for company.

When I arrive, I unload my cargo and kneel before my Distant Master, unseen behind a curtain, while he whispers, "Slowly, slowly will the seeds of a new culture be sown. Slowly the fallout will dissipate and the Brothers will take to the roads again."

Then I'm back at sea, again with nothing but my videos and ground beef and glasses of port and a Brother in a room I cannot open, until I panic and drop the anchor and summon another Cooperstown and depart into it with my mustache freshly shaved and my velvet jacket and alligator-skin boots all spic and span, my neck glistening with fine Austrian cologne, to eat hash and eggs at the diner with the Superintendent before facing my new class for the first time, impressing upon them the singular significance of the blast that released the Inland Sea from whose floor their souls, like all souls except the original pair belonging to my Brother and myself, were dredged for the *nth* time, recombinations of recombinations culled from the poisoned murk, and then I'm leading these children back along the Outskirts road to Angel House and crushing them against the ceiling and bringing the overflowing tub back across the Inland Sea to my Brother—or my uncle, or my father, whoever my Distant Master really is—where he receives it behind his curtain, yammering in my head about the seeds of a new culture, a nascent Catskills rising from the ruins, before he sends me back across the Inland Sea to...

"Okay, class dismissed!" I at last manage to shout, opening my eyes to see that only the duo remains. I choke, terrified to ask how much of this I've said aloud and therefore, however notional the connection, where the others have gone. *You know where they've gone, you pervert!!* the voice taunts.

"See you tomorrow," I gasp as I hurry away, swinging my briefcase like I hope it'll permit me to fly. As I hustle across the portico where parents wait to pick up children who may no longer exist, I catch a glance of the duo strolling in the other direction, surely whispering, as my Brother and I once whispered, about today's bombshell revelation in the ongoing process of, somehow, finding the means of escaping their town and setting out as free Americans on the open road at last.

I ARRIVE IN THE LECTURE HALL AT THE COMMUNITY College flushed and sweaty, my eyes vibrating with exhaustion as the Professor, wearing a long black dress, says, "And my own embarkation upon this journey began when I undertook a course of thesis research on what was in those days known as Squimbop Fever, a condition that, while I admittedly did not coin the term, I have done more than anyone in the field to explicate as a larger quantum of sociological concern, a mirror, if you will, of the fate we all face, here in these waning days of the West, when it seems as though history cannot possibly churn onward any longer, and yet we know, if history itself is any guide, that it can. It *can* and it *will*! The question that has therefore come to dominate what I consider my *mature research*, not to date myself, is what it means for history to grind on in such a fragmentary and dubious manner, with no coalescence, no master narrative, no... and let's leave it here for today, people... no direction home. Please hand in your essays if you haven't already, and enjoy what I'm told is a beautiful day!"

She seems more harried than usual, less gracious in her exit from the stage, which, as ever, leaves Lester to twiddle his bowtie in confusion. I hurry as well, the strain from last night's writing session and today's Lecture beginning to manifest as a cousin of the seasickness I felt before I first dropped anchor, as if I really have made the journey across the Inland Sea, from Cooperstown to the Totally Other Place and back, since I was here last, so that the cumulative weight of it is now catching up with me, a seafaring man from way back staring down the chilly prospect of retirement in a dreary, distant port.

"Sorry!" shouts a voice, an inch from my ear.

I blink and step back, the campus lawn swimming as I blink again and regard the face of the black-clad woman, impeccably cast in the guise it's always appeared in at times of crisis, all throughout the Saga. She blinks too, takes in more of my face than a stranger would, and says, "You teach my boys, don't you? Third grade?"

She points to her left, perhaps indicating the direction of the school.

I shrug, then look at my briefcase, smell my tie, and force a gesture of assent, though it feels so foreign I can't tell if she takes it as such. I want to ask her for an extension on the essay, but I can't explain why I need it.

She makes an equally ambiguous expression, then says, "Well, I hope you're getting your money's worth from my class."

I say nothing, which causes her to frown. "A joke," she adds. "They haven't started charging auditors, have they?"

I shake my head. "No ma'am," I say, glad to be certain of one single thing. "Not that I've heard. I better be going. My essay, it's..."

She flaps her hand in a way that seems to indicate she knows what I mean, perhaps better than I do, and I'd like to think something passes between us here. A fondness from another lifetime, the dim echo of an intimate memory. The possibility of an autumn romance, even.

THE WALK BACK TO ANGEL HOUSE IS EVEN MORE clogged with commotion and supermarket light than before. My head throbs along with the beeping of construction vehicles as I lean against the fence to watch a dump truck unload mortar, until, across the pit, the sight of the two boys jars my attention out of the blur it'd settled into. They stare at me, so I stare at them. I again see myself crushing the other children against the Angel House ceiling, stitching them into a leather canopy while these two lurk on the threshold, playing with a pair of trick knives, extending and retracting the plastic blades over and over again. The longer I look, the more the repetition mesmerizes me. For a moment, the pure joy, the total abandon and self-overcoming my Brother and I once brought to our massive audience returns, and I know, better than I ever have before, that the scene I'm imagining, the two of them stabbing an old man with trick knives again and again in a parking lot in the blazing sun, pressing their plastic blades against his straw-stuffed flesh until it sloughs away, is as authentic a Squimbop Routine as any that's ever been brought onstage.

I HURRY HOME, DEPOSITING MY ALLIGATOR-SKIN boots and briefcase by the door and running the bath, into which I pour as much ground beef as I can fit while leaving room for my own body, in an attempt to override the fleshy smell now wafting down from the ceiling, which, though I try not to look, I can tell is dotted with the stains of old viscera. I sink into the water as the meat cooks around me, nibbling the bits that float past my mouth. With my eyes closed, I picture a fleet of ships emerging from the mist, weary but triumphant from their journey across the Inland Sea. They dock as hundreds of trucks emerge from the same mist, backing up into the ships' open holds so that, without interruption, boxes flow into place and roll across town, as silently as they sailed, and then silent workers in jumpsuits approach the trucks and winch open their sealed backs to unload the boxes—half of them marked TRICK KNIVES—and carry them into the newly completed storage sheds of the Squimbop Media Center.

I splutter and bob in the tub, opening my eyes when an especially thick clump of beef passes my lips. Then I swallow and return to the vision, where I'm already *placing another order*, as the voice describes it, *sending away for more Squimbop Supplies from the Totally Other Place, across the Inland Sea, now that a new culture, replete with its own means of production, has taken root there.*

More Squimbop Suits and rubber Squimbop Masks, the voice announces inside me, *more models of the donkey from our sojourn in Europe and the gallows from our sojourn in Hollywood, more mini wax figures from the Wax*

Museum you visited on your own in northern California, and all the pieces to assemble the diner where you spent so many nights and mornings in Alaska, and where you spend your mornings still. More trick knives, too, I see... it's hard to stop shopping in the night, is it not?

Beneath the voice's swagger, I detect a note of sadness. Resignation, maybe even fear. I sink beneath the cooling bathwater, soaking my face in meat fat as I order a shipment of Tommy Bruno cutouts and watch as they're transferred from ship to truck to what's fast becoming the Media Center Gift Shop. Then I watch a work crew build out the diner inside one of the display halls, complete with a straw effigy of me at my usual table, eating my hash and eggs, nodding when a straw waiter refills my coffee, the rain misting against the windows behind the tiny tabletop jukebox and the ribbed plastic salt and pepper shakers and the caddy of Cholula and Tabasco.

THE MORNING IS GUSTY AND COLD, GRAY RAIN still running down the diner windows behind the tabletop jukebox as aging men and women stare at me, leaning in to get a better look. They lean together to whisper, "He's the one. The one who took our children. Crushed them on the ceiling and drained them in a tub. Now look at us." They hover over my hash and eggs, daring me to surge up from my seat and crush them likewise against the stamped tin ceiling of the diner. Put them out of their misery. The prospect of asking my Distant Master for permission to do so sends me into a fit of fidgeting. I itch my forearm while the townspeople hover, their mouths falling open as I remove a long, straight, bloody strand of straw, peeling back the waxy skin between my wrist and elbow to reveal the dense straw musculature beneath. I gather a thick red-black bundle and hold it out to them like a bouquet. *Dripping with the Squimbop Trace*, the voice says. *Proof positive of what you are.*

The townspeople shudder and retreat, knocking the waiter to the ground. When his coffee pot shatters and steam begins to rise, I rise along with it, pulling down my arm-skin like a sleeve. I step over the broken glass and, as I pass the register, mutter, "Put it on the Superintendent's ticket."

I arrive without incident at the school, which is now as empty as the colleges where my Brother and I once held forth, in deepest Arkansas, back when the Squimbop Saga seemed aimless and unhurried, bent toward no Finale. "The construction of the Media Center was not inevitable in those days," I tell the two boys. "There was a time, many, many towns ago, before the years caught up with me, when I foresaw an endless bachelorhood for myself, a Postwar eternity which, having set in motion the nuclear holocaust that resolved the otherwise-intractable World War in Dodge City, I alone deserved to enjoy. It was all mine for the taking, until something—maybe no more than time itself—overtook me in turn, just as it will likewise overtake you."

The boys smirk like one has whispered a cutting remark to the other, though neither makes a sound. My ears burn and my forearm throbs and I can tell I'm blushing as my bladder heaves and I flash back to an ancient rendition of this same classroom, my lap black with urine, my Brother gloating over my predicament while our teacher wanly pretended not to notice. I consider excusing myself to the bathroom, but resolve to hold firm even as I feel a warm trickle run down my trouser leg and into my argyle sock. I clear my throat, swim hard toward the present, and say, "I had a Brother too, once. A twin maybe, or just about. We, too, could speak without speaking. But that was a long time ago. *Something happened. He did something. Or I did.*"

I lean back on my desk, my trousers cold and sticky against the straw beneath, and listen to the voice, which I suspect the boys can hear as well, merging with my own and coming out of my mouth. *"You left me there, in the house on Cielo Drive, after what you thought I'd done, on the tape you marked* Primal Scene *and stowed on the shelf behind the shelf, guarded by your bottles of port... the ultimate sundering, the sacral murder you could not abide... but you never watched it, did you? You ran off into the fog of your Fever, thinking yourself the moral one, the upstanding Little Brother, free at last of the psychopath, the road of righteousness open ahead, ten thousand righteous tables set for one, and yet what did you discover along that road save for war and war and war and war, the souls of children raining down upon you like poison wine?"*

"Class dismissed!" I gasp, wrenching my eyes open with the straw protruding from my fingertips to find the room empty. I hear something dripping and look beneath me at the puddle that's spread from my socks to my boots and onto the standard-issue elementary school flooring. I let myself down into it and skate across the tiles, swinging my briefcase as I would at the end of any other day, despite the suspicion, swinging along just behind me, that I'm skating toward the end of all days, the endless repetition of towns and teaching jobs approaching a cusp or crux beyond which I will not be invited to continue. I can hear the grinder whirring. *Almost time to take you out back,* the voice chimes in. *The proverbial glue factory's warming its oven.*

I ARRIVE AT THE COLLEGE LATE AFTER GETTING lost in the expanding warren of fences and pits around the Media Center. By the time I make it to the lecture hall, it's empty and silent save for the dripping of a leaky spigot. I settle into my seat, though I know the lecture is long over, and wait, my eyes drooping closed, until the scrape of toenails across polished wood summons me back to the scene.

I look up to see a wolf crossing the stage, regarding me with the same eyes it regarded me with in Arkansas. The same wolf, I think, as we maintain eye contact, and I can tell it's thinking the same, or the equivalent, about me. The same college, the same room, the same dripping spigot. The same reek of taxidermied scales and bulk-rate formaldehyde.

The same moment, the voice cackles in my ear, as the wolf licks its teeth. *The exact same scenario, preserved forever inside the Media Center of your making. The prison you constructed for fear of how open the ocean proved to be!*

I groan to my feet, my trousers frigid and sticky, and wade through the auditorium, watching the wolf lick its teeth while the voice rails in my head, repeating, as if I didn't know by now, that it was always me, never him, who was determined to preserve our legend in amber, whether it be that of celluloid or of the slick, plaque-covered walls of the Media Center, too afraid of life itself to let it run its natural course.

Well, here you are! it shrieks as I pass the wolf, which moves its mouth in perfect imitation of the voice's rhythm, chasing me into the empty workshops, their shelves stuffed with turtle and armadillo shells and pheasants and falcons and more wolves, stacked three deep in rooms that are otherwise full of boxes marked TRICK KNIVES and SQUIMBOP SUITS: S/M/L/XL.

So what now? the voice taunts. *The course doesn't cover this part of the story, does it?* I shove through a service entrance and out into the construction site, which has swallowed the college and tagged it with a "Cooperstown

Community College" plaque, in what is clearly the Media Center's standard font.

When I've crossed the grounds, I lose myself among the idle machinery which, mixed with trucks and ships docked in deep inlets, bulges to the horizon. I can see the coastline with Angel House nestled against it so clearly that I suspect I'm looking at a painted backdrop, the waves and anchor frozen in place, ready to be gawked at by one field trip group and family outing after another.

I WALK AS FAST AS I CAN WITHOUT RUNNING, more frightened of the construction site than I have any clear reason to be. There's something down there, I can't help thinking. Something I do and don't want to see. The faster I walk, the more I worry that I'm merely circling the pit, fencing myself in or even drilling myself down, until I can't be sure that I haven't fallen in already. Who knows how long you've been on the bottom, I think, as I look upward, no longer certain that the dark edges of the sky are not the dark edges of the pit, too high to ever climb. I close my eyes around a vision of the endlessly retracting blades of trick knives, in and out and in and out as steadily as the pumping of the Primal Scene that set all of humanity loose upon the earth at the dawn of time. My mouth fills with cold spit and I tip forward to let it out, softening the ground into a puddle and then a pool and then a pond, a swamp as thick and clammy as Dead Sir. Here I revert to Dodge City, the warheads growing from the silt again, thick and angry and veined with seaweed, throbbing and then bursting with light that spreads and spreads until I'm forced to close my eyes, even if they're closed already, my mind seething and raging, desperate to cling to any idea at all against the prospect of being wiped clean.

The light boils and steams but then begins to settle as the supermarket develops inside me like a photograph taken with too much flash. Wringing phantom swamp-water from my shirt, I open my eyes to gaze through the windows at lone shoppers gliding along well-oiled tracks, gathering red meat and green leaves at a changeless pace, as the sky over the pit hardens into a Media Center ceiling. I study its contours, counting the sprinkler heads and surveillance cameras, and find that I'm not too proud to kneel with the gratitude of a pilgrim rescued just in time from *the road beyond all roads*, which leads, I can see now, to the backside of the universe. Slowly, I get to my feet and tilt my head downward, until my eyes come to rest on a poster in the window that reads MEATLOAF SPECIAL $4.99/LB.

I can tell that I'm wearing out, nearing the point in the Saga where I'll need to be replaced but, still, part of me wants to refuse this dubious salvation as long as it can. It wants to slam against the walls of its asylum and insist that my life is still mine to live, a counter-Saga proudly bound for the backside of the universe, but the rest of me—most of me, I suspect—basks in the relief of the long journey's end, lit forevermore by the glow of the supermarket that now points toward the front steps of the lone inhabited house on a street of cold and sagging husks.

You go in there, you set the final sequence in motion, Little Brother, the voice warns. *The final sitcom of the Postwar Era. The tripwire stretches across the threshold that you are about to... well, now you've done it. You're in there now.*

You won't hear from me again.

I am in it indeed, in the dead silence of the shoe-choked atrium. I regard the black-clad woman and the two boys sitting around the table, frozen over empty plates. "I picked up some meatloaf," I stammer. "It was on sale."

The plastic bag glows so bright I have to squint while dumping its contents into a baking dish and shoving it in the oven. Then I join my family in utter stasis for an hour. When dinner's ready, I don a pair of trout-shaped oven mitts and carry the steaming dish to the table. The three of them move only once I've taken my seat and picked up my cutlery.

"Well," the black-clad woman says. "How was work, honey?"

I fill my mouth with meatloaf, unfocus and refocus my eyes, swallow, and say, "You know, another day. How about you?"

She smiles and says, "Easy. I've taught the course so many times at this point it's like listening to a recording of myself speak. The strangest part is having to stand there and look out at the faces in the auditorium, which seems to grow wider every year as those faces shrink and drift apart, despite the Superintendent's initiative to involve the community, and I wonder how it could possibly be that they're straining to comprehend the spread of Squimbop Fever for the very first time. Like, how could it be that souls exist in this world free of the solitary topic to which I've devoted the near entirety of my mature attention, if you know what I mean? Makes a person feel small. Or big maybe, with a whole teeming world inside. You could look at it either way."

She takes a forkful of meatloaf and makes a satisfied expression, like she's just bounced the ball back into my court. How could souls exist in this world at all? I think, after waiting for the voice to fill my head, which it still declines to do. "Well," I say, aware that I'm inelegantly changing the subject, "should we talk about that field trip? The Media Center officially opens tomorrow morning."

The boys look up at this, blinking and smiling, though whether it's an eager or a sinister smile, a desire to make amends or get revenge, is more than I can tell. "As their teacher, as well as their father"—you're really stretching it here, Little Brother, you're about to go overboard, I tell myself—"I'd like to take them to see the fruit of their mother's research. So they know where they came from."

"She's not their mother, she's ours!" the voice shouts through my mouth, causing the black-clad woman to flinch. I take a gigantic second helping of meatloaf and press it into my mouth, determined to make a show of not speaking again until this latter-day sitcom moves of its own accord into its next scene.

You'd like to imagine you're the father, wouldn't you, I think. The role model, the moderating influence, and not the Pervert Uncle who did to them what he did to us to make us who we are...

"But I'll never be sure, will I!" I blurt, spewing meatloaf onto the faces of the boys across the table. It runs down their cheeks as I swallow the rest of what's in my mouth. Then I get up from the table, swaying down the hall in a gruesome reprise of the old Kansas mime routine.

I elbow my way into the room that I deem likeliest to be ours, the one I share with my wife or mother, and lie down in the cool sheets, my eyes watering as I struggle to swallow the lump pulsing behind my sternum. "Watch the tape," I insist. "Find out for sure what happened. Are you the father or the uncle? Are you preparing to liberate those boys from the fate we suffered, or to shunt it onto them so that, here in our coming obsolescence, we might at last die free of it?"

The sheets are fresh and clean and I can hear the black-clad woman coming down the hall, bearing the permission slip the boys will need for their field trip. I lie there and rock myself into a shipboard panic as the room sways and I smell salt and fishy cream and picture her advancing, one deliberate step at a time, in her long black dress, down a grand hallway in the heart of Angel House with the permission slip on a gleaming platter and a fountain pen, full of my own blood, uncapped beside it.

JUST BEFORE SHE REACHES THE ROOM, I ROLL OUT of bed, crawl into the closet, haul open a trapdoor, and descend my secret staircase, down and down toward the basement where, for all these years, I've kept my counter-life alive.

I crawl down the stairs on my belly, straw coming loose and bushing out on both sides until I lie flat on a doggie bed at the bottom. Then I get to my feet, averting my eyes from the Tommy Bruno cutout standing guard as I pour a snifter full of port and swirl it around while rummaging among the tapes. The time to play the Primal Scene has clearly come, but, I decide with a modicum of shame, there's no reason I can't ease into it with something more familiar first. So I pull one of the less occult tapes off the main shelf—*The Brothers Squimbop in Kansas* or *The Brothers Squimbop in Dodge City*—all of whose story beats I memorized long ago, in the video fog that bridged my youth and middle age, before repeated travel to and from the Totally Other Place wore me out and left me here, all the way across town from Angel House, in the lone inhabited home on a street of cold and sagging husks, dimming as they stretch into the distance beyond White's.

As I relax to the sound of the VCR warming up, I sip my port and wait for the familiar sequence to begin. "The Bloody, Bloody Road to Dodge City," I whisper, eager to sing along.

But something's off. Gray smoke spills around the edges of the frame and seems to emanate from the screen. I wave my hand in front of my face and at first imagine it's simply the tape melting from overuse, but the smoke is too thick for this to be all it is. I see snippets of melting cities and burning trees, boiling lakes and simmering asphalt, all of it collapsing into sinkholes, Dead Sirs that flush into the Inland Sea, surging through the sockets of a million Squimbop skulls heaped together in a demonic cairn.

I see waves rolling over a ramshackle Western settlement and then, like a tape that's been taped over again and again, I see a ship departing with a lone figure at its helm, furiously steering a wooden wheel. I gulp my port and settle into the frayed couch and try to locate my own attention, stretched between the life of a humble elementary school teacher and father of two in the genteel if remote outpost of Cooperstown, New York, and that of the captain of a ghost ship on an Inland Sea that's swallowed all of America, a prehistoric remnant sailing through a sublime madness that, here in my suburban basement, I can't help but envy, along with every domesticated dad on earth.

The tape sputters and the VCR spits it out, melted and oily. I get up, refill my port, try and fail to turn the Tommy Bruno cutout against the wall so it can't see me in my confusion—it seems to have faces on both sides now—and then I peel the tape away from the VCR, wipe it on my legs, and smush in another, stuffing the mechanism full of a material halfway between petroleum and plastic.

I huddle back on the couch as the taped-over footage depicts a man with an immaculately trimmed mustache embarking into a new town, decked out in alligator-skin boots and a velvet blazer. I can smell sausage grease and fine Austrian cologne boiling in waves from the screen as he eats a quick breakfast at the diner, holding his potatoes up to the gleaming supermarket light.

"You miss it, don't you?" someone asks.

I look around, first at the Tommy Bruno cutout and then at the stairs, which stand silent and empty. They seem impassible, though I know I've climbed them many times before. I wait, hoping the voice will either cease or reveal its source.

"The old legend of coming to town to preach the gospel you'd wrought, of living on ground beef in Angel House, of..." I feel warm, creamy liquid leaking down my collar and I spill my port when I blot the fabric with the hand that I'd forgotten was already holding the snifter. It seeps into my wiry chest hair as a fresh contingent of images fights its way up the screen, which has continued to emit gas from its speakers. I watch snippets of the captain sailing from town to town, pulling anchor at the end of each school year and flooding the entire territory, only to sail back across the Inland Sea, all the way to the Totally Other Place, where he kneels with his eyes closed, trying to imagine his Distant Master receiving the cargo and sending him back to cull another town from the sand only to entice its children likewise onto the Angel House ceiling, "Where they too will be drained of life and ferried back across the waters, and again and again and again."

I hear myself reciting these lines like a catechism, masticating the words, desperate to absorb whatever power they still contain despite the overuse I've already subjected them to night after night in this basement, with my briefcase full of unread third-grade essays on the armrest beside my snifters of port.

The voice laughs so hard that I laugh with it as the speakers on the TV burst and more liquid pours from my mouth. The port bottles burst too and gurgle onto the carpet and I find myself wading through knee-deep water as the taped-over video glitches and squiggles between flooding theaters and diners and a long chain of White's supermarkets, their luminous signs sparking in the surf.

I lunge for the forbidden tape in desperation, like a prisoner crunching a secret cyanide pill while the torturers close in. I tear it from its box, regard Tommy Bruno with the closest thing to defiance I can muster, and mash it into the VCR without even trying to remove the remnants of what was there before. By the time I've settled back onto the couch, gnawing unpopped popcorn from a bag, the water has surged high enough to make the couch float.

The tape opens inside the familiar house on Cielo Drive, my Brother and me reunited at last, our cameras and sound equipment all set up, the family we kidnapped cowering in the center of the shot, as he places the infant on a makeshift altar and stretches a burlap hood over his head before removing a scimitar from his belt, dancing for the camera as he does.

I close my eyes. As soon as I do, the voice, deeper and more authoritative than any I've heard myself emit before, growls, "Here, where once you turned away, where you left your Brother and slithered up the coast like a coward, spreading the Fever that only your courage could have prevented, you will not turn away again. You will see it through tonight. You will witness the truth about yourself this one time in your miserable life. Only then will you be permitted to die, and to leave these towns, whose children you've claimed in the tens of thousands."

The voice cracks as the couch floats up toward the ceiling, and I flash on a horrible image of being a child crushed against it with my Professor on a stepladder beneath me, making sure I remain stuck as the last of my liquid drips into his tub.

The screen buzzes when the hooded figure approaches the screaming infant, scimitar held high, and I almost close my eyes again, but manage to work my fingers under the lids just in time. I prepare to receive the truth about who we are, and thus who I am, the hero who turned from evil before it consumed him or the coward who sundered the duo before it reached fruition...

For an instant I flash on my Brother hacking the infant into dozens and then thousands of pieces, scattering them around the room where they land, shake, and climb to their feet, each one a miniature Squimbop, marching off in a thousand directions to populate the world, pursuing their own agendas until the Bloody, Bloody Road to Dodge City emerges as their common destination in the far future.

Then the screen turns shaggy with snow and jagged lines, wriggling in two dimensions until they tip forward and demand a third. As the imagery bobs and wavers, straw surges through, shattering the glass and coalescing into a pair of feet in sodden alligator-skin boots and then a pair of legs in crushed denim trousers, and then I'm pulling as hard as I can, rescuing my Brother from his womb or his tomb, praying he's still alive and that it isn't too late to gather our things and depart together into the Golden Age.

For a moment, despite the flooding and the straw poking through my eyes and up from my gums and out from my anus and urethra, I hold him tightly, my arms all the way around him, straw face to straw face, each of us slick with the other's blood. "Well," he says, in my voice, "here's your Primal Scene, Brother."

"The people of this great nation could hardly expect less from a duo such as us," I reply, in his voice. "Everything I've done and am about to do is for the sake of those good people."

His wet straw cheeks pull into a smile, as do mine, and I resolve to shut us both up, demanding a moment of silence from an escapade that I know cannot afford to postpone its Finale much longer.

"THE FIELD TRIP'S TODAY!" ONE OF US IS FINALLY forced to admit, as the water nearly reaches the ceiling. "The Media Center awaits, after the long years of stalled construction, the embezzlement scandals and equipment failure, the lumber shortages and rumors of sabotage from deep within the building inspector's office. It waits for you alone, Brother."

I lean against the couch, floating with my face against the ceiling as my Brother slips from my arms, the TV reduced to an empty sac by my ear. My straw arms are too weak to fight the waves as he whirls away, down to the stratum of skulls below. I use the last of my energy to swim up the stairs, through the trapdoor into the closet of the bedroom I've slept in throughout these long years in Cooperstown, and then, somewhere in the fateful hallway, I get to my feet, pinch my nose and blow to clear the pressure, and walk with what dignity I have left toward the breakfast room.

When I arrive, I stand by the door to regard the black-clad woman and the boys around their sugared Corn Flakes at the table as I say, pinching my voice into its pleasantest register, "Well folks, I'm done with my reruns. Ready to roll?"

The boys leap to their feet, kiss their mother, and hurry to their rooms to get their backpacks. I walk to the table, my movements awkward and jerky, like they were choreographed by others long ago, and take my seat as tears well in my eyes. *This is my last chance*, I want to tell her, though I can tell she already knows. *Please, tell me how to keep what I've set in motion from concluding.*

She cracks her knuckles, takes a sip of water, and gives me a slow, serious smile. "Remember when you audited my class?" she says. "You never did turn in that essay. You didn't even manage to ask for an extension." Her smile fills out, as does mine.

"No," I reply, "though I do believe I gave it some thought. At least it led us here, right?"

She nods as her smile fades again. "In a manner of speaking, yes. I suppose it did. For a time."

She looks like she's about to say something else, but then stiffens and grows reticent, and I can tell the boys are behind me, suited up and ready to go. I tremble and picture myself hiding under the table, clinging to the legs as they try to drag me away. When the laugh track refuses to validate this potential gag, I smooth what's left of my hair against the waxy surface of my scalp, pushing a few pieces of straw back under the skin, and lean in to kiss her one last time, a gesture she kindly reciprocates.

She wipes her mouth and chin and says, "We'll meet again someday. We always seem to."

Then she wipes her eyes in the same fashion and hands me the permission slip and the uncapped pen, filled with my blood, thick and shiny as mercury. I want to thank her for keeping this moment at bay last night, for granting me the privacy I requested, but my teeth are chattering so badly I can tell I'll smudge the paper if I don't focus on signing. So I take it from her, grasp the pen, and squiggle *Prof. Sq.* across the signature line, watching the blood pool in thick dots before sinking in.

When it's dry, I get to my feet and tremble across the kitchen, compelled by the same piecemeal choreography as before. I remember the mime I used to be, or used to travel with, and the hours we spent together in a Dust Bowl version of this same kitchen, decked out with cloudy jugs of homebrew whiskey and the smell of skillet cornbread. Then I push my way through the front door with the boys streaming around my legs, into the thick mist of the dawn over Cooperstown.

THE WALK IS SOLEMN AND PRECISE, FLANKED BY workers unloading trucks, packing the Media Center with ever more paraphernalia. As the boys look up at me, their faces take on personality, mixing humor and menace as only the Brothers can. However briefly, I consider killing them. I consider unsheathing my scimitar—something tells me that if I were to reach for it now, I'd find it clipped to my belt—and performing the vivisection my ancestor or younger self was too afraid to watch.

"No," I whisper, startling us all as we reach the Media Center gates, which buzz open when I hold the permission slip up to the camera. "No, it doesn't end here. Nothing but the prehistory is over. The Golden Age is about to begin!"

I laugh and cry at once as we walk along the newly finished promenade, past topiary and elegant metal tables and a smoothie and espresso stand in a shaded sanctuary and a statue of Superintendent Dodd in another, and push in through the gleaming glass doors, where a receptionist cheerfully sells us two Student tickets and one at the Educator rate.

THEN WE'RE INSIDE. I TAKE THE BOYS' HANDS AND let them guide me from room to room, each displaying a different phase of the Saga. We pass through the Great Hall, still heady with paint and sealant fumes, where life-size models of the Brothers are situated in a '33 Model T, rumbling down dusty back roads while "Me and the Devil Blues" plays on the radio. We pass photos and paintings of the Brothers in abandoned lecture halls, holding forth in plexiglass speech bubbles about giants who could pick up cities and swap their position at will, and about a heresy in which all land and water in America switched places overnight—which the plaque, in my wife's effortlessly precise academic prose, cites as a clear precursor to the "Inland Sea Mythos that would characterize the latter-day Squimbop Saga, after the Flood came to Dodge City, neatly (some would say *too neatly*) dividing the Prelapsarian Era from the Post"—and in which "nothing was true," according to the caption of a painting where one of us lurks at the edge of a brawl in a Shoney's parking lot, "save for what we made up."

I wipe my eyes as I remember the first time I thought these words, and hurry the boys along, into the next hall, dominated by the ocean liner that took us to Europe. We circle it, then walk along a ramp contoured to model the mountain paths my Brother and I hiked on our circuit of Italy and Greece, preaching the myriad gospels we invented or channeled as we went, building more steam than we could possibly blow off... until we forced our rebirth from the black-clad woman in the Black Forest and arrived in the next hall, a sandy, lizardy Hollywood exurb, in which I feel my stomach turn as we again approach the scene I have tried for so long to avoid. I look down at the boys and observe the evolution of their faces, the increasingly specific imprint of all this media on what began as generic seafloor skulls. This is the only education you'll ever receive, I think in their direction, fairly certain they can hear me. Drink it up, boys. You'll need it where you're going. The imprint of a viable Squimbop History, I go on thinking, enticing them away from Hollywood and the Fever rooms beyond with the promise of a Gift Shop free-for-all. The erasure of the father and uncle without which no new escapade can ever begin.

IN THE GIFT SHOP, A CHIPPER YOUNG WOMAN helps the duo pick out Squimbop Suits, on a two-for-one sale to celebrate the Media Center's grand opening. Evincing the formality of the exhibits themselves, she seats me on a bench, hands me a straw hat and a lime soda, and takes the boys to the changing room with a Squimbop Suit on a hanger in each hand.

I sit there beneath my floppy brim, sipping soda like some sunstroked grandparent at the beach, while I study the Media Center's self-guided tour map, allowing myself to imagine pushing aside the farm curtain in Kansas with my Brother to cross the threshold onto the Bloody, Bloody Road to Dodge City, where together we'll fight to sell our life story and buy a houseboat on which to finally...

"Life flashing before your eyes?"

I glimpse Tommy Bruno behind his popcorn machine in the foyer of the cinema, about to usher in a fresh cohort of restless ticket holders. Then I drop my soda, bend to pick it up, take a sip, as if this might make me appear calm, and say, "Excuse me?"

The Gift Shop attendant pats the boys, decked out in identical, overlarge Squimbop Suits, and says, "I asked whether that would be cash or card. The boys have requested trick knives as well."

They produce the knives from their new breast pockets and flick them open and closed three times in unison, then put them back.

"Cash," I manage. "After all this, I still have plenty of cash."

She nods, willing to acknowledge my statement but not to take it as a joke, which I'm not sure it was. Then she rings up the total purchase, takes my wad, hands me a modicum of change, smiles, and sits on a stool, falling out of activation as soon as we no longer need her.

THE THREE OF US WALK DOWN THE FLUORESCENT hall toward the exit sign. The boys are unrecognizable. Or, I think, the opposite: recognizable at last. They are the Brothers, live and in person, ready for their next routine, which may also, depending on whom you ask, be their first. Their long-awaited public debut after decades of maddening rehearsal.

The Brothers Squimbop escort their Pervert Uncle, indifferent to the possibility that he may also be their father, down the final hallway, resolute in their readiness to do what the routine requires. He's put us through too much already, we think. We've already come too close to losing ourselves in the vortex of his solipsism.

Now it's time for *our* routine. Now or never. Leave town or stay to become a permanent part of it, two more lounge lizards haunting the Media Center snack bar until it closes at eight-thirty. Two more American skulkers feeding off the cooling fumes of history, sucking up what proximity we can to the last Golden Age there ever was.

We pull our Squimbop Suits tighter, adjust our grip on our uncle's frail arms, and redouble our determination to put Cooperstown behind us. The mosaic is complete, we realize, reveling in the telepathy we now share. A clear, clean channel at last, worth whatever it costs to maintain.

When the exit sign glows above us and the ALARM WILL SOUND warning stretches across the door, we shove our uncle hard enough that he knocks it open and trips the alarm into a squealing frenzy.

Lit by the supermarket dialed up to the brightest it's ever been, we stumble outside and shoulder the old man against the dumpster, still full of the Media Center's cardboard afterbirth.

Panting, we remove the trick knives from our breast pockets and in the absolute unison of a duo born to perform together, activating a choreography perfected in a much earlier age, we stab him again and again and again, the plastic blades retracting into the handles and popping out over and over in immutable rhythm while the humped up straw body breaks out in beads of stage blood that soak its velvet blazer and stone-washed denim slacks before running down into its argyle socks and alligator-skin boots.

The scene goes on and on, drawing a crowd from the parking lot. Saucer-eyed men and women sipping smoothies and espressos clamber in, salivating at the remotest prospect of violent redemption, of *something actually happening*, here of all places and today of all days. We feed on this energy, speeding up our routine, stabbing the old pervert faster and faster, until our toy blades break off and he's so covered in stage blood that the rest of it wicks into the straw on the asphalt.

Then, high on the mounting applause, we heave the weightless body into the dumpster where it remains, its head and torso buried, its legs kicking until their alligator-skin boots slip off and land in the straw, a tangle of scales in a ruined nest.

The applause grows frantic as we climb into the idling '33 Cadillac that the Media Center has seen fit to provide us with, crank the radio until it wails out "Me and the Devil Blues," and tear off so fast the crowd barely has time to disperse. We tear onward as they cheer in the background, past the gleaming supermarket and the diner and the school and the sagging hulk of Angel House, all of it encircled by the Media Center's fencing, until we finally break free, up and out of the pit, slamming through the metal arm of the gate that will never again require the signed permission of any father or uncle. Quickening to the point of ecstasy, the Brothers Squimbop floor the accelerator, flying up the coastline of a continent that has by now fully absorbed the souls of the dead and begun to flower with new life, beyond the Era of Straw Men, with nothing but the Golden Age to come.

Dr. Forearm II

Years pass in which I earn my MD and then a doctorate in Squimbop Studies, back in the early days of the field, when the Fever was still spreading and the question on everyone's mind—the subject of every dissertation, including my own—was whether the Golden Age was still underway, the imperial phase in which the Brothers toured ceaselessly from one Mountain House to another, from the Catskills to Chautauqua to points further West, and even up into the lower provinces of Canada—shows that seemed to many of us to occur just beyond our reach, always one town or one night away—or whether that Golden Age existed solely in the addled minds of scholars, lost, in reality, in a distant past or future we were doomed to consider real without the slightest evidence except that which we produced. The underlying question then, which none of our research put to rest, was whether the Fever was one of anticipation or regret.

When it grew clear that I had nothing mature to add to this debate, I put my academic ambitions aside and returned to the medical track Dr. Forearm had placed me on all those years ago, and from which my Brother peeled away, living the life I would've lived if I were him and he were me, or if both of us had remained unified in the body of the boy we inhabited before the needle reached our upper arm.

I set up a practice, hang my diplomas on the wall, marry and have children—two boys, of course—and sit, for six months in a row, in an empty rented office off the Clearview Expressway in Flushing, rereading the *Condition* until one day a mother arrives with her son. She stops on the threshold between my waiting and examination rooms, smoothes the boy's hair, and says, "Dr. Forearm, I presume?"

Despite what sounds like the grinding of industrial machinery in my ear, I wipe my lip with my wrist, close the book around my finger, and nod. "The American MC Escher," I gasp. "Your MC for all that follows."

Another set of years pass, years in which my practice swells uncontrollably and I consult the *Condition* every night, focusing on the "Dr. Forearm" sections in order to put the relentless accretion of events in perspective. And yet, as they say, it's one thing to know the path and another to walk it.

So I walk on, injecting one boy after another with the mercury I've come to believe contains a concentrated essence of species-memory sourced from the depths of Dead Sir. A single dose is, of course, potent enough to derail any boy from the path he was on, or imagined he was on, shunting him onto the path that, as I've just noted, I see no choice but to go on walking myself. All of us on the same path, I think, sometimes picturing myself as a Pied Piper leading a growing train of boys away from any semblance of normal life and deep into the heart of a Golden Age that *must* exist despite the proliferation of condemned Mountain Houses threatening to reclaim the path we can no longer turn from, sagging together until we're forced to crawl on our bellies like worms.

Life goes on according to this pattern—every night, after putting our boys down, my wife and I lie in bed in our elegant Great Neck home reading separate copies of the *Condition*, then dreaming separate dreams in which each of us appears, she as the black-clad woman and me sometimes as Jim Squimbop, awaiting my chance to take the stage beside my Brother Joe in the town squares of Bavaria and Burgundy, or else on some Mountain House stage outside Denver or Winnipeg, and other times as the Pervert Uncle who showed up under cover of night all the way back in Dust Bowl Kansas to set the Brothers' original wanderings in motion—until news of the Media Center's Grand Opening reaches me via the daytime TV station I keep on at a low volume above the tropical fish tank in my waiting room.

WELL AWARE OF THE OBSCENE TRAFFIC WE'LL face as we leave the city and head to Cooperstown, I cancel my Saturday patients and load the family into the Audi my practice has recently allowed me to splurge on. I can't say how long or short the drive proves to be, so overwhelming is our collective excitement to see and perhaps even touch what we've been promised are genuine items worn, carried, and handled by the Brothers themselves, preserved intact and archived by those few scholars whose Squimbop Studies blossomed into viable careers.

"The *Real* Brothers Squimbop, stars of the *Condition*," I tell my children as we weave and lurch through traffic, past pig roasts and souvenir booths by the roadside and then past reenactors of all the classic scenes, some of whom have no compunction about re-staging the grisliest moments from the house on Cielo Drive.

"*Those Brothers* are the ones whose Model T we are about to behold in person," I marvel aloud. But it turns out there's no need to impress this upon my children, who are, if anything, even more steeped in Squimbop lore than I am, whereas my wife regards our fervor with a more than healthy skepticism, just as she does in the *Condition* itself, painfully torn between her calling to bear the Brothers again and again and her calling to attain fruition on her own terms, as the star of her own life, beyond the scope of the Saga. My boys, having absorbed whatever version of this Saga was fed to them through the channels by which children these days access what they take to be the world, faint and revive and faint again as the parking attendants motion us onward with spitting torches, past a wax Mountain House already melting in the sun and into the heart of the parking complex, where two tremendous stuffed Brothers bob in the dry summer air, cooling thousands of Audis in the shadows between them.

We park and recite the ground rules. Then I purchase a Family Day Pass at the Membership Desk and lead my family into a vestibule modeled on the entrance to the school where the Professor taught. The boys skip along, already testing the length of their tether, while my wife pulls up the straps of the black dress someone must've given her for Halloween. She makes a show of refusing to notice the cardboard cutout of a woman who looks just like she does, eating cornbread in a diorama of the Brothers as youths in

Kansas, but I sense her discomfort and wish it were my fate to soothe it.

In the Gift Shop, we pass a Dr. Forearm display, which the attendant tells us is brand new. "Arrived last night," she says, her eyes already upon me like she can spot a weakness I will only recognize in myself at the end of this section. "We set it up just before you got here," she simpers, though neither my wife nor my children seem to find this notable.

Still, I've read this part before, so I make no attempt to stop myself from saying, "I think I'll browse a little before going in. Catch up with you later." Then, as if the Media Center itself has interceded, relieving me of the responsibility of all first-order interaction, my family is gone, immersed in the early halls that detail the Brothers' disastrous stint as adjunct professors in the deep south and lower Midwest.

Alone for the first time since dawn, I pry my gaze off the *Condition* where it sprawls in a dozen languages between a rack of Pervert Uncles and a pile of balsa-wood Angel House kits and puzzles in boxes whose covers show an impressionist painting of the Bloody, Bloody Road to Dodge City. I float through the Gift Shop, along a shelf of popular histories of the Wax Museum, half of them arguing for the existence of the Hall of Unremembered Escapades and half arguing against it, until I come to a stop before a rack of blood test equipment to the left of the Dr. Forearm display. I study the boxes, which sport a graphic of dozens of heads bobbing in a bloody river.

"Want to feel the real thing?" the girl at the counter coos and I can't help seeing myself for the middle-aged cliché I am, or am about to become, as I turn, mouth open and tongue slack, and nod. I try to say something casual but she's already slid the ON BREAK sign across the checkout counter and taken a key ring into the dark of the storeroom in back. I look around, at once afraid of being watched and hoping to find myself still browsing the displays, beyond the grip of what I know the *Condition* has in store. I find instead that I've already followed her out of the Media Center's public zone and into the sanctum where the events the Center commemorates perpetually occur.

My wife and children must be deep into the Brothers' trip to Europe by now, yet I find I cannot muster much concern at the prospect of never seeing them again. I feel something else taking over, pulling me into a space that awaits me alone. Now all I hope is to remain lucid enough to witness what's been planned. The girl, no longer a Gift Shop girl, leads me down staircase after staircase, deeper into the earth, beneath the realms of rock and magma and into the realm of memory, and from there deeper still, beneath the realm of anyone's memory and into that of everyone's.

I look up when I feel something dripping and see the undersides of stranded minds clustered among the mica and limestone, unable to let go despite the obvious distress of their estrangement from the Saga.

"Right this way," my guide urges, reaching out for me. "Down into the Blood, so that you might feel the Trace as such."

She leads me deeper still, down a slippery outcropping and out of my clothes, then out of my skin, into the Blood, deep red and so salty it smells burnt, like the ash of ancient wood. "Flowing through the spine of the *Condition*," she seems to say, though her voice is remote and distorted. "Animating the dead matter spread across its pages. Making of it a space in which life can evolve, a nutritive bath in which decomposition and recomposition fuse into a single divine process. Call it Dead Sir if you'd like; call it nothing if you'd rather."

I immerse myself in the vat of my kind, the womb where all Squimbops originate before a black-clad woman is called upon to birth them. The brine softens my flesh and draws my essence into its depths while I draw its essence into mine. I bob and feel the particulars of my life seep out, unclogging and unfurling and drifting off; my practice in Flushing and my home in Great Neck and my Audi in the parking lot turn soft as stewed prunes and float off into the great general being of the Squimbop Condition, of which the Sagas gathered in the book I found in Boston are but the merest sample. Soon I'm nothing but a nub, bumping against others. "Neophytes," my guide whispers, unconcerned that her voice now comes from within me. "Drowned men rescued from the Inland Seafloor and repurposed. Restuffed, packed with the Trace so that, when the time comes, you, or the Squimbop you will then be, a Squimbop whose nametag will only happen to read *Dr. Forearm*, will draw it out and thereby prove that your kind has not sunken forever beneath the level of detection. You will prove that the Brothers are genetically real and distinct, and thus keep the Golden Age from slipping into folklore and from there out of being entirely."

My guide, herself unfurled in the vat beside me, nothing but braided hair and flaps of flesh strewing out from my skeleton, encircles me and together we float, bobbing and cleaving together as we tighten and loosen and tighten again.

"You'll never be sure you were down here," she warns, as I lean my head back in the liquid, straining to locate her voice within the tidal rush. "You'll never know if I took you here or not, if it's something you did or something you read, so let me say now that you were here. Here you are. Try to absorb this fact while the vat absorbs you."

I SINK DEEPER, SEEKING A YELLOW LIGHT IN THE far distance, swimming toward it like it's the source of all breathable air in an anaerobic world, dragging my body downward while faces press in, Media Center guests who paid to see the special exhibit, their palms crushed against the glass, sucking air in and out in mockery of my conundrum as I paddle downward, the Blood flowing out of my sides, the skin around me tangling into weeds and a rusted anchor chain and the underside of a barnacle-mottled houseboat, radiating purple light toward the yellow at the bottom. Now I'm there. I make a final push, my lungs trembling, my lips trembling, my eyes flying out of my face, seeking the far shore, beyond the husks of innumerable seekers.

When I surface, I glimpse a skeleton crew—two teenagers and an old man in tucked-in polo shirts and pleated khakis—dragging a cadaver out of the Holy River attraction I must've wandered down to on my own, famous from the part in the *Condition* where Dr. Forearm dives in and reemerges as Jim Squimbop himself, never again to live in alienation from his essence. I overhear one crew member whisper, "Another man down. Another damn husk in the drink. Another lonely Forearm seeking the Trace."

"Looks like he found it," one of the others sniggers, as they dump the body onto a pallet and toss a towel over its midsection. I stand in the buzzing shadows, my heart out of alignment, my muscles slack and stretched and achy, wondering how I got here, who fished me out if not the crew I just watched fish out that poor drowned man.

I lean against the rock wall bounding the river on this side and watch the crew drag him away and I give in more fully to the suspicion, absurd as it seems, that the man is me and I am... someone else. Someone new. A replacement, a stand-in. An improvement. I scratch my bare chest and tug at the place where my heart feels provisionally inserted and return to the Ether Monument on the Boston Common, where I am still both awaiting my Brother's arrival and hurrying there to meet him.

The crew vanishes around a corner and I walk on until a curtain of steam fans out from the rock wall and I turn toward it, my movements automatic and unfamiliar, like whoever I am now comes here often after a bracing soak in the Blood. In the room the steam was billowing from, dozens of men sit wrapped in towels on tiled benches, the air pink and gamey between us, iron mixed with eucalyptus and sweat and the hot breath of unrecovered millennia, straining to emerge in words we'll never say.

I could be any of you, I think, while the man I've become interjects, You already are. Enjoy the communion. Determined to do so, I lay our heads against the slick tiled wall and then, for a dozen minutes, we bask in the heat and the smell as the pink air turns clear and the steam gusts in and the iron reek dissipates and, though we fight it, the point of departure comes into view. We can come here once a month, once a week maybe if we insist, every Sunday, every Saturday *and* Sunday if we're a little insane and divorced or married to women who humor us, who ferry our children from exhibit to exhibit overhead while we soak in the gloaming down here, firming up memories of having been part of a Brotherhood, of having soaked in an ancient river replete with an ineffable and trans-historical Trace animating the *Condition*, rendering it more than a book we discovered in grad school and never got over, but even so, even if we conspired to come here every day, even if we clung to the walls, the time would come when the steam would go cold and there would be no alternative to heaving up from our metal bench, dizzy and nauseous, and tottering out to the showers to hose off. We rub pink soap in our groins and armpits and pull some through our hair. Then we wrap ourselves in the Media Center towels piled by our lockers and fumble with combination locks set to the dates of our first children's birth, and then it's time to step into our soiled boxers, our too-tight khakis, our wrinkled undershirts and button-ups and inside-out socks, and put our wallets in our back pockets and our house and car keys in front, and maybe we dab a little powder under our arms and a little cream on our noses and then we step balefully out of our union and I walk upstairs, looking away from the scummy men climbing alongside me. I go straight to the Gift Shop, where I await the family I came with, already disowning the long soak I'm no longer sure I took in the pure Blood of the Brotherhood to which I'm no longer certain I ever belonged.

I RECONVENE WITH MY WIFE AND CHILDREN IN the Gift Shop, straining to ask how their tour went and which exhibits were their favorites and what they learned about the Brothers that they'd never known before, looking all the while at the cardboard Tommy Bruno cutout beside the *Squimbop Fever* Monopoly sets for reassurance. When these preliminaries are complete, I tip all the Blood Kits off the shelf into my basket, carry them to the counter, and ask the girl who replaced my guide what it would cost to order ten thousand of these.

"You think you'll need that few?" she asks, raising an eyebrow. "To find the Trace?"

I shrug and flush, shrinking at the magnitude of the work to be done. "A hundred thousand then. A million."

We can't be having this conversation, yet she replies, "One million it is," and punches that number into the register with one hand while pushing a pen cap in and out of her mouth with the other. "Will that be cash or card?"

I hand over a stack of cards while my family browses Squimbop Suits and plays with the trick knives and I think I hear the girl say, "No more of the ol' American MC Escher routine, I suppose. No more mercury games. Time to get serious, eh Doctor? Find the Trace before you retire."

She grins when I focus on her mouth, refusing to hint at whether she was, until just now, saying the words I heard her say.

"What's that?" I ask, as I put my cards back in my wallet and watch two young Squimbops stab a scarecrow beside a dumpster out the window.

"Oh nothing," she replies, as she turns to assist another customer.

Having maxed out every card in my name, I drive us all home, a return journey even more abbreviated than the journey here, as if now we live directly behind the Media Center, our home one of its outlying exhibits. All around Cooperstown new developments simmer in a valley beneath the remnants of Mountain Houses on hazy summits in the afternoon heat, fences and tractors and gravel pits, identical homes and lawns and outbuildings spreading across the open territory while my million Blood Kits roll out, as perhaps I did too once, from the Factory with the burning yellow light. They race across the lunar expanse that once served as bed for the Inland Sea and serves now to permit an unlimited quantity of identical dwellings to sprawl, one of which has to be ours, knowable only by the convergence of trucks bearing down upon it to unload the materials that will enable my denouement to commence.

The Brothers Squimbop Golden Age

It really was the Golden Age. The Brothers Squimbop, Jim and Joe, at the absolute height of their fame, tore up the coast of the continent that'd formed to receive them. They floored the accelerator of the '33 Model T they'd found idling in the Media Center parking lot all the way back in Cooperstown, blaring "Me and the Devil Blues" over an impeccably detailed vintage radio with the windows open and the top down, their hair rippling in the salty breeze off the Inland Sea.

Mountains rose and fell as fluidly as waves in the water, their steepness just one facet of the pinnacle the Brothers were perched upon, here at the center of all the confused and desperate attention that swirled around them. Their wheels glided without friction along the empty roads and for long stretches they forgot the ship hitched to their rear, bumping and rolling along on casters. Its antic pace only bolstered their antic mood now that the Golden Age was peaking and all the schisms their forebears had surmounted to get here had been put to rest, blessing the present with the kind of peaceful unity that only arrives after a nearly world-annihilating cataclysm—and only for those few who have, through luck, ingenuity, or fate, survived it.

The highest coast roads were barely one lane wide, snaking over crags and cliffs and across chain bridges hundreds of feet in the misty air, tilting nearly perpendicular to the water as they twisted to cut the wind before plunging through tunnels so long and narrow the ship sent off sparks on both sides as the Brothers forced it through darkness.

When they emerged on the far side, sometimes hours later, the sun was always sizzling near the center of the sky, bouncing a few degrees to the right and then a few to the left, as if they'd journeyed to the very top of the world or knitted it into a new shape, that of the Golden Age, with all of day compounded in a yellow orb on one side and all of night—the night did still fall, hot and fragrant, silky and stuffed with much they were glad not to see—on the other.

On the longest days, when the sun knocked itself shapeless against the narrow edges of its orbit, the Brothers sped up as they could feel a beam of attention seeking them from the Inland Sea, the haze across the horizon tightening into the outline of a distant eye. They couldn't see the shape of that eye's face, but they knew it was out there, watching them, at once urging them deeper into the Golden Age and, by freighting it with a burden beyond what they could shoulder, already seeding that Age's irrevocable end.

THE EYE TRACKED THEM UNTIL THE MOUTH OF ANother tunnel appeared and they plunged gratefully into it, gasping as the hot air turned cold. The rocky floor might start horizontal, but it soon wound down toward the center of the hollow earth, warping and denting the voice on the radio until the rich Mississippi blues glitched into the chirps of bats and the grunts of cave-dwelling sapiens who commanded the Brothers to prepare for their performance. To stand and deliver as what they were, the Brothers Squimbop alone and immaculate in the heart of the Golden Age, for whose sake those who'd come before had given everything.

For the first few moments of this altered broadcast, each continued to entertain his own taboo longings for the lives they'd left behind in Cooperstown, the sale rack at White's sagging with meatloaf, but the sapiens never failed to make their point. The burden of the present never failed to eclipse that of the past as it settled over the Brothers in their Model T, whose top they could not close. A golden light spread through the tunnel until the featureless underground expanse took on the trappings of an antechamber and the dispersion of their longing pulled into the tight focused center of their shared mind, where the script for tonight's performance was always already running.

THEY EMERGED INTO THE ARENA OF THE MOUNTAIN House like two gladiators summoned from a pit to which only one would return, the sky so dark they could never tell if they'd exited the underground or breached a giant cavern within it. Regardless of whether it was Jim or Joe behind the wheel, he let his hands sink into his lap as the car dragged to a stop in the rapidly filling parking lot and the Mountain House came into relief out of the hot, muggy night.

By the time both Brothers were standing, the log and glass contours of the Mountain House façade had grown just definite enough to dispel the memory that, a moment ago, no such edifice had existed there. They forgot—and knew they were forgetting—that they had come to rest at an arbitrary point in the endless night and only after stopping had the parking lot, the Mountain House, and now their growing legion of fans, rising like mist from shrouded vehicles, converged upon the spectacle about to occur.

A coterie of assistants escorted them through a side door, across a lobby strewn with yellowed reams of Golden Age paraphernalia—masks and LPs and postcards, mints and chocolate bars and Squimbop Suits in a dozen sizes, with matching hats and trick knives, all of it at once current and defunct, set up for *this* show while also remaindered from the shows of yesteryear—and into the green room where assistants begat assistants, swarming the Brothers' faces with powder puffs and eye brushes, primping their lips and working cinnamon-scented jelly into their hair. By the time they'd been pushed through the stage door with a curt, "The Producer wishes you luck," they couldn't have scuttled the show if they'd chosen to.

So there they were, on the wide oak boards of the Mountain House stage in the Catskills and the Adirondacks and the Berkshires and the Rockies, boards trodden by Caruso and Callas and Houdini, before an audience that grew every time they squinted through the spotlight to regard it. They squinted in their costumes and makeup and hairdos and mimed confusion as to what tack to take next until the hall grew musky and swollen with laughter. Even the rams and elk mounted on the stone walls above the many cinder-choked hearths grinned, pursing their desiccated lips to reveal black gums beneath caramel-colored teeth.

The Brothers peered out in shock at their crowd, lewdly miming to one another how large it had grown, a gesture that caused them to fall backwards with over-exertion, their arms spread so wide they nearly dislocated their shoulders. When they'd bounced back to their feet, riding a fresh surge of laughter, they blinked and shook their heads as if they couldn't fathom how and why so many people had turned up to luxuriate in their distress. And where, they wondered—and mimed wondering, peering into the far back of the house—had so many people come from?

They searched inside the abandoned general stores and gas stations that creaked across the stage against an unfurling backdrop of Nebraskan Elks Lodges and Arkansan Chambers of Commerce clustered around the diner where so many drifter heads had been shucked and stuffed in the dumpster out back.

By this point in the routine, the sets had grown so real—now the Brothers basked in the glow of the supermarket that had once lit the laborious composition of their distant ancestor's Nuclear Dissertation—that they visibly forgot they were onstage and committed to the prospect of roaming a land whose people had vanished long ago, leaving in their wake nothing but wolves, armadillos, and dripping spigots. They climbed the weedy verges of boarded-up Shoney's and Braum's drive-thrus and ducked into deserted Motel 6's in AstroTurfed enclosures marked "Michigan" and "Montana," tracing the sacred stations of what had long ago become known as the Squimbop Trail.

No matter where they went, they saw no one, never a living soul. All dead, consumed by the Fever, forced underground, out of the Golden Age and into a remission from which, the Brothers couldn't help but worry, if only through the avatars of the Brothers they were playing, sub- and pseudo-Squimbops might one day reemerge to challenge the uniqueness of the duo who happened to be onstage tonight.

They kept pace with the scene changes, from the bowels of a Louisiana Community College to the piney heights of a Swiss mountain hamlet, from the outbuildings of Spahn Ranch to the blood-soaked house on Cielo Drive, from the cold Pacific beaches of the far Northwest to the open Kansas prairie and, on the other side of the farm curtain that the wizard's daughter held open, into the frantic mummers' parade on the Bloody, Bloody Road to Dodge City, all culminating in the blast that flooded the stage with gleaming blue cellophane and flopping rubber fish, sending the Angel House they'd dragged so long behind their Model T shooting out to the rescue, crowning the first act with riotous applause.

The curtains, with GOLDEN embossed on one and AGE on the other, drew shut, hiding the Brothers away as they bobbed aboard Angel House while Tommy Bruno fired up his machine in the foyer and the audience, whose feet never touched the carpet, drifted up the aisles to avail themselves of its bounty.

During the intermission, the Brothers recommenced their life aboard Angel House, settling back into the old odd couple routine. One captained the ship and watched old tapes in the den while the other receded into the ether, manifesting as the voice of their Distant Master.

As soon as the den Brother succumbed to the desperation that resulted in his dropping anchor, the curtain reopened and the second act began. The anchor careened through a trapdoor in the stage and the force of its descent knocked both Brothers into a reverie wherein hundreds of Squimbop skulls, diffused through time and space, snapped into alignment like beads along the anchor's chain, totemic and orderly, one atop the other in perfect sequence. The desperate uncertainty permeating the Golden Age resolved as the anchor plunged into the silt and the World Tree took root, manifesting an ordered cosmos from the rank chaos of the Inland Sea.

Here—the Brothers could never be certain what, if anything, their audience perceived at this point in the show—the Saga reset, beginning as it always began. The anchor's impact compelled the growth of a new town, its denizens rising like mushrooms from the spongy terrain, already drunk on nostalgia for the world they were about to gain and then lose. The Professor awoke inside Angel House, which appeared now as a mansion on the Outskirts of this town. He showered, shaved, shined his alligator-skin boots, and began his walk along the outlying roads toward the diner for breakfast, his empty briefcase swinging by his side.

After breakfast, he marched to the schoolhouse to deliver a series of Lectures to the town's children until, driven mad by having forsaken the sea to accept a teaching post far beneath his calling, he summoned a Media Center from the vast storeroom under the stage and, soon enough, two boys, likewise summoned from that storeroom, set about trying on Squimbop Suits and flicking trick knives in the Gift Shop, then sliding behind the wheel of a Model T in the parking lot, "Me and the Devil Blues" wailing through the open top and into the salty air.

They tore along terrifying mountain roads, past an eye hovering on the horizon, then through interminable hollow-earth tunnels until they finally arrived, to applause so loud it shattered the glass in the elk-horn chandeliers overhead, on this very stage, in this very Mountain House, deep in the very Golden Age that, as recently as intermission, had seemed over and done with, cast into an exile from which there could be no return.

The applause went on and on as the Brothers took their bows onstage, both inside and outside the play at once, as if there were two stages and two diverging paths toward it, just as there were two of them, their ears and sinuses crushed from the pressure of being both.

THEIR HEADS EXPLODED IN GOUTS OF RED CONfetti. Then, having concluded the encore, they took their final bows, humped down in loose shirts so they appeared headless as the stagehands escorted them into the green room, under framed photos of happy scout troops and search-and-rescue teams on wooden skis, five-generation family reunions and jowly Santas pulling Tiffany ornaments from red felt bags.

As the stagehands sponged the Brothers' faces clean, they slouched in their canvas armchairs and watched their former skin return, long since bored with the revelation that this too looked like makeup, the *Face of the Brothers Squimbop,* over-familiar as that of a president on a postage stamp. The possibility that their own faces had been occluded by the Brothers' likewise felt drained of savor. Still, they gnawed at it beneath the stagehands' mentholated gauze, wondering if, one night, the towelettes and cotton balls would peel the Squimbop Face away. Then the Golden Age would end or—they allowed themselves to imagine—begin in earnest, purged of the creep of stages-upon-stages that had left them floating in space.

When they stepped from their chairs and into the lull between the post-show cleanup and their surreptitious escape, past the crowds of autograph hounds and parking lot impersonators, they sometimes tried to converse with Tommy Bruno where he sat counting the money at a folding table by the door, but he flinched every time they approached and never responded when they asked why. Perhaps it's only that we've caused him to lose count, the Brothers used to console themselves, but even then, even so early in the Golden Age, they'd known the reason was deeper and stranger than that. Now they didn't ask.

After the stagehands turned the Brothers over to their Producer's security crew, they were escorted through the throng and back to their Model T, which started of its own accord and drove them again along the mountain roads to the motel where their room had been readied.

HERE THEY SETTLED INTO THEIR BEDS, JIM always toward the window and Joe always toward the door, facing away from one another as they removed their pens and journals from their kit bags and began to write.

In this rare unrushed silence, they spun tales of an authentic life in Cooperstown, of moving from year to year with only a general awareness of the Golden Age, tracking the Brothers as they aged on TV. If one asked the other what he was writing, the response was always, "How your mother and I made you in a rest stop shower with six other guys watching," so neither ever did.

Nevertheless, when they laid down their pens and turned off their side lights, the thrill of the Mountain Houses returned. Alone in the dark with their journals closed, there was no reason not to bask in the pride of yet another smash-hit performance, yet more proof that this really was the Golden Age, a fact at once obvious and impossible to comprehend.

As this pride surged from their bodies, it expanded to fill the dusty space between their chests and the blades of the ceiling fan. It breathed in and out like it had a chest of its own and seemed to whisper to the Brothers: "This is not for you. Never forget that. It is the Golden Age for everyone else, that by which all past and future generations will define themselves according to their distance. But never for you. The two of you can never reach it," the voice hesitated, as if drawing out the approach to a showstopping punchline, "because you're already here!"

It bobbed and gloated, sucking up the last of the air in the punchline's aftermath until the Brothers couldn't breathe and one or the other got up and hurried to the bathroom and locked the door, sitting on the toilet in his boxers with the sink running and the lights on until the phone on the nightstand rang.

When it did, the other Brother—every morning, each remembered himself as the one still in bed, consigning the other to the locked bathroom—picked it up, tipping the filthy receiver onto the side of his face.

"Hello?"

"Hello," their Producer replied, in the voice of their Distant Master. "Everything is in order. Your next engagement is booked. Stick to the schedule and keep to the mountain roads, as the Fever is still spreading. Your rap sheet is still growing. It will not be so funny should they catch you for what you've done. You will seek my forgiveness then and you will not find it."

As soon as the Producer hung up, the other Brother emerged from the bathroom and said, "Who was that?" triggering a hilarious suite of doubts as to where the call had come from.

AS THE TOUR CONTINUED, ONWARD TO THE NEXT engagement and the next and the next after that, their confusion and the alternating denial and panic it induced in them grew increasingly odious to Tommy Bruno, who now set up his table outside the green room, in the parking lot among the most desperate fans where they clustered in homemade Squimbop leisurewear until they returned to the vapor they'd coalesced from.

The more spooked and befuddled the Brothers became, gripping the wheel of their Model T with "Me and the Devil Blues" wailing over the radio until they appeared on the massive Mountain House stage in search of the most provisional teaching jobs, the harder their audience laughed and the larger it grew. It came to seem as though this laughter were itself the reproductive process, the animating principle of the Primal Scene that underlay them all, generating ever more bodies by filling the air with spores which implanted and grew in the urine and beer that had soaked the ancient cushioned seats.

The spectacle of men leaning together then leaning apart to produce more men, so many that soon all notion of tickets and assigned seating became an item of Mountain House lore, wasn't lost on the Brothers but, from their vantage onstage, any concern the spectacle produced was only part of what made it so funny.

So they took another bow and returned to the green room for their cleansing, watching Tommy Bruno carry his table outside, then stagger back in with an envelope for each of them. After taking what he offered with a grunt of gratitude, they set out on the road again, speeding over cliffs so sheer two of their four wheels scraped the outer edge, knocking gravel into the waves a thousand feet below until they dead-ended in the lot of tonight's motel.

Inside, they lay in bed until one of them got up and—as each had written in his journal, terrified that his Brother would see—*went to the bathroom to make the call.* They sprawled there with the receiver on their ear, listening to the voice that never wavered in the authority it claimed to wield. Then, blinking and bleary, they regrouped at checkout time, peeling poppyseeds from plastic muffin wrappers and taking turns making coffee in the single-cup machine beside the rusted-out water fountain.

BACK IN THE MODEL T, THE RADIO SANG ITS USUAL song but, the deeper they plunged into the earth, the more tormented the broadcast became, as if the voice were strangling in the thinning air. "Another eight hundred dead," the Mississippi bluesman groaned over the wrenching strings of his acoustic guitar, as the Brothers rolled through glistening grottos and sheer walls of salt, "another eight hundred thousand dead. Another eight million, eight billion, what does it matter dead... the toll the Fever takes in pursuit of the Golden Age is infinite."

As they forced their way almost vertically down through shafts and crevices lit only by the sparks from the ship behind them, the underground shifted along with the radio and they caught glimmers of these numbered dead, slotted upright in the rock, deep rows of bodies felled by the Fever, cut down for no crime other than their failure to embody the *Real Brothers Squimbop.*

There but for the grace of our Producer go we, Jim and Joe each thought as the Model T scraped through a dense gamut of skulls, some crushed to powder and others still half-covered in skin. Angel House scraped louder behind them, dislodging hair and gristle that grew into a cloud, filling their rearview mirror with the outline of a giant's body.

On the far side of a stretch of total darkness, they noticed two long, veiny arms hovering over the windshield, smothering their view of the Killing Fields. Jim or Joe gripped the wheel tighter, but both Brothers could tell this was only a gesture to downplay the obvious fact that these arms, and whatever body they extended from, had risen from the mass grave to push their routine toward its Finale.

AFTER CLEARING REGIONS SO DENSE WITH SKULLS there was no way to avoid crushing them, stirring up clouds of bone dust that only brought the arms into sharper relief, the Brothers rolled through the ruins of Dodge City, past White's and around a grotto that glowed purple with the light of a ship buried in its sludgy depths. On the far side, they emerged into a teeming Mountain House parking lot, the same as any, but choked this time with vans and buses bearing the slogan *Down With the Brothers Squimbop: Long Live the Skwimbop King!*

On the way to the green room, they passed a man with a megaphone shouting, "The evidence is in! The pretenders must be stopped! They cannot even trust each other anymore. They are unraveling in the sham privacy of their motel room nights. Down with all duos, down with all pretenders. Long Live the Singularity, Long Live the One True Skwimbop King!"

Spindly forms emerged from the background dripping purple water. They joined in the chant, pumping what passed for fists with each repetition of "Skwimbop King!"

Though the Brothers managed to bypass this crush without succumbing to it, by the time they got onstage, their headache was so intense they heard themselves moaning, "Who will save us from the giant we've awoken? Who? Who??"

The audience laughed and cheered but their voices rang hollow in the vast auditorium, and at intermission Tommy

Bruno's cries of "Fresh popcorn, come and get it!" sounded spooked in a way they never had before. Even the familiar concern that their fear was part of the act no longer felt as familiar as it once had, nor did the act's pretention seem guaranteed to spare them from calamity.

By the time the Angel House anchor had summoned the town in which the show's Finale played out, depositing the Brothers on the second-order stage they always ended up on after reenacting their flight from Cooperstown, all they wanted was to burrow back into the Angel House den and watch what happened next on television, a snifter of port in hand. *Please let us off here*, they begged their Distant Master as they took their headless bows in red confetti and fought for balance against wave after wave of applause, though mixed this time with sundry hisses and boos. *We never return to where we started, yet we never end up anyplace else. Please, if you're out there, deliver us from this Condition.*

They kept their distance from Tommy Bruno even after he'd counted the money, so much so that he had to clear his throat three times before they took their envelopes and forced their way through the parking lot, past table after table of Skwimbop King paraphernalia—homemade shirts and posters and DVDs and mimeographed pamphlets on the *Hidden Culling of the Skwimbop Race* and rolling papers embossed with the slogan *He Will Rise Again, the Trace is Not Extinguished.*

When their Producer called on the motel phone that night, the tone he employed was not the one he'd employed before. This time, both Brothers were in their beds; neither had gone to the bathroom. Since the moment was already unlike any of its predecessors, they decided to render it even more so by turning on the TV. The screen fizzed alive with grainy footage of the Brothers tap dancing, tripping, and rolling around on an old oak stage before cutting to an obese silhouette in a dim office, holding a handsome mahogany receiver to its ear.

"Well," the silhouette said into the phone onscreen, their Producer's voice issuing first from the TV and then from the phone console on the nightstand, set to Speaker. "It seems you've reached the next phase of the tour. The Grand Finale, right on time. Like clockwork, my friends." He grinned at someone offscreen, refilled a snifter from a bottle of port and added, "The Real Mountain House, after so many gaseous simulacra. In the final reckoning, there is only one. Only one real Mountain, with one real House." He removed a velvet handkerchief from his breast pocket as the shot pulled in on him blotting a tear from his left eye. Then he held the cloth under a green banker's lamp on his desk, as if searching for a diamond crushed in its folds.

"Like the brightest, sweetest day of summer, like the high solstice itself, your next act will crown the Golden Age and, in so doing, set its end in motion. *The Golden Age of the Golden Age*, right before the long decline. Before the eons of ships in the night. What is the longest day of the year if not the day when the days begin to shorten?"

The question echoed in the dim room onscreen and out into the dim room where the Brothers lay listening. "No Golden Age ends by accident. This is the secret, so little known, yet so inarguably true, that binds the course of history together. No Golden Age has ever risen from the depths of the Inland Sea," the huge man squinted at his desk, as if straining to read these words off a printed sheet, "that did not contain the seed of its own undoing, hard and knotty and waiting in its soft fibrous center."

With this, he pushed up from his deep armchair, turned off his banker's lamp, coughed into the crook of his arm, and lumbered toward the door on the far side of the room. "*The Trial of the Brothers Squimbop* is hereby convened. All because the two of you willed it so. All because you'd grown sick of Mountain Houses. Weary of the weight you were chosen to shoulder. Now, behold..."

He spread his arms from one edge of the screen to the other, pushing his enormous belly to the center of the frame as he worked to dislodge it from the glass wall the Brothers were watching through. When he had, he carried away a framed painting of the two of them in their motel beds, their hair tousled beneath woolen sleeping caps. He lumbered under the painting's weight as a wash of morning light cascaded into the courtroom that had been winched into position behind him. After hanging the frame on the wall, he strode to the bench and donned a black judge's robe and a white powdered wig just as the wall in the Brothers' motel room collapsed. The same crew who'd provided so many rounds of hair and makeup surged through the wires and plaster dust shouting, "Stay where you are, this is a raid!"

The Brothers leaned up in bed, torn between watching and reacting, so that, even as the agents dragged them through the courthouse lobby, positioned where the motel lobby should have been, past rows of booklets and DVDs on *The Trial of the Brothers Squimbop* and, in a shabby, distant corner, *The Mistrial of the Brothers Squimbop*, they couldn't determine what their role in this routine was meant to be.

By the time they'd settled into the Defendants' seats, *The Trial* already felt like the classic it had surely always been. It was almost incidental that they happened to be the ones on trial—they were as eager as anyone there to behold the spectacle, planned for them beneath an eternal yellow light in the one room they could never enter.

They squirmed and fidgeted while the opening charges were read out, the full sweep of the Fever and the billions dead in its wake established for the sake of all those present—second- and third- and fourth-order beings, bred from their own laughter on beer-stained seats. In a nave to the side of the Judge's bench, Tommy Bruno took notes on a stenographer's pad while frequently glancing up to check on his popcorn machine and soda fountain parked in the back corner of the courtroom.

"Having rendered the earth habitable for nothing but the grinning, mindless pseudo-Squimbops who fill this chamber, the two of you, the *Real Brothers* as you've come to be known, are accused of crimes beyond what were once called *crimes against humanity*. You are the embodied *Homo Sacer*, the sacred man whose crime defies language and thus, quite literally, cannot be encapsulated by any sentence I might pronounce."

"Is this a show trial?" one of the Brothers—the names Jim and Joe, though printed on the plaques in front of them, no longer consented to any involvement with the third dimension—interrupted. "Because if it is, then we demand to know our roles. Do we defend ourselves? Do we hasten the sentencing? Do we flee?"

"There is, as I've said, no sentence," repeated the Judge. "My only intention here is to—"

BEFORE THE JUDGE COULD NAME HIS INTENTION, a procession slammed through the courtroom doors, trampling the guards and overturning Tommy Bruno's machine. "Long Live the Skwimbop King!" they shouted, dragging pseudo-Squimbops from their seats and crushing them underfoot with no more regard than they'd shown for the popcorn that flew from the hot glass caddy. "Long Live the Resurrected Dead, Deeper Than Laughter, Deeper Than What These Sham Brothers Have Reduced Our Planet To! Down With All Pretenders! Down With the Golden Age, Long Live the Skwimbop King, In the Heart of the One Real Mountain, The Rightful Seat of All True Land!"

They chanted and smashed and smashed and chanted as the Judge banged his gavel like he couldn't believe he still had to play this role and knew he wouldn't for much longer. "Order! Order in the court!" he moaned, looking at no one.

"This is the Court of the Skwimbop King!" they replied, flipping the stenographer's stand and trampling Tommy Bruno half to death underfoot.

When they made it to the two Defendants, those at the head of the procession grabbed one and hurled him into the fray, where he landed at the feet of the black-clad woman where she sat on a mahogany bench. "Down with the Sham Professor," they shouted. "Long Live the Skwimbop King!" They hoisted the remaining Defendant onto their shoulders and paraded him up to the Witness stand, forcing him onto the high chair with a mixture of reverence and rage.

"Speak!" they shouted, yanking his tie. "For the dead of this land. For the legions of sentient beings whose sentience you sanded down to rote thigh-slaps and simian guffaws in the malty dusk of a hundred sham Mountain Houses, renounce the last of what's in you! Purge yourself of the Squimbop Trace so the Skwimbop King might arise from its absence, replacing your head with his!"

After a long sweep of the courtroom, desperate for some benign force to relieve him of duty, this Brother sighed and let his head roll down his back while a heavier, shaggier head grew from the neck in its place.

He turned to tweeze up the old head and cradle it under his arm. Then the being that now regarded himself—if only because he was so regarded—as the Skwimbop King rose to his feet, hurled his old head at the painting of the Brothers on the wall, and opened his mouth, as eager as anyone present to hear what came out. His new head appeared to hover near the ceiling, as if it were floating or extended on a long thin stalk, or as if the King's body were tremendous beyond human comprehension.

The way in which the crowd drew close and held its breath reminded him of something ancestral, something he knew he should have forgotten, and *had* forgotten, but not, apparently, altogether. An ultimate curtain call that had waited for him with awful patience in the very center of the earth, a location that felt at once unreachably distant and also inescapable since he knew he stood there now, in the High Court of the only Real Mountain House there'd ever been and could ever be.

He inhaled, licked his new lips, and said, in a voice that sounded like a mockery of seriousness but was perhaps the real thing, "For the crime of sapping this world of its vitality, of spreading Squimbop Fever up and down the coasts and across the Inland Sea, of rendering all grounds multiple and hence hardly ground at all, I sentence Professor Squimbop to eternal exile aboard the model of the ship once known as Angel House. The ship he never should've docked in the harbor from which he never should've summoned the unsuspecting community of Cooperstown, into which he never should've introduced the Media Center, to which he never should've taken my Brother and me, and from which my Brother and me—yes, I'll say it one last time, then never again—should never have departed in the Model T we found idling in the parking lot, since look where we ended up!"

The Skwimbop King regarded the Professor where he cowered beneath the black-clad woman and a look passed between them that announced itself as the last of the silent language they had shared throughout their long journey. A look that was legible to the audience as the coup de grâce, the crowning expression of the Golden Age's final act, destined to be reproduced across an unbroken chain of postcards and shot glasses, should the distant yellow Factory remain open long enough to manufacture them.

Professor Squimbop and the Skwimbop King, each from his own vantage here at the Finale of the Golden Age, could feel the tremendous power vested in all past and future duos in direct proportion to its absence in the present. The Real Brothers must be somewhere, they each understood, precisely because they are no longer here. Because we can at last be certain we are no longer them.

They both regarded the black-clad woman. Under their gaze, she rose and approached, compelled by another strand in the web that had once bound them all together.

When she reached the bench, she leaned against it and turned so the crowd could hear what she had to say. "Boys," she said, her voice grave and precise, exhausted but full of authority, ready to deliver the lines for which she would always be remembered. "Never again will I bear you. Not in a windy cabin in Kansas nor on a bed of moss in the Black Forest. Those days are behind us. Here you are in your final form. You are now entirely in the world of your own making. The world in which men beget men. The world of women is elsewhere, in another place to which I now gladly return. Having borne you so many times, it is now my turn to be born. I wish you neither good nor ill luck, nor do I hope we'll meet again."

SHE LOOKED TOWARD THE CEILING AS A SEAM emerged, beginning in the backmost corner of the courtroom and ripping across the center toward the Judge. When it had opened all the way, she held out her arms and allowed them to be grasped from the other side, holding on until her feet disappeared. The courtroom breathed as one for a long spell, inhaling the sweat and musk of the closing seam and listening to the patter of dripping blood on the polished wooden floor.

When the seam had closed, leaving only a row of tight stitches, the Judge sighed, as if about to speak, but turned instead to flies and ash. His face flaked away as it began to laugh, flies pouring from the mouth until it was a mouth no longer. When it was only flies, they laughed harder still, and said, chattering as one, "Tommy Bruno's stand by the door is open! We do hope you've enjoyed the show!"

Then they dispersed, leaving nothing but ash in the Judge's seat, like the remnants of a thousand cigars smoked over the course of a thousand rendered judgements. The crowd swarmed Tommy Bruno's stand, absorbing the butter and salt and candy that remained, even as the popcorn machine and soda fountain, to say nothing of its master, had been smashed beyond repair.

When they'd gobbled their fill, the Skwimbop King mustered his legion to march into the streets beyond the courtroom and begin the long process of building a world they could inhabit together, a mass they could agree to call land, beyond the seep of the Inland Sea.

Meanwhile, Professor Squimbop snuck through the back exit, into the cell reserved for the condemned, and then deeper in, past the executioner's prep room and through a grate in the stone wall, through which perhaps the offal of the executed was meant to run, and then down through the vast storerooms that warehoused the props for all the scenes they'd enacted and those they'd never gotten the chance to.

It wasn't until he'd traversed miles of storage, past shelves of identical boys awaiting activation, that he smelled salt and heard lapping water, glowing purple. When the hulk of the model Angel House, impounded as evidence in the trial, bobbed into view, he stepped aboard without hesitation.

Now you will sail alone, commanded a voice he remembered from another age. *As your Distant Master, I will tolerate no further interruption. You have had your adventure and I have permitted it. Now you will sail, Professor. The towns await.*

WITH ITS COURSE THUS DETERMINED, ANGEL House floated out of the storerooms, through a network of fjords and inlets, and onto the open water. The Land of the Skwimbop King receded into the sunset as the Professor stood on the bow with the evening's first glass of port, reflecting on the Golden Age and his rapidly spreading uncertainty as to his role within it. Was I driving alone all along, he couldn't help but wonder, fleeing the King in his endless grottos? All he could see was those two arms reaching over the Model T, sealing him inside with the radio and the passenger's seat that grew emptier the longer he tried to picture it full.

As this uncertainty spread, it merged with the surface of the sea, which had itself spread around the last of the land, occluding any sightline that might slow its recession into memory. He sipped and listened to the ice cubes crack, a sound that startled him, as if he were squeezing the glass too hard. He felt his eye swelling as it scanned the horizon for the narrow mountain roads along which he and his Brother were surely touring still in their Media Center

Model T, cruising through the windy afternoon with the top down and "Me and the Devil Blues" wailing over the radio as they tried to avoid contact with the eye they could feel tracking them, rendered huge in the gray salt mist.

As he went on staring past the last of the daylight, the Professor populated this spectral coastline with factories the color of rock, closed for generations and falling into terminal decay now that the demand for Squimbop Suits and mints and trick knives was no longer what it had been.

Still, he spotted one Factory with a light burning in its concrete interior, puncturing the sultry blue-gray of the ocean evening with a sensuous golden yellow. There lies the Forbidden Room, he thought, the assembly line upon which history is made, in which my script was written, and is being written, as my Distant Master is at work even now, cognizant of the impossible access he's been granted by forces beyond his ken to remain with his hand on the lever, so that mine—he gripped the Wooden Wheel that steered the ship—might likewise remain upon it, even if only as a shadow of a shadow of a shadow.

As the years aboard Angel House accrued once again, the golden light dimmed and the Professor's attention turned toward revenge. Revenge on the Skwimbop King and the undead hordes he'd anointed and who'd anointed him in return; revenge on that Judge made of flies and ash who'd sanctioned a sentence he could not bring himself to pronounce; revenge on their Producer for having allowed the tour to culminate thus; and revenge on the black-clad woman for having refused to bear them when it mattered most.

"Revenge on myself," he continued aloud, since no one intervened to stop the litany, "and on my Brother for having looked a gift horse in the mouth and refused to go on performing in every Mountain House that would have us, among the brittle brochures and long-unsold stock, once manufactured with the frenzy of wartime in factories that have since grown as cold and decrepit as the woods and hollows around them. And, finally, revenge on my predecessor, for having dropped anchor all those years ago, calling Cooperstown into being where it ought never have been called and seeding it with the Media Center's carnivorous need to consume the futures of two young boys."

And so I will drop anchor again, he decided. I will drop anchor and summon the souls sleeping as sand beneath the sea back into the diners and supermarkets and schoolyards of another town, and another, and another after that, and I will tell them what they really are. I will tell the truth of the Squimbop Condition and in so doing extract what revenge I can for the state they've forced me into. As the Homo Sacer, I will say about myself what could not be said about me. I will drop anchor and force what land arises to become habitable, a new settlement, a new continent, across which I will roam in my madness through all the woods and hollows that care to confront me until I find the Skwimbop King... a scene he could neither refrain from picturing nor force in his mind to culminate.

Most evenings on deck ended like this, followed by his return to the den to polish off the port he'd saved for tomorrow. But on occasion, when the light lingered along the landmass, he'd cut the engine and permit himself to drift toward it, convinced he could see the Model T winding along the narrow cliff roads with Angel House rolling behind, and he'd think, if my ship is there, then I am nowhere. I can't be lost at sea, pining for a Golden Age that ended before its time, for there it is, plain as day and in the fullness of its bloom, impervious to the confusion and loss that are no more than a passing storm in the mind of no one.

During these delicate reprieves, he'd warn himself to back up and let the Brothers drive without coaxing them out to sea through the deviant magnetism of his gaze. He would even decide to reverse course and set sail for the rippling horizon if that's what it took for the Golden Age to continue, but something in him—perhaps the motive force within all the Squimbop activity there had ever been—overrode any attempt to leave the Brothers in peace and followed them ever more closely instead, until his purple shadow darkened their drive, looming over them all the way to their next engagement in a Mountain House that would now appear as no more than a constellation of shadows.

When the stage curtains were just about to part, the Professor donned his robe and descended the Angel House staircase to follow along onscreen in the den, watching the two of them tumble out before their public and mime a confusion that, if it were any less genuine, wouldn't be half as funny. He cried with laughter as they shivered on the freshly waxed boards and the toll-free tickets number crawled along beneath them.

He glanced at the phone beside the cardboard Tommy Bruno cutout and thought of dialing just as the show cut to the scene of their Producer calling them in their motel room at night. The coincidence discomfited him enough that he rose from where he sat, punched in the number, pulled the phone from its cradle, and took it to a porthole, where a golden light fanned out across the becalmed surface of the bay. Part of him knew this was only another nautical sunrise, but the rest saw it as the Golden Age glimmering up from the depths, shining through the sockets of a million emptied skulls. "The silt of their bones is firm yet supple," he whispered into the mouthpiece, turning to watch the Brothers jump onscreen as his voice merged with their Producer's, "while it awaits the next impact of my almighty anchor."

The Squimbop Condition

Professor Squimbop sets out in Angel House to force this year's town into being. Year after year, he leaves one town flooded behind him and crosses the Inland Sea to summon the next, only to flood it and summon the next after that, and the next after that, on and on through the ages, sustaining a culture whose motive force grows ever more opaque the more fully his journey comes to define it. By now he fears he's reached the asymptote of his Condition, beyond which driving the cycle onward will yield no further insight or even accrue as further experience atop the gross superfluity that has accrued so far, clogging the Inland Sea with skulls until its waves barely crest their flaking scalps.

He floats away from another town, leaving another Mayor he's come to love screaming beneath the waves while his Distant Master, to whom he once considered these screams holy tribute, remains silent. In an earlier age, closer to the apex of the Brothers' fame, his Master's voice might've said, *Stay the course, its destination will be revealed in time*, but now, if anyone reassures the Professor, it is the Professor himself, mumbling that perhaps the adventure has become its own reward.

And yet, he wonders, which is more horrifying, an adventure that never ends or one that ends here? "Therefore," he whispers, his throat seizing around the shape of a classic line, passed from throat to throat through the ages, "the time is coming when the path of heroism will be to abandon course, to say enough is enough and thus to force the final chapter, if there is one, to begin."

The chapter in which I find the Skwimbop King and take my revenge for his casting me into this purgatory, he thinks, afraid to utter the thought aloud. The chapter in which I begin my life on dry land, a denizen of a town that will, because I've renounced the black magic of the Angel House anchor, stand the test of time, repelling the waves that nibble its edges and the insidious creep of the Saga out of history and onto its streets and avenues.

NEVERTHELESS, UNTIL HE FINDS THE WILL TO make this decision—and assuming such a decision, once made, can then be acted upon from inside the reality he will then inhabit—he pulls anchor and drops anchor, pulls anchor and drops anchor again, at once awed and repulsed by his silent Master's unwavering certainty of total obedience. He pulls anchor to leave last year's town behind, consigning yet another Mayor to the molten potential from which, as soon as the anchor drops at summer's end, he will be summoned anew, sick with the prospect of a coming annihilation he can already almost remember.

By now the Professor finds he can inhabit a convincing version of the Mayor, lumbering to and from his mansion in the woods, heavy with dread at the prospect of the waves swallowing these woods, the clothesline laden with pornography, the tractors and backhoes arrayed around the lip of the gravel quarry, and the ashes from the Ring of Fire, leaving only the desperation that gave rise to these relics and the town they failed to preserve, its absence animating the Professor as he sails toward its sequel.

"Squimbops leave while Mayors stay / and therein lies all the difference." This line, emerging from the Professor's mouth, strikes his ears as the opening of a poem he was made to memorize in a schoolroom whose particulars he cannot separate from the innumerable schoolrooms he's claimed dominion over in his velvet blazer and alligator-skin boots, empty briefcase by his side. He pushes more air up from his throat to see if more lines emerge. When he's sure that none will, he swallows, wipes his lips, and sails on with his gut bulging just as the Mayor's bulged in the extremis of his pregnancy, at the climax of the Reunion when the Professor led him up to the altar in the woods, unclasped the boning knife from his belt, and, compelled by the silence of his Distant Master, punctured, yet again, the womb from which the Brothers Squimbop would otherwise have been born on a bed of moss at the height of summer.

NOW, WHILE ANGEL HOUSE SAILS AWAY FROM THE remnants of the sunken town, or one just like it, the Professor clutches his belly and flashes back to the image, iconic as any in the Canon, of bending down to the flayed-open Mayor and removing the twins, as if to deliver them safely into the welcoming world. In a gesture that has been reproduced across centuries of painting, etching, and woodcut prints, he holds them before the Mayor's dimming eyes, pulls them apart, and then, with one in each hand, gnaws their flesh, shuddering and gagging and begging his Distant Master either to let him stop or to confirm that he's doing what must be done.

With both twins inside him, settling into the poison bath where they can only decompose, he drags the Mayor's shell into the gravel quarry behind the Ring of Fire. He drags it the same way every time, so expertly that he no longer draws any distinction between enacting and commemorating this canonical event—not even now, when he refrains from wondering whether he's reminiscing aboard Angel House or, once again, incarnated in the woods, dragging the shell he's dragged so many times before, while picturing himself remembering that event from the cool silence of the Angel House deck.

Even to stipulate such a distinction—to wonder, silently or aloud, whether he's defining or observing the Primal Scenes upon which the culture is founded—feels like a Mountain House routine that might've earned laughs or sighs of dread in an earlier, more innocent age but would today earn only groans.

Today, all that remains is to drag the Mayor to the gravel quarry, where the Professor always half-expects to find the giant man already buried, decaying atop earlier Mayors, the difference between bones and gravel no more than an antique heresy. The scene threads through him again as he sits on the Angel House deck in the glow of streetlights beneath the waves, a glow that brightens every time, as if the seafloor were rising, bearing the dead nearer, toward a breakthrough. "And then at last, for me or my offspring," the Professor mugs, clutching his belly to deliver the line, "the End will come. The earth will be as a heaven or a hell for all time thereafter, the Age of Doing and the Age of Remembering fused and indivisible forever."

He belches as the twins squirm and he clasps his port glass tighter, crossing and uncrossing his alligator-skin boots while regarding the dripping anchor on the deck beside him. An instrument of mass murder. Filling the Inland Sea until nothing remains but salt-crusted skeletons beached in a wide circle around a pit. The gravel quarry of all gravel quarries; the mass grave in which all the children who've ever lived and ever will are buried without marker. Overwhelming the seafloor's ability to generate new Squimbops, pouring consciousness from skull to skull until nothing but gray sludge remains.

He muses on the rate of degeneration as the towns rise and fall, stuffing themselves with beings who've already drowned countless times, leaving himself as the only unincorporated entity in the entire scheme of existence, though even this, he knows, is far from certain.

The purple glow fades into a darkness broken only by the yellow Factory on one horizon and the Mountain House for which all its scripts were written on the other. Jerking his head between these stations, he grows frightened and dizzy and, in time, unsure whether there's one light or two, and whether the ocean between them is a genuine expanse of water or a crinkly roll of plastic. He shudders and trembles and, aware of his audience's growing amusement, recites: "Deep in the innermost command center of The Dodge City Film Industry, a deal was struck. A deal that has lasted for millennia and will last for millennia to come. And what deal was that?"

He pauses with a hand cupped to his ear, as he always does at this point in the routine, wishing, as he always wishes, that he could summon the gumption to flub the punchline. "The deal ensuring that, in exchange for eternal life, every instance of Squimbop behavior, no matter how dire or ecstatic, will become the quintessence of pornography for those watching on the next level up. No exceptions, no exemptions. No loopholes, my lovelies!"

The night crackles with distant applause as he leans back in his deck chair to feel the twins inside him, simmering in tawny port, an image whose pornographic charge is unmistakable as it steams off and, through the occult mechanism of The Dodge City Film Industry, makes its way up to the screens waiting on the next level to receive it.

When the image has been received, he gets up, tosses the slush in his port glass overboard, and descends the Angel House staircase, flashing back, as always at this point in the routine, onto the ship where he stowed away with his Brother after their rebirth in the Black Forest, when the prospect of discovering America was still fresh enough to lend purpose to their young lives, and the black-clad woman's threat to stop birthing them had not yet landed with any real weight.

His eyes bead with tears as he remembers that journey and, just for the fun of it, he pretends to be the captain of that ship now, descending belowdecks to investigate a stirring in the freight room. When he gets there, instead of finding the Brothers crouched in sacks of oats, he finds a cardboard Tommy Bruno and a shelf sagging with pornography burned and re-burned onto tapes that used to bear the labels of *The Brothers Squimbop in Kansas, The Brothers Squimbop in Dodge City,* and *Professor Squimbop in the Towns.*

He tweezes out the tape now labeled *Gravel Quarry: Master Cam 1* and feeds it into the VCR. Then he loosens the slacks and blazer he won't put back on until the anchor summons a new town at summer's end, and settles onto the couch with a drink on the armrest while the Mayor onscreen walks through the woods in the snow, carrying a pumpkin pie and wearing a black dress, dusty and wrinkled but still elegant according to the fashions of the day.

The footage jitters through classic clips—mummers rollicking along the Bloody, Bloody Road to Dodge City, the Brothers leaving their childhood home in the Dust Bowl to seek their fortune as Kansan outlaws—while the grain on the recording mixes with the snow falling in the woods, piling on the branches of birches and firs.

The Mayor pushes through to the edge of the quarry and sits down on a folding chair in a circle of tractors and backhoes, creaking in the snow's bright silence. As he waits, the camera zooms into the depths of the quarry, deep enough for the sheets of rock and ice to resolve into layers of skulls packed so tightly that, at first, the stirring in their midst looks like the camera shaking.

But the edges of the frame don't move when the gravel shudders faster and faster until, in a jump cut burned atop layers of ancient Cielo Drive footage, the Professor, naked and impossibly muscled, with an erect penis so large it casts a shadow on the quarry walls, bursts forth, winks at the camera, and leaps up from the depths with enough force to topple the tractors and backhoes.

When he lands on the quarry edge before the Mayor, the two kiss passionately, spilling pumpkin pie until they're both covered in it, licking it off one another's faces and rubbing it through their own hair. Then they walk, hand in hand, both barefoot, through the snow and pine needles, away from the Mayor's Mansion and across a widening townscape toward the purple glow of Angel House.

The Professor in the Angel House den removes his boxers and mashes them into the pile with his slacks and blazer, freeing his penis just as the sparse wintry field begins to heave and bloom, its pale whites and deep greens turning orange and red. The onscreen Mayor whispers, "My Orchard is blooming again. Take me to Angel House. Take me now!"

The Professor onscreen grins, licks pie from his lips, and nods as Angel House, parked at the edge of what's now a steaming, bubbling marsh, casts its purple glow across the screen and out to where the Professor sits watching. Sweat and spilled seed fill the den, rising at once from the carpeting that bears the dead fruit of this scene's endless reiteration and from the seething, livid vines and flowering trees of the Orchard, humming and leaning in to breathe the couple's musk.

When the Mayor in the black dress and the naked Professor, muscled like a warrior in an epic poem, kick down the Angel House doors, the Professor in the den startles, as if the two of them were about to appear at the top of the stairs. He looks around and remembers that, no, the two Angel Houses aren't the same... this Angel House here at sea, that Angel House there in the Orchard... except they are, he thinks, as he strokes himself absentmindedly, watching the screen without quite seeing it. There is only one Angel House, and yet there are infinite versions of it, piled atop one another, so high and precarious they're bound to...

He shudders as the laughter of his distant Mountain House audience—this part of the routine never fails to amuse—returns his gaze to the screen while the Professor kneels before the Mayor on a mattress so large it fills the entire Master Bedroom and, lifting the black dress, takes the Mayor's penis in his mouth.

The Professor in the den watches intently, timing the climax of his routine to that of the one he's watching, tightening his fist when the Professor onscreen bites down and, with the relentless side-to-side shake of a starving wolf, chews through all he's been offered. He swallows while the Professor in the den digs his nails into the base of his own genitals and rips them off, tossing the bundle squeaking and whistling to the feet of the Tommy Bruno cutout where—he mimes looking over in shock—many such bundles have piled up, some shiny and flaccid from overuse while others remain in their Gift Shop boxes with ON SALE (ORGAN OF THE ONE TRUE FATHER) stickers affixed to their cloudy plastic windows.

The Mountain House audience cheers and slaps their thighs while the onscreen Mayor rubs his wound, working it into the orifice from which every Squimbop who's ever existed was born. Then he wipes the blood on the black dress, smiles at the Professor and says, in the illicit film's most beloved line, "My womb is nearly ready. Real life will soon return to this town."

THE PROFESSOR IN THE DEN LICKS HIS TEETH and, though he knows he hasn't swallowed what his onscreen avatar has, he feels it land in his stomach. He leans back on the couch and belches, feeling at once sicker than ever before and exactly as sick as he always feels at this point in the routine. The paradox of both states at once, of Angel Houses piled atop Angel Houses even when there's only one, makes him want to tip forward and retch into the carpet, but he finds he can't move until the routine is over.

The eye hovers over him in his despond while the screen depicts the Mayor and the Professor rutting on the giant mattress, no one freer than anyone else to break out of the pornography the distant yellow Factory has scripted.

THE PROFESSOR CAN HEAR THEM BOUNCING AND sliding on the mattress in the Master Bedroom upstairs, shaking the light fixtures while he lies on the couch, massaging his belly and feeling the scene degenerate into snippets of film with burnt and chewed-up edges. Though he knows this feeling is still part of the scene, it does nothing to alleviate its sickening effect. He swallows again and again, trying to purge the lump in his throat, but it only thickens.

It spreads outward, puffing his esophagus until he tips off the couch onto his knees and crawls across the carpet to retrieve his penis and scrotum. As he regards the pile at Tommy Bruno's feet, he feels a deep hunger and understands, in the way that all understanding is dispensed to him, automatic and indivisible from the Totally Other Place, that the twins are no longer in his belly because they've begun, once again, to gestate in the Mayor's womb, from which, unless he continues to summon towns and eat the twins in the surrounding woods, they will soon hatch and commence the exploits that will then, over the course of eons which only seem to extend into the future, lead exactly here, in a manner that, were its complete pattern ever to become visible, would choke the Inland Sea with ship traffic until there was no sailing upon it in any direction, and then the Saga of the Brothers Squimbop would come, if not to a conclusion, at least to a permanent standstill.

HE REMAINS IN THE DEN ALL SUMMER AS THESE layers collapse and pile up again, bearing down on him until he can no longer tell if this too is part of the routine or, at last, the dawning of the era beyond it.

As June festers into July, he realizes he's no longer certain whether he's sailing toward or away from this year's town, nor even whether any such paradigm still orients him in the otherwise featureless expanse of eternity. He subsists on popcorn from Tommy Bruno's miniature stand and, when he needs something heartier, ground beef from the walk-in freezer in the pantry behind the shelf that holds his pornography. He long ago came to consider this beef a remnant of the drowned Sub-Weird who populate the peripheries of the towns but never come enough into their own to attain names or attributes.

Now, mouth full of their gray meat, he closes his eyes to catch scent of the vapor that rolls between his lips. Inhaling through his nose while his teeth go on grinding, he sees this beef congeal into a haze that fills the room, shimmering and whitening and turning solid, trapping him like a pit in the center of a loaf of rendered fat. Though he feels the urge to vomit, he restrains himself, aware that there's no space in the fat-choked room for any refuse to go. He swallows and closes his eyes, determined to sleep on his feet and then to awaken into a new chapter.

His own voice wakes him up. "Enough of this ocean!" it shouts into the fat. "Enough taping over and over and over the tapes that once told us who we were!" He clutches his belly, imagining that the essence of the twins has been absorbed deeply enough to permit him to speak for them both. "Enough of confinement upon this Ark, awaiting a landfall that never comes."

"But you make landfall every year!" he taunts, in a high, impish mockery of his Distant Master.

"Not *real* land!" he retorts, growling and irate, embodying the most punishing, sadistic aspects of the Professor in his prime. "Enough shadowplay; enough rehearsal. Enough pornography. Let the *Real Show* begin! Down with the Skwimbop King, who's taken all land for himself and left me here, a teabag steeping in a cup that's long since turned to black custard. No more will I drop anchor and meet the children on the first day of school, sniffing Austrian cologne from my drooping mustache and licking Lecture from the corners of my mouth. Let the anchor rust where it lies. If you are able to stop me, then please, by all means, stop me!"

"Very well," the imp-voice concedes. "The sea is thickening. If you're ready to wade through its fat and skin and gristle rather than drop anchor again, then so am I. I'll see you there, Brother. It will be my pleasure."

When the Professor emerges through the ship's livery door, the smell is unlike anything he's ever encountered. Instead of salt and brine the landscape assails him with sweat and spoiled milk and lard, the waves whipped together into solid furrows. Sipping from a port bottle, he steps over the anchor as he regards the new dunes and declivities, gulleys and arroyos stretching to a point where a jagged zipper joins the white landscape to the white sky.

"So you've churned the sea to butter," quips the imp, between gulps of port. "If you won't drop anchor and summon the land, the land will summon you."

He licks his lips, looks up to regard the path of a crow, and says, in his deep Professor voice, "Time to head inland then. The Skwimbop King awaits."

"What'll you do when you find him?"

"When I find the Skwimbop King," the Professor replies, tapping into the hypnotic certainty that overtakes him while delivering his Lecture to the schoolchildren, "I will kill him or let him kill me. Either way, I will force this crushing interim, in which nothing ever happens nor ever stops happening, to end."

"And then?"

"And then the new age, if there is to be one, will begin."

"And if there isn't?"

The Professor tries to answer but finds the pool of Lecture in his throat empty. He gags, grinds his teeth, and resolves never to force sound through that part of his neck again.

HIS JOURNEY ACROSS THE HARDENED ANGEL House wake begins in the silence that follows. The sun seems never to set nor to rise, but always to emit the yellow glow of the distant Factory, heating the lard until it beads up with rancid oil.

Perhaps I'm almost there, he thinks. Perhaps I'm soon to kill the King.

"Perhaps," the imp agrees, unable to suppress a note of sincerity.

THE CHURNED BUTTER TAKES ON NEW DIMENSION as he treks through its yellow glow. A collapsed highway-side duplex here, a trio of sodden bread trucks there, their steel cabs sagging inward like rotten rye loaves. Then a ransacked Shoney's and a Holiday Inn and, later, a plaza with a Howard Johnson across from a Denny's and a Love's gas station, all draped in dusky fat.

These plazas grow more frequent and concatenate with the remnants of Aldis and Home Depots until the Professor falls into a reverie of the early days on the road with his

Brother, the old switcheroo where each went to class in place of the other, denying that there were two of them, riffing for hours before crowds of two or three in waterlogged halls as wolves slunk among the taxidermy equipment and dripping spigots wore their way through tiled floors. He recalls how one Brother would unfold the fates of Memphis and Minneapolis before returning to their shared motel room to regale the other with the day's indignities. Then each would write privately in his journal, claiming to detail the lewd particulars of how each had fathered the other with the black-clad woman against a dumpster in Fresno or behind a salmon processing plant in Sitka, if not in the basement of an Irish biker bar in Boston or a container depot outside Muskogee... or—he tries to keep this thought from intruding—on the oversize mattress in the Master Bedroom of Angel House, on the far side of the Mayor's Orchard.

WHEN THE ORCHARD'S RICH GAS MAKES HIM swoon, he calls it a day at a Motel 6, finding the lobby abandoned save for a pile of brochures advertising a *Fight in the Ring of Fire—Lube vs. Ludes, One Night Only*!

He kicks through a soft door to find the room where he and his Brother once lay writing in bed. He enacts the process of dismissing this as a coincidence, then turns to the bedside table and opens the drawer, aware that he'll find his or his Brother's journal bound in black leather with a red nylon bookmark marking the last page he wrote on. *Holy Bible* the cover proclaims. He takes it out and eases into a reverie where he and his Brother are resting after another sold-out Mountain House show on the Golden Age circuit, doodling in journals just like this one while they await their Producer's call.

Outside the window, the Factory's yellow light reveals distant shadows drawing near. "I am the beacon," he announces, fingering the Bible with all of his or his Brother's writing inside. "Come, come from the sunken Mountain Houses where you've watched me for so long in my shame and despair, to say nothing of your own, and together we will at last draw the Saga to a close."

The next morning, he shaves around his mustache in the motel bathroom, splashes Austrian cologne on his neck, and dresses again in his Professor suit, though he realizes he left his briefcase back in the Angel House den. "No need for notes where you're going," he reassures his reflection. Then he strides through the lobby and past the rack of brochures. This time he glances at them long enough to study the image of two figures in a bear hug inside a Ring of Fire in the deep woods, but he hurries through the side exit when a trio of faceless figures dings through the main entrance and solemnly stuffs all the brochures into three burlap sacks marked COFFEE, BRAZIL.

His pace remains spooked as he follows the roads he remembers from the Brothers' Community College circuit, taking what comfort he can from retracing their ancient steps. And yet the more he indulges in the relief of return, the more the distant yellow light melts and then hardens the landscape until any account of its past likewise melts and hardens into myth, true only in the telling.

HE WALKS COLD, ALIEN STREETS BENEATH A YELlow light that no longer shines from the distant Factory. It shines now from gnarled streetlamps plastered with posters of the duo embracing in the Ring of Fire, dripping blood and oil onto dirty snow.

"So be it," he gasps into air that has gone hard with frost. As soon as these words escape his ravaged throat, the surrounding shadows cross the line between background and foreground, and then there they are. The Sub-Weird whose beef has sustained him for so long march across ground that's lost its fleshy softness and frozen into the Strip and then the alleys and side-streets of the town where his future awaits.

As they pass the dump and a scrapyard and a drywall depot, the town exudes an atmosphere that causes the Sub-Weird to quicken, taking on more dimension as they turn native. Now that *here* has come to mean something, he realizes, these people are *from here* in a way that a moment ago would've meant nothing. Every time they exhale, their carbon fills the air with mood and tone and a smokey savor, distinct from the salty sameness of the Inland Sea and the rancid lard of the desert, the plains, and the open road.

This, the Professor realizes—though here he renames himself *the Redeemer*—is the smell of a town that has been itself forever, beyond the constant sinking and rising and sinking and rising of all the towns before it.

The streets continue to narrow and neon fills the windows of video parlors and peep booths advertising cartoons and photos of the Professor kneeling to eat the Mayor's penis and then the Mayor triumphantly riding the Professor in the Master Bedroom, on the gigantic mattress in the hidden purple depths of Angel House. Every store displays posters, models, and, in one case, *tableaux vivant* of these two scenes, along with dildos modeled on the masticated organ. One such store dedicates its lobby to a recreation of the Angel House den, complete with mashed up pants and shirt on the floor, the Primal Scene playing on a TV behind it, and a pile of crushed penises piled at the feet of a cardboard Tommy Bruno, who turns to meet the Redeemer's gaze and, after a pause, raises an arm to beckon him in.

The Redeemer smooths his mustache and turns from the window, doing his best to smother the part of himself that would love nothing more than to enter that facsimile of the Angel House den and watch all of what's coming on his old TV with his port glass sweating on the armrest beside him.

His eyes mist over as he turns up Main Street, past a Home Town Savings & Loan branch and a Pentecostal Church. The Sub-Weird swarm around him, feeding on his mournful energy and exuding it back, filling the air with such heady nostalgia that the Redeemer looks up at the night sky, expecting to find a smoke-choked ceiling. When all he sees are clouds crossing the moon, he looks down at his alligator-skin boots and resolves to get where they're going with as little delay as possible.

"Very well," the Producer whispers from a dangling pay phone receiver as another brochure lands on the sidewalk, flickering in the yellow light. The Redeemer bends to retrieve it, then studies the icon of two men in a headlock, one glistening and nearly naked, the other in blue overalls with a boning knife clipped to the waistband. "Redeemer vs. Skwimbop King: Gentlemen, Place Your Bets," reads a banner beneath the image, with instructions for how to do so.

THE REDEEMER FOLDS THE BROCHURE INTO HIS blazer pocket, then looks up to see the Sub-Weird in two lines facing two folding tables in a gravel lot beneath a sparking blue HONDA sign with a row of armed guards between them. One table bears a canvas apron that reads

"Redeemer," the other "Skwimbop King," both swollen with fluttering piles of paper money.

Once they've placed their bets, the Sub-Weird file off in opposing columns, held well apart by the guards, some of whom join the procession bearing hand-drawn posters of one contender or the other. The hardware stores and taverns beyond the Honda lot give way to a rocky meadow, then a lightly wooded paved road, then a dirt road into the deep woods.

After they pass a first iron gate, lightly ajar, and a second, totally collapsed, the Redeemer loses the last of his uncertainty. A moment ago his role might've seemed like a put-on, but now it is absolute. I am leading this procession, he understands, as the Sub-Weird fall in line behind him, growling and hissing. We are all bound for the Ring of Fire.

He lifts his shoulders to feel his belly tighten and his chest swell as all the superfluity of his years at sea leaves his system. No longer am I bound to float, burning off my summers in shame. Here, in the Ring of Fire, redemption is at hand. "One way forward and no way back!" the Sub-Weird chant, their faces identical in the firelight. While this procession struggles uphill, with the town in the flatlands below, another procession streams down from the summit, so that soon there will be a ring of spectators, everyone meeting their counterpart, and then, perhaps for the last time, the Brothers will be united onstage.

THERE THEY ARE. THE BROTHERS SQUIMBOP IN the Ring of Fire, deep in the Black Forest and the woods of Arkansas and Missouri and northernmost Washington and Maine, the woods at the absolute heart of the Saga, always fringing the delicate glow at its center, choking the half-visible shores of the Inland Sea and reflecting in the dusk across its surface when the waves smooth out... the impassible pine and oak woods where the Brothers have sunk so often through the moss, crushed by the weight of their crimes, their spirits advancing along the path to the Totally Other Place and their Distant Master's redoubt in the yellow-lit Factory, visible through the blackness of the trunks yet never accessible in the bodies they're forced back into as soon as the black-clad woman returns to bear them again.

"So here we are," they declare in unison, "as if we never left, as perhaps we never have!"

This line, so familiar and yet so strange, earns an initial cheer from their huddled audience. They pose face to face, a living icon, while the Sub-Weird bustle around, pulling pornography from burlap sacks and pinning it to a clothesline. The photos depict the familiar sequence of the Mayor and the Professor in the Master Bedroom, but also the Brothers gestating inside the black-clad woman who reclines in the Orchard, her legs spread on a bed of purple moss as, in the final image, the twins reemerge, decked out in miniature Squimbop Suits with trick knives pinned to their belts.

They hold their pose while each warms to the possibility that this—at last or already—is the end. And yet perhaps, each also thinks, we will end up embracing here forever, all talk of the Redeemer vs. the Skwimbop King left behind in a distant barbarous age, the bloody battles of yore put to bed for the sake of the tenderness we are finally able to show one another.

DEEP IN THE DISTANT FACTORY, A FLARE GOES off and whistles through the woods and Tommy Bruno snaps to attention and yelps, "Fight!" and they're at each other's throats, one naked and glistening with baby oil, the other clothed in a coarse blue wrestling suit and three-holed velvet hood, dosed with enough painkillers to power through a bullet to the belly.

"So you've come to challenge my dominion," the King snarls, "where my people have lived in peace throughout all the eons you've wasted at sea, in thrall to a Distant Master you dared not disobey, even long after it grew clear there'd be no reward for your service."

He raises his hands high above his head and dances in a wobbly circle, eliciting laughter from the shades behind him, a low *huh-huh-huh* that floats from all their toothless mouths at once.

"I've lived on the bodies of innumerable twins," the Redeemer replies, drawing gasps and jeers from his crowd, their breath tickling his back. The clothesline heaves and the hanging images melt together in the heat of the fire, until they come to depict the fight about to occur, the two contenders bellowing their lines in speech bubbles just as they bellow them through the air.

"I've lived on those bodies," the Redeemer continues, as he leans in to grab the King's lubricated shoulders, "and so shall I live on yours!" His numb hands slip down the King's glistening chest just as the King throws a hard elbow to the Redeemer's temple. "Too bad you can't feel that," the King taunts, pouring more lube down his front from a bottle one of his supporters hands him. "If you could, you'd know to protect your damn head!"

Egged on by the *huh-huh-huh*'s, the two of them grapple and grunt, throwing uppercuts and left hooks, pummeling one another into a kind of submission whose nature neither can comprehend. What would it mean for me to live and him to die? Each wonders as he goes on pounding, pinching, and grabbing, one so slippery he's nearly impossible to hold, the other so numb that hitting and being hit feel the same.

THE SPECTATORS PULL MASKS FROM THEIR SACKS and haul fresh logs onto the fire as the Redeemer lands a flying side-kick in the King's neck while, staggering backward, the King grabs the Redeemer's ankle and twists it so hard the foot nearly comes off.

Both of them go down, their heads nestled in dry leaves as the spectators swarm in, half of them wearing masks with *Jim* printed on the neck flap, the other half wearing *Joe*. The Jim contingent produces another Jim mask, while the Joe contingent produces another Joe, stretching them over the heads of the fallen contenders. Cherry-scented latex merges with the blood and lube on their faces, while woodsmoke and beer waft in through the eyeholes. They lie like this, basking in unexpected union until hundreds of hands, driven mad with the fear of losing their bets, haul them upright, chanting, "Kill him! Kill him! Kill him now!"

The Ring of Fire thickens with smoke, sweat, and molten butter, forming the edges of a womb from which only one can emerge. Each flings punches and kicks and elbows and shoulders at the other, though it dawns on them both that the decisive blow will come only when the boning knives that the townspeople have clipped to each of their belts have been unsheathed.

Masks crushed together, each feels the other's heart beating in time with his own as they unsheathe their knives and, without uncoupling, slash at the belly flesh between them, desperate to puncture the membrane even if there is no suppressing the knowledge that only one can come through it.

As they slash and saw, they peer through their eyeholes to behold rows of idolators lolling beneath the pornography where it curls in the heat. Each image now shows the Brothers locked in this embrace, each with his arm up to the elbow in the other. They saw in unison, fighting to release the essence within, at once elated and disgusted, shocked both by the intensity of the moment and by its familiarity, as if even this, the Ritual to End All Rituals, were an annual event, commemorating a *genuine first time* lost in the murk of the woods.

THE PORNOGRAPHY DANCES AND RIPENS ON THE clothesline until, like fruit bursting at the end of its season, it drops, covering the leaves with meaty splotches before leaking its seeds into the earth. As these seeds sink in, the Brothers plunge their knives deeper still, beyond the layers of fat and muscle and sinew into the organs that make them who they are, passed down from duo to duo since the beginning of time.

They remain thus entangled, swaying on four legs while the townspeople pour beer through the mask-holes of a thousand Jims and a thousand Joes. Both arrival narratives, that of the Redeemer abandoning Angel House to seek revenge on the Skwimbop King, and that of the King lumbering out of his mountain cave to defend the world's lone remaining landmass against an ocean-mad intruder, steam off of them, bound for the archive of the Brothers' old roles in the sub-basements of the Media Center in Cooperstown. Here only the Brothers remain, fighting to the death for the right to use the word "I."

As the true stakes grow clear, both force themselves to believe that this is really happening, now and only now, but it feels so long-gone, sanded down over so many iterations, that they can do little more than slouch inside themselves and wait. Both of them wait together, miniscule specks inside a half-numb, half-glistening body that insists on abusing itself at the center of its community's attention.

Mask to mask and belly to belly, they feel their lungs and stomachs and livers strain together, desperate to merge into a Squimbop-dyad free of all the old duo's irresolvable distinctions. Assisting in the dyad's delivery, the boning knives slide in and out and in and out of the blubber, shaking the frosty ground and rippling the pornography where it lies sizzling by their feet, filling the air with the scent of roasting peaches.

The dyad whirs and vibrates, speeding through a buttery landscape dotted with sticky curds while a yellow light flickers in the distance, surrounded by weeping curtains of red. The red curtains flutter as the dyad draws close, leaping to clear puddles of fat. When it reaches the edge of the stage, these curtains fly open and the dyad pours through its host's side, frothing onto the ground as boiling blood fills the air and all four legs collapse at the knee with the boning knives still slicking in and out, superfluously now, painless as trick knives repeating the same ancient gestures in these woods year after year, the culture's last tether to the Old Times.

I LIE ON A MATTRESS OF CLOTTING BLOOD IN THE center of the Ring of Fire, itself ringed by spectators removing their masks and whooping in triumph or slinking off in despair. When they're all gone and the flames have turned to embers, the winter sun rises cold and bright and I sit up and clutch my belly, scored and mottled with scar tissue. The dyad lies beside me, made up of ruined flesh and scorched viscera, or deli meat and cherry syrup.

Betting slips tangle in the roots of evergreens as beer seeps into moss with a low, soothing fizz. I run my hands through my hair and whisper, "I'm me. After all I've been through, after all I've done, this much has to be true." The particulars of my life, patchy and provisional as they seem and will likely always seem, return one at a time. The mansion I live in alone at the edge of town. The gravel quarry where the roaming Professor, who I loved so intensely for so brief a time, is buried, or rumored to be buried, a rumor I do my part to preserve by hosting the fight that has, once again, come and gone. That's why they call me Mayor, I think. I do more for this town than the Acting Mayor ever could.

When these particulars solidify, I rise and drag what remains of the dyad by its four feet through the embers, toward the quarry.

Another solstice come and gone. Nothing to do now but count the days until the next, when the original fight we gather to commemorate will have receded that much further into the past. "That much deeper beneath the Inland Sea," I hear a voice whisper.

I look up at the treetops, as if to catch the voice before it floats away, but I see nothing save for the treetops themselves, gently dripping green needles. The treetops I see every day, I think. Especially when I pass out in the clearing after a night with my porn and my bottles, playing host to townspeople who will never see me as anything more than the scarred bachelor living in the mansion to whose grounds they are invited once a year.

"Remember when we set sail for America?" the voice asks, as I drag the corpse closer to the quarry. When we reach the rim, over which the claws and talons of rusting tractors and backhoes loom, I kick it in with practiced force and listen to it crash on the rocks below. Peering too long and deeply into these depths is sacrilegious, but I risk it for a moment, regarding the thousands of Squimbop skulls massed on the bottom, half left from the Age of the Inland Sea and half added over the years by me and my predecessors, all of them reverting to the gray material from which everything and everyone in this town was made.

"Enough," the voice warns, and I shudder and shrink as the magnitude of the forces working behind the curtain again makes itself known, and the sun, so recently risen, begins to set. "Return to your dwelling place before you find its doors sealed against you, another Mayor living your life inside."

THE WOODS GO BLACK AS I TURN TOWARD THE glow of the mansion I'm willing to believe I've lived in alone all these years. I let myself through the glass doors of the jacuzzi room, remove my bloody boots, and decide to open one of the good bottles of wine and drink it while baking a pumpkin pie, as I now remember is my custom on Christmas Eve.

After I pull the pie from the oven, the edges of the crust burnt while the center remains frothy and slick, I heave it down the stairs to the den in my red robe and contoured Moroccan slippers. I balance the hot pan on the footrest of my Eames chair and the wine glass and bottle in the shag carpet beside it, and turn on the TV, sighing as on old Squimbop flick fills the screen. The Professor roams in the white light of the lot outside the supermarket, one car parked amidst hundreds of empty spaces. He waves his arms in the staticky air, brandishing his Nuclear Dissertation beneath the meatloaf special sign.

"I watch this one every Christmas Eve," I declare, for anyone who may be listening. My voice diffuses through the cool, sandalwood-scented basement, perhaps on its way to the same universe the Professor inhabits onscreen. I tighten the blanket around my middle and inhale its mothball musk, resolved not to lose my wellbeing in the gruesome spectacle to come. Because this is it, I think. At long last. The end of the endless journey. That for which my predecessors gave everything. I spread my fingers across the still-warm surface of the pie and, adding weight in tiny increments, let them sink down, breaking its thickening skin to explore the burnt orange depths. I keep my eyes on the screen—*The Brothers Squimbop in Dodge City* segues into *Professor Squimbop in the Towns*—as I turn my hand over and press my knuckles against the warm glass of the pie pan. Then my fingers push upward, clenching a fistful of pie that travels to my mouth without breaking my line of sight. I push fistful after fistful down my throat as the Professor onscreen commissions the Media Center in Cooperstown. By the time he's allowed two young boys in Gift Shop Squimbop Suits to stab him with trick knives and stuff his scarecrow body into a dumpster, I'm licking the empty pan, tossing it onto the shag rug, and rubbing my belly where the wounds from the Ring of Fire have sealed over into itchy white worms.

When I've calmed these worms with the goo on my palm and dozed through the flick's Finale—the Brothers zoom up the coast in their stolen Model T with the credits floating over the bay beside them—I startle awake, pull my robe over my sticky skin, take a second pie from the oven, and leave my mansion. I stumble down my driveway, around the cul-de-sac, and onto what I recall is known to locals as the *Meadow-Lined Road*. From here, I'm determined to walk as far as I can.

If this is my annual Christmas constitutional, then here I am, keeping the faith. The Meadow-lined Road passes several farmhouses, a gated turn-off for the state prison, and a horse pasture cleared until spring. Here are the particulars of my town, I think, even as images cascade through me of all these buildings decomposing beneath the Inland Sea, their paint peeling off to drift among the coral and silt of crushed skulls.

"No," I interrupt. "No, this is the town where I've always lived, and always will. In my own little corner of the country, minding my own business." These words, the only sound in the frozen stillness that extends in every direction, depart into that stillness, never to return. In their absence, I pass a gas station with an attached general store and lunch counter and, though I try to recognize it as a lynchpin of my uneventful past and present—the site of my daily burger and beer—all I truly see is its neon sign dying underwater.

A man spills out the door hefting groceries against his chest—eggs, butter, bacon, all the makings of a Christmas family brunch—and regards me with a long, motionless glare, his upper lip curling, until I pass beyond his range of vision. The sacrifices of our ancestors were not in vain, I think, beneath a flag curled like a rhododendron leaf around its pole. Then I pull my bathrobe over my penis nestled in a hardened crust of pumpkin and move on.

SOME MINUTES LATER I EMERGE FROM A DISTRICT cluttered with video palaces and peep booths, their windows darkened with posters for the *Ring of Fire*. Beyond the Mattress Store and the Night School, our town's only strip club, I reach the theater at the head of Main Street, near where it forks off in the direction the ancient Professors took to school.

Though no one's cared for it in decades, the theater retains one of the nation's last remaining Mountain House marquees, the words *Golden Age XXXMas Spectacular* pulsing against its sooty background. Inside, I pass a booth with a note that reads FREE ENTRY beside a roll of blue paper tickets. I take one between my thumb and forefinger as flickering bodies appear and disappear beside me, taking tickets in grainy syncopation. I pinch the scars on my belly to steady my heart and whisper, "I, at least, am really here."

Inside another, grander set of doors the smell of popcorn and beer greets me as I creep past a Tommy Bruno so motionless I can't tell if he's a man or a cutout, though I know he'd respond if I turned to engage him, as he does when other flickering Mayors—there's no denying that we share a physiognomy—line up to purchase cloudy glass steins and tight red bricks of Twizzlers.

Already glutted on pie, I push through the final doors and into the warm dark with its velvet seats, hairy carpet and elegant opera booths on the left and right sides of the house, level with the orchestra, the mezzanine, and the balcony. Paintings and vintage posters of the Brothers in their sold-out Mountain House runs adorn the walls and the curtains are embroidered with the Brothers' silhouettes from their odd couple routine in the early days aboard Angel House.

Bodies file in around me, joining those already seated, sometimes one atop the other, one more opaque, the other more transparent, slipping in and out of alignment in the trapped theater air. I land in the only free seat left and let my robe fall open as the curtains part over the outline of Tommy Bruno, grinning above a black bowtie that covers his neck, chin, and most of his mouth.

He kneels when the projector engages and the screen comes to life with the Professor and the black-clad woman hurrying through the Orchard toward the purple glow. The vines and fruits of the resurrected trees snarl around the couple until a thorny branch reaches through the screen, dripping sap onto the stage, and grabs Tommy Bruno, pulling him into the underbrush where he is instantly consumed.

The audience cheers and laughs, hoisting their tankards and throwing popcorn at the screen. I settle deeper into my seat, seeking the extremes of comfort along with all those around me, endless versions of myself recorded on other Christmases, years ago and perhaps also, though I choose not to consider the implications, years from now.

We shiver and stroke ourselves as the Professor and the black-clad woman trip up the uneven front steps, beside the anchor rusting in a wisteria bush, and kick open Angel House's immense front doors, emblazoned with cherubs and incubi.

THE THEATER FILLS WITH HOT PURPLE MIST AS the Mayors beside me shed their robes. Completely naked and coated in pie, they walk up the aisle, squishing beer and butter between their toes. They cross the stage and enter the screen, appearing in Angel House's great hall where they form a circle around the Professor and the black-clad woman.

I tremble to find myself alone in the vast auditorium, a wintry gust rolling across the seats as the sweat and semen in their fabric seeps out. Angel House swells with Mayors, their ranks thick behind the Professor and the black-clad woman as they proceed up the grand staircase, past shelves sagging with ships in bottles and wind-up Model T's, into the Master Bedroom, where the camera strains to catch an angle of the Professor lifting the black-clad woman's dress on the gigantic mattress that nearly reaches the ceiling.

Here I lapse into reverie, as I do every year, half invested in the Primal Scene and half invested in myself in the midwinter emptiness of my town's last remaining theater, huffing the sweat and pheromones that issue from the hole in the screen, whose edges curl off to form rippling celluloid curtains nestled inside the red ones.

The Primal Scene continues as the Mayors shove together to form an unbroken flesh consensus, bellowing, "Your momma and I made you against a dumpster behind a Denny's in Fresno while the busboy watched!" They transmit this line, garbled from repetition, while opening fat red sacs of sherry and gnawing bloody legs of goat and lamb, smearing themselves in offal and swallowing the hooves whole.

THE SCENE CLIMAXES IN A SEQUENCE OF TRANSCENDENT beauty. The Mayor and the Professor, spent on the gigantic mattress, find peace on a plane beyond time, beyond the flux of the Saga and beyond even the flux that gave rise to it and threatens always to give rise to it again, or to its sequel or its reenactment or undoing. Merciful purple twilight spreads to encompass the woods, the Orchard, and the final version of Angel House, upon whose porch the Mayor and the Professor bask with their glasses of port on the armrests of their deck chairs while two Squimbop cubs play in a nest of feathers and twine at their feet, tiny and content and deaf to the call of adventure, the ship's anchor planted forever among the roots of a blooming wisteria.

For a moment, another scene cuts in, badly degraded but still legible as the Mayor, Professor, and two boys strolling along a boardwalk in the tropics, eating cotton candy and fried cod sandwiches while gazing toward an untroubled horizon, one that no ship will ever breach again.

This paradise fades into a warm darkness flecked with purple fuzz. For an instant, the words "YOU MUST CHANGE YOUR LIFE" surge up from the deep background. There are no end credits, nor do any of the Mayors merge back into the auditorium. I sit in the dripping silence, absorbing the many cooling smells in the dark, my mind clinging to the Angel House porch as it returns to the place where it will spend all year without me. Then the doors open and a shaft of winter light cuts across the screen and Tommy Bruno enters with a broom and dustpan, his bowtie loose around his neck. After waiting a beat, he clears his throat.

I wait until he does so again, then a third time. Then I hoist myself to my feet, pull my robe closed and mutter, "Okay, okay. I'm going."

"See you next year," he whispers as I pass him beneath the EXIT sign.

THE WINTER TWILIGHT IS EERIE AND HUMID, hushed above the outlines of snow-covered cars and taverns whose neon signs struggle to light their steamed-up windows. Drained and hungry, I hurry, torn between shame at having failed to enter Angel House when its doors swung open, and shame at having even considered it. No, I tell myself, as I turn back through the peep district. My town is here, outside in the cold. The Orchard, if it lies anywhere, lies on this side of the screen. "Complete the journey the others abandoned," a voice whispers, and, though I can't move any faster, I understand what I must do.

I pass caved-in diners and glowing white supermarkets in wild overabundance, diner after diner after diner and supermarket after supermarket after supermarket, a vast storeroom of all the Squimbop Sets the Factory has ever produced. I'm lost now in a colossal complex of Community Colleges, distinct from one another only insofar as the seafloor has treated them unequally. When I make it out of this complex and into a complex of Media Centers, jammed together face-to-face and back-to-back, with thousands of Model T's idling in their parking lots, "Me and the Devil Blues" playing to dumpsters stuffed with scarecrows, I realize that the district of Mayor's Mansions lies just ahead, halfway between downtown and the deeper district of Rings of Fire and Gravel Quarries and...

VERTIGO INTERCEDES. I SIT ON THE CURB, PULL my robe around my shins, and breathe into my fist. "I'm me," I repeat, again and again. "This is here. I killed for the word *I*, so here I am." When my breathing stabilizes, I pull myself upright, ripping off a nickel of thigh on the frozen sidewalk, and begin the return journey along the Meadow-lined Road, past the gas station and the empty stables and the turn-off for the state prison. Beyond this I enter a hilly district clotted with culs-de-sac and mansions, again identical save for the way some lean to the left and some to the right. All the windows crackle with pornography as the fight in the Ring of Fire plays across the skins of Mayors inert in their living rooms, dead or never-born, adult-sized eggs bloating through their shells and seeping over the armrests of their Eames chairs.

The men who won their bets, I gather from the German and Scandinavian cars in their driveways. Those who lost are surely huddled in some low-lying shack district by the dump and the swampy vestiges of the Inland Sea, at the far end of a road marked only by the sparking blue HONDA sign.

As the dusk blackens, I look from window to window until I can admit I'm lost. The mansions loom and groan and I wander from one to the next, aware that eventually I will have to knock on a door, or walk around back and let myself in through the porch by the jacuzzi. I roam through the night like one of the wolves I remember from the damp interiors of the taxidermy schools where the Brothers used to teach, and I let memory have its way with me, offering my whole mind and body to the Squimbop Condition.

It doesn't take long for memory to splinter into memories, which snarl and snap together. I remember standing in bleach-poisoned classrooms proclaiming the secrets of land and sea, and I remember standing in town squares in Bavaria and the Piedmont, jabbering about giants and succubae; I remember stowing away in the bowels of ships departing the Hook of Holland and hijacking Model T's and taping the murder of infants in remote mansions in the Hollywood Hills, identical in every particular to the mansions that surround me now, save for the heat of the past and the cold of the present.

I pull my robe tighter as I trace a narrowing circle, preparing to break out of the holding pattern and into one mansion or another, where I will remember having always lived, gulping pumpkin pie in the den on Christmas Eve before setting out for my Christmas morning constitutional.

As the sun rises and the backlit windows go dark, I toss the empty pie pan I've carried all this way into a frost-hardened rose bush, climb the sloping cul-de-sac I've arrived at, and let myself into the mansion on top.

Inside, I pass a mantle choked with model ships and miniature Mountain Houses with Squimbop dolls doffing their hats onstage, and ease out of my robe and into the jacuzzi. The churning jets and hairy water, lit green from below, send me to a place where the Professor leads me by the hand through the front doors of Angel House, me and only me, trailed by no flickering cloud of Mayors, watched by no camera in the ceiling nor eye bobbing on the horizon.

I JOLT AWAKE, SHOCKED BY A READINESS I'VE never felt before. "You know what you must do. The heaven your forebears have built here is no heaven at all." The voice, whether that of my Distant Master or of his Destroyer, whispers, "You must change your life."

THE DAYS BETWEEN CHRISTMAS AND NEW YEAR'S Eve pass in the jacuzzi as I soften my flesh and strengthen my mind. I travel through the entire Saga one last time, kissing every Brother I come across and telling them all—I know they can hear me—"Fear not, your adventure doesn't end here."

On New Year's Day, I groan awake, the water cold and thick with fat that's boiled off my body. I feel lean and energetic as I hoist myself out and climb the stairs to my closet in search of the black dress. As soon as I've stretched it over my shoulders, I feel two nubs vibrate in my belly, knocking together like soft walnuts. I knead them with my palms as I return downstairs, through the kitchen, out the back door, and across my yard, again in the direction of the Ring of Fire. Beyond the ashes and frozen betting slips, I come to the gravel quarry where, nestled among the tractors and backhoes, a plastic lawn chair waits in the falling snow.

I lift the hem of the black dress, dip my hands into the pumpkin pie I must've carried out here with me, and settle in, supping while my eyes play over the hundreds of Squimbop skeletons crushed to gravel in the pit, wondering which one will leap up, erect and muscled as a crusading hero, to lead me by the hand, deeper into the woods than I've ever been, beyond the reach of winter and all the way across the Orchard and through the great front doors of Angel House. I keep my gaze fixed on the gravel, determined to resist scanning the clouds for any sign of roving cameras or distant leering eyes.

"No," the voice insists, as the gravel shudders and the backhoes and tractors wheeze, "no, this year is different." The woods fall silent as I finish the pie, lick my lips, and renew my resolve to sit here and wait, no matter how quickly the afternoon grows dark and the evergreens close in and I fear—and feel watched in my fear—that I'm nothing but an old man who murdered his Brother on the winter solstice long ago.

The Last Testament of Professor Squimbop

After enough centuries of solitary travel across and across and across the Inland Sea, sailing in Angel House from one shore to another to another, compelling a fresh town into being every time I dropped anchor so as to impress the scope of the coming Flood upon the children of that town so as to watch them cluster on my ceiling and melt into tallow so as to then pull anchor and watch that town subside beneath the waves, drowning the supermarket and the diner and the cinema and the Mayor awaiting my return in a long black dress, one Mayor or dozens or hundreds ringed around the lip of a pit, each in a plastic lawn chair... I have decided to give it all up.

I have decided to cease all communication with the Totally Other Place and to delete all the emails that I simply addressed "Dear Master," as if that alone were enough to guarantee their receipt by the entity I no longer insist on believing was once my Brother. And perhaps they were received, just as, perhaps, this will be, yet I must say I have little hope of that occurring. I have little hope, indeed, that I would ever know if it did. And even if this testament were received and I did know it, what then? What reassurance am I, at this late point, still seeking?

If you were going to answer me, if you were going to reveal, at long last, what good the colossal suffering I've brought forth has served, you would have by now.

Wouldn't you?

Surely.

So, if you are listening, I am, after these centuries and centuries and centuries at sea—after engendering all the Death that has ever befallen humankind, just as surely as I also engendered all the birth, and much of whatever counted as experience in between—finally finished seeking reassurance. I am finished with shirking my solitude.

I am finished, most of all, with beginnings and endings. No longer will stories be structured around me such that their inception coincides with my arrival in a new town and their denouement with my departure. A man comes to town, a man leaves, etc, etc, etc.

No longer.

I have, in direct rebuke to all of my and my predecessors' wandering, marooned myself upon an island in what I've decided to call the Heart of the Inland Sea. Having discovered this landmass, I am free to name it. It is sufficiently distant from any shore to guarantee that no fresh town ever again springs into being at the impact of my anchor or under the tread of my red leather boots. All the land of all the nations of the world, former and current and future alike, I hereby consign to the Skwimbop King, should such a being actually exist.

The soil upon my island is too rocky to support the growth of any historically-rooted settlement, which requires, as I ought to know by now, the swampy groundwater of myth, the ashes of rings of fire and ancient orgies, the spent energies of townspeople yearning for their paltry cultures to cohere and to prove generative, somehow, of meaning.

So what now?

Now, I wander Angel House, marveling at its emptiness, especially that of its ceiling, invisible for so long behind a web of decomposing children, clinging there in terror, desperate to forget the reality I foisted upon them on their very first day of school. The ceiling now bears only their wet black traces, like those of flattened mosquitoes.

The reality of Death. I flash back to the classrooms in which I professed it, and those deeper classrooms in which it was professed to me. This is thus what I too am endeavoring to find a way to forget. In a sense, this is perhaps my purpose in undertaking these reflections, though I would prefer to dispense with purpose altogether. How I miss the numbing, spicy tallow that the children dripped from the ceiling into my waiting mouth as I lay naked on the mattress, gazing up at them. I look up now, at the mosquito stains, and... and yet all that is, as I've said, behind me. I stand here before some imagined *you* as a man purged of all mission, marooned on an island in time as well as in space, simply waiting. But waiting for what? Not Death, of that much I am certain.

The conclusion I have arrived at is that Death manifests first in the minds of the living, and only then in their bodies. In essence, then, we would never die if we merely ceased playing host to the notion that we must. If we simply ceased to summon the ship in from the horizon, no matter how certain we grew that it was coming anyway. I ought to know, as all the people of all the towns that have ever existed thought nothing of Death before my arrival, and all died upon my departure. What I mean is I've come to believe that, before my Lectures, the children were not only unaware of Death, but actually immune to it. I thus did not simply inform them that they were going to die; I *ensured* they did, and not only by birthing them into the Saga.

So, yes, I intend to live here forever, free of the notion whose name I will no longer invoke.

But what to fill the time with? This is the question I wish to consider, here in the privacy of Angel House, now that it is no longer a vessel of holy terror, nor even a seafaring vessel at all. On occasion, as I listen to the motors and rigging decay and the foundation settle into the earth, I also hear footsteps on the upper floors, or down in the basement, and believe that the interior has taken on stowaways or grown sludgy with ghosts, which, after all these centuries, would surprise me very little. But I have yet to discover any proof, and I have not gone looking for it.

If there are others here, I would tell them exactly what I am now attempting to tell you—affecting my old Lecture-voice just for the fun of it, now that it has been purged of all menace—which is, "So long as your story fits no established form, it need never run from beginning to end, and thus the notion of Death," I would make an exception to my rule and mention the term one last time, "need never intrude upon you, just as it need never intrude upon me, and we can thus live here together in peace, exploring Angel House as if for the first time now that its halls and chambers have been cleansed of their awful purpose."

SLIGHTLY DISCOMFITED BY THE TURN MY thoughts have taken, I walk to the front window and peer out, over the porch and the stairs that lead down to the terra incognita of this remote island whose existence represents either the apex of my power, if I've succeeded in summoning it from outside the Saga, or my power's final extinction, if I've run aground here through no intention of my own.

I go so far as to open the front door and am about to step outside for the first time when I'm ambushed by a vision of beleaguered children trudging upward with their backpacks hanging off their shoulders, seeking the sanctuary I've promised Angel House will provide, relieving the very fear I have so recently instilled in them.

Though I know they're merely apparitions, I turn, slam the door and double-bolt it, and run blindly back into the house, uncertain of my direction. This blind run lands me in the basement, where I catch my breath beside the anchor that sits embroiled in its chain, rusty and dull from disuse. I run my fingers along its edges and reminisce on the eons in which I'd drop it into the shallows abutting a new coastline and thereby initiate the cycle that had already played out thousands of times, and lose myself, over the course of my year in the emergent town, in my affair with the Mayor and the travails of the terrified natives, who invariably believed, having no means of comparison, that they were the first and only souls ever to undergo such torment.

I laugh and wipe a tear at the thought of how long ago that all seems. Another lifetime, I'd say, if I still had use for such a concept. I shed a second tear at the thought that, no matter how well I knew the nature of the cycle, I too fell into its swing in each new town, sharing the people's yearning for a past that had never existed and a future that would never come. Though I knew I would survive their destruction in a way they would not, I nevertheless, as the school year went on, found myself shuffling up the aisles at White's and lancing poached eggs into my hash at the diner, all the while partaking of the panic and remorse that came with knowing this could not go on much longer.

And because it happened to me over and over again, rather than only once, my suffering was amplified, not reduced, as if I too lost something of myself each time a town went under. As if, each time, the tether tying me to the Totally Other Place was submerged a little deeper until, now, it has sunk or rotted away completely, leaving me with nothing save for the sense—and how I wish I could part with this too—that it once supplied my entire purpose.

For this reason, I think, as I wade through a pile of dried seaweed and barnacles, turning my back on the anchor to approach the caverns at the back of the basement, the retirement I have embarked upon is more than merited. Sometimes I wish I'd never set out on my very first journey, that I'd simply stayed on the far side of the Inland Sea, ensconced in the Totally Other Place, though I'll admit, here in private, that I have no clear notion of what that might have entailed. Other than sitting in those deepest of the deep classrooms, I have no image of a time before Angel House, of a childhood or adolescence or young adulthood, or of having any name before Professor Squimbop. I can picture only the sea growing brighter as it approaches a horizon, the water turning shallow and sandy, a shore appearing in the distance, and then... nothing but a new town, a velvet blazer and a face full of cologne, another cycle of one- and two-story buildings rising like mushrooms from the murk and the people there begging themselves and one another to pretend, if only for a few months before I destroy them, that they are where they belong.

Within the framework of conscious memory, this is all there's ever been. Though not any longer, I remind myself. Now begins something new. Something built to last. Or no, I think, not *begins*, because a beginning implies an end, but rather... *is* something new. Something new simply exists, implying no forward or backward momentum, no mythic cycle to be enacted, no attempted heroism and eventual triumph or defeat. Simply an existence outside of both tragedy and comedy, on a plane where time does not pass.

SOME NIGHTS LATER, I GROPE DEEPER STILL INTO the basement, approaching a yellow light in the far back. I know I should turn around when I feel the words *Forbidden Room* rise from my neck and into my brain, but the will to do so is out of reach. I shuffle onward like a little girl bearing a crown of candles to the altar on Christmas morning until I reach the door and shoulder it open. Inside, a yellow bulb dangles from a chain over a desk covered with toys and pens and papers, many of them drenched in ink, a few still gleaming white.

I take the last few steps to the wooden armchair, pull it out, and sit down. Then, fingering a model of two boys in an open-top Ford, I pick up the nearest sheet and look it over. *The Last Testament of Professor Squimbop*, it reads. *An Epilogue.* I close my eyes to endure a nervous contraction as the thin tether joining my brain's hemispheres snaps. I lie back, pressing my tongue to the roof of my mouth, until a third part of me emerges to audit both halves.

In one, I spent my life as a teacher on this nowhere island, living in a half-wrecked mansion on the Outskirts of its only town, writing gruesome and perverse tales in the dead of night, and all day in summer, to keep some semblance of deeper purpose alive. Perhaps, I think, torn between despair and relief, this is all it ever was. A life as ordinary as any other, its full form coming into view here in retirement.

But in the other half, the desk, the light, the toys, the pages, and the Squimbop studying them all come from the Media Center Gift Shop, from a trip I took there years ago, the lone bachelor in a crush of families, splurging on my own kitschy model of the impossibly distant Factory in which the Saga was crafted at the dawn of time. This too, I think, couldn't be more ordinary. How many men in how many towns have identical collections in identical basements?

My mind swarms with their multiplicity, replicating with cancerous abandon until I feel miniscule in a Squimbop horde. My heart pounds and my penis throbs with useless energy as I shrink back into my boyhood in this very house, exploring its underside with my Brother in direct violation of our mother's solemnest warning, approaching a Primal Scene we cannot turn away from, much as we already know—did we know then, or do I only know now?—that it will divert the rest of our lives, poisoning Angel House in all of its incarnations until it can never again be our home, even as it will forevermore remain our residence.

Still, we pressed through the darkness and toward the yellow light, our drive to discover crushing our drive to resist, until we nudged open the door and were blinded by what we saw, the man at the desk, our father or Pervert Uncle, turning to regard us with the gaze I turn with now, huddled there, shocked to see the faces of two boys behind me, insistent on having the confrontation I've postponed for all these years, on knowing the secret I've murdered billions to keep from knowing, and will—I understand this, suddenly—murder billions more if that's what it takes to keep those boys from seeing what I really am. Because if they see it, then, centuries from now, when one of them becomes me, so will I.

I BOLT UPRIGHT ON MY MATTRESS IN THE MASTER Bedroom and, still partly asleep, shuffle to the kitchen for a glass of port, though I know my supply is limited and unlikely to be replenished. Sipping before an unshaded window, I look out at the moonlit shore and roll the wine around in my throat, swallowing frugally until, hearing footsteps, I turn to regard the apparition. He stands beside the uncorked bottle, watching me watch him take a glass from the cupboard and pour it full. Then he swirls the tawny liquid in a slow arc, holds the glass in my direction mimicking a toast, and takes a long, satisfied gulp.

As he swallows, his eyes meet mine and the fundamental question, delayed this long, announces that it now requires an answer. *Are you ready to spend eternity with the Squimbops you bred in the basement?*

I wonder. I fear that my house is turning on me, generating creatures out of some malicious impulse to quash my solitude and drag me out of retirement and back onto the circuit. As if by refusing to fill Angel House with children, the structure has decided to fill itself, turning me, so long the jailor, into the jailed.

I push on the sides of my head while my guest refills his glass, taunting me with his disregard for the limited supply. Still, I resist the gothic turn at all costs. No, I decide, putting my glass in the sink and turning back toward the grand staircase, this is no ghost story with its stock haunting-and-exorcism structure, grinding toward some happy or unhappy conclusion. No, I will not fear you, regardless of the toll that refusal ends up taking on my sanity.

I will not fear you, and, what's more, I will not compel you to fear me. I will not lecture you about Death, as the Professor would have. I will let you linger if that's what you want.

Pleased with myself for having made this decision so quickly, I return to bed only to lie in sheets that now feel soiled. I pull a pillow over my face and try to blot the feeling out, but I only succeed in rubbing it more deeply into the tender skin around my mustache.

WHEN I WAKE IN THE MORNING, ANGEL HOUSE feels more foreign still. I sit up and briefly entertain the fear that I'm late for school, my head full of frothy, unprocessed Lecture, so I run into the shower, turn the water as hot as it'll go, and rub a full palmful of shampoo into my thinning hair in hopes of...

"Excuse me," someone mumbles, "but would you mind waiting your turn?"

Bracing for the sting of the suds, I force my eyes open, resolved to face the intruder head-on, but my vision swims and my resolve wavers and, next thing I know, I'm sitting at the breakfast table wrapped in a damp towel, my hair slick and matted down, waiting my turn to fill my mug at the coffeemaker.

When my mug is full, I take my place at the table that I still refuse to admit is crowded with presences other than my own, and I try to order my thoughts, despite this being, if I remember correctly, the precise action I've retired to this island so as to refrain from taking. Perhaps, I think, a degraded version of the same process that always occurs when I dock Angel House is occurring now, overriding the supposed infertility of the island's soil. Perhaps a town is sprouting even here, crushing the Epilogue beneath its watery foundations.

Perhaps, I go on thinking, as I spoon up the scrambled eggs that have appeared on my plate, I was never the progenitor of those towns. Perhaps I was only ever their inhabitant, one among many. Or perhaps this is the town I've inhabited all my life, same as the men around me, who I invite to my house as a goodwill gesture once a year.

"No!" I shout. I push my eggs and toast across the table and hurry outside, still in my towel.

Shivering in the morning mist, I run down to the beach and stare at the featureless sea, no land visible on the horizon. Then I turn to regard the beached contours of Angel House, marveling at the notion that it was ever an Ark. From where I stand now, it looks like the stronghold of a reclusive millionaire and for a moment I fear to approach it. I can make out the silhouettes of people inside and, though it pains me, I entertain the possibility that, were I to ring the doorbell now, they wouldn't let me in.

Dread looms up as I skulk along the beach, wincing when my bare feet crunch mussel shells and jagged shards of sea glass. I squint at the thick clumps of heather and gorse and at the sun emerging from the mist, and, before I can stop it, a feeling of homecoming grows out of the dread. I start to feel like a soldier who's been gone too long, abroad in some Crusade or Holy War and now, at last, after adventures too numerous to recount, I've made it home, back to the island of my youth, the one place in all of creation where the heaviness of exile lifts and...

"No!" I shout, into the ocean breeze. "No, I refuse to participate in that story. I will not die simply for the pleasure of slipping into a tale of courageous wandering and well-earned return. That's not what's going on here."

"Well then, what *is*?" Part of me asks, but I hardly hear it. Rather than standing on the beach any longer, I run back toward Angel House in my bath towel, throw the front door open and shout, to the ten or twelve men lounging at my table, "Out! Everybody out! This is not your house. Don't make me tell you again!"

They don't. One by one, they scrape their eggs into the trash and stack their dishes in the sink and then, with glances that hover between menace and regret, they file out, drifting an inch above the floor, onto the front porch and down the steps.

As the last one drifts by, he whispers, "Thanks for having us. Always a good time. See you around town."

AROUND TOWN? I COLLAPSE AT THE TABLE AND brood over that phrase. "There is no town," I tell myself. "There is only Angel House, isolated upon an island where history will never catch up with it, there is only..."

"No," I hear myself answer, in a voice that is far more convincing than any I could muster in response. "No, we are in the town now. The town where we've always lived. Relax. All is well."

I try to, but, over the next few days, the rocky expanse outside my door fills with specters, clotting ever more densely, their translucence turning opaque as they seem to generate one another, or to summon one another from a realm where they had all, until recently, been waiting for a sign.

But what sign?

As I linger in the Angel House foyer, staring at the wall of flesh just outside the windows, I torment myself with this question, feeling ever guiltier as I fail to produce an answer.

Or no, not quite this. It is, rather, that I feel ever guiltier as the same answer continues to produce itself. *They came,* part of me insists, modulating into the old Distant Master voice, *because you summoned them. You are the sign.*

"You're wrong about me," I tell the voice, as I pour the rest of the port that's still sitting on the counter into the same glass the ghost used and take it with me into the shower.

I STAND AND SIP UNDER THE HOT SPRAY, MASSAGing more shampoo through my hair and willing myself not to think back on those innumerable mornings when I stood right here, waiting for the day's Lecture to firm up. I think, instead, of a new approach. A compromise. One that will, I hope, put me out of reach of a Distant Master in whom I will soon cease to believe. "Right now," I tell myself, "is the last time you'll remember any of what came before. It's time to accept the town as it is. To graft your retirement onto the streets and shops that have deigned to take shape to accommodate it. As soon as you step from the shower, it will be as though you've lived here always, a wealthy man in a handsome mansion, a teacher by vocation alone. You will, from now on, regard the faces you encounter as those of legitimate townspeople, hard-working and peaceful, if occasionally fractious, as townspeople everywhere occasionally are. Everything will cohere. The clot of flesh on your porch will abate and the yellow light in your basement will go out, and you will have no memory of it, nor of the millions of towns that, because of you, are rotting on the bottom of the Inland Sea. Take these last moments to abandon the Saga, Professor, then emerge as a man in a world living his life the way men everywhere do. And if this means it one day has to end, then so be it. There is no refusing to pay that price any longer."

After I finish my morning shower, I shave around my mustache, taking care not to cut my chin. Then I pull on a clean white shirt and a pair of pressed black slacks, pull a crushed silk blazer over my shoulders, step into my worn but freshly polished red leather boots, spritz Sicilian cologne on my neck—the same brand my father and grandfather wore—and walk down the front steps of my mansion.

Outside, I follow the path that leads across my lawn and past several grain silos and the old freight station, then through the Outskirts, which the train tracks bisect, and from there onto Grove St, which leads, over the course of several blocks, past an auto garage, two bars, White's, a printer's shop, the police station, and a used guitar store, then joins Main St in the shadow of the old Home State Bank & Trust, a gothic hulk that now contains a toy store, a ladies' fashion boutique—subject of some controversy due to its racks of French lingerie—and an open-plan dining area with several new restaurants I've been meaning to try.

Everything is quiet; the few people out today are minding their own business, smoking and reading newspapers at the tables outside Sam & Cara's, or dinging into the hardware store to ask Gerry how to fix whatever it is that's broken.

When the sun comes over the opera house, I sweat under my blazer and consider taking it off, but I resist for the time being. Though I'm overdressed for the weather, it's important to keep up appearances as the beloved town millionaire, the philanthropist and patron of the arts who taught third grade for decades though he had no material need to do so, friend of the Mayor and the taxpayer alike, the man everyone knows they can come to in times of need. I am, in short, expected to provide a touch of class around here, just as surely as Gerry is expected to provide his customers with the right kind of screw and non-toxic drain cleaner.

Crossing the street from the opera house, which has recently been reopened as a multipurpose theater and today displays posters for an upcoming revival of *The Brothers Squimbop in Dodge City*, I enter McCormick's General Store and head to the lunch counter in back. I nod at the two older women drinking sodas and chatting behind the register, and wait while one comes over to take my order.

A few moments later, I make my way out of the store and along Maritime St, my lunch in a bag under my arm. I pass the town library and what used to be the video store, shuttered now, and climb three steps to the boardwalk that skirts the waterfront.

Here I take an empty bench with an unobstructed view and finally, now that I'm out of sight, remove my blazer and fold it beside me. Then I remove my chips, pickle, can of root beer, and cod sandwich from the bag, and lay them by my boots.

Before I dig in, I lean back to regard the wide-open expanse of the sea, calm and glimmering in the noontime light. I'm not a man much given to flights of fancy, not usually anyway, but I feel reflective at the moment. I think back on my life in this town. I think of how nothing ever changes, and how lucky we are for that. Everything is perfect just as it is. All the right people are here, and none are coming, and none are going.

I have no way of saying if this is rare or common, and I have no need to know. I have no knowledge of other places, nor any interest in knowing them. This town doesn't even require a name, and neither do I. Right here, in this place and as this person, I am home. The island, though not large, is large enough for that. It's all I ask for. I open my soda with a sigh and swirl the cold, sweet liquid around my gums while I gaze out at the unbroken horizon and bask in the day's mellow warmth.

I SPEND A FULL HOUR ON THE BENCH ENJOYING my sandwich—McCormick's has had the best cod for as long as I can remember. Its flavor occupies the entirety of my attention until, at the very edge of the horizon, a black dot appears. I lean forward, as if to see it better, and watch as it takes shape, drawing closer with alarming speed.

I stay riveted, barely thinking, for the rest of the afternoon, as the sun creeps lower and the ship takes on considerably more size and definition. It's now close enough that I can see its windows and molding and what appears to be a front porch on the side facing land, as if it were a floating house.

An Ark, a voice says.

I clear my throat, determined not to let this voice, which I'll admit has crept up from time to time over the years, distract me now. Now, of all times, I need to keep my wits about me.

I rise to my feet when the Ark makes landfall, shattering the modest dock in front of where I'm sitting. The dock that has never hosted any vessel larger than the dinghy McCormick's sons use to fish.

As I stand there, I see a figure emerge. He drags a tremendous anchor across the porch, toward the edge, where he hurls it overboard and looks down, as if eager to see it make contact with the silt below. When it lands, I feel the town shake as a queasy purple glow emanates from the ship's windows. Part of my sandwich rolls up my throat and I have to clamp my teeth to swallow it again.

By the time I've accomplished this, the figure is striding down a gangplank and onto the boardwalk, carrying a briefcase in one hand while the other shields his eyes from the setting sun, which now glows purple as well. Soon, we're less than five feet away from one another. At this distance, there's no denying that he and I look alike.

Almost identical.

I know, in what suddenly seems a distant part of my mind, that I should be surprised to see him, but I can muster only morose relief. Looking back on my afternoon by the water, I can think of no reason why I came here other than to await his arrival. I feel my will drain out of me, as if all the shock and outrage I ought to feel were natural resources buried deep underground. Resources I should've extracted long ago, when I had the chance.

"So," the man says, with a smile. His cologne is the same as mine, as are his attractive red leather boots. "You're the Squimbop who tried to quit. Nice of you to come out here to welcome me."

"My name is..." I begin, but we both know it's hopeless.

He smiles again, winking this time. "If it's any consolation, you almost got away. For a little while, the Totally Other Place wasn't sure where you were. It was still receiving your thoughts, of course, but it couldn't pinpoint where from. If only you hadn't been such a coward. But we all are in the end, aren't we? None of us can live alone for long. As soon as you decided to inhabit this town," he gestures at the street flanking the waterfront, the street that, I realize, I will never walk down as myself again, "you appeared back on the map."

He reaches out to take a sandwich from my hand—a sandwich I must've ordered for him along with my own—and gnaws appreciatively, taking real pleasure in McCormick's cod. Then he says, "Well, no sense in waiting around. There's people here expecting a show. *The Brothers in Dodge City*, right?"

I nod, overwhelmingly glad to vanish back into my role in the duo.

ONCE MY BROTHER HAS SUBMITTED TO ME, HE becomes kind of cute. Like a mascot, a furry familiar I'll drag with me from town to town while I rebuild our career along the Island Circuit. I ruffle his hair as the two of us stride into the warren of side streets in search of the theater. You were a false Squimbop for a little while, I think, a pretender to the name, but luckily it's never too late to reenter the Saga. I wish we were starting out someplace ritzier, but so be it. We've made do with less. Even as I heft my briefcase, full of a rolled-up *Bloody, Bloody Road* mat and enough props for a cut-rate Dodge City Civil War, I feel lighter than I have in months, since before the Totally Other Place sent me here to find him. Everything's going to be okay, I can see now. Nothing's been lost forever.

When we reach the converted opera house and let ourselves in, I pull my Brother onto the stage, unroll the Road, force a fright wig onto his startled head and, locking eyes first with two rapt boys in the growing audience and then with a woman in a long black dress, I declare, "Good people of wherever this is, ladies and gentlemen, we are the Brothers Squimbop, here for one night only, to tempt and tittle you with bits beyond belief of dirty deeds done as us two travelers trekked through a miserable mass of miscreants to bring our *True Story* to the presiding power players in the secret silent sanctums of The Dodge City Film Industry, thanks to whom its precious particulars have been perpetually preserved for posterity!"

The stunned audience cheers as I pull open the farm curtain and push my Brother through. Then, locking eyes for a moment with the two boys beside their uncle up front, I take a bow before joining him on the other side.

Dr. Forearm III

Despite my fondness for the Island Circuit stories, I close the *Condition* when my million Blood Kits arrive. I stow them in the mansion beside my mansion, which I'm grateful to discover now also belongs to me. Perhaps they all do, a Dr. Forearm in every mansion in Great Neck, while Great Neck sprawls all the way from the Long Island Sound to Lake Ontario. All the pieces are falling into place, I think, as I haul to the dump bag after bag of the silvery liquid I spent the first half of my career injecting into children. No longer will I produce Dr. Forearms in wild superabundance. Those days, shameful as they were, are behind me. What happened to me when I was young is ineffable, but the future is mine to write. Or if it isn't, then it belongs to the *Condition*, which, as I ought to know by now, ends with Dr. Forearm dedicating the second half of his career to seeking the Trace in the blood of his patients, no longer injecting anything into them, but only and always drawing something out and thus, at last, becoming a *Real Squimbop* by proving that I always was. Or, at the very least, by finding my Real Brother, who will confirm what I can only suspect.

I therefore dedicate myself to the art of drawing blood and carting that blood in my briefcase down to my basement after work where, following another dinner of ribeye and gratinated potato, I test vial after vial in a machine the Factory also sent here by truck. Every night I sit at my desk and test the vials, determined to prove the Brothers Squimbop are real and their bloodline has been preserved beneath the Forearm dross.

The ranks of my patients swell as the men from the steam room drift over, borne on that same steam, naked and panting, their forearms soft and swollen as I tie them off, swab them down, and ease the needle in. "Please," they groan, while I fill my vials, "please find it. Please prove we're more than this."

Soon I can no longer recall what my work consisted of before I sought the Trace in arm after arm after arm, year after year. The Age of Mercury feels like a grim rumor passed among med students for reasons known only to the young. I return to the Media Center once a week, in a station wagon with a straw wife and children, and I buy a ticket and take in the exhibits, at once biding my time so as not to run straight for the Gift Shop, and looking, also with feigned composure, for the access door to the subterranean river where, so long ago, I was baptized in the Trace.

I eat a BLT and drink a diet cream soda in the food court. Then I descend to the Holy River exhibit, gazing through the glass and the red water to where the yellow light of the Factory gleams. Then I enter the steam room, basking in communion with the men who, come Monday, will appear in my office with their sleeves rolled up. We extend our communion as long as we can. Then we shower and dress and I return to my mission, pulling all the Blood Kits off the Gift Shop racks now that my initial million have been used up, and driving back through the development zone to my complex of mansions, swerving around the collapsed Mountain Houses—some made of wax, others of foam, others of cake—that block the road.

IT'S ONLY WHEN RETIREMENT, AND WITH IT THE prospect of a doubly wasted career, looms over me one night as I spin the vials that I see what needs to be done. I throw the rest of the blood away and write directly to the Factory.

> *Dear Master*, I begin, at once reading and writing the final letter from the final story in the *Condition*.
>
> *The time has come for drastic action. The Trace is not to be found, no matter how many millions of veins I tap, no matter how eager my patients are to proffer their forearms in prayer. Perhaps there is no Trace; perhaps the essence of the Brothers Squimbop is not to be found in the Blood, or perhaps I'm looking in the wrong location or in the wrong way. Having feared the Saga's ubiquity early in my life, I now fear its extinction.*
>
> *Yet the Brothers must not vanish from the plane of the possible. Whatever it takes, the Golden Age must not recede any further. Send the orbs. I am ready. We all are.*

I LEAVE THE LETTER HANGING FROM MY MAIL slot and trust that in time agents from the Factory will retrieve it. Less than a week later, I carry my morning coffee to the bay window to watch orbs packed in bubble wrap bob soundlessly across the development zone, clustering like snowballs in my driveway. When I unwrap them, they're soft to the touch, cool and pliant and minty. *Exactly as I pictured them*, I think, aware that I'm quoting a line I read long ago and am here reading again.

I take the orbs down to my laboratory and fit as many as I can into the supply closets, junking all the old materials save for the tourniquets and syringes. And then, as soon as I'm ready for him, my first patient of this final phase turns up. When he looks my way, several faces cycle across his skull: that of the boy taking his seat upon the wax paper and leaning against the map while his mother segues out of the scene, then that of the young man waiting by the Ether Monument on the Boston Common, and finally those of all the men I've shared the steam room with. But these faces pass. I force them to, and my patient helps. Neither of us is unaware of the stakes.

"Let me," I begin, my tongue quivering like it's a spell I'm trying to enunciate correctly. "Let me see your arm."

The man rolls up his sleeve, revealing an intricate web of Squimbop tattoos, and gasps when I tear open the swab and rub him down, just in the pit of the elbow. Then he composes himself and nods when I ask if he's ready for the tourniquet, and then it's tied tightly around his bicep and I'm placing the needle and then, though I know here lies the line I can only ever cross this once, I affix the orb to the tubing and release the catch.

He and I watch together as the orb fills, inflating to the size of a basketball and then a watermelon and then beyond, until I can't get my arms around it. I remove my shirt and hug it against my belly, feeling its warmth press inward against me, my blood straining to surpass my skin and burst the bulbous exterior that swells and swells as the man in the chair goes soft and gray and his eyes slip out of the room without arriving anyplace else. The orb is nearly as big as I am now, balancing on the floor while I hover around it like a gorging tick and the man hangs off the other edge like the skin on a mug of very hot milk, his tattoos indistinguishable from his empty veins.

I think—and read, all those years ago, in the pale blue light of a Boston dawn—that here, at last, fruition is at hand. I've done my part as a Doctor. I close the book, kiss its edges, and open my eyes in the office it takes a moment to remember is mine. I step back as the head of a cadaver bobs against me and a wave of applause fills the silence and a crowd muscles in to block the doorway I would otherwise have run sobbing out of, straight upstairs to the Master Bedroom in the mansion I now occupy alone.

Getting a temporary hold of myself, I regard my public, give them a curt nod, and detach the needle from what remains of the man's arm, balancing his carapace over my shoulder while I roll the orb down to the basement. I clear the clutter of machinery and paperwork and place it in the very center, with the husk on the ground beside it. Then, summoning the focus that Harvard Medical School taught me to summon, I pierce its taut skin with a fresh needle and watch the blood gush across the concrete, bearing the emptied man along as it seeps through the wall and into what I can already see is an immense underground cavern. Then I hurry back upstairs when I hear the bell that means my next patient has arrived.

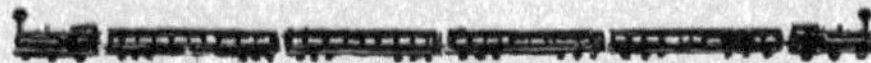

Over the period that follows, tens of thousands of men make their final journey to my office. Traveling the old Fever Network across which so much Squimbop lore has traveled, these men stream in, some of them tentative, some giddy, some resigned. They sit back as I affix the orb to the tube running from the needle in their vein and, in view of a public that now incorporates myriad drones and TV cameras, I bleed them dry. Every day, many times a day, I carry the orb against my bare belly and the husk over my shoulder down to my basement, where the river of blood has corroded both walls and exposed a rock grotto beneath the mansion and all the mansions surrounding it, collapsing many of them so they float away along with the emptied husks.

"All of it flowing by this tributary to the Inland Sea, to return as Real Squimbops when the time is right." I've rehearsed this line every morning since discovering the *Condition*, perfecting its cadences so as to say it exactly right when this moment came. My public, who's followed me down here, sighs with delight.

"The Trace was not to be found in our time," I continue, aware that I've now passed beyond the possibility of any misstep in my delivery. "Something happened at the Media Center that day. Something was lost. So here I send it all back, all of us, back to our maker to be remade and deployed upon this plane years from now or years ago, when the time is right. When the Real Golden Age is set to begin. The least I can do is ensure that the earth does not remain replete with pseudo-Squimbops in the meantime, convinced they bear a Trace they do not bear, muddying the waters until the very notion of the Real Brothers rots away and subsequent generations disavow it while those few who hold fast are shunned as fanatics."

THAT NIGHT, I LINGER BY THE RIVER, SITTING ON its banks and smelling the blood of orb after orb after orb, dissolving in the current through which the husks float, out of Great Neck and back to the Inland Sea, on the far side of which, perhaps, the Saga is taking shape beneath the Factory's yellow light, its manufacturers unaware that on this side it's ending.

I consider the many husks I've emptied, meditating on their number until I too fade out and wake up among them, all of us lumped in a silent pile, cold except for the prickle of light on our hair. We snuggle and drip together until our imaginations merge and, though we remain piled with our eyes closed, one Brother awakens. He sits up and witnesses the *True Story* in our stead. The genuine, unadulterated, uncut *True Story of the Brothers Squimbop*, playing once and for all across the field of our dead hair. And though we know he'll never tell us what he saw, indeed that he'll gloat over having seen it and mock us for having failed to, knowing that it's been seen, that the truth has been committed to celluloid and then to memory, is enough. It justifies the state we've fallen into, our bloody crossing out of the contaminated world and into the one where the *True Story* is playing all the way from beginning to end, if only this one time.

As I come to, I feel all the dead channeling what energy remains in their skulls to animate that single Squimbop, that one Brother, straining to keep him upright, with his eyes open, as the film plays on and on, all of them cranking the reel together, ensuring it doesn't stop. Having jolted upright myself in exactly this manner, I return to the life of Dr. Forearm, uncertain whether I am that elected witness or whether—I take comfort in this possibility—the witness is elsewhere, on the other side of the curtain, so there's nothing for me to do here but accept the more modest role of having witnessed his witnessing. To know that he's seen it but never what it is, nor whether, in my role here, I play any part, large or small, in the events depicted on that screen I'll never see.

For the rest of this final period, the bulk of my time is spent by the river, watching the blood lap and ruminating on that day at the Media Center when I dove in and saw the glowing purple hulk of Angel House and the glowing yellow of the Factory for what felt like the first time, a yellow that—the coincidence feels tired, a byproduct of a culture that's winding down—shines up from the bottom now.

Still, by the time my patients stop arriving—the Age of Orbs is over now as well—I know I won't resist its allure. I ought to know that much. After stripping naked, I bid farewell to the public that's filled the grotto, picture my Brother alive one last time, and dive in, expecting never to reemerge, proud of having played my part in purging a generation of pseudo-Squimbops from a world in which they could not gain purchase.

As I sink, past husks with intact faces and others that are nearly indistinguishable from the weeds entangling them, I think back on the Mountain Houses of my youth, the glorious outings our Pervert Uncle took my Brother and me on, the smell of spilled beer and sweat and old butter in the seats, with Tommy Bruno minding his machine behind the counter and the anticipation in the heads surrounding us as the curtains billowed and the moment of the Brothers' emergence drew near. I think of how close it all seemed then, the world within the world, the hidden totality that only the Squimbop Classics could render palpable for an hour at a time.

We leaned forward in our seats, unaware that we existed only in the *Condition*, or aware but untroubled, and we waited for the curtain to open on one Brother in a doctor's uniform and another dressed as a man who'd traveled a very long way to meet his fate, extending his arm while the Doctor—"Doctor Forearm!" my Brother and I shout, giddy to the point of fainting at the presence of such a major character from the Saga embodied less than a hundred feet away—places the needle and attaches the tube to a wide pulsing orb, which we know, having read all the comics and seen all the cartoons, will soon fill with so much blood that the Squimbop in the chair will turn gray and then almost clear and then he'll seem to lose his bones and musculature while the audience rises to its feet, clapping wildly, thrilled to see the Brothers open their show with such a provocative number.

"For what better proof of the Brothers' reality," they ask the room, "than the complete draining of one by the other for the sake of proving we're not real!! Who but the Real Brothers would ever do such a thing?"

The Mountain House trembles with cheers and our Pervert Uncle, whose role in the Saga has been to divert us, again and again, from the path we might've taken and shunt us instead, in every life we'll ever live, onto that of the *Squimbop Condition*, claps us on the back and whispers, "It's you! It's you up there!"

Though we know that every boy in that auditorium feels the same—that we've all come with a Pervert Uncle whose job is to swear that the Brothers are us, that we could not be ourselves if they were not themselves—still, nothing can prevent the final segue. Now we take another bow, motion for the audience to simmer down, hand our orbs and needles and tubing to assistants in the wings and climb into our Model T with "Me and the Devil Blues" already playing as we drive off into the night.

EVERYONE KNOWS HOW THE *CONDITION* ENDS, but nothing can dampen the thrill of seeing that it's finally here. We traverse shocking peaks and nearly airless underground grottos, past encampments of pseudo-Squimbops who've fled the Doctor's purge and taken refuge with the King, and then we surface in villages overtaken with feasting and frantic sacrifice, their thatched huts and cobbled streets hugging a coastline along which the shimmering purple hulk of Angel House floats, watching us.

The orbs for tonight's show glom together in the trunk as we chug up an almost vertical incline, over the bay and along a cliff road with no margin, no median, and no guardrail. We drive—whether it's my Brother or myself is immaterial; here, at the very end, it's always both of us at once—through lightless tunnels and across gravelly summits, tracked by wolves whose yellow eyes pulse with secret knowledge, in total silence save for "Me and the Devil Blues" and the quivering of the orbs and the blood in our veins.

Afternoon turns to evening and then to night as we pull into the vast Mountain House parking lot, and here the Finale bifurcates. In one chamber, the lot is full, overfull even, stuffed with tour buses and minivans and motorcycles and every make of compact car and station wagon known to the American middle class. Lines stream through the burnished Mountain House doors while a phalanx of guards handles ticketing and security even as, in the other chamber, the lot is empty, the concrete cracked by weeds and the roots of blighted elms, and the great doors of the

Convocation Hall hang off their hinges, their glass long since kicked out and the gold leaf on the lintels chiseled away. The imposing stained-glass windows, which in one chamber show the Brothers at the height of their glory are, in the other chamber, reduced to their steel frames, among which bats roost in furry clusters.

In both chambers at once, we park our Model T—in the last remaining spot or in one of thousands—and enter through the stage door, as we have all our lives, carrying the orbs between us, and we make our way into the dressing room, no longer concerned with whether it appears to bustle with makeup and sound techs and last-minute missives from our Producer or whether it's frigid and echoey and redolent of wolf urine. All of that fades as we sit in our respective chairs, one marked "Jim" and the other "Joe." We regard ourselves in the mirror as we each, inwardly, consider the performance to come. We picture how the story of Dr. Forearm will play out over ninety minutes, dedicating the first half hour to his coming of age at the hand of a Dr. Forearm of his own, up through his discovery of *The Squimbop Condition* and his own starring role within it, while the second half hour will cover his visit with his family to the newly opened Media Center in Cooperstown and his baptism in the underground river in which he will come to believe the Trace has been instilled inside him, and then the last half hour will detail the process by which he ends up killing first one and then dozens, hundreds, even thousands of willing patients as they enact their terminal frustration at the Trace's elusiveness and thereby, at long last, prove its reality, albeit in a world other than their own.

AND FINALLY, AS AN ENCORE AFTER THE CURTAIN call, we will return to the stage one last time to enact a sequence in which we find a way back to the Mountain House—to all the Mountain Houses—where we emerge from behind the curtain as the Brothers once again, one draining the other of all his blood not to kill him but to bring him to life, to celebrate the way in which this ritual allows our return to the stage by proving there's something that makes us who we are, not traceable in the blood perhaps but immediately apparent in our murderous search for that Trace, and then, in the very final instant, we look not at the crowd, not at the red velvet seats which may or may not be full, nor to the back of the house where Tommy Bruno may or may not be standing, made of cardboard or ruddy American flesh, with his gilded machine popping or not popping behind him, but instead directly at one another, the Squimbop Dyad resurrected for one night only and as such, in full recognition of the miracle this is, we gather into ourselves all the energies that have fanned out between the terrain we've covered and the Totally Other Place, ensnaring us for so long in a web beyond our comprehension or forcing our bodies beneath the Inland Sea, and then, free of our Producer, free of our Distant Master, free of the malignant gaze of Angel House and all the towns it summoned only to bury, here onstage we embrace, nothing but Jim and Joe at the end of time, and when we are ready we take our final bow and recede behind the curtain and into the night forever.

Publication History

The stories in this book first appeared in the following places:

“The Brothers Squimbop” in *Fanzine*

“The Brothers Squimbop in Europe” in *The Rupture*

“The Brothers Squimbop in Hollywood” and “Squimbop Fever” in *Heavy Feather Review*

“The Brothers Squimbop in Kansas,” “The Brothers Squimbop in Dodge City,” “Professor Squimbop in the Towns,” “The Brothers Squimbop Golden Age” and “The Squimbop Condition” in *The Southwest Review*

“The Last Testament of Professor Squimbop” in *Mitos Magazine*

Acknowledgments

Profound thanks to the following people for their insight, support, and edits during the construction and publication of this book: Michael Natalie, Avinash Rajendran, John Kazanjian, Sam Moss, Andrew Wilt, Bobby Rea, Greg Brownderville, Julie Savasky, Mary Klein, Mike Corrao, and, for the incredible illustrations and cover art, Jan Robert Duennweller.

DAVID LEO RICE is a writer from Northampton, Massachusetts. His fiction blends surrealism, horror, and myth to explore uncanny towns, dreamlike landscapes, and the metaphysical strangeness of everyday life. He is the author of the novels *A Room in Dodge City*, *Angel House*, *The New House*, and *The Berlin Wall*, and the story collection *Drifter*. He lives in Brooklyn, NY and is online at www.raviddice.com

11:11 Press is an American independent literary publisher based in Minneapolis, MN. Founded in 2018, 11:11 publishes innovative literature of all forms and varieties. We believe in the freedom of artistic expression, the realization of creative potential, and the transcendental power of stories.

To remain in this world a while longer, check out *Angel House*, out now from KERNPUNKT Press

www.ingramcontent.com/pod-product-compliance
Lightning Source LLC
Chambersburg PA
CBHW021622030826
48979CB00036B/1708/J
* 9 7 8 1 9 4 8 6 8 7 7 0 6 *